Cry
No
More

By Linda Howard

LINDA HOWARD

Cry
No
More

BALLANTINE BOOKS • *NEW YORK*

A Ballantine Book
Published by The Random House Publishing Group
Copyright © 2003 by Linda Howington

All rights reserved under International and Pan-American Copyright
Conventions. Published in the United States by The Random House
Publishing Group, a division of Random House, Inc., New York, and
simultaneously in Canada by Random House of Canada Limited, Toronto.

www.ballantinebooks.com

Library of Congress Cataloging-in-Publication Data
Howard, Linda, 1950–
    Cry no more / Linda Howard.– 1st ed.
      p.   cm.
    ISBN 0-345-45341-7
      I. Title.

    PS3558.O88217C79 2003b
    813'.54–dc22

                                                          2003045140

Book design by C. Linda Dingler

Manufactured in the United States of America

First Edition: November 2003

10   9   8   7   6   5   4   3   2   1

To my friends Beverly Barton, who has smashed her share of dishes, and Linda Jones, both of whom cried when I told them what this story is about.

To Kate Collins, my editor, and the Ballantine production team, for work above and beyond the call of duty. You guys are great.

To Robin Rue, my agent, who sniffled along with me. *Do you realize we've been together almost twenty years???* Some marriages don't last that long.

And to William Gage Wiemann, who's supposed to make his appearance on January 5, 2004. I'm betting he'll arrive on the eighth.

Cry
No
More

1

Mexico, 1993

MILLA HAD FALLEN ASLEEP WHILE THE BABY WAS NURSING. David Boone stood over his wife and child and watched them, aware of the silly grin on his face, of the fullness in his chest. His wife. His child.

God, his world.

The old fascination, the obsession, with medicine remained, but it was tempered now by something equally as fascinating. He'd never suspected that the process of pregnancy and childbirth, of the rapid development of the infant, could be so engrossing. He'd chosen the field of surgery because of the sheer challenge of it; obstetrics, in comparison, had seemed kind of like watching grass grow. Well, sometimes things went wrong and the obstetrician had to be on top of things, but for the most part babies grew and were born, and that was that.

He'd thought that until it came to his own child. Clinically, he'd known every detail of fetal growth, but he hadn't been prepared for the sheer emotion of watching Milla round out, of feeling the small kicks and flutters of the baby grow into stronger, more demanding ones. And if the sheer emotionalism had blindsided him, how had Milla felt? Sometimes, even during the physical misery of the last month of pregnancy, he'd caught an expression on her face, a rapt, absorbed look as she unconsciously stroked her belly, that told him she was lost in a world inhabited only by herself and the baby.

And then Justin had arrived, squalling and healthy, and David had felt light-headed with relief and euphoria. In the six weeks since, each day seemed to bring some small change as the infant grew; the dark fuzz on his head had become blond, his eyes were more blue and alert. He was noticing things, recognizing voices, waving his arms and legs in a jerky, uncoordinated rhythm as his little muscles grew in strength. He loved his bath. He had an angry cry, a hungry cry, an uncomfortable cry, and a cranky cry. Milla had been able to tell the difference within days.

The changes in his wife were fascinating, too. Milla had always had a way of holding herself apart from the world, as if she were more an observer than a participant. She'd been a challenge from the moment he'd first seen her, but he had stubbornly courted her until she couldn't help but notice him as a person rather than a moving part of the scenery. He could remember perfectly the exact moment when he'd won: they had been at a New Year's Eve party and in the middle of all the laughter and drinking and general silliness, Milla had looked at him and blinked, a faintly startled expression crossing her face as if he had suddenly come into focus. That was it; no hot kiss, no heartfelt exchanges in the night, just a sudden clarity in her gaze as she finally, truly *saw* him. Then she smiled and took his hand, and with that simple touch they were linked.

Amazing.

Okay, it was also amazing that he'd surfaced from his stud-

ies and work long enough to notice her at one of the deadly
dull staff parties his professor parents often hosted, but once
he had, he couldn't get her face out of his mind. She wasn't
beautiful; maybe she barely qualified as pretty. But there was
something about her, in the strong, clean lines of her face and
the way she walked, an almost gliding stride that made him
think maybe her feet didn't quite touch the ground, that had
kept consciousness of her nagging at him like a persistent
mosquito.

Learning about her had fascinated him. He liked knowing
that her favorite color was green, that she didn't want pepper-
oni on her pizza, that she enjoyed action movies and, thank
God, yawned at the idea of chick flicks, which was surprising
because she was so essentially feminine. As she explained it,
she already knew about woman stuff, so why would she want
to watch more of the same? Trivial stuff, mostly. He was be-
guiled by her serenity; if she had a temper, he'd never seen it.
She was the most evenly balanced person he'd ever met, and
even after two years of marriage he still couldn't quite believe
his luck.

She yawned and stretched, the move popping her nipple
out of the baby's slack mouth, who grunted and made a few
sucking motions, then was still. Fascinated, David reached out
and stroked one gentle finger over the plump mound of her
bare breast. He admitted it; he was delighted with the new size
of her breasts. Prepregnancy, Milla's shape had been lean, like
a long-distance runner's. Now she was rounder, softer, and
the postbirth moratorium on sex was driving him crazy.
He couldn't wait until tomorrow, when she had her six-week
checkup from Susanna Kosper, the team's ob-gyn. Actually,
because of a couple of emergencies that played havoc with
Susanna's schedule, it was almost seven weeks now, and he
was close to howling at the moon. Jerking off relieved the

tension, but was a long way from being as satisfying as making love to his wife.

She opened her eyes and drowsily smiled at him. "Hey, Doogie," she murmured. "Thinking about tomorrow night?"

He laughed, both at the nickname and how she'd read his mind—not that reading his mind was any great feat. He'd had little else besides sex on the brain for two months now. "Nothing else."

"Maybe Doogie Jr. will sleep all night." She stroked a gentle hand over the baby's fuzzy head, and he responded by making more sucking motions with his mouth. Simultaneously both adults said, "I doubt it," and David laughed again. Justin had a voracious appetite; he wanted feeding at least every two hours. Milla had been concerned that her breast milk wasn't rich enough, or that she didn't have enough, but Justin was clearly thriving and Susanna said there was nothing to worry about, the baby was just a pig.

Milla yawned again, and, concerned, David touched her cheek. "Just because Susanna will give you the all-clear tomorrow doesn't mean we *have* to make love. If you're too tired, we can wait." Susanna had made damn certain he understood how exhausted a new mother was, especially if she was breast-feeding.

Interrupted in mid-yawn, Milla glared at him. "Oh, yes, we do," she said fiercely. "If you think I'm going to wait another minute—Justin will be lucky if I don't leave him with Susanna while I hunt you down at the clinic."

"Gonna hold a scalpel on me and make me strip?" he asked, grinning.

"It's a thought." She caught his hand and pulled it to her breast again, rubbing her nipple against his fingers. "It's been over six weeks. We don't have to wait for Susanna's official okay."

He wanted to go with that idea. It had, in fact, occurred to him before, but he hadn't wanted Milla to think that all he cared about was sex. He was relieved she had brought up the idea first, and temptation gnawed at him. He glanced at his wristwatch and the time made him groan. "I have to be at the clinic in ten minutes." Already people would be lining up outside the clinic doors, prepared to patiently wait for hours to see a doctor. He was the team surgeon, and in fact had a surgery scheduled in half an hour. He barely had enough time to get to the clinic, change, and get scrubbed. Not that he'd need more than ten seconds to climax, the way he felt, but Milla definitely needed more time than that.

"Tonight, then," Milla said, turning on her side and smiling at him. "I'll keep Justin awake as much as possible so he'll sleep."

"Good plan." He stood and reached for his keys. "What are you doing today?"

"Nothing much. I'm going to the market this morning before it gets so hot."

"Get some oranges." He'd been on an orange kick lately, as if his body craved the vitamin C. He'd been spending long hours in surgery, so maybe he did. He leaned down and kissed Milla, then brushed his lips against Justin's satiny cheek. "Take good care of Mommy," he told his sleeping son, and hurried out the door.

Milla stayed in bed a few more minutes, luxuriating in the peace and quiet. Right this moment, no one was wanting anything of her. She had thought she was prepared to care for a baby, but somehow she hadn't realized the work would be practically nonstop. When Justin wasn't needing to be fed or changed, she was rushing around trying to keep up with all the other chores, and she was so tired that every step was like slogging through water. She hadn't had a good night's sleep in what felt like months. No, it *had* been months; about four of them, since the growing baby had gotten large enough to press on her bladder and she'd had to pee practically every half hour. She had carried him low, which Susanna said made it easier to breathe, but the trade-off was peeing a lot. Being a mother was anything but glamorous; rewarding, but definitely not glamorous.

She knew she was beaming as she examined her sleeping son. He was so gorgeous; everyone said so, exclaiming at his blond hair and blue eyes and the sweetness of his mouth. He looked like the Gerber baby, that idealized, big-eyed infant whose image graced millions of baby-care items. Milla was entranced by everything about him, from the tiny fingernails to the dimples that were forming as he gained weight. She could just sit and watch him all day long ... if she didn't have so much else to do.

Immediately her mind switched into work mode as she re-membered everything that needed to be done today, such as laundry, cleaning, cooking, and, whenever she had a spare moment to sit down, catching up on the clinic's paperwork. And sometime today she needed to take care of girly things like washing her hair and shaving her legs, because she had a hot date with her husband tonight. She would never get tired of being a mother, but she was definitely ready to be something else, too, like a sexually desirable woman. She missed sex; David made love with the same total concentration he gave to everything else that interested him, which was very nice when one was the recipient of said concentration. Actually, it was better than nice. It was pretty damn wonderful.

First, though, she would go to the market, before the day got too hot.

Only two more months here, she thought. She would miss Mexico: the people, the sunshine, the slowness of time. The year David and his colleagues had donated to the free-care clinic was almost over; then it would be back to the rat race of practicing medicine in the States. Not that she wouldn't be glad to be home, back with family and friends and such niceties as an air-conditioned supermarket. She wanted to do things like take Justin for walks in the park or visit with her mom during the day. She had missed her mother a lot during the long months of her pregnancy, and sporadic phone calls plus one quick visit home just hadn't filled the need.

She had almost decided not to come to Mexico with David; she found out she was pregnant just before they were scheduled to leave. But she hadn't wanted to spend such a long time away from him, especially while she was carrying their first child. After meeting Susanna, the ob-gyn part of the medical team, she had decided to stick to their original plan. Her mother had been horrified—her grandchild would be born in another country!—but the pregnancy had gone by the book, without any medical problems arising. Justin had arrived almost on time, just two days past her due date, and since then Milla had felt as if she existed in a fog composed of equal parts love and fatigue.

This was so completely opposite to how she had imagined her life would be that she couldn't help but feel amused. Armed with her grand liberal arts degree, she had planned to change the world, one person at a time. She was going to be the kind of teacher people remembered when they themselves were grandparents, the kind of teacher who made a real difference in her students' lives. She was comfortable in academia, even the highly political side of it; she had planned to continue her education until she received her doctorate, then teach at a university. Marriage—yes, after a while. Maybe when she was thirty or thirty-five. Children—maybe.

Instead she had met David, a wunderkind of medicine. He

was the son of her history professor, and when she became the professor's student assistant, she learned all about him. David's IQ was way above genius level; he'd finished high school at fourteen, college at seventeen, blew through medical school, and was already a practicing surgeon at the age of twenty-five when she met him. She'd expected him to be either an arrogant know-it-all—with some justification—or a total egghead.

He was neither. Instead he was a good-looking young man whose face was often lined with exhaustion from long hours in surgery and augmented by a bottomless need for more knowledge that kept him poring over medical books long after he should have been asleep. His smile was sweet and sexy, his blue eyes full of good humor, his blond hair usually shaggy and disordered. He was tall, which she liked, since she was five-seven and liked to wear high heels. Actually, she liked everything about him, and when he asked her out she hadn't hesitated at all.

Still, she'd been surprised, at a New Year's Eve party, to catch him staring at her with dark, potent desire in his eyes. Realization had hit her like a blow to the stomach, as if Joshua had blown his horn and all the walls had come tumbling down. David loved her, and she loved him. It was that simple.

She had become his wife at twenty-one, as soon as she got her degree, and now at twenty-three she was a mother. She didn't regret a minute of it. She still planned to teach, when they returned to the States, and she still planned to further her education, but she wouldn't undo a single decision that had led to the small miracle that was her son. From the moment she'd realized she was pregnant, she'd been consumed by the process, and so in love with the baby that she felt as if she were lit from the inside with a powerful, incandescent glow. That feeling was even stronger now, to the point that she felt the tug between her and Justin even if he was just in the next room sleeping. No matter how tired she was, she reveled in that connection.

She got out of bed and carefully placed the pillows around the baby, even though he couldn't yet roll over. He didn't move while she quickly washed, dragged a brush through her short, curly hair, and then dressed in one of the loose sundresses she had brought specifically to wear after giving birth. She was still fifteen pounds heavier than she'd been before getting pregnant, but the extra weight didn't bother her ... much. She kind of liked the motherly softness, and David certainly liked the way her breasts had expanded from a B cup to a D.

She thought of the coming night and shivered with anticipation. A week ago David had brought home a box of condoms from the clinic, and the mere presence of the box had made them both a little crazy. They had used condoms for a short while when they first became lovers; then she had been on birth control pills until they had decided to have a baby. Having to use the condoms again made her feel as if it were the first time all over again, when they were in a frenzy to have each other and everything was so new and intense and scary.

Justin began squirming a little, his mouth pursing as if searching for her breast. His blue eyes opened, his tiny fists began waving, and he made the grunting sound that preceded his "I'm wet, change me," cry. Pulled from a daydream about making love with his daddy, Milla got a clean diaper and bent over him, cooing as she changed him. He managed to focus his gaze on her face, and he stared at her as if nothing else existed in his universe, his mouth open with delight, his arms and legs pumping.

"There's mommy's baby," she crooned as she lifted him. As soon as she settled him in the crook of her arm, he began rooting at her breast. "Make that 'mommy's pig,'" she amended, sitting down and unbuttoning the front of her dress. Her breasts tingled in response, and she sighed with pure pleasure as the baby latched onto her nipple and began sucking. Gently she rocked back and forth, playing with his fingers and toes as he nursed. Her eyes closed dreamily, and she hummed a lullaby, drifting in the moment. She could do without the dirty diapers and loss of sleep, but she loved this part of being a mother. When she held him like this, nothing else mattered.

He finished nursing, and she put him down again while she grabbed a quick bite of breakfast. After brushing her teeth, she draped a blue denim sling over her head and put the baby in it. He settled down with his head resting where he could hear her heartbeat, his blue eyes already drooping shut as he dozed. Grabbing a hat and a basket, with money in her pocket, she set out for the market.

The walk was only about half a mile. The bright morning sun promised to deliver scorching heat by midday, but for now the air was cool and dry, and the small open-air village market was busy with early shoppers. There were oranges and brightly colored peppers, bananas and melons, yellow onions on strings. Milla browsed, occasionally chatting with some of the village women as they stopped to admire the baby, taking her time in picking out the produce she wanted.

Justin was curled in the ball shape of the very young, his legs still automatically drawing up into his prebirth position. She held her hat so it shielded him from the sun. A soft, pleasant breeze played in her short, light brown curls and lifted the baby's wispy blond fuzz. He stirred, his rosebud mouth making sucking motions. Milla set down her basket and patted his tiny back, and he lapsed back into sleep.

She stopped at a display of fruit and began carrying on an animated, if fractured, conversation with the old woman behind the stacks of oranges and melons. Her understanding was better than her speech, but she managed to make herself understood. She used her free hand to point to the oranges she wanted.

She didn't see them coming. Suddenly two men were bracketing her, their body heat and odor assailing her. Instinctively she started to step back, only to find herself blocked by their bodies closing in on her. The one on the right pulled a knife from the sheath at his waist and grasped the straps of the sling, hastily slicing through them before Milla could do more than give a startled cry. Time seemed to stutter, giving her freeze-frame impressions of the next few seconds. The old woman fell back, her expression alarmed. Milla felt the sling that held Justin to her begin to drop, and in panic she grabbed for her baby. The man on her left snatched the baby from her with one hand, and shoved at her with the other.

Somehow she kept her balance, terror twisting in her chest as she leapt at the man, screaming, fighting to wrest her baby from him. Her clawing nails scratched down his face, leaving bloody furrows, and he reeled back from the assault.

The baby, startled awake, was wailing. The milling crowd scattered, alarmed by the sudden violence. "Help!" she shrieked over and over as she tried to grab Justin, but everyone seemed to be running away from her rather than to her. The man tried to shove her away again, his hand on her face. Milla bit him, sinking her teeth into his hand and grinding down until she felt blood in her mouth and he was yelling in pain. She clawed for his eyes, her nails sinking into spongy softness. His yells turned into shocked bellows, and his grip on Justin loosened. Desperately she grabbed at the baby, managing to catch one tiny, flailing arm, and for one heart-bursting moment she thought she had him. Then she felt the other man moving in close behind her, and a searing, paralyzing pain shot through her back.

Her body convulsed and she dropped like a rock to the

ground, her fingers scrabbling helplessly in the grit. With the baby clutched like a football under one assailant's arm, the two men raced away, one holding a bloody hand over his face and screaming curses as he fled. Milla lay sprawled in the dirt as she tried to fight through the agony that gripped her body, fight for breath to scream. Her lungs pumped wildly but didn't seem to be dragging in any air. She tried to get up; her body didn't respond. A black veil began closing over her vision, and she managed to whimper, over and over, "My baby! My baby! Someone get my baby!"

No one did.

David had already repaired a hernia and was washing up while Rip Kosper, Susanna's husband and the team anesthesiologist, did a final check of the patient's blood pressure and heart rate to make sure he was okay before turning him over to Anneli Lansky, the nurse, for monitoring. They had a good group working here; he'd miss them when the year was up and they all returned to regular practice in the States. He wouldn't miss the cramped, one-story concrete-block clinic, with its cracked tile floors and barely adequate equipment, but he'd definitely miss the group as well as his patients—and he'd miss Mexico itself.

He was thinking about the next case, a gallbladder, when he heard a commotion in the hallway just outside the door. There was shouting and cursing, some scuffling sounds, and high-pitched wails. He dried his hands and started for the door just as Juana Mendoza, another nurse, began yelling for him.

He hit the door, already running, and skidded to a halt in the hallway before he rammed into a knot of people that included Juana, Susanna Kosper, and two men and a woman who were clumsily carrying another woman. The crush of bodies hid the wounded woman's face, but David could see that her dress was drenched with blood and he immediately switched into emergency mode. "What happened?" he asked as he kicked a box out of the way and dragged over a gurney.

"David." Susanna's voice was tight and sharp. "It's Milla."

For a moment the words didn't make sense and he looked around, expecting to see his wife behind him. Then Susanna's meaning kicked in and he saw the wounded woman's unconscious, paper-white face, saw the froth of soft brown curls around her face, and everything tilted out of kilter. Milla? This couldn't be Milla. She was at home with Justin, safe and sound. This woman who looked as if she'd bled out just resembled his wife, that was all. It wasn't really Milla.

"David!" This time Susanna's tone was even sharper. "Snap out of it! Help us get her on the gurney."

Only his training enabled him to function, to step in and lift the woman who looked like Milla onto the gurney. Her dress was bloody, her arms and hands were bloody, her legs and feet and even her shoes were bloody. No—just one shoe, a sandal that looked just like a pair Milla often wore. He saw the pink nail polish on her toenails, and the delicate gold chain around her right ankle, and he felt as if all his insides caved in.

"What happened?" he asked, his voice hoarse and faraway and not his own, even as his body moved into action and they rapidly wheeled Milla into the surgical bay he had just left.

"Knife wound to the lower back," Juana said, listening to the babble of voices around them before they closed the door and shut out most of the noise. "Two men attacked her at the market." She caught a shuddering breath. "They took Justin. Milla fought them, and one of the men stabbed her."

Rip, alerted by the hubbub, burst back into the room. "My God," he blurted when he saw Milla; then he fell silent and began readying his equipment.

Justin! David reeled from the second shock, and he half turned toward the door. Two bastards had stolen his son! He actually took a step away from the gurney, toward the door, to race out and search for his baby. Then he hesitated, and looked back at his wife.

They hadn't had time to clean the operating room, or restock the supplies on the trays. Anneli ran in and began grabbing what they'd need. Juana wrapped a blood pressure cuff around Milla's limp arm and swiftly pumped it up, while Susanna used the shears to cut away Milla's clothing. "Blood type O positive," Susanna was saying. How did she know? Oh, yeah, she'd typed Milla's blood before Justin's delivery.

"Sixty over forty," Juana reported. Moving so fast her actions were a blur, she started an IV line in Milla's arm and hooked up a bag of blood plasma.

He was losing her, David thought. Milla would die right in front of him, unless he snapped out of his shock and acted. From the position of the wound, the knife had probably hit her left kidney, and God knows what other damage had been done. She was bleeding out; she had only a few minutes left before her internal organs began shutting down–

He pushed everything else out of his mind, and shoved his hands into the fresh pair of gloves Anneli held out for him. He didn't have time to scrub up; he didn't have time to search for Justin; all he had time to do was reach for the scalpel that was promptly slapped into his palm and call on every ounce of skill he had. He prayed, he cursed, and he fought time as he cut into his wife's body. As he'd suspected, the knife blade had hit her left kidney. Hit it, hell; it had all but sliced the organ in half. There was no saving the kidney, and if he didn't get it out and the blood vessels tied off in record time, there would be no saving Milla, either.

It was a race, savage and merciless. If he made one misstep, if he hesitated, if anything was dropped or even fumbled, then he lost, and Milla lost. It wasn't surgery as he was accustomed to doing it; it was battlefield surgery, fast and brutal, with her life hanging on every split-second decision and action. While they poured all of their available blood into her, he fought to keep it from pouring out of her just as fast as it went in. Moment by moment he stemmed the bleeding, searched out every severed vessel, and slowly he began to win the race. He didn't know how long it took; he never asked, never found out. *How long* didn't matter. All that mattered was winning, because the alternative was more than he could bear.

2

Ten years later
Chihuahua, Mexico

Paige Sisk leaned against her fiancé, Colton Rawls, her eyes drifting shut as she took a big hit of weed and passed the joint to Colton. Oh, man, all those dweebs who had gone on and on about the bad things that could happen to her in Mexico were so totally wrong. Mexico was the best. I mean, she wasn't an idiot, she knew better than to score weed in front of some Mexican cop, though she'd heard all you had to do was flash them some green and the problem went away. Like she wanted to waste her money on bribes.

They had been here four days already. Colton thought Chihuahua was the coolest. He had some serious thing going about Pancho Villa; until they got here she thought it was, like, some house where ponchos were made. The only Pancho she'd ever heard of was in an old, old western where this silly-looking dude kept saying, "Oh, Pancho," to an even sillier dude in a big hat, but Colton said no, this Pancho was the real thing. Like there were fake Panchos. But whatever. Colton dug it. They had gone twice to see this shot-up old Dodge where supposedly the real Pancho had been turned into Swiss cheese, just like Bonnie and Clyde.

As far as she was concerned, Pancho Villa was just a dead old fart. She didn't care about his stupid Dodge. Now, if he'd driven a Hummer, that would have been cool.

"If he'd driven a Hummer," she said, "he could have run right over those assholes who were shooting at him."

Colton surfaced from his fog to blink in confusion. "Who drives a Hummer?"

"Pancho Villa."

"No, it was a Dodge."

"That's what I'm saying." Impatient, she elbowed him. "If he'd been driving a Hummer, he could have smashed them flat."

"No such thing as a Hummer back then."

"God!" she said in exasperation. "You are so literal. I said *if*!" She grabbed the joint and took another hit, then got up from the bed. "I'm going to the bathroom."

"Okay." Happy to have sole possession of the joint, Colton settled back on the pillows and gave her a little wave as she left the room. She didn't wave back. Going to the bathroom didn't make her happy; there was only one on this floor, there was a magazine instead of toilet paper for wiping, and it smelled really bad. But Colton had insisted on staying here instead of in one of the nicer hotels, because the rooms were so cheap. Well, of course they were cheap; what fool would pay top price to stay here? And it was really close to the marketplace, which was neat.

She felt really mellow from the weed, but not so mellow that the bathroom didn't bother her. The lock was broken, too. A shoelace had been tied around the knob, a nail driven into the frame right beside the knob, and to latch the door you wrapped the loose end of the shoelace around the nail. It did hold the door shut, but she didn't put a lot of faith in the method. So whenever she had to be in there, she absolutely raced to finish her business.

Oh, shit; she'd forgotten to bring the flashlight. The lights hadn't gone off yet when she was in the bathroom, but everyone insisted it *did* happen occasionally, and she was afraid of the dark, so that was one warning she'd listened to. She tried to hurry, but really, you can piss only so fast and she had waited until she was miserably full because she hated using this bathroom. Crouched over the toilet–no way was she going to sit on that thing–she kept going and going and going, and her legs began to ache so bad she thought she might actually have to sit down after all, and then what could she do, boil her butt?

But finally she finished, blotted herself with a page from the magazine, and groaned in relief as she stood from her awkward, crouched position. If she could ever get Colton away from Chihuahua and Pancho Villa's bullet-riddled Dodge so they could continue their vacation tour, she was going to insist that they stay at better places.

She pulled up her shorts, rinsed her hands, and dried them on her bottom because she'd forgotten to bring a towel with her, then unwound the shoelace from the nail. The door swung open and she turned out the dim light as she stepped into the dark hallway. She faltered, coming to a stop. There was supposed to be a light on in the hallway. There had been when she went into the bathroom. The bulb must have blown.

Chills ran down her back. She *so* didn't like the dark. How was she supposed to make it back to their room when she couldn't see a thing?

A board creaked, to her left. She jumped a foot high and tried to scream, but her heart was in her throat and all she could manage was a squeal.

A rough hand clamped over her mouth; she got a dose of really bad B.O., then something hard slammed into her head and she slumped, unconscious.

El Paso, Texas

Milla's cell phone rang. For a moment she thought about not answering it; she was dead tired, dispirited, and had a throbbing headache. The temperature outside was 107, and even with the air-conditioning in the SUV set on high, the heat coming through the windshield burned her arms. The image of Tiera Alverson's battered face and the fourteen-year-old's sightless blue eyes staring up at nothing wouldn't leave her mind. In her dreams tonight she would hear the sound of Regina Alverson's harsh sobbing when she heard that her little girl was never coming home again. Sometimes Finders succeeded, but sometimes they were too late. Today, they had been too late.

The last thing Milla wanted to do right now was take on someone else's heartache; she had enough aches of her own. But she never knew who might be calling, or why, and after all, she herself had made finding people her personal crusade. So she opened her eyes just enough to find the right button to punch, then immediately closed them again to shut out the ferociously bright late-afternoon sun. "Hello."

"*Señora* Boone?" The accented voice on the speakerphone filled the Chevy SUV. Milla didn't recognize it, but she spoke to so many different people every day that there was no way she could recognize everyone. This was definitely business, though, because only when it concerned Finders was she known as Milla Boone. After the divorce, she had taken back her maiden name of Edge, but the public so associated the name Boone with the cause of finding missing children that she'd been forced to use it in all publicity and anything to do with Finders.

"Yes, this is she."

"There is a meeting tonight. Guadalupe, at ten-thirty. Behind the church."

"What kind of meeting—" she began, but the voice cut her off.

"Diaz will be there."

The phone went dead. Milla sat up, her headache forgotten as adrenaline buzzed through her system. She clicked off the phone and sat very still, thoughts racing.

"*Which* Guadalupe?" Brian Cusack said from the driver's seat, mostly in frustration, because he'd heard everything.

"If it isn't the closest one, then it doesn't matter." There were several Guadalupes in Mexico, ranging in population from about fifty thousand down to a collection of only a couple of hundred souls. The one closest to the border qualified as a village.

"Shit," Brian Cusack said. *"Shit."*

"No joke." It was after six; no one would be at the office to provide backup. She could try to track down people at home, but there wasn't time to spare. If the meeting was at ten-thirty, then they needed to be in position at least an hour beforehand. Guadalupe was about fifty miles from El Paso and Juarez. In this traffic it would take them forty-five minutes to an hour to get to the border. It would be less hassle to park the SUV, walk across the bridge into Mexico, and pick up transportation there, rather than go through the paperwork involved in driving across, but the operative phrase was *"less* hassle," not *"no* hassle." When time was short, any hassle at all could mean the difference between success and failure.

They both had their passports and their multiple-entry tourist cards for Mexico; that was standard procedure, because they never knew when they'd be called on to cross borders. That was about all they had, though, other than a couple of night-vision devices that they had used searching for little Dylan Peterson—a successful find, thank God—and that had been left in the duffel as they then swung immediately into the search for Tiera Alverson. They hadn't needed a lot of stuff in the Alverson case; the job had taken them to Carlsbad, New Mexico, and had required patience and time, not survival gear.

They would have to make do with what they had, because there was no way she could pass up an opportunity to get Diaz.

Diaz. The man was as elusive as smoke on a windy day, but maybe this time they'd be lucky.

"We won't have time to pick up any weapons," Brian said evenly as he seized an opening and muscled the big SUV around a poky white Toyota with huge rust spots on the door.

"We'll have to make time." They never took the chance of smuggling weapons through at the border; instead they had arrangements to buy weapons once they were across. Most of the time she didn't need weapons—all she was doing was talking to people—but sometimes common sense dictated they be able to protect themselves.

She tried Joann Westfall's number, hoping she could catch her second-in-command at home, but the answering machine came on. Quickly Milla left a message filling Jo in on the admittedly sketchy details of where they were going and why. It was her own rule that none of the Finders went off by themselves, or without letting someone else know where they were.

After two years, her first real shot at Diaz!

Her heartbeat thudded in her chest. Maybe this was the break she'd been hunting for ten years.

Justin's kidnapping was shrouded in mystery, rumors,

suspicion. No ransom had ever been demanded, and the men who had stolen the baby from her in the tiny village market that day had disappeared. But eventually she began hearing snippets of information about a one-eyed man who was never there when she tried to track him down. Then, two years ago, a woman had whispered to her that a man named Diaz perhaps knew about the matter. For the past twenty-five months Milla had stayed on his trail like a bloodhound, and except for maddening rumors, she'd come up empty.

To find Diaz, said an old man warning her away from her quest, was to find death. Best to stay far away from him. Diaz knew about, or was behind, the disappearance of many. She heard that the one-eyed man's name was Diaz. No, that was wrong; the one-eyed man worked for Diaz. Or Diaz had killed the one-eyed man for mistakenly snatching an American baby and causing such a furor.

Milla had heard all of that, and more. People seemed afraid to talk about him, but she asked questions and waited, and eventually some sort of muttered reply would come. Even after all this time, she still had no clear idea of who or what he was, only that he was somehow involved in Justin's disappearance.

"Someone's setting Diaz up for a fall," Brian said suddenly.

"I know." There was no other reason for that phone call, and that worried her. She didn't want to get involved in a plot of betrayal and revenge. First and foremost, she wanted to find Justin. That was what Finders concentrated on, finding the lost ones, the stolen ones; if justice was served, fine, but that was police business. She never hindered an investigation, in fact often helped, but her objective was simply to return children to their families.

"If things turn ugly, we'll just stay low and out of sight," she said.

"What if it turns out he's the one you've been looking for all these years?"

Milla closed her eyes, unable to answer. It was one thing to say they'd stay out of whatever trouble was brewing, but what if Diaz was indeed the one-eyed man who had stolen Justin? She didn't know if she could control her rage, which still seethed and bubbled inside her like a hidden volcano. She couldn't just kill him; she needed to talk to the man, even if he *was* the one, to find out what he'd done with her baby. But oh, how she wanted to kill him. She wanted to tear him apart as surely as he'd torn her apart.

Because she had no answer, she concentrated on the here and now. She could do that; she'd gotten by for ten years by focusing just on what she could do right *now*. She and Brian were tired, hungry, and they faced a long night. Nothing she could do about the last point, but she dug into their stash of PayDay candy bars and opened one for each of them. The peanuts in the candy bar would give them energy. Now that he knew the candy was going to be his supper, instead of the steak he'd been fantasizing aloud about all the way home, Brian grabbed the PayDay and downed it in three bites. Milla handed him another one, which lasted slightly longer.

She always carried fruit on the jobs, too, but because they thought they were headed home, she'd allowed the supply to get low. They were down to one banana. She peeled it and broke it in half. Brian was already reaching for it before she got the thing peeled.

"Anything else?" he asked after he'd allowed her to eat her half.

"Let's see. Two more PayDays. A roll of Life Savers. And two bottles of water. That's it."

He grunted. They'd need the PayDays to keep them going on the trip home. "Guess that's supper, then." He was clearly unhappy. Brian was a big boy who required constant refueling.

She wasn't thrilled with the idea, herself. She opened the

bottles of water, but they drank only a few sips each. The last thing either one wanted now was an overloaded bladder.

They had been to Guadalupe before, but she went through the box of maps until she found one that included the town, and studied the layout of the place. "I wonder how many churches are in Guadalupe. I can't remember."

"I hope to God only one, since that guy didn't give us a name. Give me that roll of Life Savers."

She handed over the Life Savers and Brian tore into the roll. He didn't let the candy melt in his mouth; he put in three or four at the time, and crunched.

Milla got out her cell phone and called their contact in Juarez, Benito—no last name had ever been given. Benito was a whiz at providing them with wheels whenever they needed them, and not the rental agency variety of wheels, either. Benito specialized in beat-up, rickety pickup trucks that no one paid attention to, and which weren't likely to be vandalized if left on the street unattended. That was because there was nothing left to vandalize in Benito's vehicles. They were bare-bones, really not worth stealing. But they ran, and the one he delivered to them on his side of the border would be full of gas. The paperwork was always in order, too, in case they were stopped by the police.

Arranging for weapons was trickier. The Finders didn't often have a need for weapons, and doing this always made her uneasy. Mexico had strict weapons laws; not that there weren't plenty of weapons to be had; it was just that if they were caught with guns, they'd be in very deep doo-doo. She didn't like breaking the law, but when you were dealing with human snakes, you had to be prepared. She reached their contact for illegal weapons and placed her order: nothing fancy, just basic self-protection. She never knew exactly what would be provided, but she expected cheap .22 revolvers, which they would dispose of before they returned to the States.

As she had expected, it was seven-thirty and getting dark by the time they parked the SUV, walked across the bridge, and cleared their paperwork. Benito was waiting patiently for them with a truly remarkable excuse for a truck, an ancient Ford that was more rust than painted metal. There was no tailgate, the passenger door was wired shut—presumably to keep it on the truck—and the windshield was held in place with duct tape. Literally. Despite their hurry, both Milla and Brian had to stop and blink at the derelict.

"You've outdone yourself this time, Benito," Brian said in awe.

Benito grinned broadly, showing the gap where he was missing a tooth. He was short and wiry, age anywhere between forty and seventy, and he had the most consistently cheerful expression Milla had ever seen. "I try," he said, with a New York accent. Benito had been born in Mexico, but his parents had crossed the border with him when he was small, and he had very few early memories of the land of his birth. Later he returned to his roots and settled down very happily, but he couldn't shake his accent. "The horn doesn't work, and if the headlights don't come on when you pull out the knob, push it back in real hard and then kind of ease it out again. You gotta get the knot in just the right position."

"Does it have a motor, or do we have to push it with our feet?" Milla asked, peering inside. She was only half joking, because part of the floor had rusted out and she could see the ground.

"Now, the motor's a work of art. It purrs like a kitten, and there's more power than you'd expect. Might come in handy." He never asked questions about where they were going or what they were doing, but he knew what the Finders did.

Milla opened the driver's door and climbed in, gingerly scooting across the seat and avoiding the hole in the floor. Brian handed her the case containing the two nightscopes, the one blanket, dark green, they'd had in the SUV, and the two bottles of water; she securely stowed everything while he slid behind the wheel.

The truck was so old there weren't any seat belts; if the traffic police stopped them, they would almost certainly have to pay a fine. As Benito had promised, however, the engine turned over at the first turn of the key. Brian maneuvered through Juarez's busy streets, then stopped in front of a *farmacia*, a drugstore. Milla waited in the truck while he went inside, where he met their contact, a woman they knew only as Chela. She was very distinguished-looking, neatly dressed, and looked to be in her late forties. She gave Brian a Sanborn's shopping bag; he passed her some money so slickly that no one knew the transaction had taken place; then he was back in the truck and they were on their way to Guadalupe.

Darkness had fallen by then, and he fiddled with the knob for the headlights until they came on. Driving in Mexico at night wasn't recommended, for anyone. Not only was that when most highway robberies occurred, but the heat retained in the pavement drew livestock to the highways. Hitting a horse or a cow was never good, for either animal or vehicle. There were also potholes and other hazards, which were more difficult to see at night. To make driving even more adventurous, Mexicans sometimes deliberately drove at night without their own lights, the better to see oncoming cars on hills and curves and avoid them, which was okay unless two cars traveling in opposite directions *both* had their headlights off. Then it became more like a game of blind chicken.

Brian loved driving in Mexico. He was still young enough,

only twenty-five, that he enjoyed pitting his night vision and reflexes against whatever waited for him on the road. He was steady as a rock and didn't know the meaning of the word "panic," so Milla gladly left the driving to him, while she held on with a death grip and prayed.

It was almost ten o'clock when they finally reached Guadalupe, perilously close to the time for the meeting. It was a small village of maybe four hundred people, with a single main street that was closely lined with shops, the inevitable cantina, and a variety of other buildings. Here and there hitching posts still stood in position. The road had deteriorated to mostly dirt and gravel, though there were patches of pavement.

They drove down the main street, verifying that there was indeed just one church; behind it was a cemetery, closely dotted with crosses and tombstones. Milla wasn't able to see much during the drive-by; she couldn't tell if there was an alley between the church and the cemetery, though she assumed there had to be room enough for a car to drive.

"No place to park," Brian muttered, and she turned her attention back to the street. He was right; while there was physical space for parking, there wasn't anywhere that wouldn't attract the attention of men who didn't like being spied on.

"We'll have to go back to the cantina," she said. Several cars and trucks had been parked there, providing camouflage for their truck. Brian nodded and continued past the church, keeping his speed slow and steady. He took the next right, down a narrow lane. When it intersected, he took the right turn, then worked his way back to the cantina.

He parked the truck between a 1978 Chevrolet Monte Carlo and an original-style Volkswagen Beetle. They waited and watched, looking for people on the street. Noise poured from the cantina, but a dog nosing curiously around doorways provided the only movement they could see. They each took a pistol and night-vision scope. Before Brian opened the door, Milla automatically reached up to turn off the dome light, only to discover it had been removed.

They slid from the truck and quickly blended into the shadows. The dog looked their way and gave an inquisitive bark, waited a moment to see if they responded, then returned to its search-and-eat mission.

There was no sidewalk, just the street with its obstacle course of potholes and chunks of pavement. By chance they were dressed fairly well for nighttime clandestine work, Brian in green cargo pants and a black T-shirt, and Milla in jeans and a sleeveless burgundy blouse, and they both were wearing rubber-soled work boots as well as dark green baseball caps with "FA," for *Finders Association*, in light blue on the front. Brian was darkly tanned, but Milla's bare arms were noticeable, so she draped the blanket around her shoulders. Now that night had fallen the temperature had cooled dramatically, and the blanket felt good.

They didn't run, or slink from doorway to doorway; either would attract the attention of anyone watching. They walked purposefully, but without obvious haste. The bad news was that it was less than fifteen minutes until the meeting was supposed to take place. The good news was that only tourists were on time in Mexico, where punctuality was considered bad manners. That didn't mean no one would be watching the church, but it improved their chances of getting into place unseen.

Seventy-five yards from the church, they left the main street and ducked down a tiny alley that brought them out on the near side of the cemetery.

"What's the plan?" Brian whispered as he slipped one of

the pistols into his pocket, then took out one of the night-vision scopes. "Do we get the jump on them, find out which one is Diaz, and take him away for questioning?"

"I doubt it'll be that easy," she said dryly. Because Brian was young and big and strong, and running over with testosterone, he had so far been able to handle everything that came his way. The crucial phrase was "so far." She was much more aware of how quickly things could go horribly wrong. "We do exactly that if there are only two men, but if there are more, we don't."

"Not even if there are just three?"

"Not even." If there were two men, she and Brian could catch them by surprise and keep both of them covered. Milla didn't mind holding them at gunpoint while Diaz answered her questions. If there were more than two . . . she was neither stupid nor suicidal, and she certainly wouldn't risk Brian's life. It might be two more years before she had another shot at talking to Diaz, but that was better than having to bury someone. "Can you work your way around to the other side of the cemetery?"

"Has a cat got a tail?" Brian was not only ex-military, having joined the army straight out of high school, but an east Texas farm boy who had grown up ghosting through the woods while deer hunting.

"Then pick a spot where you have a clear view of the entire back of the church, and I'll do the same on this end. Remember, if there're more than two, all we do is watch."

"Got it. But if there are only two, what's the signal for moving in on them?"

She hesitated. Normally they used radios, but they'd been caught without much of their equipment. "Exactly three minutes after they both show up and begin talking, we move. If the meeting is shorter than that, we move when they do." If the men meeting here were on the alert, the three minutes would give them time to settle down—she hoped. This wasn't the best method of synchronization, but it was the best she could come up with under the circumstances. God only knows how long they would have to wait.

Brian faded away into the darkness, and Milla edged in the opposite direction, first away from the cemetery, then around it to the back. Taking cover behind a tall tombstone, she used the night-vision scope to look all around her, searching for someone—other than Brian—who was doing the same thing she was doing. There was no one lurking around the church that she could spot, nor was there anyone hiding behind another tombstone.

Still, she waited a few minutes and scanned the area again. Still nothing. She cautiously moved up to another tombstone. This part of Chihuahua State was desert, with cactus and brush, so there was no grass to muffle any sound she made. She went down on one knee and a rock dug into her leg, making her wince, but she controlled her reaction and didn't make any sudden movements, just carefully shifted her position.

Something crawled across her hand. It felt tiny, like an ant or a fly. Again she controlled her flinch, but her skin crawled, and she had to fight the urge to shriek and jump up and down to fling the bug away from her. She hated insects. She hated being dirty. She hated lying on the ground, in close proximity to both dirt and insects. She did it anyway, and had trained herself to ignore the dirt and bugs. What she was doing was dangerous and she knew it; her heart was already pounding with sickening force, but that, too, she had learned to ignore. She might cringe inside, but no timidity at all showed on the outside.

She picked up the rock that had been digging into her knee, her fingers sliding over the smooth, triangular shape, kind of like a small pyramid. Hmm, that was interesting. Automatically she slipped it into her front jeans pocket. After a moment she realized what she'd done and started to dig the rock out of her jeans, to toss it aside, but she couldn't make herself do it.

She had been picking up rocks for years now, always on the lookout for smooth ones or ones with unusual shapes. She had quite a collection of them at home. Little boys liked rocks, didn't they?

After once again surveilling the cemetery and surrounding area, she moved in a crouch up and to the right, then again to the next tombstone, slowly working her way into position. Cupping her hand over her wristwatch, she pressed the button that illuminated the face: ten thirty-nine. Either the caller's information was bogus, or the people were in no hurry to get here. She hoped it was the latter, and she and Brian hadn't gone to all this trouble for nothing.

No. It wasn't for nothing. Sooner or later, she would find her son. All she had to do was keep running down all leads. She had been doing this for ten years and she would do it for another ten, if necessary. Or twenty years. She couldn't imagine ever giving up on her little boy.

Through the years she had tried to imagine what Justin's interests would be, how they would change as he grew, and she had bought toys she'd thought he would like. Would he be fascinated by balls and toy trucks? Would he make motor noises as he crawled along? When he was three, she imagined him on a tricycle. By four, she thought, he would be picking up rocks and worms and things like that, putting them into his pocket. She couldn't make herself pick up a worm, but the rocks . . . she could do rocks. That was when she'd begun collecting them.

When he was six, she wondered if he was learning how to play soccer, or T-ball. He would probably still like rocks at that age, too. But just in case, she'd bought a baseball and a small bat.

When he was eight, she imagined him with his adult teeth growing in, too big for his face just yet, though his cheeks would be losing the chubbiness of childhood. At what age did children start playing Little League? He'd have his own bat and glove by now, surely. And maybe someone had taught him how to skip a flat stone on the water; she began looking for the smooth, flat ones, so she'd have them for him just in case.

He was ten now, maybe too old for throwing rocks. He'd have a ten-speed bicycle–a gear for each year, she thought. Perhaps he was into computers. He was definitely old enough now for Little League. And maybe he had an aquarium. Maybe he could put a few of the prettier rocks in his aquarium. She had stopped buying toys, and though she did have a computer, she didn't buy a bicycle, or an aquarium. The fish would just die, because she wasn't home often enough to keep them fed.

Milla's jaw set and she stared blindly across the night-darkened cemetery. She couldn't let herself think that he might not be alive, so instead she imagined that he was living a normal, happy life, that he'd been found or bought or adopted by people who loved him and were taking good care of him.

That was the theory, anyway, that he'd been stolen and sold to an illegal adoption ring that provided black-market babies to people in the States and Canada who wanted to adopt. These people had no idea the children they'd adopted had been stolen, that families had been devastated and parents left bereft. She tried to believe that. She tried to comfort herself by imagining Justin playing, growing, laughing. The not knowing for certain what had happened to him was the worst, and anything was better than thinking he was dead.

So many of the stolen babies *did* die. They were stuffed into car trunks to be smuggled across the border, and if the heat killed eight out of ten, well, the ten hadn't cost anything but effort, and the two remaining ones could be sold for ten, twenty thousand dollars each, maybe even more, depending on who wanted a baby and how much they could afford. The Federales had tried to comfort her by telling her that extra care would be taken with Justin because he was blond and blue-eyed, and therefore worth more. Oddly, it was a comfort, though her heart ached for the tiny Hispanic babies who wouldn't receive that extra care because they were dark.

But what if—what if he was one of the unlucky ones? Did the bastards who trafficked in stolen babies and ruptured lives even take the time to bury their tiny victims? Or did they just toss them in a ditch somewhere, to be eaten by—

No. She couldn't go there. She couldn't let the gruesome thought finish forming in her mind. If she did, then she would lose control, and that was the one thing she absolutely couldn't do right now. If the tip played out and someone actually showed up at this secret rendezvous, she had to be ready.

Scanning the cemetery once more, she picked out her destination tombstone, one heavier and more ornate than the others, with a nice thick base that would completely conceal her if she was lying down. She got down on her stomach and belly-crawled the rest of the way, lying prone and positioning herself behind the tombstone so that she was at a slight angle and could easily move her head just a little to the right and see the entire width of the church, as well as down the right side of it. Now all she had to do was wait.

The minute hand on her watch crawled around. The hour hand moved to eleven, then past. Finally, at eleven thirty-five, she heard the sound of a car engine. She was immediately alert, though she knew it could just be a farmer heading home from the cantina. She watched closely, but there was no flash of headlights, just the sound of the engine growing closer and closer.

The dark hulk of a car turned at the far back corner of the church, and crawled to a stop about a third of the way down.

Milla drew a deep breath and tried to control the sudden leap of her heart. Most of the time these tips led to nothing but a wild-goose chase, but this time the geese were actually within reach. With any luck, she was about to get her hands on Diaz.

3

WITH THE SCOPE SHE COULD SEE THERE WERE TWO MEN IN THE car, and her heart sank. Obviously others were supposed to join them, unless the meeting consisted of the two men sitting in the car talking to each other, which she doubted. She studied the two in the weird green light of the scope, but they remained in the car and she couldn't get a good look at their features.

She hoped Brian followed the same reasoning that she had and stayed in place. She hadn't spotted him, though she had looked. Wherever he'd hidden himself, he had done a good job of it.

The minutes ticked past, and she still didn't see Brian. Good. He thought the same thing she did, that someone else would be arriving soon.

Almost ten minutes later, she heard another car engine. The vehicle pulled slightly past the church, then backed into the narrow lane so it was trunk to trunk with the other car.

Two men got out of the second car. The doors on the first car opened, and those two men got out as well.

Milla trained her scope on the newcomers as they approached, facing her. The driver was a tall, thin mestizo, his black hair worn long and slicked back in a ponytail. The passenger was somewhat shorter, stockier. The moment she focused on him, her blood ran cold.

For ten years she'd tracked the bastard. The day Justin had been stolen was mostly a blurred horror in her mind; the days afterward, as she fought for her life in the tiny rural clinic, were lost forever. But in the strange way time had of sometimes standing still, she had a few perfect, freeze-frame memories of the attack, and especially the face of the man who had wrenched Justin from her arms.

She wouldn't recognize her little boy now, but the man who had taken him ... she'd recognize him anywhere. She clearly remembered the sensation of his eyeball popping under her digging, clawing fingernails, remembered the bloody furrows she had raked down his left cheek. She had maimed him, marked him, and she was viciously glad. No matter how the bastard aged, she would always know him by the damage she had done to his face.

After ten years, he was walking straight toward her. His left eye socket was empty, the lid scarred and twisted. Two deep lines were clawed straight down his face.

It was *him.*

She could barely breathe. Her lungs ached; her throat ached; her vision blurred with rage.

Don't move if there are more than two of them, she'd told Brian. He was smart; no way would he figure just the two of them could handle four men, all of whom were possibly, probably, armed.

But the bastard was *here,* right in front of her. She'd known this could happen, and still the force of her reaction was so violent it almost blinded her. Red mist swam in her vision, and there was a roaring in her ears.

Her muscles were shaking with intensity. She wanted to tear him apart with her bare hands. A small part of her brain knew it was insanity, but almost as if her hand didn't belong to her, she felt it reaching for the pistol in her pocket, and she began to rise.

She never even made it to her knees. Something hard and heavy hit her in the middle of the back and smashed her to the ground, smothering all movement. Several things happened simultaneously, so fast she had no time to react. Legs hooked around her legs and held them tight, a hand clamped over her mouth and jerked her head back, and an iron-hard arm locked around her throat. In what felt like a fraction of a second, she was immobilized.

"Move or make a sound, and I'll snap your neck."

The voice was cold and menacing, the words spoken so low she could barely hear them, but she understood them perfectly. The arm cutting off her oxygen was plain enough on its own. She was pinned to the ground, unable even to bring her hands up to defend herself.

Dizzily she tried to think. Was this a scout, maybe, sent ahead to make certain the meeting place was unobserved? But if it was, he would have seen Brian, too, and common sense would have dictated he take out Brian first. Maybe he had. Maybe Brian was lying dead on the other side of the cemetery, his throat cut or his neck broken. But if this was a scout, why had he told her not to make any noise?

He couldn't be with the four men. Whatever his interest was in the meeting, he was there for his own reasons. So maybe Brian was still alive, and maybe, if she was very still, she'd make it through with her spinal cord still intact.

She couldn't breathe. Her vision blurred and she managed a small gasp. The arm around her throat loosened the tiniest fraction, but it was enough for her to drag in some air.

Her head was arched back at such an angle she could see

the four men only out of the corners of her eyes, and without the night-vision scope she couldn't make out details. They had opened the trunks on both cars, and two of them now were dragging something out of the trunk of the second car and transferring it to the other trunk.

The rock in her pocket was digging into the sensitive area where her leg joined her hip. Her breasts were flattened painfully into the dirt, and her back ached from her neck being so forcefully arched. There was no softness in the man's weight bearing down on her, no give; he felt like iron. In this position the side of his face was pressed to her head, but though she could feel his chest moving in slow, even breaths–the bastard wasn't the least bit winded or nervous–there was no movement of air on her skin as he exhaled. It was creepy, as if he weren't quite human.

He wasn't paying any attention to her. Now that he had her subdued, he was completely focused on the four men behind the church.

With whatever transaction they had made completed, they were getting back into their respective cars. The man who had stolen Justin was leaving. After ten years she'd finally found him, and now he was getting away. She strained upward against the man holding her, her entire body tightening in protest, and he pressed harder on her throat with his arm. When her vision blurred again, she went limp in despair, a sob convulsing in her chest. In this position she was as helpless as a turtle on its back.

The second car slowly pulled away, turned the corner, and disappeared. The first car began reversing down the narrow lane. The man holding her suddenly lifted his weight and flipped her over on her back. "Take a nap," he growled, and his fingers pressed hard on the base of her neck.

She tried to struggle, but she was already oxygen-deprived

and teetering on the edge of unconsciousness. He leaned over her, a black, featureless weight oozing menace, and the world went blank.

She came to lying propped against Brian's knee, while he anxiously patted her face, her shoulder, her arm. "Milla? Milla! Wake up!"

"I'm awake," she mumbled, the words slurred. "Nap."

"Nap? You took a *nap*?" Disbelief made his voice get louder.

She fought to gather her scattered wits, but she felt as if she were underwater, every movement an effort. "No. Man– jumped me."

"What? Shit!" Brian's head came up and he glared around him. "They must have had a lookout that we didn't spot."

Slowly she heaved her weight off his knee and sat up. Her entire body ached, as if she'd been slammed to the ground. Oh, wait–she had been.

"No, he wasn't one of them."

"How do you know?"

"He told me he'd break my neck if I made a sound." And he'd come close to doing it anyway, if the way her throat felt was any measure of his intent.

"Why would he do that, unless–"

"–he was watching them, too," Milla finished, when Brian broke off the sentence as he worked through the logic.

"But why jump you? We were just watching. He could have stayed where he was and we'd never have known."

Anguish tore through her as she remembered how close she'd been to the man who'd taken Justin. She closed her eyes. "I was about to do something stupid."

"Like what? You don't do stupid things."

"One of the men in the second car–the passenger–is the one who stole Justin."

Brian drew in a long breath, then blew it out. "Shit. Damn."

He was silent a moment. "I guess you were going to go for him, huh? Even though there were *four* of them?"

Her silence was answer enough. She pulled off her baseball cap and ran her hands through her matted curls. "I've dreamed of seeing him again. I've thought of it for ten years, imagined getting my hands on him. I was going to choke answers out of him, if I died doing it."

"And you would have; all four of them were packing, in case you didn't notice."

She hadn't; after seeing the face that had haunted her dreams for a decade, she hadn't noticed anything else. Evidently the guy who'd jumped her had inadvertently saved her life.

Groaning, she got to her feet. The blanket she'd had draped over her was lying a few feet away, and she retrieved it. The night-vision scope had rolled against the base of the adjacent tombstone. The pistol that had been in her pocket, however, was gone. Her assailant must have taken it.

The headache she'd had earlier was back with sickening force, pounding in her temples, and she felt slightly nauseated. "Let's go home," she said tiredly. She'd come so close, but achieved nothing. The bitterness of it was an ashy taste in her mouth.

Silently they made their way back to the truck. As they passed the cantina, fury rose in her again and impulsively she turned, shoving the door open so hard it banged against the wall. Rough, startled faces turned toward her, hazy in the dim light of the smoke-filled little room.

She didn't step inside. Instead she said, in the Spanish she'd honed over the years, "My name is Milla Edge. I work for Finders in El Paso. I will pay ten thousand American dollars to anyone who can tell me how to find Diaz."

There had to be a million Diazes in Mexico, but judging

from the sudden stillness of the men in the cantina, they all knew who she meant. Rewards had been offered before, of course; ten years ago, there had been one for any information about the kidnapping of Justin Boone. She also regularly handed out bribes, *mordidas,* and paid what seemed like a small army of informants. Announcing a reward in a dingy little cantina in a tiny village probably wouldn't produce any different results, but at least she felt as if she was doing *something.* The man who'd destroyed her life ten years ago had just been here in this village, behind the church, and "Diaz" was the only possibility she had for his name. A stab in the dark sometimes brought blood.

Women weren't welcome in Mexican cantinas unless they were prostitutes. One of the men began to get to his feet, and Brian stepped up close behind her, making his imposing presence known. "Let's go," he said, taking her arm, and the force of his grip said he wasn't kidding.

She climbed into the disreputable truck and Brian got in behind her. The motor fired as soon as he turned the key, and they were already in motion when two of the cantina's patrons stepped to the door and watched them drive away.

"What was that for?" Brian demanded hotly. "You always tell us not to take chances, then you walk into a cantina? That's just asking for trouble."

"I didn't go inside." She rubbed her forehead and sighed. "You're right. I'm sorry, I wasn't thinking. The sight of him— after all these years . . ." Her voice thickened and she swallowed. "I'm sorry," she said again, staring through the duct-taped windshield into the night.

Having said his piece, Brian didn't keep on nagging at her. He concentrated on his driving, on the lookout for potholes, cows, and people driving without headlights.

Milla's nails dug into her palms. Ten years had passed

since she'd seen his evil face. She hoped they had been long, miserable years for him, though there was no way they could have been as long and as miserable as they'd been for her. She hoped he suffered from some medical condition that was incurable and hideously painful, but nonfatal. She wanted him to live a horrible existence, but she didn't want him to die. Not yet. Not until she got the information she needed from him, and found Justin. Then she would gladly kill him herself. He had destroyed her, so why shouldn't she destroy him in return?

The years ticked themselves down in her mind, like a countdown.

Ten years ago, Justin had been stolen from her.

Nine years ago, David divorced her. She couldn't blame him. Losing a child put so much stress and strain on the parents that marriages often dissolved. In their case, David hadn't just lost his son, he'd also lost his wife. From the time she'd regained consciousness after being stabbed, her every thought, her life, had focused on finding Justin. There simply hadn't been anything left in her for David.

Eight years ago, while following yet another lead that had produced no information about Justin, she had recovered a stolen baby. The infant had been more dead than alive at the time, but had survived, and Milla had found some comfort for herself in seeing the mother's hysterical joy on having the child returned. She herself didn't have a happy ending, but perhaps she could produce happy endings for others.

Seven years ago, she had organized Finders. It was a group, some paid employees but mostly volunteers, who mobilized to hunt missing children, whether they were simply lost or had been stolen. Police departments across the country were underfunded and understaffed, and they simply didn't have the time or manpower to adequately devote to the problem. The

difference between finding a lost child dead or alive sometimes boiled down to how many bodies could be brought into
the search. Milla was good at mobilizing. Thanks to her high
visibility after Justin's kidnapping, she was also very good at
fund-raising.

Six years ago, David had remarried. It hurt more than she
could have imagined. Part of her resented that he had rebuilt
his life without her, without Justin, but for the most part she
simply hurt. She'd loved David so much. She still loved him,
though their time for being *in* love had ended the day Justin
was stolen. David was, simply, the best man she'd ever known.
Everyone handled grief differently, and David had handled his
by throwing himself into his work, by saving lives that would
otherwise have been lost. He'd had the practice of medicine to
get him through the pain. And Milla had continued her unre-
lenting search for her son.

Five years ago, Finders had accepted its first missing per-
sons case. They didn't just search for lost children now, they
would look for anyone who was lost. The pain of those left behind, wondering what had happened, was too great for her to
ignore.

Four years ago, David and his new wife had had a child.
Milla had been agonized when she heard his wife was pregnant. What if it was a boy, another son? It was small of her and
she knew it, but she didn't think she could bear it if David's
child was a boy. To her immeasurable relief, they'd had a
daughter. And Milla kept looking for her own child.

Three years ago, at the family Christmas celebration at her
parents' home in Ohio, her brother, Ross, had brusquely told
her it was time to get on with her life and stop letting something that had happened seven years before dominate all their
family get-togethers. To her horror, her sister, Julia, hadn't spoken up in her defense, and had refused to meet her gaze. Since

then, Milla saw her parents only when her siblings weren't also visiting. The holidays were lonely, but she didn't think she'd ever be able to forgive Ross for his callousness.

Two years ago, she'd heard the name Diaz for the first time. After eight years of nothing, finally, there was a whisper of information that could possibly have a connection to Justin.

A year ago, David and his wife had a second child, a son. When she heard, Milla cried herself to sleep that night.

Tonight ... tonight, she'd seen him, the monster who had destroyed her. She'd been so close, only to come up empty-handed once again.

But he was still alive. That had been a deeply buried fear, that he would die before she could talk to him. She didn't care what happened to him, so long as she could find out from him what he'd done with her baby. And now that she knew for certain he was alive, and what area he was in, she would intensify her search. She'd hunt him down like a rabid dog, or die herself in the effort.

4

A LITTLE AFTER FOUR-THIRTY, MILLA LET HERSELF INTO HER condo. She was bone-tired, and so dispirited she wanted nothing more than to crawl into bed and hide under the covers.

So close.

She couldn't get the refrain out of her head. For years she'd kept her hope and determination alive with almost nothing to go on, yet now that she'd actually seen the man and knew he was still alive, knew what area he was in, she felt nothing but despair for having failed to capture him.

"I won't let it get me down," she said aloud, going into the bathroom and stripping off her filthy clothes. "I won't." That was how she'd gotten through the hell of the past ten years, by simply refusing to give in. Sometimes she felt like one of the Japanese soldiers after World War II, fighting on long after the war was over because they couldn't accept the outcome.

You'll never find him, people had said. Get on with your life, her own brother had told her. Justin had been so young when he was taken that she had no idea of how he would look, no way of identifying him short of DNA tests, and she couldn't go around the country demanding that all ten-year-old boys have DNA tests. That was assuming he was even in the United States. He could be anywhere. He could be in Canada, or still in Mexico. One well-meaning but totally demented woman had even told her it might help to have a funeral for him, and lay him to rest.

The fact that the woman was still alive was a testament to Milla's self-control.

Justin was *not* dead. If she ceased believing that, she wouldn't be able to function.

Her bathroom mirror reflected back a face that was drawn and pale with exhaustion, with dark circles under her brown eyes and a grim set to her mouth. Tonight, she looked older than her thirty-three years. The streak in her untidy hair was stark under the fluorescent lights. Within days of the kidnapping, one of the nurses at the clinic had noticed that a strand of her hair was growing in white. The streak always stood out in the photographs that were taken at fund-raisers, a reminder to everyone that she knew all too well the agony parents went through when their child was lost. The rest of her hair had remained the same, light brown, curly, but the streak was what drew the gaze.

There was another fund-raiser tomorrow night, she thought; her tired brain caught itself. No, *tonight*. Just because she hadn't been to bed yet didn't mean another day hadn't arrived.

But after she'd showered and pulled on a nightgown, then fallen into bed, sleep wouldn't come. Tonight she hadn't just come close to the man who'd stolen Justin, she had come close to getting both herself and Brian killed. If she had charged those four men, pistol in hand, they would have shot her and, inevitably, Brian, who would have charged to her aid. In retrospect, her lack of control horrified her. Brian had been right to be so upset with her. The Finders weren't vigilantes; they weren't trained to go into gunfights. The core group all had some firearms training, just so they would know how to protect themselves if necessary, but that was all. Brian, with his military background, was the most qualified of them all when it came to weapons.

But because it involved Justin, she had lost all reason, all sense of caution. She would have to do better than that, or she'd never find him, because she would be dead.

She finally dozed, and she dreamed of Justin. It was a recurring dream, one that she'd often had in the first few years after he was stolen, but now her subconscious seldom produced it. As dreams went it was but a small snapshot, and heartbreakingly realistic. She was rocking him while he nursed, and in the dream she felt the small weight of him in her arms, the warmth of his little body against hers. She smelled the sweet baby smell, touched his blond hair and felt the softness, stroked her finger over his cheek and reveled in the velvety texture of his skin. She felt the release of her milk, the tug of his rosebud mouth on her nipple ... and she was at peace.

She woke crying, as she always did. In the perverse way the body had when it was really tired, she wasn't able to go back to sleep. After trying for half an hour to put the dream out of her mind, she gave in, got up, and put on some coffee; then, while it was brewing, she stripped off her nightgown and did some stretching and yoga, which was her favorite form of exercise.

Because she never knew what a case would demand of her, whether it was running down a city street or climbing rocks, she worked hard at staying in good physical condition, but none of it came easily or naturally to her. She intensely disliked sweating, almost as much as she disliked bugs and getting dirty. She did it, though, because she had to, just as she had learned how to handle firearms even though she hated the noise, the smoke, the smell, everything about them. She was at best mediocre in her marksmanship, but she had kept practicing until she had achieved at least that. To track the men who had stolen Justin, she had learned to deal with many things that she disliked, had turned herself into someone else. The woman she'd been before couldn't have dealt with these things, so Milla had forced herself to change.

No, it was those bastards who had changed her. She had been changed the instant Justin was wrenched from her. From the moment she'd regained consciousness in that little clinic, too weak to move, racked with pain, she had been a different woman, focused on only one thing: finding her child.

That was why David had divorced her.

Divorced her, yes, but he hadn't walked away from her. He'd insisted on buying this condo for her in El Paso's Westside, and he paid her forty thousand dollars a year in alimony. Both gestures enabled her to concentrate full-time on Finders rather than having to find a conventional job that would, of necessity, have severely curtailed her ability to track down any and all leads that came her way.

If she had let him, David would have beggared himself buying a lavish mansion for her and giving her a ridiculous amount of money each year. This condo was strictly middle-class, about two thousand square feet, with two bedrooms and two baths upstairs, and a half bath downstairs. It was twenty years old, cozy without being lavish. The forty thousand dollars was about fifteen thousand dollars a year more than she was comfortable with, but she understood it was David's way of helping her in the search. He couldn't do what she did, so he did what he could, and considering he had another family now, that was more than generous.

Her exercises done, she poured a cup of coffee and took it upstairs with her to dress. No jeans and boots were necessary today, thank goodness; she could dress in a skirt and sandals, which were much cooler. Because small luxuries helped get her through the hard times, she always took advantage of nontravel days by taking the time to smooth her skin with moisturizers, take extra care with her hair and makeup, wear perfume; just little things, things she did for herself, but they soothed a need within her. Though some days she might look like a cross between GI Jane and Thelma and Louise right before they drove over the canyon lip, inside she was still a woman who enjoyed feminine things.

Because she took that time with her appearance, she was late getting into the office. Finders was located on the top floor of a warehouse, the space donated by True Gallagher, an El Paso businessman who in the past few years had become involved in helping bankroll Finders. The bottom floor of the warehouse was still in use, and she was accustomed to the sound of tow motors zipping around below, the shouts of the workers, the rumble of eighteen-wheelers arriving to pick up or deliver machinery.

Upstairs, the offices were bare-bones. Naked fluorescent bulbs, cracked linoleum tile on the floor, and industrial green paint were the predominant features. The secondhand metal desks were battered, most of the office chairs were patched with duct tape, and there were only two private offices—semiprivate, that is, since the top half of the front wall in each office was a huge window.

The phone system, however, was state-of-the-art. Finders put its money where it would do the most good.

Milla loved her staff. God knows they didn't work there for the pay, which was barely adequate. They worked long hours, including most Saturdays, and sometimes even on Sunday. She herself took no pay, not even a nominal amount. Most of the people in the Finders network were volunteers, spread out all over the nation, who offered themselves and their time whenever they were needed to look for people who were lost in their particular area. The core of Finders, however, the group of people here in El Paso, devoted themselves full-time to the job and were on the payroll.

Most of the volunteers did it out of the goodness of their hearts. Some of her full-time staff were the same, but some of them had personal reasons for being there. Joann Westfall's best friend in grade school had become lost while on a family camping trip and died of exposure before she was found. Debra Schmale's ex-husband had disappeared with her two daughters, and it had taken her over two years to locate them and retrieve her children. Olivia Meyer, Harvard-educated, staunch New Yorker, chose to live in hell–her term for El Paso, which greatly offended the locals on staff–because her elderly, senile grandfather had wandered away from his house one November day and spent hours walking the cold city streets without even a sweater for warmth before a cop picked him up and took him to a precinct station.

The best way to find lost people was to flood the area with searchers. All of her people understood that and devoted themselves to the task.

Brian was at the coffee machine when Milla entered. "Want a cup?" he called, and she nodded.

Joann looked up with an anxious gaze. "How did it go last night? Did you find out anything?"

"The man who took Justin was there," Milla said baldly, and there was a collective gasp from everyone within hearing distance. People shoved back chairs and hurried over.

"What happened?" Debra asked, her blue eyes huge. "Did you talk to him?"

Brian approached and shoved a polystyrene coffee cup into

Milla's hand. "No. There were four of them, just two of us." He flicked a glance at her that said he wasn't going to spill the beans about her loss of judgment.

She wasn't about to dissemble, though, so she came clean. "That was the idea, anyway, that we wouldn't try to talk to them if there were more than two people. When I saw him, though, I lost my head. All I wanted was to get my hands around his throat."

"Omigod," Olivia blurted. "What happened? Did they shoot at you?"

"They never knew we were there. I was jumped and knocked out by another man."

"Omigod," Olivia said again. "Were you hurt? Did you see a doctor?"

"No, to both questions."

"I don't get it," Joann said. "This other man obviously knew you were there, so why didn't he tell the others?"

"He wasn't with them. He was watching them, too."

"Well, that's a twist," someone else muttered.

"Any idea who he might be?" Debra asked.

"Not a clue. I didn't get a look at him. Whatever he was up to, though, he saved our lives by jumping me. And since I'm confessing, I also went in a cantina and offered ten thousand dollars to anyone who could tell me where to find Diaz. So if you get any phone calls asking about a reward, that's why."

"That explains that," Olivia said, her eyebrows rising. "First thing this morning I got a threatening call, telling me to stay away from Diaz or die. I think that's what she said, anyway. That was pre-coffee, so my Spanish comprehension wasn't up to full speed yet. I told her I don't have a boyfriend named Diaz."

"Her?" Milla asked, her own eyebrows going north.

"Definitely a 'her.' That's why I was thinking angry girlfriend. Sounds like you pulled on someone's chain, for sure."

Yes, it did. This was interesting, and exciting. "Did you get the number?"

"Sure." Olivia went over to her desk and checked Caller ID. "It says 'El Paso,' but I don't recognize the exchange."

Brian ambled over and looked at the number. "Phone card," he said. "Untraceable."

There was something about Brian that always got on every last New Yorker nerve Olivia possessed. "Really." Her tone was ice cold. "I suppose you can tell age, sex, and weight from the phone number, too, O Great White Hunter." The last was a subtle dig at his military background; Olivia was a staunch dove who had only with the greatest reluctance learned anything at all about firearms.

"Not sex," he said, grinning. "I use another method for that." He topped things off by ruffling her hair before prudently retreating out of reach. "Not only that, I buy phone cards to use for long-distance calls, so I know how the numbers show up on Caller ID. With my vast expertise, I'd say that's an AT&T card, easily purchased at any Wal-Mart and a gazillion other places."

Milla had often bought phone cards to use while she was on the road and cell phone service was spotty, but she doubted Olivia, with her moneyed background, had ever even noticed the cards for sale practically everywhere. If she needed to make a call and didn't have cell service, she would simply charge the call to her credit card or her home phone, thereby guaranteeing astronomical rates.

Getting back to the subject, Milla said, "Let's lay out the facts. Late yesterday afternoon, I got a call on my cell phone giving me the tip on Diaz. The caller was a man. I didn't notice the number, but I'll check it, see if it matches up with today's call. Brian and I both thought it might be a setup, not for us, but for Diaz. Someone wanting him out of the way.

"We get to the meeting place, and the man who took Justin

is one of the men who show up. He's the only one I recognized. The odds are *he's* Diaz, because the coincidence is fairly large."

Milla noticed that as she talked, Joann was busily writing down each point.

"The four men arrived in two cars, two in each car, and took something out of one car trunk and transferred it to the other. I couldn't see what it was–" Because her head had been pulled back at a painful angle.

"A body," said Brian, his tone flat. "Wrapped in a tarp or blanket."

A chill went down Milla's spine. She should have realized, but she'd been too focused on the one-eyed man. This was yet another illustration that she had to get control of her emotions; she was missing things that should have been obvious to her.

"I was knocked down by an unseen assailant who was also very interested in the four men, and not at all interested in what I was doing there. When the four men drove away, he used the carotid-artery thingie to knock me out–"

"You didn't tell me that," Brian interrupted, his gaze sharpening.

"Knocked out is knocked out. At least I didn't have a concussion."

"No, but unless you know what you're doing, you can cause brain damage if you press too long. Though I guess in most cases you wouldn't care, considering you're cutting off someone's blood supply to his brain. Or her brain, in your case."

That was a perspective she could have done without, to realize how easily she could have been left impaired. Not that there was anything she could have done to protect herself, other than not be there in the first place, and withdrawing from the search simply wasn't an option.

She shook away her retrospective alarm. "I assume the man then followed one of the cars, but he might not have. He might have followed Brian and me. I can't think of any reason why he would, other than curiosity, but it's still a possibility. I offered a ten-thousand-dollar reward to a cantina full of men, for information leading to Diaz, and this morning a woman calls telling us to stay away from Diaz or die." She paused. "Does anyone else have anything to add to this hodgepodge?"

No one answered. Joann studied the flow of facts. "I'd say the only anomaly is this guy who assaulted you. Everything else connects. I'd say the one-eyed man is Diaz and someone tried to set him up. When you went into the cantina and made that announcement, he heard about it, obviously figured out you'd been very close to him that night, since you were in the same village at the same time, and he had someone call to warn you off."

Milla had already formed the same opinion, but not as concisely. Joann had a knack for clarity that made Milla prize her even more.

"It's obvious someone—my original caller—wants us to find Diaz, for whatever reason. Probably a rivalry, but I don't care why. All we can do now is wait for him to contact me again."

That went against the grain. She wanted to scour the area around Guadalupe, even though logic told her it would be a waste of time. She wanted to be actively doing something, anything, instead of waiting around for a call that might not come for days, weeks, if it ever came at all.

The phone rang right then, and a staffer hurried to answer it. After listening for a minute, he looked up and said, "Amber Alert in California, San Clemente area."

It was a call to battle stations. Within seconds, they were all on the phone, raising their army of volunteers in the San Clemente and surrounding sectors, getting people on the freeways and highways, searching for the vehicle in question, a blue Honda Accord. According to witnesses, a man had grabbed a twelve-year-old girl in a fast-food parking lot and shoved her into his car. One woman had managed to get a partial on the license plate as the car fishtailed out of the parking lot.

With that information, the Finders would set up observation points, people with binoculars who searched for blue Honda Accords with a man driving. When one was spotted, information was relayed to the Finders in vehicles who would zero in on the car and check the license plate. Finders didn't try to apprehend; if they located the vehicle, they would in turn notify the area law enforcement and let them take over.

Milla checked the time: eight forty-three in California. Traffic would be very heavy, which might or might not help. If a commuter was listening to his radio, he would hear the Amber Alert, but if he was playing a CD or listening to an MP5, he wouldn't; he would just be in the way.

She shoved last night's events away, and concentrated on recovering the little girl in California while she was still alive.

She hadn't been able to do this for her own child, but she could do it for someone else's.

5

THE FUND-RAISER THAT NIGHT WAS HELD IN A LOCAL HIGH school gymnasium. Finders generally didn't rate a black-tie event, which suited Milla, though occasionally she found herself at more ritzy affairs. She had invested in one suitable evening gown, which meant it cost the earth, but she didn't want to spend the money to buy more than that one. She did have several good cocktail dresses, and tonight she wore her favorite, needing that pick-me-up to keep her going when she was so tired. The ice blue did wonders for her warm complexion, and the shoes that went with the dress were comfortable enough that she wasn't in agony by evening's end.

She had left the office a couple of hours early and spent the time pampering herself: facial, manicure, pedicure. She even fit in a short nap, which would keep her going for several more hours. She fussed with her curly hair and, though she never quite managed to tame it, did at least achieve a style that said it was intentional. The facial had brightened her complexion and made her look less tired, and she used a gentle makeup job to soften her face even more. Perfume, hosiery, jewelry—she loved the ritual of it all, the way it made her feel. She so seldom had the opportunity to indulge in being overtly feminine that she reveled in the fund-raiser occasions. They were crucial to Finders' financial health, but in a more subtle way they were just as crucial to her mental health.

She drove her six-year-old white Toyota SUV to the high school, where the parking lot was already filling with an assortment of cars, trucks, and SUVs, with the latter two far outnumbering the cars. Well-dressed people were walking purposefully toward the gym, because only an idiot stood out in the heat in El Paso in August. Even though the sun had gone down and twilight was gathering, in the short walk to the gym Milla felt perspiration gathering between her breasts.

She always came alone to these fund-raisers, though she could easily have asked Brian or any of the other men who worked at Finders to accompany her. For one thing, fund-raisers were deadly dull and she didn't want to inflict them on anyone else. For another, she was always painfully aware of how she appeared to the people whom she was asking to give money to her cause.

The facts of her particular case were well known, that her baby had been stolen and a year later her marriage had broken under the strain, that she had devoted her life since to searching not only for her child but for other lost ones, too. For some reason, the fact that she was solitary seemed to loosen purse strings. If she started attending fund-raisers with a different man every time, people might begin to think she was spending more time dating than attending to business. When you stayed in business by begging money from these same people, what they thought was important.

She opened one of the heavy double doors to the gym and stepped into blessed cool air. Round tables that seated eight to ten each had been set up on the gymnasium floor, which had been covered with green felt to prevent it from being scuffed and dented. The tables had been covered with white table-cloths, the place settings and napkins precisely arranged, and fresh flowers stood in the middle of each table. At the head of the room was a long table on a makeshift dais, and a podium. She would be sitting up there with the organizers of the event, the mayor, and the social lights of El Paso who made an effort to help.

She always spoke at these events, and after so many years she no longer needed prepared notes. Her speech was always essentially the same, though details might change; she always told about searches Finders had made, with both good and bad endings. The good ending was to illustrate that Finders pro-vided a beneficial service; the bad ending was to illustrate that, with proper funding, they could do even better. Tonight, Tiera Alverson was very much on her mind. A fourteen-year-old girl shouldn't end her life in a dingy, roach-infested dump, her veins fried with drugs.

Smiling, speaking to people she knew, she began making her way toward the dais. She was about halfway there when a hard, warm hand closed over her elbow to bring her to a halt, then immediately released her. She turned and smiled when she met True Gallagher's narrow, dark gaze. "Hello, True, how are you?"

"You look tired," he said bluntly, ignoring the social niceties.

"Thanks," she replied, her tone wry. "Now I know I wasted a lot of effort."

"I didn't say you look bad. I said you look tired."

"Yeah, but the effort was to make me look less tired."

"Maybe it worked." He surveyed her with his shrewd gaze. "Just how tired are you?"

"Exhausted," she said, and smiled.

"Then it worked."

True was a self-made businessman, a man who had clawed his way out of poverty, and the struggle had made him into a powerful man. That power was still more in the force of his personality than it was in his financial base, but she had no doubt True Gallagher would die a multimillionaire. He was determined and ruthless, and he didn't allow anything to get in his way. Yet from the time he first began enjoying some success, he had been interested in Finders and was one of their steadiest donors.

She didn't know how old True was; he could have been anywhere between thirty-five and forty-five. His face was darkly tanned and weathered by long hours in the west Texas sun, his build was still lean and strong. He was tall, about six-three or -four, and possessed of an animal magnetism that women automatically noticed. Sometimes he brought a date to these events, but just as often he attended alone. Since he didn't have Miss August clinging to his arm, Milla assumed this was one of his stag appearances.

"Long night?" he asked, a hand on her back urging her to continue to the front of the room and falling into step beside her.

"Last night was. I hope tonight is quieter."

"What happened?"

She wasn't about to do a recital of the entire evening. Instead she said, "It was a bad day. We found the runaway we were looking for, but she was dead."

"Yeah, that's tough. How old was she?"

"Fourteen."

"That's a hard age. Everything feels like the end of the world, and you can't reason with someone who can't see tomorrow."

She couldn't imagine True Gallagher ever suffering from teenage angst, or drug addiction, or any other weakness. She was surprised he even knew about them. He was like iron-wood, impervious to his surroundings.

His strength drew her. She enjoyed the not-quite-flirting banter with him, though she was always careful to keep from crossing the line. He was an influential sponsor, and ever letting their relationship become personal would be immensely stupid of her. Business didn't mix very well with pleasure under the best of circumstances; when she depended in part on his largesse to keep Finders operating, having a brief fling with him would have been a recipe for disaster.

Besides, right now she didn't have time for a fling, brief or otherwise. Not only was she incapable of giving her full attention to a romance, her job dictated that she travel a lot. She had tried dating, off and on, since her divorce; if the man was remotely interested in her, he didn't like the amount of time she spent out of town. Unfortunately, that wasn't something she would compromise on, period. She had tried having a couple of affairs, only to have them wither from neglect. She had eventually come to the conclusion that it wasn't fair to either the man or herself to waste his time and hers until the day came when she could devote herself to something other than searching for Justin.

And in her heart, she knew she hadn't yet met a man who could measure up to David in her affections. She was no longer *in* love with him—time and life had taken care of that—but a part of her would always love him for the man he was. She didn't pine for him; she didn't lie awake at night yearning for him. There was a stark line of demarcation in her life, and David belonged on the other side of the line. But she knew what it was to love, and no one since had kindled that kind of emotion in her.

True Gallagher was thinking of trying. She sensed it, the way women always know those things. The truth was in the way he touched her—always in a public, proper way—but still *touching* her. He hadn't yet made the effort to take their relationship further, but the thought lay there, in the back of his mind. She had no doubt he would eventually get around to trying.

And she would have to find some graceful way of refusing him that wouldn't harm Finders.

The gym was rapidly filling, and Marcia Gonzalez, the chief organizer of the event, was motioning to her and True to take their seats. Milla slid into the seat True held out for her, next to the podium, and somehow she wasn't surprised when he took the seat next to hers. She automatically tucked her legs to the side so there couldn't be any accidental brushes of his leg against hers.

The catering service began delivering the plates of rubber chicken and green beans that were de rigueur for fund-raisers. The chicken was roasted, the green beans had slivers of almonds in them, the rolls were dry. She would have preferred a taco, a hamburger, anything other than more chicken and green beans. At least it was a relatively healthy diet, and she was never tempted to overeat.

True stabbed his chicken as if he were imagining killing it. "Why aren't we ever served roast?" he grumbled. "Or steak?"

"Because a lot of people don't eat red meat."

"This is El Paso. Everyone here eats red meat."

He was probably right, but if anyone in the city didn't eat red meat, they would be in the crowd who attended charity events. The organizers had wisely played it safe. Unfortunately, safe meant chicken and green beans.

True pulled a small shaker from his suit pocket and began sprinkling something red over his food.

"What's that?" Milla asked.

"Southwestern spices. Want some?"

Her eyes lit up. "Oh, please."

She wasn't as liberal with the shaker as True had been, but her taste buds wept with gratitude.

"I've been carrying that shaker around for a couple of years now," he admitted. "It's saved my life."

The woman on the other side of him leaned around. "May I borrow it?" she asked, and soon the shaker was making its way down the table, people were smiling, and the level of enthusiasm visibly lifted.

Milla eyed his strong face as they ate. There was something about the cast of his features that made her wonder if he was part Hispanic. She did know that he had strong contacts with the Hispanic community, on both sides of the border.

True had grown up in the mean streets. His contacts weren't with just the movers and shakers, but with the seamier elements as well. She wondered if he would be able to find out anything about Diaz that she couldn't.

"Have you ever heard anything about a man named Diaz?" she asked.

Maybe it was her imagination, but she thought he froze for a split second. "Diaz?" he said. "It's a common name. I know probably fifty, sixty people named that."

"This one works the other side of the border. He's somehow involved with smuggling people across."

"A coyote."

"I don't think so. I don't think he actually does it himself." She hesitated, thinking of Brian's certainty that the four men last night had been handling a body. "He's probably a killer, too."

True took a sip of his water. "Why are you asking about someone like that?"

Because she thought he was the son of a bitch who had stolen her baby. She bit back the words and resorted to her own water glass. "I'll track anyone who might lead me to Justin," she finally said.

"So you think this Diaz was involved?"

"I *know* the man who took Justin has only one eye, because I clawed out the other one." She drew a deep, trembling breath. "And I *think* his name is Diaz. It may not be, but the name keeps surfacing. If you could find out anything about a one-eyed man named Diaz, I'd appreciate it."

"Just having one eye narrows it down. I'll see what I can learn."

"Thank you." She was aware he might use her request as a bridge to other things, but that was a situation she'd have to handle if and when it occurred. He'd heard the name, she thought. Yes, he probably knew a lot of people with the last name of Diaz, but still, it had meant something to him in the context she meant. For some reason he was being cautious, hiding his cards. Maybe he'd had dealings with Diaz in his more disreputable past, and he didn't want it known.

Dessert was being served, yellow cake with chocolate icing. She waved hers away but accepted coffee. The time was approaching when she would have to speak, and she wanted to gather her thoughts. These people had paid forty dollars a plate for some truly unremarkable food, and some of them would write a separate check to Finders afterward; she could at least give them a coherent speech.

By ten-thirty, speech made, thank-yous offered, and hands shaken, Milla wearily climbed into her vehicle. As she was about to close the door, True called her name and strode over to her.

"Will you have dinner with me tomorrow night?" he asked, with no lead-up or preparational flirting, which she greatly appreciated, because she was so tired now she didn't think she could handle even a mild verbal dance.

"Thank you, but I have another fund-raiser in Dallas tomorrow night." And she looked forward to it almost as much as she would have looked forward to having a tooth pulled.

"And the day after tomorrow?"

She smiled wryly. "The day after tomorrow, I have no idea where I'll be. I can't guarantee anything."

He let a few moments of silence tick by. "That's a hard life, Milla. There's no time for anything personal."

"Believe me, I know." She sighed. "I couldn't go to dinner with you anyway, because of the situation."

"Which is . . . ?"

"You're a sponsor of Finders. I can't risk damaging the organization with my social life."

Another moment of silence. "You're honest," he finally said. "And up front. I admire it, even though I think I'm going to change your mind."

"I think you'll try," she corrected gently.

He laughed, the sound deep and masculine and delicious. "Is that a challenge?"

"No, it's the truth. Nothing on this earth means as much to me as finding my son, and I won't do anything to jeopardize that. Period."

"It's been ten years."

"I don't care if it's been twenty." Because she was so tired, her voice was sharper than she'd intended. What he'd stated was too much along the lines of what her brother, Ross, had said to her, that it was time to put it behind her and get on with her life, as if *Justin's* life was over and done with, as if love had a time limit on it. "I don't care if it takes the rest of my life."

"It's a hard road you've set for yourself to travel."

"It's the only road I can see."

He lightly slapped her door and stepped back. "For now. I'll find out what I can about this Diaz you're hunting, and get back to you. Until then, be careful."

That was an odd thing to say. She stared at him, the words penetrating her bone-deep weariness. "You know something, don't you? About Diaz."

He didn't answer directly, instead saying, "I'll see what I can find out." He walked toward his own car, and Milla stared after him.

Yes, he definitely knew something. And what he knew must not be good, for him to be warning her to be careful.

A chill ran down her spine despite the heat that lingered even this late at night. She was on the right track. She knew it. And following it might well get her killed.

6

SOMETIME DURING THE NIGHT, MILLA WOKE WITH A THOUGHT crystal clear in her mind: she hadn't looked at the cell phone display of the number for the call telling her about the meeting in Guadalupe. The number might not be important, but then again ... it might. Still groggy from fatigue and sleep, she stumbled out of bed and turned on the overhead light, blinking in the painful brightness. She retrieved the phone from her purse, turned it on, then went through the menu to the most recent calls. There it was, and it was an El Paso exchange.

She had already hit *redial* when she glanced at the clock and saw it was twenty after two. Hastily she pressed the *end* button. Whoever it was would wait until the morning, and probably be more cooperative for it.

She wrote the number down, turned out the light, and went back to bed. This time she dreamed disjointed fragments that made no sense and were immediately forgotten each time she roused enough to realize she was dreaming. Despite her restless sleep she woke at her usual time, five-thirty, feeling almost normal. Today was Sunday, she realized, the one day of the week she didn't go to the office–unless something came up. At least half the time, though, something came up. Children didn't care what day of the week it was when they wandered away from home, nor did kidnappers fret about it.

She stayed in bed another fifteen minutes, luxuriating in the lack of urgency. She so seldom got to sleep late that she almost never *did,* even when she had the chance, but it was nice not to have to leap out of bed and get a start on the day.

Just as she was about to get up, the phone rang. She groaned as she threw back the covers and jumped up. She was accustomed to calls at all hours of the night–and early morning–but they almost always meant a job and her stomach tightened as she answered the call.

"Milla, this is True Gallagher. Did I wake you?"

Surprise had her sitting down on the bed. "No, I'm an early riser. So are you, I see."

"Actually, I've been up all night gathering information for you, and I wanted to talk to you before I go to the office."

"You stayed up all night?" She hadn't intended for him to put himself out that much. Then she said, "You go to the office on Sunday?"

He chuckled. "Not usually, but there's something I have to deal with today."

"I hate that you stayed awake all night on my account. I'm sorry. It wasn't urgent; you could have waited until tomorrow."

"The people I needed to talk to aren't people you can catch during the daytime."

"I understand. I should have realized that." She herself certainly dealt with that sort of character often enough.

"I've got good news and bad news. The good news is that I did dig up some info on the Diaz I think you're hunting, but the bad news is it probably won't do you any good."

"What do you mean?"

"You're looking for the man who took your baby, aren't you? That would mean he was operational in Chihuahua ten years ago. This Diaz wasn't. He started popping up about five years ago."

Sharp disappointment speared her, because that name was the only one she'd ever heard mentioned in connection with kidnapping. "Are you certain?"

"As certain as I can be, under the circumstances. This guy doesn't exactly leave a paper trail. But be glad he isn't the one you're looking for, because he's bad news all the way. The word is he's an assassin. If you want somebody to disappear, you put the word out, and Diaz will contact you. He tracks down his target and takes care of your problem. He's supposed to be damn good at it, too. People hear he's on their track and they run, but he always finds them. In some circles that's the only name he has, the Tracker."

"Are you sure this Diaz isn't one-eyed?"

"Positive."

She grasped at the only other straw she had. "I heard a rumor that perhaps he employs a gang of coyotes, so maybe the man who took Justin works for him."

"I doubt it. I didn't turn up anything like that. As far as I was able to find out, Diaz always works alone."

She could almost feel another opportunity dying away like bubbles under her fingers, just as previous ones had, for ten years. She would hear something, get her hopes up that she was finally making progress, then—nothing. No new information, no progress, and no Justin.

"Could there be another Diaz?" She was grabbing at another bubble and she knew it, but what else could she do? Stop grabbing?

He blew out a weary breath. "Too many of them. I know a

few of them myself, men I wouldn't want to turn my back on. But I was able to eliminate some because they were otherwise accounted for during the pertinent time period."

In jail, he meant. "And the others? Do any of them have just one eye?"

"I still have a few inquiries out. But when people these days say 'Diaz,' they're talking about the killer. I'm not surprised his name surfaced when you asked questions, but I'm damn glad you won't have to deal with him."

She would gladly deal with Satan himself if it would help her find Justin. "All I want is information," she said, rubbing her forehead. "I don't even care about justice anymore. I just want to ask some questions. If you do find a Diaz who might have been involved ten years ago, can you get word to him that I won't turn him in, that I just want to talk?" That was a lie. Regardless of what the one-eyed man's name was, she wanted to kill him. After she talked to him, of course. But she would do whatever she had to do, and if letting him walk was necessary, she'd let him walk. She would hate it, but she'd do it.

"I can give it a shot, but don't get your hopes up. And do me a favor."

"If I can."

"Go through me if you need to contact anyone, or find out anything. It's too dangerous for you to be going after these guys yourself. It would be better to keep your name out of it entirely, so you aren't on their radar."

"My name isn't in the phone book. The address on my business cards is Finders' address."

"That helps, but it wouldn't hurt to put another layer of protection between you and them. I know how to deal with them."

"But isn't that putting you in danger? I've built a reputation through Finders for years now that all we're interested in is recovery of people, not in police work, so why would they trust you more than they would me?"

"Because of some people I know," he said flatly. His voice softened. "Let me help, Milla. Let me do this."

Instinct told her not to take his offer, that doing so would allow him to get closer to her than she knew was smart. He wasn't couching his offer in personal terms, but the tone of his voice was very personal. On the other hand, he was an asset she could use; he'd found out more about Diaz—assuming they were talking about the same man—in one night than she had in two years.

"All right," she said, letting her reluctance show. "But I don't like it."

"I can tell." There was a smile in his voice now that he had gotten his way. "Trust me, it's the smart thing to do."

"I know it's smart for me; I just hope it isn't a bad move for you. I can't thank you enough for going to all this trouble—"

"Sure you can. If you're in town tomorrow night, have dinner with me."

"No," she said firmly. "The reason I gave you last night still stands."

"Ah well, it was worth a try." He smoothly changed subjects. "When is your flight to Dallas?"

"Two something."

"Are you coming back tonight?"

"No, I'll stay the night and catch the first flight out tomorrow morning."

"Take care, then, and I'll talk to you when you get back."

"I will. And thank you. Oh—" she said, abruptly thinking of something. "Did you find out Diaz's first name? The assassin Diaz, that is. We can use that to sort out all these rumors we hear, and discard the ones pertaining to him."

"No, I didn't get his first name," he said, but there was the tiniest hesitation that again made her think he knew more than he was telling.

Since he was going out of his way to help her, though, she wasn't about to give him grief about his overprotectiveness. She thanked him again, said good-bye, and began preparing for her trip to Dallas.

She had laundry to do, bills to write checks for, some light housekeeping; outside of laundry, dust was her biggest cleaning problem. But she liked her house to look nice and smell nice, so she made the effort. Every week she freshened the potpourri she had in each room, so whenever she came home she was greeted by a wonderful scent. Sometimes that was the only comfort she could find.

By nine-thirty, her last load of laundry was in the clothes dryer. She put stamps on the envelopes she was mailing and decided to take them to the post office rather than leave them in her box overnight, since her credit card payment was among the bunch. She grabbed her car keys, then at the last minute checked to make certain the phone number the tipster used was still on her cell phone. Sometimes the numbers disappeared, and she didn't know why. Perhaps she was hitting some combination of keys that told numbers to go away, but for whatever reason, it happened. Sure enough, when she pulled up the menu and accessed her incoming call log, nothing was there. Nothing. Not a single number.

She puffed out her cheeks in frustration, then ran upstairs to get the scrap of paper on which she'd scribbled the number last night. Thank goodness she'd written it down. She could go by the office, take care of some paperwork, and check the number on the computer there.

The warehouse was closed on Sunday, the gravel parking lot usually empty. Today, however, Joann's red Jeep Cherokee was parked right next to the door. Milla parked beside the

Cherokee and climbed the steep flight of exterior stairs that led to the second floor. When she tried to open the door, she found it locked, which was good, since Joann had been here alone. Milla unlocked the heavy steel door and went in, calling, "Joann?" both to locate her friend and to let her know someone else was here. To be on the safe side, she locked the door behind her.

"In here," Joann called, and came out of the break room. "I'm nuking some popcorn, but I've got another bag. Want some?"

"No, thanks, I had a real breakfast."

"Popcorn is real. And I had a Pop-Tart, too."

Joann was a junk-food junkie, which made it all the more amazing that she was so trim. She was forty, divorced, had an eighteen-year-old son, who had left the week before to spend what was left of the summer with his dad before heading off to college, and she looked no older than thirty. She wore her blond hair cut almost boy-short, and her blue eyes held a permanent twinkle. Joann was often the voice of reason when emotions erupted out of control in the office, which happened on a regular basis. The job they did was so intense, and sometimes so heartbreaking, that mini-crises were the rule rather than the exception.

"Why are you here today?" Milla asked.

"Paperwork, what else? How about you?"

Milla sighed. "Paperwork. And I wanted to run a phone number through the computer."

"What phone number?"

"The one that came in on my cell phone Friday afternoon, with the tip about Diaz. It's an El Paso exchange, so I'm curious."

"Have you called it?"

"Not yet. I started to last night, but it was late—or early—and I decided to wait. And if I can find out who I'm calling beforehand, so much the better."

She went into her office and booted up her computer. While the machine was going through its digital contortions, she turned around to her desk and flipped through the stack of paperwork to pull out those things she could get finished in the short amount of time she had.

Their computer system needed updating, she thought as she listened to the beeps and whirs behind her. That was one more expense that was continually shoved to the back burner, because there was always something more important, more urgent, that took their funds. As long as their current system still worked, she couldn't justify spending thousands to upgrade.

When the booting was complete, she swiveled her chair around, went on-line, pulled up Google, and typed in the phone number. In two seconds, she had the name of the service station where the call had been placed, and the address. Behind her, she heard Joann come into the office.

"Find anything?"

"It's a service station."

Joann leaned her hip on the desk and waited as Milla dialed the number. It was answered on the fifth ring. "Service station."

An informative greeting, Milla thought. "Hello, this is Milla with Finders, and we received a call from your location about six P.M. Friday afternoon. Can you tell me–"

"Sorry," the man said impatiently. "This is a pay phone. I don't have time to watch everybody who uses it. You get a crank call?"

"No, it was a legitimate call; I'm just trying to get in touch with the man who made it."

"I can't help ya. Sorry." He hung up, and Milla blew out a frustrated breath as she followed suit.

"What did he say?" Joann asked impatiently.

"Yes," said a low, emotionless voice behind them. "What did he say?"

Joann jumped and gave a startled little squeak as she whirled. Milla stood up so abruptly her chair shot backward and crashed into her desk, and somehow she ended up standing beside Joann, frozen, staring at the man who blocked her office door. Chills ran up and down her spine, and her heart thundered in her chest. They had been alone in the office. The door was locked. How had he gotten in? What did he want?

He wasn't carrying a weapon, at least none that she could see. But though his hands were empty, she wasn't reassured, because his eyes were the coldest, most remote eyes she'd ever seen. She was looking into the eyes of a killer, and though she was so frightened she was shaking, there was something mesmerizing about that gaze and she found herself unable to look away. Like a cobra, she thought, hypnotizing its prey before it struck.

There was a preternatural stillness about him, as if he wasn't quite human.

Beside her, Joann was breathing in rapid little gasps, her eyes round as she stared unblinkingly at the intruder. Milla touched Joann's hand in reassurance and Joann immediately grabbed her hand in a death grip.

The man looked briefly at their clasped hands, then back up to their faces. "Don't make me ask again," he said, still in that totally empty tone.

That voice. She knew that voice. But panic was still beating through her veins, and she couldn't solidify the memory. Milla swallowed and managed to get the words out of her tight throat, but her voice was strained. "It was a pay phone. The man said he didn't know who used it, that he was too busy to pay attention."

A slight dip of his eyelids was the only acknowledgment the intruder gave of her answer.

There was no way they could get past him. He wasn't a

huge man, but he was big enough, about six-one, maybe six-two, with a lean, hard build that said he was all muscle and strength, with a dash of rattlesnake quickness thrown in. He was darkness, a shadow filled with almost palpable menace.

Then she knew, and she felt dizzy as blood rushed from her head. She reached out and grabbed the edge of the desk for support. "You're the man who knocked me down," she said, the words thin and shocked. And in that instant she realized something else, something that made her knees shake and almost give way. *"You're Diaz."*

Still his expression didn't change. "I heard you wanted to talk to me," he said.

7

Oh, God. *Diaz.* She remembered what True had said, that Diaz was an assassin, and she believed him. She had no doubt at all.

She should have expected this. True had told her just a few hours ago that people would put out the word they wanted Diaz, and he would find them. She had announced to a cantina full of men that she would pay a reward to anyone who could give her information about Diaz, knowing he was in the area, maybe even listening. Maybe she should be surprised it had taken Diaz thirty-six hours to show up; he could have been waiting for her yesterday morning. Then she remembered giving the men in the cantina her real name, *Milla Edge,* instead of *Milla Boone* as she usually did. Her telephone was listed under "Edge"; when she'd told True that her name wasn't listed in the phone book, she'd meant "Milla Boone." True himself had her home number only because she'd scribbled it on the back of one of her business cards. If Diaz had been on the ball, he could have broken into her condo before she'd even gotten up that morning.

Or maybe he'd just had something more interesting to do.

He stepped inside the office and closed the door, then moved to the side so his back wasn't to all that glass. In doing so he blocked their exit past the open end of Milla's U-shaped desk; if they wanted out from behind the desk, they would have to vault over it.

He dragged one of the chairs over and sat down, then stretched his legs out and crossed one booted foot over the other. "I'm here," he said. "Talk."

Part of Milla's mind was blank; what did one say to an assassin? Hello, nice to meet you? But the other half of her brain was connecting dots and reaching obvious conclusions. Obviously, Diaz wasn't the one-eyed man. But he had been observing the meeting on Friday night, so he was either hunting one of the men involved or was following them, expecting them to lead him to his target. She suspected the latter, because all he had done was watch them. And if anyone could find the one-eyed man, it was Diaz. He might know where the bastard was at this very moment.

Slowly she pulled Joann to the side, and stepped in front of her. It wasn't fair that Joann should be dragged into the middle of this when it was all Milla's doing, and her problem to solve. Milla pulled her chair out of the protective U of her desk and sat down, her knees almost touching his legs, though she was careful to keep that precious inch of space between them.

"I'm Milla Edge," she began.

"I know."

His complete lack of facial expression was unnerving. Everything about him was unnerving, yet she knew she could have walked past him on the street and not looked twice. He wasn't a slavering madman, as would have befitted a homicidal maniac; instead he seemed very controlled and detached. His black hair was cropped short and his jaw was covered with a day's worth of stubble, but that wasn't disreputable. His olive drab T-shirt was clean, as were his black jeans and black rub-ber-soled boots. The short sleeves of the T-shirt clung to his bi-ceps, but his arms were sinewy rather than bulky, roped with muscles and veins. If he had a weapon on him, she thought, it had to be tucked into one of his boots. That wasn't terribly re-assuring, nor was the fact that he was sitting in such a relaxed posture. A snake could strike without warning, but the line of poetry that began running through her head wasn't about snakes; it was about a panther. Ogden Nash had said, "If called by a panther, don't anther." And yet she had called one to her, and now she had to deal with it.

Except for the brief time he'd glanced at Joann's grip on her hand, he hadn't once looked away from Milla's face, and that was the most unnerving thing of all.

"I'm told you find people," she said softly.

Behind her, Joann made an abrupt movement. "Milla—" she began sharply, and Milla knew she was going to say this wasn't a good idea, maybe she should reconsider, and all the other sensible things that could be said. Diaz's gaze didn't waver, and Milla lifted her hand to forestall her friend's objections.

"Sometimes," Diaz said.

"The one-eyed man, at that meeting Friday night. I want to find him."

"He's nothing. He isn't important." There was a slight in-flection to his speech, not in his tone but in the way he shaped his words, as if perhaps English wasn't his first language. He spoke English perfectly and with a west Texas accent, but there was still something, beyond his name, that spoke of Mexico. If he'd been born in the United States, she'd find a hat and eat it.

"He's important to me," she said, and drew a breath. Success was once again singing its Lorelei song, beckoning to her. This man gave her a real shot at finding out what had happened to her son, and if she was dealing with the devil, then so be it. "Ten years ago, my six-week-old son was stolen from me. My ex-husband is a doctor; he and some of his colleagues had set up a free clinic in one of the poorer areas of Chihuahua and we lived there for a year. My baby was born there. I was at the market and two men jerked him away from me, but I fought back, and clawed out the left eye of the man who had my son. The other man stabbed me in the back, and they both escaped. I haven't seen my baby since."

Something was glimmering in his gaze, some minute change that signaled a sharpening of his attention. "So you're the one."

"The one?" she parroted.

"Who blinded that pig Pavón."

Pavón. Oh, my God, that was his name. After ten years, *she knew his name.* She closed her eyes and drew in a deep breath, her hands clenching into fists. Her heartbeat had been settling down a bit, but now it was thundering even harder in her chest, deafening her with the roar of blood through her veins. She wanted to scream. She wanted to cry. She wanted to jump up and find him *right now*; she wanted to slam his head against a wall until he gave her the answers she wanted. But two of those things she couldn't do, and one she refused to do, so instead she pressed her violently trembling fists against her eyes and fought for control.

"Do you know his first name?" she asked in a constricted voice.

"Arturo."

Arturo Pavón. The letters branded themselves in her mind. Just as she had never forgotten his face, she would never forget his name, or this moment. For so long she had struggled and persisted with practically nothing to go on; now all of a sudden things were changing so fast she felt as if her world had tilted on its axis. Logically, she had known she would likely never find Justin. Emotionally, she had been unable to stop looking. Now, at last, the real possibility existed that she might at least be able to find out if he had *lived*. And if she could actually find him, find her little boy . . .

"Can you find him?" she asked, leaning forward as if by sheer force of will she could bend events to her wishes. "I want to talk to him. I want to find out what he did with my son–"

"Your baby was sold," he said flatly. "Pavón wouldn't know to who. He's a *pendejo*, a *gañan*."

Milla blinked. *Gañan* she understood: "thug." But unless she was mistaken, Diaz had also called Pavón a pubic hair. Obviously she missed some of the nuances of idiomatic Mexican Spanish. "He's a what?"

"He's nothing. He's a little man who follows orders." Diaz shrugged. "He's also a mean, worthless son of a bitch, but the bottom line is he doesn't have any authority."

"He's still my only link, and I have to follow the chain to find my son."

"You can follow the chain, but the odds are it won't lead anywhere except back on itself. Smugglers don't keep records. He'll remember *you*, of course, and probably your baby, but all he'll know is that the baby was taken across the border and sold. That's it."

She couldn't accept that the trail led nowhere. Pavón wouldn't have been in any shape to take Justin to the border himself; the most likely person to have done that was the second man, the one who stabbed her. Pavón would know that man's name. And when she found that man, he would know another name. If she just kept digging, eventually she would find Justin.

"I still want to find him," she said stubbornly. "You were watching him that night, you kept me from–"

"–getting yourself killed."

"Yes," she admitted. "Probably. Not that protecting me was your intention, you just didn't want them to know anyone was watching. But since you're trailing him anyway, why can't you–"

"I'm not tracking him in particular," Diaz interrupted. "I'm following the snake back to its head."

"But you know where he is."

"No. I don't."

She felt like screaming in frustration. She wouldn't accept a dead end now; she simply wouldn't. "You can find him."

"I can find anyone. Eventually."

"Because you don't give up. I can't give up, either. If it's a matter of money, of course I'll pay you." She couldn't in good conscience let Finders foot the bill, but she would give him every penny she had in savings, and beg more from David if she had to. Not that there would be any begging to it; David would do anything to help her find Justin.

Diaz regarded her with a faint gleam of curiosity in his eyes, as if she were an alien species and he couldn't figure out what made her tick. He was a man who evidently felt very little; she was a woman who felt, perhaps, too much. Since she couldn't appeal to his emotions, she tried instead to appeal to his logic. "Finders has a huge network of people, contacts you can't imagine. If you help me, I'll help you."

"I don't need help." His gaze was cold and remote again. "And I work alone."

There had to be something she could offer him. "A green card?" She could pull in some favors, get some corners cut.

For the first time there was a real expression on his face: amusement. "I'm an American citizen."

"What, then?" she asked in frustration. "Why won't you take the job? I'm not asking you to kill anyone; just help me find him." Or maybe that was it; maybe he got off on the thrill of the hunt, the struggle to the death.

"What makes you think I would kill anyone for you?" His voice had gone soft again, his face hard and blank.

Normally she was discreet about her informants, but her nerves were like jagged shards of glass slicing at her. Somehow, any way she could, she had to convince Diaz to help her. "True Gallagher pulled together some information for me, on anyone named Diaz who could have been connected to my son's kidnapping."

"True Gallagher . . ." he repeated, as if trying out the name on his tongue.

"He's one of our sponsors."

"And this information said . . . ?" he prompted.

"That you're an assassin." She didn't hide the truth, or try to be coy about it. Perhaps he wasn't an assassin, but she still had no doubt he could kill and had killed. And if he was, knowing that she had both eyes wide open concerning him and was still willing to hire him might make a difference in his decision.

Joann made a small sound of shock, but he didn't look at her.

"Your informant is wrong. There are reasons for which I would kill. I may get paid, but the money isn't why I kill."

Which in no way said that he hadn't killed, or that he wouldn't kill again. But oddly enough, she believed him, and felt reassured. At least he had some sort of moral compass, a standard to which he held himself.

He steepled his hands, watching her over his fingertips as he seemed to be contemplating something. Finally he said, "Tell me about this tip you got about me on Friday night."

"I don't have a lot to tell. The caller was a Hispanic man. All he said was that you would be at a meeting behind the church in Guadalupe, at ten-thirty. The call was made from that service station, and the owner doesn't know anything about it."

She couldn't read what was going on behind those cold, dark eyes, but she could imagine he was sorting through acquaintances and possibilities.

"At the time, I thought Pavón's name could be Diaz," she explained. "All I had were vague rumors that a man named Diaz was involved in some disappearances. I thought you could be the one-eyed man, because your name kept coming up in connection with him."

"I have no connection with him."

"I heard that he works for you."

His eyes went even colder.

"The point is, I've had feelers out for information about you for two years. Anyone could have called." She paused, another point occurring to her. "Though, since I've been offering rewards from the beginning, it's strange that I'd get an anonymous tip and there wasn't any effort to collect on the offer."

"Not just anyone would have information about my whereabouts."

And he didn't like it.

"Who knew where you would be?" she asked. "Anyone you told, obviously. And the person who gave *you* the tip about the meeting."

"I didn't tell anyone, so that narrows the list of possibilities. The question is, why?"

"Brian and I thought you were being set up, but that obviously wasn't the case. Pavón and the others had no idea you were there."

"Brian," he said. "That would be the man hiding on the other side of the cemetery?"

So he'd seen Brian, too. She nodded. "He works for Finders, too. We'd been out on a case and were on our way home when I got the call."

Something was going on. It was almost as if she had been deliberately thrown in Diaz's path. She didn't have to read his expression to know what was going through his mind, because she was having the same thoughts.

"I'll help you," he said abruptly, and flowed to his feet. "I'll be in touch."

He left the office and a few seconds later they heard the sound of the outer door closing. Milla and Joann stared at each other, then turned as one and raced to the window to see where he went.

The stairs to the office were empty. So was the parking lot. There was no sign of him, and though Milla opened the door and listened for the sound of a car engine being cranked, she heard nothing. It was as if he'd disappeared.

"I know how he got out," she said, bemused. "But how did he get in?"

"I don't know," Joann moaned, collapsing into the nearest chair. "My God, I've never been so scared in my life! He was probably already in here when I arrived. If he'd wanted, he could have done anything."

Milla went from window to window, checking to see if any of them showed signs of being forced. She wasn't a detective; nevertheless, she didn't see any new scratch marks on the latches, nor were any of the windows broken. Whatever method he'd used for gaining entrance, he hadn't left any obvious evidence of it.

Joann was visibly trembling. "I can't believe you sat down and talked to him, as cool as pie. That's the scariest man I've ever seen."

"Did I look cool?" Milla swallowed and found herself a chair, too. "I couldn't have. I was shaking so hard I could barely stand, so I had to sit down."

"I didn't notice. I thought he was going to kill us. His eyes—it was like looking at my own death."

"But he didn't kill us, and he gave us information I've been trying for ten years to get." Milla closed her eyes. "Arturo Pavón. I have a name. Finally, I have a name! Do you know what this means?" Tears scorched her eyes and seeped from beneath her closed lids. "I have a real chance now of finding my baby; for the first time I have a chance!"

8

THE FUND-RAISER IN DALLAS WAS MORE SUCCESSFUL THAN SHE'D hoped; not only did the event produce money, but Finders also picked up a corporate sponsor, a software company that had promised to upgrade their computer system. Visions of new computers danced in Milla's head, but that wasn't what kept her awake in her hotel bed that night.

Excitement zinged through her every time she thought of what had happened that morning. She felt as if she had plunged headlong into a fire and emerged unscathed; she was almost giddy with hope. She wanted to call David, wanted to tell him that at last she was making real progress, that she had the kidnapper's name and an expert—what else could she call Diaz?—was helping her locate him. She wanted to share her elation with someone, and who better than Justin's father?

But that was a call she refused to let herself make. David wasn't her husband now. He had another family, and Milla was very wary about intruding on it. She didn't know, and wouldn't ask, if David's wife had a problem with the money he gave her every year. As much as possible Milla had tried to make the break a clean one, to not give the new Mrs. Boone any reason for anger.

The *new* Mrs. Boone? Milla had to laugh at herself. David's wife's name was Jenna, she was a very nice woman, and she had been married to David twice as long as Milla had been.

When she had something concrete about Justin, then she'd call David. She didn't keep him abreast of every rumor and development. He called her about twice a year, and that was when she brought him up to date on any progress, which for ten years had been precious little. To keep things as smooth as possible in his private live, she never called him. Period. A surgeon's wife had enough everyday hassle, with her husband's long hours and emergencies that seemed timed for whenever he sat down to dinner or they were about to leave for vacation. There was no need to add calls from an ex-wife to the turmoil.

She couldn't contain the excitement, the sense of expectation, so she gave up trying to will herself to sleep and instead went over and over everything that had happened and been said that morning, from the time of True's call to the moment Diaz had vanished.

The biggest mystery for her–though perhaps not for Diaz– was who had called her about the meeting in Guadalupe, and why. The reason couldn't be the reward, since the call was anonymous. But someone had put her in Diaz's way, and she didn't know if the intent had been to help or to harm. Diaz could just as easily have killed her, rather than knocking her out. And after meeting him, she didn't think killing her would have cost him any sleep.

She wracked her brain but couldn't come up with any

logical reason for the call, and finally she decided to simply count her blessings. Perhaps Diaz was a mixed blessing, but still, in the space of a few minutes he had given her priceless information and offered her the best chance she'd had yet of finding Justin.

She couldn't believe she'd actually talked him into helping them. She couldn't believe she had sat down so close to him that only a couple of inches had been separating their knees, and pretended she wasn't terrified of him. His were the coldest, emptiest eyes she'd ever seen, as if no emotion touched him. She would almost call him a sociopath, except he did seem to have some internal braking mechanism on his inherent violence. He *knew* right from wrong, she thought, but he didn't *feel* it. If he chose to do what he perceived as right, it was a mental decision rather than an emotional one.

But because of that, she thought she could deal with him. They—the Finders—weren't in danger from him. He could have killed her and Brian that night in Guadalupe, simply for being in his way, but he hadn't because they weren't a threat to him— to his purpose, maybe, but not to *him*. So long as she was fairly certain of his boundaries, she thought she could trust him and work with him.

She hoped.

Considering True's reaction to Diaz's name, she decided to keep it quiet that the man himself had turned up in her office. True had a protective streak that she found charming even though she knew she had to keep her distance from him. He might call the police, which was the last thing she wanted.

She thought about asking True to find out what he could on Arturo Pavón, but decided against it. For one thing, he would want to know how she came up with the name, and she didn't like the idea of outright lying to him, when he had been so helpful. For another, Diaz wouldn't like it. She didn't know how she knew that, but she was certain of it. Diaz liked to work alone, with very few people, if any, knowing his whereabouts or what he was doing. If both he and True were searching for Pavón, they might very well cross trails. No, he wouldn't like that at all. He might even stop helping her, and no way would she risk that.

So, the fewer people who knew about Diaz, the better. She made a mental note to call Joann first thing in the morning, before she went to the office, and tell her not to mention Diaz to anyone.

She caught the first flight out of Dallas for El Paso, swung by the condo to leave her luggage, then continued on to the office. As early as it was, the heat was already becoming oppressive, reminding her of how much she looked forward to winter.

When she entered the office, she saw at once that Brian was in a playful mood, which always took the form of teasing Olivia and trying to drive her mad. Today he was giving her fashion advice, and it wasn't going over well at all, much to the amusement of everyone else within hearing distance, which was most of the staff.

"You should try a new hairstyle," he was saying as he lounged on the corner of her desk. "Something flirty. And bigger. You know, with waves and swoops and things."

Every feminist principle she possessed insulted, Olivia gave him a long, cold stare. "Who do I look like, Farrah fucking Fawcett?"

"No, but you could try," he said seriously.

Brian was young and big and fast, but for a moment Milla thought that might not be enough to save his life. Olivia slowly stood up until they were almost nose to nose, which, at five-two, she was able to do only because he was sitting on her desk. "Little boy," she said deliberately, "I've destroyed better men than you: used them up, wrung them dry, and thrown them away. Don't try playing out of your league."

Brian did *obtuse* really well. "What?" he said, looking bewildered. "I'm just trying to help. You know, give you some pointers and stuff."

"Really. I didn't know Neanderthals were fashion experts."

He grinned. "A little fur goes a long way."

"I'm sure you'd know."

Joann caught Milla's eye and gestured toward Milla's office. Milla looked and almost groaned aloud when she saw who was waiting for her. Mrs. Roberta Hatcher was searching for her missing husband, who had disappeared one weekend several weeks ago while she was in Austin visiting her sister. Since Mr. Hatcher's clothing was also missing, as well as his car and half the money in their checking account, the police had correctly concluded foul play wasn't involved, that Mr. Hatcher had left of his own free will, and there was nothing they could do. She had then turned to Finders for help, and refused to take no for an answer.

Casting a cautious look at Brian and Olivia–Milla hoped Olivia's antiviolence philosophy would continue to hold–she stepped into her office and smiled at Mrs. Hatcher. "Good morning, Roberta. Would you like a cup of coffee?"

Roberta shook her head. She was a pleasant, graying dumpling of a woman, in her late fifties, with the kind of round, cheerful face that looked most natural when wreathed in a smile. Since Benny Hatcher had disappeared one sunny afternoon, however, her eyes were often red-rimmed from weeping and Milla had yet to see the woman smile.

If she could get her hands on Mr. Hatcher, Milla thought, she would gladly strangle him. How dare he put his wife through this? If he wanted to leave, he should at least have had the guts and the courtesy to *tell* her, instead of leaving her twisting in the wind like this. Her heart would still be broken, of course, but at least she would know what was going on, that he was alive, and what her legal status was. She was in limbo, she was suffering, and Mr. Hatcher needed to have his ass kicked.

"Please help me," Roberta said in a low, scratchy voice, as if she had cried so much her throat was raw and swollen. Milla knew all too well how that felt. "I know you said he isn't a missing person, that he walked away under his own power and of his own accord, but don't you see, I don't *know* that, not for certain. What if some con man talked him into something, and now he's lost all his money and he's ashamed to come home, or he's hurt or even dead? I checked into a few private detective agencies like you told me to do, but I can't afford them. Even the cheapest one is way out of my budget. Please."

"I can't," Milla said, just as upset as Mrs. Hatcher. "We're in the same boat you're in. We don't have unlimited funding; we pinch every penny and make do with what we have or we do without. Look at this office. You can see we save most of our funds for our searches. The odds are that Mr. Hatcher left you and didn't have the courage to tell you. How can I justify using our resources to locate someone who almost certainly left of his own free will?"

"But can't you check his social security records to find out if he's working somewhere?"

"That takes a special subscription service, and we don't have it. The people we track are lost, not hiding." She rubbed her forehead, trying to think of a solution. "Have you tried the Salvation Army? They locate lost relatives. I believe it's a one-time-only free service and I don't know if they do it under these circumstances, but perhaps they can help."

"The Salvation Army?" Roberta murmured. "I didn't know they did things like that."

"They do, but as I said, I don't know their requirements. If they can't help you, then please see a lawyer. Do what you can to protect yourself legally."

A single tear dripped down Roberta's cheek. "I haven't told the children," she said raggedly. "How do I tell them their father just walked away?"

She had two sons, both married and with their own children. "You just tell them," Milla said. "You have to, rather than letting them find out some other way. What if he calls them? Then they'll be angry at you for not telling them what was going on."

"I suppose." She wiped her cheek. "I guess I keep hoping he'll come home and they'll never have to know."

"It's been almost three weeks," Milla said gently. "Even if he did come back now, would you take him back? Do you still want him?"

Another tear rolled down. "He doesn't love me, does he? If he did, he wouldn't have done this. He *couldn't* have. I know I've let myself go a tad, but I'm almost sixty and it's all right to be gray-haired when you're sixty, isn't it? Benny always kept himself in good shape, though. And he has only a little gray in his hair."

"Could he have a girlfriend?" Milla hated to say it, even though she knew the police had already asked Roberta the same question. At the time, in shock, worried out of her mind and terrified that her life was falling apart, Roberta had automatically rejected the idea.

Now, however, her face crumpled and she put her hand over her eyes. "I don't know," she sobbed. "He could have. He played golf almost every day. I never checked up on him. I *trusted* him."

Milla supposed there were people who willingly played golf even in the most searing heat, but every day? She doubted it. And so did Roberta, now that she was seeing things from a different perspective.

"Please, see a lawyer," Milla said again. "And change your bank account. I bet you haven't done that, have you? His name is still on the account. What if he empties it out? What will you do then?"

"I don't know, I don't know," Roberta moaned, rocking back and forth a little in her distress. She began blindly pawing through her purse. Guessing what she needed, Milla pulled a tissue from the box on her desk and pressed it into Roberta's hand.

After a few moments of wiping and blowing, Roberta took a deep breath. "I guess I've been acting like an old fool these past few weeks. I need to wake up and see what's what. He left me. I might try the Salvation Army thing, but you're right: first off, I need to change the bank account and protect what's left." Her chin quivered. "I'll call the boys tonight and tell them what's happening. I can't believe he's done this. Leaving me is one thing, but what about the boys? He's always had such a good relationship with them. He has to know this will change everything, so I guess he doesn't care about that, either."

Milla didn't say anything to that, though she suspected that eventually Mr. Hatcher would contact his sons, say he was sorry and so on, and expect everything to be as it was before. Some people simply didn't see the consequences of their actions, or they figured they could work things out. She didn't think this could ever be worked out, but it wasn't her call.

Roberta's eyes were red and swollen but her head was up and her stride brisk as she left the office. The door was barely closed behind her when Milla's phone rang. She punched the button and sank into her chair, feeling exhausted already.

"This is Milla."

"Hi, sweetie. Are you free for lunch today?"

It was Susanna Kosper, the obstetrician who had delivered Justin at the tiny free clinic in Mexico. Life was funny sometimes; Susanna and Rip, her husband, had liked the Mexican people so much that they had settled in El Paso to practice. That way they were still in the United States but close to the culture they enjoyed. They still made at least two trips a year into different parts of Mexico.

Susanna made an effort to stay in touch with Milla, and considering an obstetrician's busy schedule, that was saying something. There was a link between them because Susanna had been in the clinic that awful day, and she and Rip had been part of David's desperate struggle to save Milla's life. Sometimes a couple of months would slip by without contact between the two women, because of their hectic schedules, but whenever they could they'd have lunch together. Such plans had to be spur-of-the-moment, but somehow they usually made it work.

"Unless something comes up," Milla said. "Where and when?"

"Twelve-thirty. Dolly's."

Dolly's was a trendy little café that served chick food and was always busy at lunch, packed with women who wanted something lighter than the usual fare. A few businessmen ate there, but for the most part men stayed far, far away from the dainty chairs and tables in Dolly's.

As Milla hung up, Joann stuck her head in the door. "I haven't mentioned him," she said in a low voice, and she didn't have to elaborate. "He called first thing this morning. At least I think it was him. His voice gives me the creeps, and I got big-time goose bumps with this call, so I'm pretty sure who it was."

Milla wasn't even hearing his voice, and her skin roughened with a chill. Absently she rubbed her arms. "What did he want?"

"He didn't say. He asked if you were here. I said no, told him what time your flight would be in and what time I expected you, and he hung up."

"Did you give him my cell phone number?"

Joann looked worried. "No. I started to, but I didn't know if you wanted him to have it."

Since he probably already had her home phone and address, thanks to her slipup of using her real name instead of her business name, Milla couldn't see how giving him her cell phone number could hurt. "I'll give it to him when I see him again."

"See who?" Brian asked from the doorway.

Their office could use a tad more formality, Milla thought as she looked around. On the other hand, Finders was a partnership of people dedicated to what they did, not a corporation. She was the figurehead and the operational head, but other than that, the structure was very loose, and she had encouraged that feeling. While she might tell Brian about Diaz later—she wasn't sure how to explain how she had entered into an agreement with a man who was essentially a vigilante, and that was being charitable—she wasn't ready to tell him now, so she deflected him by changing the subject.

"Brian, I know you're only teasing when you start ragging on Olivia, but I'm not certain *she* knows. I don't want the office upset—"

"She knows," he said, stuffing his fingers into his jeans pockets and grinning at her, that wide, white aw-shucks-I'm-just-a-country-boy grin that he used to keep people off guard. "We're having fun."

"If you say so," Joann said doubtfully. "From the way things looked a minute ago, you were about to get clocked."

"Nah. She's a pacifist; she doesn't believe in hitting."

"Unless you push her to her limit," Milla said. "And I think you're getting close."

"Trust me." He winked at her. "What did you say to Mrs. Hatcher? She looked like a woman marching off to war when she left here."

"I convinced her to change her bank account and see a lawyer."

"Thank God," Joann said. "She should have done that as soon as she realized he'd taken half their money."

"She wasn't ready to hear it. The shock had to wear off before she could listen."

"I hope he comes crawling back in a few months and finds out she's divorced his ass," Brian said. "The shithead."

"Amen." Milla looked at the pile of paperwork on her desk and sighed. "I'm having lunch with Susanna, unless something comes up. Is everything quiet?"

"Under control. First thing this morning I got a group in Vermont out looking for an elderly lady with Alzheimer's who wandered away from home, but they found her within the hour. And some college kids hiking in the Sierra Nevada didn't come home on schedule, so things are getting organized there."

"How late are they?"

"One day. They were supposed to be home last night, but the families haven't heard from them."

"Let's just hope they have sense enough to stick together." And that none of them were injured. And that at least one of them had given their itinerary to a parent or a friend. Milla was always amazed at how many people set off into the wilderness without telling someone where they were going.

She told the staff the news about their new sponsor from

Dallas, and the promise of a new computer system, then she settled down to wade through the growing stack of paper.

An hour later, Olivia stuck her head in the door to ask a question, and Milla took advantage of the opportunity. "If Brian's teasing gets to be too much, just let me know."

"I can handle him," Olivia said, smiling. "It's okay, really. He thinks he's getting a rise out of me and I enjoy busting his chops. When he stops dancing around and works up the nerve to ask me out, I'll make him forget about big hair and small brains."

Ask her out? Milla's eyes opened wide. Was that what was going on? "He's ex-military," Milla blurted. "He's conservative. He's macho to the max—"

"He's also ten years younger," said Olivia, the smile widening to a grin. "Sounds good, doesn't it? I doubt we'll get around to discussing social issues, but if we do, I can hold my own with him. Who knows? I might convert him to my way of thinking."

Bewildered, Milla stared after Olivia as she walked away with a real bounce in her step. Sexual chemistry was an amazing thing. She had to adjust her thinking to see Olivia and Brian together, but in an odd way they meshed, because they were both strong-minded enough that neither could be dominated by the other.

Well. This had been an interesting morning.

Lunch with Susanna was as pleasant as usual. Susanna always asked about Finders; from the beginning she had shown real interest and occasionally turned up at fund-raisers. She never pried, never rehashed that awful day when Justin was taken, but she always asked how things were going. If Milla had any new leads, she'd tell her about them, but for the most part she had nothing to tell. Today, she did, but when Susanna asked, Milla just shook her head. Because Susanna sometimes attended fund-raisers, she was in the same general social circle with True Gallagher, and Milla didn't want to take the chance her friend might say something to him. Even if she asked Susanna to keep the news private, Milla knew it wouldn't be. Susanna would tell Rip, Rip would tell someone, and before Milla knew it, True would be on the phone raising hell and Diaz would disappear. She couldn't risk that, so she kept quiet.

The meal was almost finished when Susanna dipped her spoon into her papaya sorbet and casually asked, "Are you seeing anyone lately?"

Milla burst out laughing. The rumor mill had certainly been efficient! "If you mean True Gallagher, the answer is no."

"That's not what I hear." A tiny smile was playing around Susanna's well-shaped mouth, and her blue eyes were laughing.

"He asked, I refused. That's all there is."

"I hear he walked you to your car Saturday night."

"But that's all he did."

"For goodness' sake, why won't you go out with him? He's a . . ." Susanna paused, and gave a delicate little shiver. "He's a *man*, with a capital *M*."

"I know. He's also one of Finders' sponsors."

"Which means?"

"That I won't do anything to jeopardize our funding, whether it's from True or someone who wouldn't like the way it looked if I dated one of the sponsors."

"You didn't take a vow of chastity," Susanna said, annoyed.

"I know. It's my own choice. Finders is more important to me than my social life, even if the man in question wasn't part of our funding."

"Is that why you keep breaking up with the guys you date?"

Milla smiled. "Actually, they broke up with me, not the other way around. And there have really only been two since David and I divorced."

Susanna's mouth fell open. "Two? You've dated only two men?"

"I didn't say that. I've dated, some, when I can. Which isn't all that often, and not at all lately. But there've been only two quasi-relationships. Do you remember Clint Tidemore?"

"Vaguely. You dated him once or twice."

"More than that. He was one of my quasies."

"Cute guy."

"Yes, he is. He wanted me around more than I could manage, and I wasn't willing to delegate, so we parted ways."

"You didn't say anything. I thought he was just a casual date."

"There wasn't any point in rehashing everything when I wasn't willing to compromise."

"But you have to." Susanna's gaze turned serious. "Sooner or later, you'll have to. Everyone compromises. It's the only way to get along."

"Maybe someday," Milla said. Someday when she'd found Justin, and the devil was no longer flicking his whip at her heels. Until that day, she couldn't rest, couldn't let anything else matter to her.

"Make it sooner rather than later," Susanna advised as she glanced at her watch and picked up her bill. "I have to run. Appointments start at two."

Milla stood also, and they hugged. Then Susanna dashed off, her mind already on work. Milla lagged behind, gathering her bag and leaving the tip, since Susanna had forgotten. Two other patrons got between her and Susanna at the cash register, and when Milla finally emerged from the café, Susanna's red Mercedes was already two blocks down the street. Milla crossed the street to where she had parked her Toyota SUV, her head down as she searched the bottom of her bag for her car keys. Usually she just put the keys in her pocket, but the slim skirt she was wearing today didn't have pockets.

There they were. She was almost at the Toyota when she finally spotted them. She pulled the keys out, looked up, and barely choked back a startled shriek when she almost collided with the man who had appeared out of nowhere and was now between her and her vehicle.

"I've been waiting," Diaz said.

9

"DON'T YOU KNOW YOU SHOULDN'T WALK WITH YOUR HEAD DOWN like that?" he continued, his dark eyes narrowed in the shadow of his hat brim. "And you should always have your keys in your hand before you leave a building."

Thank goodness she was wearing her sunglasses, she thought a trifle wildly, so he couldn't see how her eyes had bugged out with fright. Her heart was still galloping, and a cold sweat had broken out on her skin. She had to stop reacting to him like this, before he realized she practically jumped out of her skin every time he moved a muscle.

That wasn't to say he didn't already realize it, because she saw the tiniest twitch of his mouth. The twitch could never have been called a smile, but maybe it wanted to be one.

"I usually do," she found herself explaining as she tried to fit the key into the lock. Her hand was shaking slightly and she had to try again before she succeeded. The next vehicle she bought, she promised herself, would have remote-operated locks. As she opened the door, she said, "Joann said you called."

"Yeah." He leaned past her and hit the unlock button that released all the locks, then went around and got into the passenger seat.

Evidently he was riding with her. Either that or he didn't want to talk while standing on the sidewalk. Taking a deep breath, she got behind the wheel and started the motor, then turned the air-conditioning on high and lowered the windows to help dissipate the stifling heat that had built up in the closed vehicle.

He'd had to remove his hat when he got in, and he twisted to toss the dark brown Stetson onto the backseat. Then he buckled his seat belt.

For a moment she was so startled by the image of an assassin wearing his seat belt that the significance of his action escaped her. She blinked as she realized that he wouldn't have fastened the belt unless he expected the vehicle to be moving soon.

She put her bag on the back floorboard and fastened her own seat belt. "Where to?" she asked, in case he had any specific ideas about their destination.

He shrugged. "You're driving."

"I was going back to the office."

"Fine."

"Where's your car?"

"In a safe place. I'll tell you when to let me out."

She shrugged, checked her mirrors, and when she saw a gap in traffic, she pulled out of her parking space. The air blowing from the vents was becoming cool, so she raised the windows, sealing the two of them inside the small private space. She'd never before realized just how small and just how private a vehicle was, but even though Diaz was the most *still* person she'd ever met, he had a way of taking up space and making it his own. She felt both crowded and smothered, even though he was doing nothing more than sitting quietly beside her.

"Why did you call?" she finally asked, since he wasn't volunteering any information.

"Pavón isn't in the area now. He's gone to ground somewhere."

Disappointment hit her in the stomach like a sledgehammer. She tightened her hands on the steering wheel. "You know that already?"

"Yes. Don't worry, he'll turn up. Did you tell anyone about me?" He was checking the side-view mirror, she realized, keeping watch on the vehicles around them. He wasn't overt about it, but he hadn't relaxed his guard one iota since getting into the SUV with her.

"No, and I told Joann not to mention you, either."

"Can you trust her?"

"More than most." Until the moment those words left her mouth, Milla would have said she trusted Joann absolutely. But Diaz wouldn't believe in absolutes; to him people would be more trustworthy or less trustworthy, but not completely trustworthy. And he was right, she thought. As much as she trusted Joann, there was always the possibility something would slip during conversation.

He continued to watch the traffic, and she watched him as much as she could while she was driving. He was a neat man; his clothes weren't stained, his fingernails were short and clean. Today he was wearing dark brown jeans and a T-shirt that looked as if it had once been beige but had been washed so often it had faded to a soft cream. He wore a wristwatch, one of those highly technical things that looked as if it could plot a course to the stars, but no other jewelry. His hands, resting quietly on his thighs, were strong and lean, with prominent veins that laced upward on his arms.

His profile was tough, contained, a little grim. His jaw was still covered with stubble, his lips compressed as if he found nothing in his life to be joyous. Maybe there wasn't anything joyous, she thought. Joy came from people, from the web of relationships that bound people together, and Diaz was profoundly solitary. He might be sitting right beside her, but she felt as if part of him wasn't there at all.

"Did you find out who called me Friday night?" she asked after the silence had stretched several minutes beyond comfortable.

"No. I hit a dead end."

Did he mean that literally? Was his contact now dead?

"I'll find him eventually," he continued, and she blew out a tiny breath of relief.

Her cell phone rang. He looked around, located her bag, and hauled it up from the back floorboard. "Thanks," Milla said, fishing the phone out of its pocket. The office number was showing in the window. "Hello."

"We've got a missing four-year-old boy," Debra Schmale said without preamble. "He lives close to the state park. He's been missing from home for at least two hours." She gave his address. "The police department are the first responders. The family and neighbors looked for the boy for two hours before they called. The PD called and asked for our assistance. We're getting people in the street as fast as possible. Most of the office staff are on their way."

"I'll meet them at the boy's house," Milla said, and ended the call. She glanced at the traffic and changed lanes, accelerating to catch the next traffic signal on green. She hung a right, then another right, and headed in the opposite direction. "Where should I let you out?" she asked Diaz.

"What's wrong?"

"Lost four-year-old, close to Franklin Mountains." The

string of hundred-plus temperatures had continued today; unless the little boy found shelter from the sun, he could die of heatstroke. And if he had found shelter, that could just make it more difficult to find him.

Diaz shrugged. "I'll go with you. I know the area."

Somehow she'd never expected that. Not only was he putting himself out, but a lot of people would see him. She had thought he would shun crowds.

"What's your name?" she asked. "If you want to keep your identity quiet, I shouldn't call you Diaz."

He had a way of not answering questions immediately. He always paused a second or two, as if considering both the question and his possible answers. That little pause was unnerving.

"James," he finally said.

She punched the Toyota into passing gear and powered ahead of a sports car. "Is that your real name?"

"Yes."

Maybe it was, maybe it wasn't. But as long as he answered to the name, if it was his real one or not didn't matter.

She was glad the police department had called them. In cases like this, Finders always worked under the direction of either police departments or county sheriffs, depending on who had jurisdiction and were the first responders. Searches did better when they were organized, rather than having a bunch of panicked people taking off in all directions without anyone knowing where they were going. Both the city and the county had search-and-rescue teams, but when manpower was short and time was critical, sometimes they would call Finders. Her people knew how to search, how to follow orders and stick to the grid.

The street where the little boy lived was clogged with cars, both official and private, and people walked up and down both sides of the street calling his name. A cluster of people was in front of his home, and Milla saw a distraught young woman sobbing into an older woman's shoulder.

Her stomach clenched. She had once been that young woman. No matter how many times she saw a sobbing mother, no matter how many times a child was found safe and re-turned home, for one horrible moment she always flashed back to that little open market and the last time she'd heard her baby's cry.

She found a place to park, jumped out, and retrieved her emergency kit from the back. The Finders all carried a change of clothing with them, because they never knew where they would be or how they would be dressed when a call came in. She climbed into the backseat and hurriedly stripped off her skirt, then pulled on a pair of cargo pants and put on her socks and sneakers. While she was changing, Diaz planted himself at the door with his back turned to her, blocking anyone from seeing in and surprising her with his consideration.

Baseball cap and sunglasses went on, then she filled her pockets with a few items: one of the walkie-talkies that all the Finders carried, a whistle, a bottle of water, a roll of gauze, and a pack of chewing gum. The whistle was to alert anyone nearby in case the radio failed, and the other items were for the little boy. He might not be hurt when they found him—she never let herself think that he might *not* be found in time—but he would definitely need water, and would probably like some chewing gum.

Her group had spotted her SUV and were coming toward her. Brian was in the lead, and even though he was wearing sun-glasses, too, Milla could tell his attention was riveted on Diaz.

She climbed out of the backseat and locked the doors, slip-ping her keys into her front pocket. "This is James," she said by way of introduction, before Brian could ask any questions. "He's going to help us. Who's in charge?"

"Baxter," said Brian.

"Good." Lieutenant Phillip Baxter was a veteran of these searches, a steady, commonsensical man who could be counted on to be thorough.

"What's the little boy's name?" She could hear people calling what sounded like "Mac" or "Mike," and she wanted to be certain.

"Max. He's in general good health, but wasn't in day care today because he has an ear infection and was feverish. His mother thought he was taking a nap while she did laundry, but when she went to check on him, he wasn't in his bed."

Children did that, wandered outside to play without telling anyone. Milla had once searched for an enterprising toddler who had watched his parents latch the door, then had waited for his moment, pushed a chair over to the door and climbed up on it, and used his toy truck to help him reach the last few inches he needed to push up the latch. They knew all that only because after he was found, he proceeded to make another bid for freedom and demonstrated his tactic. Children were horribly inventive, and oblivious of danger.

It was worrisome that little Max was ill; a fever would make him even more susceptible to the heat. They needed to find him really fast. She had been out in the heat only a few minutes, and she was already dripping with sweat.

They all went to the front yard and reported in to Baxter, who held a clipboard and was coordinating the effort so that no area would be left unsearched while others were searched over and over again by different groups. His men, steady professionals, were in charge of each sector.

Baxter gave her a nod as her group approached. "Milla," he said by way of greeting. "Glad your group could make it. They waited such a long time before calling 911 that the kid's had time to put some distance between home and wherever he is now. He wanted to go to his grandmother's earlier, but because he was sick his mom said no, and he was mad."

"Where does his grandmother live?"

"A couple of miles from here. His mother says he does know the way to Granny's house, so we're concentrating most of our efforts between the two points."

Diaz, lurking behind her but always near, asked, "What door did he use?"

She was surprised that he'd brought attention to himself, but evidently he wasn't worried about the El Paso cops seeing him. That was somewhat reassuring; the odds were he wasn't wanted on this side of the border.

Baxter gave him a sharp look, then indicated the direction with his hand. "The back door. Come see."

Milla was sure Baxter had already inspected the backyard, but if he was willing to take them back there, she wanted to see things for herself, too, so they went around the side of the house to the back.

The backyard was neat and enclosed with chain-link fencing. There was a swing set and slide, several toy dump trucks where the little boy had evidently spent a lot of time moving dirt from one place to another, and a plastic tricycle against the fence.

"I figure he climbed on the tricycle, got a handhold, then made it the rest of the way over the fence," Baxter said. "It's the only way out that I can see."

Diaz gave an absent nod, his cold gaze inspecting the surrounding area for anything that would attract a little boy's attention. "A dog, maybe," he said almost to himself. "A puppy, a kitten. Hope it wasn't a coyote."

Milla's throat tightened. She hoped it wasn't any kind of predator, animal or human, that had lured the little boy from the safety of his backyard.

"You don't think he was going to Granny's house?" Baxter asked.

"Probably. But if a little dog or cat wandered by, he could have taken off after it. You know how kids are."

"Afraid so." Baxter sighed, his eyes worried.

Diaz went to the point of the fence where Max had climbed over, and squatted down as he surveyed the ground, then lifted his head and slowly surveyed the surroundings. It was something the Finders often did, got down on the missing child's level, to see things as he saw them. Adults, looking down, would sometimes miss a hidey-hole or the interesting shape of a rock.

"A lot of people have trampled the ground here," Diaz said, meaning they had obliterated any tiny sign he might have seen. "You have a dog on the way?"

"He'll be here in about an hour." To Baxter's credit, he wasn't getting sideways with Diaz's questions. But then Baxter didn't feel he had anything to prove; his goal was to find the missing child, nothing else. If Diaz could help, that was fine with him.

Diaz grunted. The little boy had already been missing for over two hours. Another hour to get the dog here, get him oriented, give him the scent—they could be looking at four hours for the little boy to be out in this heat, sick, no water.

Baxter consulted his clipboard. "Okay, Milla, let's get your people organized." Joann gave him a list of their names and he added it to his sheaf of information, then began calling off names two by two, and ticking them off the list as he gave them their instructions. He pointed to Diaz and Milla. "I want you two to head straight for the mountain." He eyed Diaz. "You strike me as a tracker, and Milla has a sixth sense where lost kids are concerned. Maybe he did follow a dog, or something."

He gave everyone Max's general description–black hair, brown eyes, wearing a white Blues Clues T-shirt, denim shorts, and sandals–then sent them on their way.

She and Diaz fell into step as they threaded their way through mostly grassless lawns and alleys, often getting down on their hands and knees and crawling as they peered under cars, bushes, structures, anything that a small boy could squeeze under. Every few feet Milla would call Max's name, then stop and listen. A sharp rock dug into her knee; a piece of glass cut her hand. She ignored all those physical discomforts, ignored the heat, concentrated on looking, calling, and listening. She had done this more times than she could remember, and yet every time her sense of urgency was just as great.

They were half a mile from the house when Diaz found a child's footprint in the dust. They had no way of knowing if it was Max's, but it was something. Milla crouched beside him and examined the print. It looked small enough to belong to a four-year-old, and the print was made by a shoe with smooth soles, rather than a sneaker.

"You're bleeding," he said abruptly.

Milla glanced at her hand. "It's just a shallow cut. I'll take care of it when we get back."

"Wrap it now. Don't contaminate the trail with your blood scent."

She hadn't thought of that. She stopped, drew the roll of gauze out of one of her cargo pockets, and began wrapping her hand. She could wrap it efficiently enough, but with just one hand she couldn't tie off the bandage. Diaz pulled a wicked knife from his boot and cut the gauze, then sliced the end into two long strips that he then wrapped around her hand and tied in a firm knot.

"Thanks," Milla said. She looked around. "Have you seen any coyote prints?"

"No."

That was good. Small animals were a coyote's food, anything from a rat to a pet to a child.

They went back down on their hands and knees, thoroughly searching everything. "Max!" Milla called. "Max!" She listened. No answer.

She was so hot she was getting a little sick to her stomach, so she took a drink of water and handed the bottle to Diaz, who also drank. If she felt like this after half an hour, how did Max feel, after almost three hours? If he was anywhere near, he should have heard them calling.

An idea struck her, and she fished out her walkie-talkie, keyed it. "This is Milla. What's Max's full name?"

A few minutes later the answer crackled over the radio: "Max Rodriguez Galarza." She slipped the radio back into her pocket, put her hands on her hips, took a deep breath, and channeled her own mother. "Max Rodriguez Galarza, you come here right now," she called in the sternest voice she could muster.

Diaz flashed her a surprised glance, and a tiny hint of amusement kicked up one corner of his mouth.

"M-mommy? Mommy!"

The little voice was faint, but understandable. Shock jolted through her that the tactic had actually worked; then the sweet flash of success made her turn a huge grin on Diaz. "Got him!" she crowed. She raised her voice again. "Max! Where are you, young man?"

"Here," said the little voice.

That was helpful, she thought. But Diaz suddenly cut across a backyard to the right of them, so maybe it *was* helpful.

"Come here this minute!" she called, so he would 'say something else. He seemed to respond to the voice of authority.

"I can't! I'm stuck."

A pickup truck was parked in the backyard two houses over, and Diaz went down on his knees beside it, peering under it. "Here he is," he said. "The back of his shorts is snagged."

Milla grabbed her radio and broadcast the good news, while Diaz went down on his belly and snaked under the truck. She got down on her knees, removed her sunglasses, and watched as he used his knife to cut the belt loop on the little denim shorts that held Max to the undercarriage of the truck. She thought of what would have happened if anyone had got into the truck and driven it away, and shuddered. Max would have been dragged to death, and if the truck's radio was on very loud, the driver wouldn't even have heard him scream.

"Gotcha," Diaz said, taking a firm hold on the little boy with one hand while he slipped his knife back into his boot; then he slithered out from under the truck with Max in tow.

Max was soaking with sweat, his little face was pale, and dark circles lay under his eyes, but he stared up at them and announced, "I can't talk to you. You're strangers."

"That's exactly right," Milla said, going down on one knee beside him and taking the bottle of water out of her pocket. "Are you thirsty? You don't have to say a thing, just nod your head if you are."

He nodded, his dark eyes round with apprehension as he stared at her. She twisted the cap off the bottle and handed it to him. "Here you go."

He grabbed the bottle in both hands, which still bore some of the dimples of babyhood but were showing signs of becoming big-boy hands. He gulped the water, tilting the bottle so high that some of it spilled down the front of his shirt. When he'd emptied half the bottle, Diaz reached out and stopped him. "Slowly, *chiquis*. You'll be sick if you drink too fast or too much."

Max stared up at him. "What does that mean?"

"Chiquis?" Max nodded and Diaz said, "Squirt."

Max giggled, then clapped his hand over his mouth. "I talked," he said.

"Be sure and tell your mommy." Diaz leaned down and scooped the little boy up in his arms. "Now, let's go see her. She's been looking for you."

"I was trying to catch a kitty," Max said, looping an arm around Diaz's neck. "It went under the truck and I did, too, but then I got stuck."

"It happens to the best of us."

"You didn't get stuck."

"Almost."

Milla listened to Max's chatter, and Diaz's relaxed answers. He was at ease with Max, and she realized he wasn't as solitary as she had imagined. At some point he'd had contact with children, knew how to talk to them, and he'd picked Max up as if he had done so hundreds of times. Max certainly wasn't afraid of him. This was a side of Diaz she would never have suspected, and it intrigued her.

Baxter and a couple of his men, plus a couple of medics, met them halfway, with Max's mother running along with them. She shrieked when she saw her little boy, and Max yelled, "Mommy! I got stuck!"

The woman grabbed Max out of Diaz's arms, hugging him close and kissing him all over his face and head, wherever she could reach. She was crying and laughing and scolding all at the same time, and Max was trying to tell her about the kitty, and the big knife the man had used to cut his shorts, and that he knew he wasn't supposed to talk to strangers.

They took Max away to be checked out, but since he'd been under the shelter of the truck, he'd escaped sunburn and the worst of the heat. Milla herself was feeling the need for some water and air-conditioning, as were all of the searchers.

They trudged back to the staging area. Her people all

reported in and dispersed in various cars and trucks, and she was on the verge of getting into her own SUV when a local TV reporter stopped her for a comment. Milla gave her standard best wishes to the family, praised the El Paso police, got in a plug for Finders, and briefly explained how Max had crawled under a pickup and his clothing got snagged. She noticed that Diaz had faded out of sight, and she didn't mention him. The last thing he would want was for his face and name to be broadcast on television.

The reporter left, Milla got into her vehicle and started it, and waited to see if Diaz would reappear. He did, opening the door and sliding into the passenger seat. They buckled up, and she executed a U-turn.

It was several minutes before he spoke. "You didn't get to have that moment."

She knew the moment he was talking about, when Max's mother had seen her child alive and unharmed, and incandescent joy had lit her face. "No," she said, her throat suddenly tight. "The last time I saw my baby, he was crying. He'd been napping against my chest, and all of a sudden he was jerked away from me. He screamed his head off." She saw that tiny outraged face as clearly now as she had at the time. She locked her jaw, fighting the burn of tears.

"I see why you do this," Diaz said after another long pause. "It was a good feeling."

She cleared her throat. "The best."

He said in a casual voice, "I don't think you'll ever find your boy, but I'll kill Pavón for you."

10

"No!" SHE YELLED, SO STARTLED THAT THE STEERING WHEEL jerked in her hands. "Not yet!" Then, appalled at herself, she said, "Oh, God," and pulled to the curb because she was suddenly shaking so hard she was afraid to drive.

"Don't you want him dead?" Diaz asked in the same tone he might have used to ask if she wanted fries with her order—disinterested, flat, eerily remote.

"Yes!" Her tone wasn't flat, it was fierce. "I want him dead; I want to kill him myself; I want to scratch out his other eye and cut out *his* kidney; I want to hurt him so much he's screaming for me to end it before he dies. But I *can't*. I have to find out what he knows about my baby. After that, I don't care what happens to him."

He waited those few unnerving beats before he asked, "'Kidney'?"

She stared at him, eyes wide, her attention totally derailed by that one word. Out of her entire tirade he had picked up on the one detail that didn't fit in with the rest. From the moment she'd awakened from surgery in that little clinic, her entire life, her very being, had been concentrated on finding Justin. She hadn't let her focus waver, had gritted her teeth and charged through her physical rehabilitation, had almost literally set her life aside because nothing else was as important to her as her son. She hadn't dwelt on what the attack had done to her body. Until those enraged words, she hadn't realized how furious she was at what had been done to *her*, the pain she'd endured, the physical cost.

She turned away, staring woodenly out the windshield. "I told you I was stabbed," she said. "I lost a kidney."

"Good thing you had two."

"I liked having both of them," she snapped. She remembered the searing agony, remembered convulsing in the dirt as the pain hurled her body out of control. She functioned perfectly well with just one kidney, of course. But what if something went wrong with it?

She drew a deep breath and forced her attention back to the original subject. "Don't kill him," she said. "Please. I have to talk to him."

He shrugged. "Your choice. As long as he doesn't fuck with me, I'll leave him alone."

Milla wasn't a prude, but his use of the word "fuck" made her uncomfortable. For her it was primarily a sex word, regardless of how it was used as an adjective, adverb, interjection, and exclamation these days. Her dealings with Diaz were already dicey enough; she didn't want anything sexual, even language, to make matters more tense. Odd how Olivia could use the word and be funny; hearing it from Diaz made Milla want to squirm.

She pulled back into traffic, concentrating on her driving so she wouldn't have to think about anything else right now. Silence reigned, and she let it lengthen, let the minutes add up.

There were times when even an uncomfortable silence was better than words.

"Don't go after him yourself," he said as he checked the traffic around them. "No matter what, don't go by yourself. Not even if you hear he's sitting outside your office, and you haven't seen me in a week. Don't go yourself."

"I never go by myself," she said, startled. "There's always someone with me when I go on assignment. But if Pavón is outside my office, I'm not making any promises."

"You were alone in Guadalupe."

"Brian was there and you know it."

"He was on the other side of the cemetery. He had no idea I was anywhere around. I could have snapped your neck, and there was nothing he could have done about it."

That was inarguable. *She* hadn't known he was there until he was on her. Besides, he wasn't telling her to do anything she didn't already practice. "I'm as careful as possible," she told him. "I know my limitations."

"Another missing woman turned up in Juarez last night. Her body did, anyway. This one was an American college student named Paige Sisk. She and her boyfriend were in Chihuahua; she went to the bathroom one night and never came back."

There was a serial killer in Juarez, she knew; numerous articles had been in the newspaper. The FBI had worked with the Mexican authorities—the first time they had ever been asked to help with a Mexican investigation—and concluded that all the murders were single homicides. If so, a lot of young women had gone missing and turned up dead since 1993. A couple of criminologists agreed: it wasn't a serial killer, it was two serial killers, possibly more. The pickings were rich in Juarez.

Finally, two bus drivers had been arrested, and supposedly the killings had stopped. Now Diaz was telling her they hadn't.

"Is it the same M.O.?"

"No." He checked the traffic again. "She was eviscerated."

Nausea roiled in Milla's stomach. "My God."

"Yeah. So do what I tell you, and stay out of Mexico right now. Let me handle this."

"If I can," she murmured, and he had to be content with that, because she wasn't going to promise him she would play it safe, not when getting some information about Justin was at stake. She wouldn't be foolish, she wouldn't lie, but neither would she let an opportunity pass by.

"It's going to rain," Diaz said in a complete change of subject, staring at the purple edge of clouds just showing on the western horizon.

"Good. Maybe it'll break the heat." The heat wave was killing old people and driving everyone else insane with misery. Granted, El Paso was usually hot during the summer, but not this hot.

"Yes, maybe," he murmured. "Let me out here."

"Here?" They were in the middle of a busy intersection.

"Here."

She put on her brakes and turned on her right signal at the same time, wedged her way into the right-hand lane, then pulled to the side. A horn blared at her, but she didn't blame the offended driver, so she didn't bother looking. Diaz unhooked his seat belt, got out, and walked away without a word of good-bye or a hint of when he would turn up next. Milla watched to see where he went, noticing the catlike way he walked, as if his legs were spring-loaded. He disappeared behind a utility truck, and didn't reappear. Still she waited, but somehow he used the utility truck, traffic signs, and other vehicles for cover, because she didn't see him again. Either that or he went down a manhole. Or had slithered under the utility truck and was clinging to the undercarriage. Or–

She had no idea where he'd gone, and she wished he'd stop doing that.

Diaz made his way back to where he'd parked his dusty blue pickup. There was absolutely nothing remarkable about the vehicle, except perhaps that it was in perfect working condition. It wasn't pretty, but it could run. He could afford a newer model but he didn't see any reason to get rid of this one. It suited him, and didn't attract attention.

He'd spent most of his life not attracting attention. He instinctively knew the best camouflage, and whenever anyone noticed him, it was because he wanted them to. Even as a child he had been silent and solitary, prompting his mother to have him tested for autism, mental retardation, anything that would explain the way he just sat and stared at the people around him but seldom joined in any conversation or activity. Even knowing that his mother had worried about him at first and later was simply uneasy around him hadn't stirred any emotion or response in him.

He watched people. He watched how their faces, their bodies, would tell a different story from their words. And contrary to his mother's belief, he wasn't an inactive child. When she wasn't there to see, or when she was asleep, he roamed the house, or—depending on where they were at the time—the neighborhood or the countryside. He was as at home in the night as the other predators. From the time he was so small he had to stand on tiptoe to reach the doorknob, he had slipped outside at night and explored. He liked animals better than he did people. Animals were honest; no animal, not even a snake, knew what it was to lie. Their body language expressed exactly what they were thinking and feeling, and he respected that.

Eventually, when he was about ten, his mother got tired of dealing with him and sent him to his father in Mexico. His old man was less concerned about socialization than he was about how much Diaz could help with the chores, so the boy fit right in. But it was with his grandfather, his father's father, that Diaz had found a like soul. His *abuelo* was as remote as a mountain snowcap, content to watch rather than participate, his sense of privacy like an iron fence around him. Mexicans in general were a friendly, highly social bunch, but not his grandfather. He was proud and remote, and fierce when crossed. It was said that he was of Aztec lineage. Thousands of people were, of course, or said they were. Diaz's *abuelo* never said any such thing, but other people did. It was their way of explaining him. And it was how, in turn, they explained Diaz.

Diaz had tried not to be any trouble. He made good grades in school, both in the United States and Mexico. He didn't act out. He didn't smoke, didn't drink, not out of any sense of social responsibility but because he saw both as weaknesses and distractions, and he couldn't afford to have any.

He liked living in Mexico. Whenever he visited his mother in the States, he felt hemmed in. Not that he visited all that often; she was too busy with her social life, with finding another husband. Diaz's father had been her third, he thought. He wasn't certain they had ever actually been married. If they had married at all, it hadn't been in the Church, because by the time Diaz went to live with him, his father had another wife and four children. His father regularly went to confession and mass, too, so he was in good standing with the Church.

When Diaz was fourteen, she took him back. She wanted him to finish school in America, she said. He did. She moved so often he spent his last four years in six different schools, but he graduated. He didn't date; teenage girls had great bodies, but their personalities left him cold. He thought he was probably the only virgin in his class. He was twenty before he lost his virginity, and he'd been with only a handful of women since. Sex was great, but it required a voluntary vulnerability on his part that he had a difficult time accepting. Not only that, women tended to be afraid of him. He tried never to be rough, but nevertheless there was a fierceness to his lovemaking that seemed to intimidate them.

Maybe if he tried it more often, he thought with black humor, he wouldn't seem so hungry. But taking care of the matter himself was easiest, so he did. It had been a couple of years since he'd seen a woman he was attracted to enough to consider having sex with–until he saw Milla Edge.

He liked the way she moved, so smooth and fluid. She wasn't pretty, not that bright American prettiness that made him think of cheerleaders. Her face was strongly molded, with high cheekbones, a firm jawline, dramatic dark brows and lashes. Her hair, worn not quite shoulder length, was a froth of light brown curls, with that startling streak of white in front. Her mouth was completely feminine, soft and full and pink. And her eyes . . . her brown eyes were the saddest eyes he'd ever seen.

Those eyes made him want to put himself between her and the world, and kill anyone who caused her one more iota of pain. Many women would have been broken by what had happened to her. Instead she fought, and she wouldn't let herself stop fighting, no matter how hopeless the cause or how difficult it was for her to keep going. Such gallantry humbled him in a way he'd never before felt. Here, he thought, was a woman he truly wanted to know. For a while, at least.

If he could keep her alive, that is. Arturo Pavón might be a *chingadera*, a fuckup, but he was a vicious fuckup. She would break her heart and her spirit trying to find her kid, and that was the best-case scenario. He couldn't let her track Pavón on her own, even though the odds were she'd learn nothing of value from him. That was if Pavón didn't kill her; it was well known he harbored a deep hatred for the *gringa* who had torn out his eye. He would love to sell her body on the black market.

Pavón was now involved in something much worse than

baby snatching, and the stakes were proportionally higher. Before, getting caught would have meant a prison sentence; now it would be the death penalty. Mexico didn't have the death penalty, but Texas sure as hell did, and from what he'd been able to find out so far, the gang was headquartered in El Paso. Pavón might not be executed, but the higher-ups would be. Diaz didn't know exactly how international law shook out on that one. If Pavón was caught on American soil, though, he thought American laws would prevail. That was what happened in Mexico whenever a stupid tourist believed the old tales about what a free and open country Mexico was when it came to drugs. If you got caught in Mexico, then you went to a Mexican prison.

The matter of law might be a moot point, though. When he was certain who was running the operation, if he couldn't get enough evidence to turn it over to law enforcement and be sure of a conviction, then he would take care of the matter in other ways.

He'd told Milla he didn't kill for money, and he'd told the truth, as far as it went. He'd killed, and he'd been paid for it, but money was never the reason he did it. There were some people whose crimes were sickening, yet if they were ever brought to trial, they would be given either light prison sentences or probation—and that was assuming they'd even been found guilty. Maybe killing them wasn't his decision to make, and maybe he'd answer for it in the hereafter, but he'd never felt bad about it afterward. A child molester, a serial rapist, a murderer—those people didn't deserve to live. To some people that would make him a murderer, too, but he didn't feel like one. He was the executioner. He could live with that.

He would help Milla find Pavón, because she would keep trying anyway and she would be safer with Diaz. But even more important, Pavón was a link to the head of the snake. If he kept following the little fish, eventually he would find the big fish.

People were dying in Juarez, and all over the state of Chihuahua. That in itself wasn't unusual. Some of these were the work of the serial killer. But more and more bodies were being found with the organs removed, and that didn't fit the pattern. Different killing methods were used. Some had been shot, some had been stabbed, some had been strangled. In a few horrible cases, evidently the organs had been removed while the victims were still alive, though he hoped they were at least unconscious when the process began. The victims were both male and female, mostly Mexican, though three of the unfortunates, like Paige Sisk, had been tourists. The bodies were found in different parts of Juarez, carelessly dumped as if they were no longer of any value. And they weren't.

How much was a heart worth on the black market?

A liver? Kidneys? Lungs?

People on transplant lists died every day, waiting for an organ to become available. What if some of those people had money, though, and didn't want to wait? What if they could put in an order for, say, a heart, from a donor with a particular blood type? What if they were willing to pay millions? *What if the donor not only wasn't willing, but wasn't dead?*

Easy. Make the donor dead.

Diaz's job was to find whoever was behind this. Not the peons, the grunt soldiers like Pavón—and he was far from the only one—who kidnapped the victims. There was likely a central place where the organs were removed and refrigerated, then immediately transferred to the waiting recipient, but he hadn't located it yet. He might be wrong; the organ removal could be carried out wherever it was most convenient at the time. What was needed other than a cutter and some coolers of ice?

Whoever was doing the actual organ removal had to have some training, so that the organs weren't damaged. Perhaps not a doctor, but at least someone with a level of medical expertise. Diaz thought of the unknown person as "the Doctor," though. Kept things simpler in his mind. The Doctor might be the head of the gang; who else was in a better position to know about the transplant lists, who was on it, and who had enough money to privately arrange for an organ?

On Friday night, behind the church in Guadalupe, he'd watched the transfer of what he was sure was another victim. It might even have been the Sisk girl. The presence of two other people watching the transfer had been a hindrance, especially when the woman started to blow the whole scenario wide open by attacking. He'd admired her guts, if not her brains, but he'd had to stop her. The last thing he wanted was for Pavón and his cohorts to know someone was onto them; they would become more careful, and that much harder to trace.

Taking care of the woman had cost him precious seconds, and he'd lost them. He'd known the person he jumped was a woman because of the curls sticking out from under the cap, and her general shape, as well as the slenderness of her arms and hands. From his vantage point, and with his own night-vision device, he'd watched the two from the moment they arrived. The guy was pretty good at ghosting around, the woman less accomplished but still competent.

He didn't know what they were doing there, but it was obvious they weren't part of Pavón's gang, so he didn't intend to harm them, even though just by being there they were fucking him up. He'd have other chances with Pavón; it was the victim who wouldn't have another chance. He could have intervened and maybe saved that one person, but he'd have had to kill probably three of the men and there was no guarantee the one remaining would tell him anything, or even know anything *to* tell him. Until he had seen which car left with the victim, he'd had no idea whom to follow.

He'd had a tip about that meeting behind the church. Then Milla had received a tip telling her that *he* would be there. Who could have known other than the person who had tipped him off? And who the hell was it? His caller had been female; a man had called Milla. What was going on? Was it coincidence that they were both sent to the church in Guadalupe at the same time, or deliberate?

He didn't believe in coincidences. It was safer that way.

11

It was almost nine o'clock when Susanna Kosper pulled into her driveway and punched the button on the garage door opener. Even before the door slid up and she saw the other parking bay was empty, she knew Rip wasn't home yet, because the big, cream stucco house was dark. When Rip was home, the house was lit up like downtown; he turned on the lights in every room he entered, then forgot to turn them off again when he left.

More often than not, now, Rip wasn't home when she got home. And even when he was, he barely spoke.

Twenty years of marriage were going down the drain, and she didn't know how to stop it. They had so much in common that she wasn't quite able to grasp how they could drift so far apart. They both loved their careers, and they enjoyed the healthy salaries they pulled down. Even though her malpractice insurance rate had skyrocketed, along with that of every other ob-gyn in the country, together they did very well.

She had once gone through a scare when she thought they

might lose everything they'd worked so hard for, but she had been doubly cautious about money since then, and her caution had paid off. Their house was a showplace, they had healthy retirement funds, and Rip made no pretense of not enjoying their success. They liked the same movies, the same kind of music; they voted the same way most of the time; they even liked the same college football team, the Ohio State Buckeyes. So what had gone wrong?

Susanna lowered the garage door behind her and let herself into the house, then keyed the code into the alarm system. She loved this moment when she first came home, when she saw the tastefully decorated rooms, smelled how clean and fresh it was, with the sweetness of potpourri that wiped out the smells of hospitals and antiseptics. She loved it even more when Rip was there waiting for her, but that seldom happened these days.

The most probable—the most clichéd—cause was another woman. A nurse, of course. Wasn't that what usually happened? A successful doctor hits middle age, starts feeling less than vital, and looks around for a younger woman to give his sex drive a boost. The only difference in their situation was that in case of a divorce, Rip wouldn't have to pay Susanna alimony, since her earning power equaled his, and she wouldn't ask for alimony anyway. But his standard of living would go down, because of the loss of her salary. Susanna thought her own standard of living would stay about the same; she would, of course, keep the house. And insist that Rip pay it off. Divorce wouldn't be a smart move on Rip's part.

She didn't want a divorce. She loved Rip. Even after all these years, she still loved him. He was funny and intelligent and warm, and though anesthesiologists usually had only brief contact with patients, he could establish a rapport and relax the patient better than anyone else she'd ever seen.

Maybe they should have had children. But when they were younger and struggling to establish their practices while still paying off their student loans, there simply hadn't been either the time or the money for children. Especially no money; she shuddered to remember how tight things had been, how desperate. People thought doctors were rolling in cash, but that generally wasn't true, at least for most. It took years to become a doctor, all the while taking on more and more debt to finance your education, then years more to establish a good practice. You struggled to pay the salaries of your office staff, your nurses, the overhead of rent and utilities and supplies, equipment, insurance. Sometimes the debt had seemed mountainous. But they had done it: paid off their student loans, gradually became more profitable, and finally had enough money to enjoy life.

But here she was, almost fifty years old, and it was too late for children. She hadn't had a menstrual period in almost six months, which was a bit sooner than average for menopause, but not drastically so. She had scheduled a checkup with another doctor, of course, just to make certain nothing was wrong. Everything was normal, she was in excellent shape, but she was definitely going through menopause. Even that was going well: no hot flashes, no sweats, no disturbed sleep or emotional swings. Not yet, anyway. Some women sailed through, some women really suffered, then there were all degrees in between. Maybe she would be one of the sailors.

She and Rip hadn't had sex in . . . four months? She wasn't certain. It had been a while. Of course, he was fifty himself, and people did slow down. But their sex life had been fairly regular, enjoyable, and then–nothing.

There had to be another woman.

She was in the bedroom changing clothes when she heard the alarm beep as the garage door opened. Rip was home. She didn't know if she was glad or dreaded seeing him. She was just stepping into the pants of her lounging pajamas when he came into the bedroom, his face lined and tired.

"Where have you been?" she snapped, though until she saw him she had planned to say not a word. "You were supposed to be home at five."

"What difference does it make?" he asked without inflection. "You weren't home, either."

"I'd like to know where you are, in case there's an emergency."

He shrugged out of his jacket. "Then you should check your messages more often."

"I checked my messages–" She stopped. She hadn't checked them since she'd left the office.

"Obviously not." He walked over to the answering machine and played the messages. There were two hang-ups, a long distance company, a friend inviting them to a party on Saturday night, then Rip's own voice telling her his partner, Miguel Cárdenas, had come down with a stomach virus and was puking his guts up, so he was having to fill in on an emergency surgery.

Susanna almost felt ashamed. Almost. Just because he was innocent this time didn't mean he was innocent all those other times he'd been out late. "What kind of emergency?"

"Car accident. Crushed pelvis, broken ribs, deflated lung, severely bruised heart." He paused. "He died."

He sounded as tired as he looked. He rotated his neck and flexed his shoulders, trying to get the kinks out as she had so often seen him do after a long day at the hospital. "Where were you?"

"Doing rounds. Felicia D'Angelo started spotting, thought she was having contractions, so I had her come in. I checked her out, ran some tests. She's fine. Who's your girlfriend?"

He didn't miss a beat, didn't even act surprised by the question. "I don't have a girlfriend."

"Of course you don't. That's why you're seldom at home, why we don't have sex anymore, why you act like you can barely stand to speak to me. Because of this girlfriend you don't have. Is it someone in your office? A nurse at the hospital?"

His eyes narrowed as heat came into them. "I'm not fucking around, Suze. Period."

"Then what's wrong?" Susanna didn't want to beg, refused to beg, but the distance between them was killing her. "Is it because I'm going through menopause?"

"I didn't know you were," he said, and somehow that hurt as much as anything, that he'd paid so little attention to her.

"If it isn't that, what?"

He was silent for a long moment; then he shrugged. "We're just different people now. That's all."

"That's *all*?" She thought she would explode from the emotions that swelled up in her, anger and frustration and pain mixing together and each feeding the other. "We're *different people*? Just when did we become *different*? Who changed, me or you?"

"Neither of us," he said softly. "That's the kicker. Maybe I just found out we've been different all along."

"Would you stop with the fucking riddles?" she yelled, clenching her fists. "I don't know what's going on! I don't know what you're talking about! All I know is we're falling apart and it's killing me! For god's sake, just say it in plain language!"

"Leave it alone." He sounded totally unmoved by her fury. "Just—leave it alone. I don't plan on leaving you; we can rock on the way we always have, keep our lives the same."

"Are you crazy? How can it be the same? How can you love someone one day and the next day it's like we haven't even been introduced?"

"I'll tell you how." Venom suddenly laced his tone. "I'll tell you in two words: True Gallagher."

Susanna actually fell back a pace, her mind going blank. "What?" Shock paralyzed her thought processes, leaving her standing there with her mouth open and nothing else coming out. Surely not. Surely he didn't–

Rip didn't say anything else, just watched her.

Then with an almost audible click her mind began working again, racing along at a feverish pace. "I'm not seeing True Gallagher! You think *I'm* having an affair with him? My God, Rip, I'm trying to set him up with Milla!"

Something moved in his eyes, flashed across his expression, so fast she couldn't read it. "Leave Milla alone," he said flatly. "She deserves better than him."

"Why do you have such a hard-on for True? What's he done to you? I swear, I *promise* you, I'm not cheating on you with anyone and certainly not with him!" She tried to think of the times she'd spoken with True in public, which weren't many, tried to think of anything they had said or done that would give an onlooker the impression they were having an affair.

"Let's just say I don't believe you," Rip said. "And leave it at that."

He turned and left the room, and somehow Susanna knew he wouldn't be sleeping in the same room with her anymore. Until now they had at least done that, though he'd been on his side and she'd been on hers, and not so much as a hand had strayed into the neutral territory between them.

She wanted to laugh. She wanted to cry. She wanted to throw something; she wanted to hit something; she wanted to hit *Rip* for being such a dumb asshole. He was being a jerk because he was jealous, of all things.

She couldn't believe how backward she'd had it. While she was suspecting him of having an affair, he was suspecting her of the same thing. She knew *she* wasn't. Unless Rip had accused her as a sly method of throwing her off his track, he wasn't having an affair, either.

Her marriage wasn't over, after all. It was just going through a rough patch. If she hung in there, things would eventually smooth over and he'd realize he was totally out of bounds with his suspicions, and they would gradually regain the warmth between them. Until then, she'd have to be very, very careful.

She didn't use the landline phone, any extension of which Rip could look at and see she was on the phone. Instead she fished her cell phone out of her bag, closed the bedroom door, then went into the bathroom and closed that door, too. Then she dialed True's number.

"Rip thinks we've having an affair," she said in a low voice when he answered. "He's very suspicious."

"So soothe his ruffled feathers. We can't afford to have him doing something stupid like following you around."

"I know. I told him I was trying to set you up with Milla, but he's so pissed he didn't like that idea, either."

"Just keep playing him. Did you make any progress with Milla?"

"I don't think so. You know how stubborn she is when it comes to that foundation of hers. She's afraid that if she goes out with you, she'll lose a dollar in funding from some old biddy who doesn't think it looks good for her to be dating a sponsor."

"Yeah, that's what she told me, too. Keep working on her, though. I don't want to push too hard and make myself obnoxious."

"I'll do my best. With our schedules, sometimes it's tough getting together for girl talk."

"Then make an opportunity. All of a sudden she's coming up with information she shouldn't have. I need to know how she's getting it, and I need to know every move she's going to make before she makes it. I can't do that unless I get close to her."

"I know, I know. Like I said, I'll do my best. I can't twist her arm and *make* her go out with you."

"Why not?" He sounded amused. "Get her to go out to dinner with you and Rip, and I'll just happen along. How does that sound?"

"I don't know if I can get Rip to do anything right now. I'll have to work on him."

"You do that, and make it good." The phone clicked as he hung up, and Susanna turned off her phone.

She took a deep breath. Well, the plan was simple: seduce her husband. Executing the plan, though, was going to be a bitch.

12

A WEEK WENT BY IN WHICH MILLA DIDN'T HEAR ANYTHING from either True or Diaz; she didn't expect to learn anything from True, now that she knew she'd been on the wrong track thinking Diaz had been involved in Justin's kidnapping, but she did expect True to at least call and *tell* her he didn't have any new information.

She felt constantly on edge, expecting to see Diaz every time she turned a corner or opened a door. Sometimes she had the sensation of being watched and she would look around, but if he was there, she never spotted him. Why would he be trailing her anyway? He was probably somewhere in Mexico, doing whatever it was he did, legal or otherwise.

She should feel more relaxed, with him gone. Whenever he was anywhere near, all her senses were on high alert, as if she were in the presence of a half-tamed animal that she couldn't fully trust. But when he wasn't there and her sense of danger faded, then her guard dropped and she would sometimes be blindsided by an insidious pang of desire.

It was insane. She'd been attracted to other men since David, had tried to have other relationships. She was aware that there was some chemistry between her and True Gallagher, though her reasons for not responding to it were valid and she didn't have even the smallest temptation to change her mind. Being physically attracted to Diaz, however, was alarming. He was the most *unsafe* man she'd ever met, and she didn't mean in terms of sexually transmitted diseases. He could be devastatingly violent. She hadn't seen it, had tasted only a small fraction of his potential the night he'd jumped her in Guadalupe, but she could read it in his eyes, in the reactions of people who had heard of him or had anything to do with him.

She would have to be a fool to consider anything other than a working relationship with him—and that was assuming he was capable of *having* a relationship. Sex, yes—relationship, no. That would require an emotional bond she didn't think he wanted to make, or was even capable of making. Besides, did she really want to crawl into bed with a man she was half afraid of?

Maybe just once, her libido whispered, which told her how tempted she truly was, because she'd never before had a problem refusing personal gratification if it interfered with her relentless search for Justin. Diaz was the best shot she'd ever had at finding out what had happened to her son, and she didn't dare do anything to upset the status quo.

Once she acknowledged the dangerous attraction she felt for him, she became even more nervous as she waited for him to turn up in that unexpected way he had. Part of her, the deeply feminine part that yearned for the touch of a strong male, wanted to see if the tug of desire was there in person, or if she had just imagined it in the safety of his absence. Logically, however, she knew she should never give him the slightest indication that she saw him as a sexual being, and the best way to do that was to stay away from him. Since that wasn't possible, the big question was could she clamp down on her response and keep him from seeing the slightest glimmer of interest? In view of his acute awareness of his surroundings and the intense way he watched people, she would have to be doubly careful.

After he located Pavón for her, perhaps—

No. She couldn't let herself even think that. She couldn't hang the possibility out there like a constant temptation, a reward at the end of the trail. She had to put her physical responses in deep freeze and concentrate on only one thing: Justin. That had worked for ten years, and it would work again. The only relationships she had allowed herself to have were with men who didn't elicit a strong enough attraction that she wasn't always in complete control. She could and had put them in second place without a moment's thought. With Diaz she was afraid she wouldn't have that control, and now of all times, when she finally had a concrete lead to Justin, she couldn't afford to give that control up.

Because she was so nervous, when Susanna happened to catch her on a night when she didn't have anything to do and asked her out to dinner with them, she gladly seized the chance to get away from her own thoughts for a while. Normally she preferred to enjoy her rare free evenings at home, but she felt as if the other shoe was waiting to drop and the mental tension was driving her crazy.

Determined to enjoy the evening, she put on one of her favorite dresses, a pale, creamy yellow sleeveless silk, with a swingy skirt that flirted with her knees when she walked. Though rain had indeed broken the heat wave and eased temperatures back down to normal, normal in El Paso in August was still hot, and the dress was wonderfully cool. Back when she and David were dating, they had often gone dancing, and this dress reminded her of the dresses she had worn then. Now that she was older, she realized what an effort David had made in his courtship of her, because he'd been in his residency program then and perpetually short of sleep. She loved to dance, though, so he had used his precious off-time to take her dancing.

The memory had her smiling as she opened the door to Rip when he and Susanna came to collect her. She had offered to drive herself and meet them at the restaurant, but Rip was protective of her, had been since the day Justin was stolen and she herself had nearly died from her wounds. He nearly always insisted on picking her up and making certain she was safely home whenever she had dinner with them.

"Hi there," he said, smiling at her. "Spiffy dress."

"Thanks." She returned his smile as she switched on a lamp in the small foyer for her return; then they stepped outside and she locked the door. "It's nice to dress up sometimes and not have to make a speech."

"You've been doing this a long time." He opened the back passenger door for her, and she slid inside. As he got under the wheel he said, "Can't someone else at Finders take on some of the PR duty?"

"I wish. I'm the face everyone associates with lost children, though, so I'm the one they ask for."

"But you need a life of your own," Susanna said, turning around in the front seat and regarding her with somber eyes.

"I have a life," Milla said. "This is it. This is what I've chosen."

"Or what was chosen for you. You don't have to keep doing it, you know. You could step down from the day-to-day grind at Finders, only do fund-raisers. The stress you're under . . ." Susanna shook her head. "I don't know how you've gone on as long as you have. You should at least take regular breaks."

"Not yet," she said. Not until she found Justin.

Susanna sighed. "At least get regular checkups, and take vitamins. Prenatal vitamins would be a good choice for you, since you're under so much stress."

"Yes, Mother," Milla parroted, making both Rip and Susanna smile. Vitamins were a good idea, though. She didn't want to get sick now, when she had the feeling that some breakthrough could happen any day. She had to be ready, had to be in good physical condition.

Susanna gave up nagging, and they began talking about mutual friends, catching up on gossip. Rip made a few comments, but it didn't take long for Milla to notice that he wasn't his usual self. His voice and smile were warm whenever he spoke to her, but there was an almost palpable tension between him and Susanna. They had obviously had an argument, which made her uncomfortable. She would rather they had canceled than force her and themselves to sit through a stiff, awkward dinner, but she was caught now.

The restaurant they chose was casually elegant, the type where a tie wasn't required but jeans were definitely unwelcome. It was, in fact, one of Milla's favorite places to eat, because they had a wonderful grill. She chose the salmon, which was grilled on a cedar plank, and set about plowing through the evening with relentless small talk. She could enjoy their company even if they didn't enjoy each other's.

The meal dragged on, but at last they were almost finished and had just ordered coffee when Milla felt a presence beside her and glanced up into True Gallagher's lean, weathered face. "True!" she and Susanna said simultaneously. She shot a suspicious look at her friend. Had Susanna set this up, when Milla had specifically told her she wasn't going to go out with True?

"I just happened to see you," he said, putting his hand on the back of her chair and touching the back of her shoulder.

"Susanna, Rip, how're y'all doing? Too bad I didn't spot you earlier, or you could have joined me."

"We're fine," Susanna said, smiling. "Overworked, as usual. You?"

"The same."

"We just ordered coffee; why don't you join us, if you aren't in a hurry?"

"Thanks, I think I will." He settled his tall frame into the empty chair between Milla and Susanna and slanted one of his intense looks at Milla. "I haven't seen you lately; is anything new going on? You look–"

"If you say 'tired,' I'm going to swat you," she said firmly.

He grinned. "I was going to say you look great."

"Um-hmm." She wasn't convinced. "And, no, nothing new is going on. Looking for lost people, trying to raise money. I did pick up a new sponsor in Dallas, a software company."

True said, "That's good."

Rip hadn't contributed anything to the conversation, hadn't even greeted True. Milla glanced at him and saw that his expression had lost all its usual warmth; his gaze was hooded in a way that reminded her of Diaz.

Damn. She had gone out with the intention of forgetting about Diaz, not being reminded of him. But what was going on with Rip? He was normally a very friendly man. What had True done to get sideways with him?

A beeping noise suddenly erupted in Susanna's purse. She groaned. "At least it waited until I was finished eating." She dug her pager out and glanced at the readout. "It's the hospital. Let me just step outside and call in, and I'll be right back." Taking her cell phone, she hurried toward the door.

"A page is never good when you're a doctor," True said. His hand was once more on the back of Milla's chair, and his thumb rubbed gently over her shoulder before he seemed to think better of it and moved his hand back into his own space. Or maybe he was just sneaky, and didn't want to give her time to move away.

Rip's jaw was tight, and he didn't respond to True's comment. Rather than sit in silence until Susanna returned, Milla said, "Did you find out any more information for me?" If she didn't ask, he'd be curious.

"Nothing that fits the time frame. I'm afraid it's a dead end."

"Information about what?" Rip asked abruptly, and though his question was uncharacteristically rude, Milla realized she had been just as rude in excluding him.

"I thought I'd finally found a name connected with the kidnapping, and I asked True to check it out." She didn't have to specify *which* kidnapping, even though Finders had been involved in many. That awful day was a center of reference for them all.

Rip didn't even glance at True. "Why not ask the police to run the name? You know they'd do it for you."

"I know, but True has contacts on the other side of the border–"

Susanna hurried back in, her expression tense as she interrupted them. "I'm sorry, I have to go. Felicia D'Angelo has a fever and her blood pressure is up. She's only twenty weeks along. I'm meeting her at the hospital."

"Which one?" Rip asked, since she had privileges at two.

She told him, then leaned down and kissed Rip's cheek, ignoring the way he stiffened. "I'm taking the car. You can get a cab, can't you?"

"Don't bother with a cab," True said, looking from Milla to Rip. "I can drive both of you home."

"No, that's too much trouble," Milla said. "We live on opposite sides of town."

"I knew that when I offered. It's no problem."

Rip said, "We'll take a cab. I'd like to see Milla safely home, so I'll have the cab drop her off and then take me home."

"That's rid–" Susanna began, then cut herself off and gave Rip a frustrated look, which made Milla think she had indeed been set up. "Never mind. Arrange things however you want. I have to go; I'll see you later tonight, I hope." She grabbed her bag and hurried out the door.

The waiter brought the coffee and poured it, and Milla sat uncomfortably between the two men while she sipped her coffee, they ignored theirs, and the polite tug of war over her continued. True was determined to take her home; Rip was just as determined that he wouldn't. She saw Rip's hold on his temper start to shred, and decided she'd better step in.

"Hold it," she said calmly. "Neither of you have asked me what *I* want to do."

Both of them immediately turned to her, and Rip's expression was faintly apologetic. "Sorry. Were you feeling like a wishbone?"

"A bit." She smiled at him, because she knew he wasn't going to like what she said. "I need to talk to True, so I'll go with him."

She was right; Rip didn't like that at all, though he had the grace not to argue once she made her decision. True didn't look triumphant, but then maybe he was smart enough to realize he wasn't going to like their talk.

"Whatever you want," Rip said as the waiter brought their bills, and he fished a credit card out of his pocket, placing it in one of the folders. True made a motion as if to take the folder containing Milla's bill, but she stopped him with a glance. She slipped several bills in that folder.

They waited until the waiter had taken both folders away, then returned with Rip's credit card and receipt for his signature. He asked the waiter to have a cab called for him, and while that was being done, he added a hefty tip, then scrawled his name and pocketed his card.

"The cab company said ten minutes," the waiter said when he returned.

"We'll wait," Milla began, but Rip shook his head.

"No, go on. It's just a few minutes. I'll finish my coffee while I wait." He stood as she and True did, and kissed Milla's cheek. "It's been too long since we did this. Don't be such a stranger."

She chuckled. "Like yours and Susanna's schedules are any better than mine."

"Ain't it the truth. Be careful going home." He nodded a good-bye to True, and sat back down as she and True left the restaurant.

"My truck's this way," he said, indicating the left and gently steering her in that direction with his hand on her back. "I get the feeling Rip doesn't like me."

She made a noncommittal sound, and waited until they were in True's silver Lincoln Navigator before saying, "I'm not very happy with you, myself. I don't like being maneuvered and manipulated."

He sat silently for a moment, the keys in his hand. Finally he said, "That obvious, huh?" as he put the key in the ignition and started the motor.

"Obvious enough." If he had denied that his being there was a setup, she might have believed him, but she respected him for not trying to weasel out of telling the truth. Something else occurred to her, and she said, "How do you know where I live?" When she had said she and the Kospers lived on opposite sides of the town, he'd said that he'd known that in advance.

"I don't, exactly. I know you live in the Westside, because I asked Susanna. What's your address?"

She told him, and he nodded. "I know how to get there." He was a native El Pasoan; he knew his way around the city.

"Was Susanna's page a real one?"

He shrugged. "So far as I know. I intended to offer to drive you home regardless."

"I meant what I said, True. I won't go out with you. I appreciate the lift home, but that's all it's going to be."

The traffic was fairly light and they caught several green lights in a row. She watched the streetlights cast changing shadows on his face, watched the way his expression hardened and his fingers drummed on the steering wheel. "You don't have to bury yourself," he finally said, his tone sharp with frustration. "God knows, I understand what drives you, but it doesn't have to be either-or. You can search for your son and still have something for yourself. You've closed yourself off emotionally; you don't let anyone in–"

"Because it isn't fair to let people expect something I'm not willing to give," she interrupted. "I won't give you one minute of my time if I think that minute could make the difference between finding out any information that could lead me to Justin, or missing the boat."

"You take the time to have dinner with Susanna and Rip."

"That's a different relationship from the one you're talking about, and you know it. If I had canceled at the last minute because I had to meet someone–and I would have, if anything had come up–they wouldn't have been upset. There's friendship, but our lives only intersect every now and then; they aren't all wound together."

"So you're saying we can't even be friends."

She snorted. "As if I believe that's what you want."

Despite his annoyance, he grinned. "Damn, you're tough. But I like a challenge."

"I'm not challenging you. This isn't a dance for position. I resent that you're putting me in exactly the spot I wanted to avoid, which is making you angry by not doing what you want. If I don't go out with you, you won't like it; but if I go out with you but don't put you first, you won't like that either. It's a lose-lose situation."

His jaw set. "What if I promise to help you look for your son? What if I go along with you when you're chasing down whatever rumor you hear? If you're dealing with coyotes and other slimy bastards like that, you need protection anyway."

"I never go alone to any meeting." She stared through the windshield. Less than two weeks ago she would have jumped at any chance to have his aid, but that was before she met Diaz. Despite his money and connections, she simply didn't think True would be as effective as Diaz in finding Pavón. Maybe she was wrong. She might be making the mistake of a lifetime, but she had made her choice and she would stick with it, no matter how inherently dangerous that choice was.

He swore under his breath, then said, "If you take someone with you anyway, then why shouldn't that someone be me?"

"Because you have strings attached. Tell me the truth: Will you stop sponsoring Finders if I don't go out with you now?"

He drew back as if she'd slapped him. "Hell, no!"

"Then my final answer is no."

His hands tightened on the steering wheel, but he didn't say another word until he turned on her street and said, "Which house is yours?"

She directed him to her condo, which was the last unit on the left, and he pulled into the short driveway, the headlight beams flashing over her front door. Her neighbor's garage butted up against hers and their driveways were separated only by the line where the sections of concrete were poured. Because she was the last unit, the right side of her condo was graced with trees and shrubbery that somewhat softened the blocky lines of the residences. Her small backyard had privacy fencing around it, to separate it from her neighbor's. Her front door was recessed in a small alcove, and she had put planters of bright flowers on each side. The yellow porch light made the flowers look more orange than red. Her house was neat and well maintained, but she knew True was comparing it with his own house and probably wondering what she used for brains.

"Thank you for bringing me home," she said as she unfastened her seat belt and opened the door.

He shoved the gear lever into park and got out of the big SUV, but he wasn't fast enough to make it around before she got out. His hand closed around her elbow as he walked with her to the front door.

"All right," he said abruptly. "I'll back off. But if you need anything, call me. Day or night. I mean it. No strings attached."

The offer touched her, and she smiled up at him. "Thank you."

He stared down at her; then he swore softly again and before she could step back she was in his arms. Even with her three-inch heels he was about six inches taller than she was, and when he bent over her, she felt overwhelmed. His hand flattened against her back and his mouth covered hers.

She put her hands against his shoulders and pushed, trying to lever herself away from him. Under other circumstances, she might have liked his kiss, might have returned it. He knew how to kiss; his mouth was warm, his breath was pleasant, his tongue intimately teased but didn't intrude. Where her hips were molded to his, she felt his erection grow.

She pulled her mouth away and shoved even harder; he dropped his arms and stepped back.

"I thought you said you'd back off," she said, angry that he evidently wouldn't take no for an answer.

"I am backing off." His expression was hard, his eyes narrow.

"But I wanted a taste of you, and I wanted you to taste me. If you change your mind, all you have to do is tell me."

That male arrogance wasn't completely unattractive, but his intensity made her wary and she wasn't at all tempted to linger. She took out her keys and unlocked the door. "Good night," she said as she stepped inside, and she closed the door and locked it in practically one motion.

She was so unsettled that it took her a moment to realize the lamp wasn't on. She froze, and as the darkness pressed down on her she realized that she wasn't alone.

13

Instead of going home, Rip had the cabdriver take him to the hospital. He used his parking card to gain entrance to the physician's parking lot, and he told the driver to wait. As he got out of the cab, he checked the vehicles in the lot, and wasn't surprised to see that his own car wasn't there. He was disappointed, but not surprised. Still, he clipped on his identity badge and went inside to the emergency department.

"Has Felicia D'Angelo checked in?" he asked the admissions clerk, who checked the computer.

"No, sir, we have a Ramon D'Angelo, but not a Felicia."

Just to be certain, Rip had the driver take him to the other hospital where he and Susanna had privileges, and he went through the same routine. His car wasn't in the parking lot, and Felicia D'Angelo hadn't been admitted to the hospital.

He hoped like hell Susanna would be at home when he got there, that the false page and her story had just been part of her misguided effort to throw Milla and Gallagher together. Despite everything, he still hoped.

But when he got home, the windows were dark. He paid the cabdriver the rather hefty fee, then trudged up the sidewalk and unlocked the front door. He automatically turned off the alarm and flipped on the light switch.

He wondered what tale Susanna would have when she got home. He wondered where she was. And he wondered what in hell he was going to do.

True might not have gotten into his truck yet; he might hear her scream. The thought burned through her mind as Milla tried to force air past her constricted throat, but it was like in a nightmare, when you try and try to scream but can't. All she could manage was a strangled sound that was cut off when a hard hand clamped over her mouth and a steel-muscled body pushed her against the wall, holding her there.

"Hush," said that low voice. "Don't scream. It's just me."

Just him? Even knowing it was Diaz didn't lessen her panic a lot. Her heart was slamming against her breastbone so hard she felt ill from the force of it. She was almost grateful he was holding her against the wall, because otherwise she didn't think her knees would have supported her.

She felt him lean to the side, heard the click as he switched on the lamp and mellow light flooded the foyer. From outside came the sound of an engine starting, then the whine of tires on pavement as True drove off.

Diaz took his hand away. His face was expressionless, his eyes cold. "You got something going on with Gallagher?"

She hit him. She slapped his arm and his shoulder; then she took her purse and swatted him on the side of the head. "Damn it, you scared the life out of me!" she shrieked, and tears of fright and relief trickled down her cheeks. Trembling, she sank down in the chair beside the lamp table while she fumbled in her purse for a tissue.

Diaz was no longer expressionless; he looked absolutely floored that she had hit him—and, probably, that he had let her. She couldn't believe it herself, not only that she had so lost control, but that he'd just stood there instead of breaking her arm or at least tossing her to the floor. She opened her mouth to apologize, and instead found herself swatting him on the knee. "Damn it," she said weakly, as more tears trickled down. She scrubbed at them with a tissue. Her makeup was probably a mess, and that made her want to swat him again.

He crouched in front of her, his eyes almost level with hers. "I didn't mean to—I'm sorry." Cautiously he reached out and took her hand, as if making such contact wasn't something he normally did and he wasn't quite sure how to go about it. His fingers were hard and hot, his palm was callused; he cradled her hand in his and stroked his thumb over her knuckles. "Are you okay?"

"You mean if my heart ever starts beating normally again?" she snapped, then abruptly found herself laughing. She was so weak from adrenaline overload that she couldn't stand up, so she just leaned her head back against the wall and chuckled while she wiped her face with her free hand.

An incredible thing happened. The corners of his mouth moved upward.

She was so astonished at the sight of Diaz smiling that she stopped laughing and stared at him. Her heart had begun to settle down, but now it started thumping wildly again, and this time it wasn't because of fear. Her entire body flushed with heat and she began trembling again. Diaz holding her hand, smiling—*now* was when she should scream, because she was in far greater danger than she'd been a moment ago.

"What?" he asked, bewildered by the way she was staring at him.

"You're smiling." It was as if he had dropped part of his

mask and was letting her see past the blankness he usually presented to the world. Astonishment, bewilderment, concern, amusement had all been visible in his expression during the past minute. The one thing she was most terrified she would see was desire, so she pulled her hand from his and began making the feminine motions of neatening herself: pushing her hair out of her face, straightening her skirt, blotting under her eyes to remove any melted mascara.

"I smile," he said, as if he couldn't understand why such a small thing would startle her.

"When?"

"Hell, I don't keep a log. I laugh, too."

"This year?"

He started to say something, then reconsidered and shrugged. "Maybe not." Amusement began curling the corners of his mouth again. "You hit me with your purse."

"I'm sorry," she apologized. "I was so scared, I lost it. Did I hurt you?"

"You're joking."

"Not really. I mean, I hit you in the head."

"Those were girl slaps."

They had been. She felt a twinge of despair. She trained and trained and trained, trying to get herself in a sort of warrior state of mind so she could handle situations exactly like that, and instead of doing anything effective, she had automatically fallen back into a purely feminine response. If this happened with, say, Pavón, then she was a dead woman.

He was still crouched in front of her, so close she could feel his body heat against her legs. His short black hair was spiked and untidy, as if he'd run his fingers through his hair while it was wet. For the first time since she'd met him he was clean-shaven, though he was dressed in his usual uniform of T-shirt and jeans, with black boots. The lamplight emphasized the stark bone structure of his severe face, made his dark eyes seem more deep-set, and his usually grim mouth was softer, fuller.

Desperately she hid her inner quiver. She had held out hope that her physical response to him was mostly in her imagination, fueled by his deadly aura. Women daydreamed about dangerous men, when in reality a nice, normal guy was far preferable. But this was no daydream, and she had to clench her hands to keep from reaching out and stroking that mouth. Diaz wasn't a bad boy, he was a bad *man*, and she would do well to remember the difference. He didn't walk on the side of the angels.

But they were alone in her house, isolated in this small pool of light, and she knew that all she had to do was part her knees and he would be between them. He hadn't made a pass or even indicated he was thinking about it, but she knew he wouldn't turn her down. He would oblige her, and then he would disappear again, the encounter having meant no more to him than a drink of water when he was thirsty.

So she remained in the chair, and kept her legs together. She refused to be nothing more than convenient sex for anyone, even herself.

"Gallagher kissed you," he said, letting her know that he'd watched them from a window, since her door was solid. Even as she watched, his face was changing, losing its brief animation and settling back into the familiar stone mask.

"I didn't want him to." For some reason, she felt as if she owed Diaz an explanation. "He keeps asking me out, and I keep refusing."

"Why were you with him tonight?"

"I had dinner with some friends and True stopped by our table. My friends are both doctors, and one of them was called to the hospital on an emergency. She took their car, so True drove me home while Rip took a cab home."

He was silent as he considered that, then shook his head. "I won't help you unless you stay away from him."

She didn't bridle at the ultimatum, because it jibed with her own feelings. "All right."

"Just like that?"

"Just like that. You know him, don't you?"

"We've met."

And yet True, when she'd asked him about Diaz, hadn't said anything of the sort. Instead he'd pretended to be looking for information. It was possible he thought she would be safer if she never crossed paths with Diaz, and if so then he was right, but she made her own decisions and took her own chances. By trying to keep her from Diaz, he'd been blocking her from information she desperately needed.

"Did you find Pavón?"

"Working on it. Got a lead. He may stay out of sight for a month or so, though, since he got word I was looking for him."

Any sane person would stay out of sight longer than that, like for a lifetime. "Then why are you here, if you don't have any new information?"

"To tell you I did run across something that might interest you. One of my informants knew something about a baby-smuggling ring going on about ten years ago."

She stiffened, chills running up and down her spine and over her scalp. She felt as if her lungs suddenly constricted, preventing her from breathing. "What did he say?" she asked, her voice stifled.

"It was a fairly high-class operation, as these things go. The kids were flown across the border in a small private plane, rather than stuffed in car trunks and driven across."

She still couldn't quite catch her breath; all she could do was gasp. A plane! She'd had nightmares, thinking of Justin dying of heatstroke in some car trunk and being tossed aside like so much garbage.

"This doesn't mean it was the same ring that kidnapped your baby," he warned. "But the time is about right, and they operated in southern Chihuahua and Coahuila. They had a contact here in Texas who arranged for birth certificates for the kids, so they could be legally adopted."

"Birth certificates." Then it had to be someone who worked in a county courthouse, or a hospital. Since Justin had been born in Mexico and all the paperwork had been done there, she wasn't sure exactly how birth certificates were issued, and she had never thought to check.

"Things wouldn't work the same way now," he said, reading her mind. "Everything is on computer. And the birth certificates could have come from any state."

"I know." Adoption records were also private, unless otherwise directed by the birth parent. That was a huge obstacle. Nor could she look for a noticeable spike in a certain county's birth rate, because the number of extra certificates would far more likely be a few hundred for one year, rather than thousands. In a county that contained a large city, with a transient population, those extra birth certificates wouldn't even be noticed. But the larger cities would also have been more likely to be computerized ten years ago, she thought. A small rural county, with limited funds that didn't cover full computerized record-keeping, would be a better bet. She said as much to Diaz, who nodded.

"What would you look for?"

"Birth certificates issued in clumps. How many babies would be born in a small county on the same day, or the same week? Even the same month? If the total in some months was noticeably higher than in other months, I'd concentrate there."

He was silent, and she waited while he processed whatever he was thinking. Finally he glanced up at her. "Supposedly, the smuggling ring stopped operating when the private plane crashed."

Her lips went numb as the feverish hope in her turned into yet another nightmare. "When?"

"Roughly ten years ago. Everyone on board died, including the six babies."

She sat staring at her hands long after he'd gone. Life couldn't be so cruel, *God* couldn't be so cruel, to let her go for so long and get this far, then snatch everything away from her. She knew Justin wasn't necessarily on that plane, that a different smuggling ring might have taken him. But this was another nightmare possibility that she had to deal with, another horrible ending to innocent little lives.

She might never find her baby, though she'd never stop looking. But she *would* find the people behind this–no, not "people," *monsters*–and she'd bring them down if it was the last thing she ever did. Something in her was changing, and she was no longer willing to overlook anything in exchange for information on her lost baby, on any lost baby. She wanted justice, and she wanted vengeance.

14

SUSANNA WAS SO TIRED HER MOVEMENTS WERE SLUGGISH AS she pulled into the garage. She sat for a moment with the door open and her eyes closed, trying to summon the energy to get out of the car. It had been a very, very long night, and now she'd get maybe two hours of sleep before she'd have to get up and do her rounds at the hospital, followed by seeing patients in the office all day, then evening rounds before she could come home and fall into bed. Coffee might wake her up, but it wouldn't make her feel any less tired.

She wondered how True had made out with Milla the night before. She knew Milla well enough to tell that she'd seen through their subterfuge, and was annoyed.

True thought he could get around Milla, but he didn't know her the way Susanna did. Milla looked like, and was, the type of woman who preferred to wear a dress instead of pants, who liked cooking and decorating and working with children. She had once even planned to teach, which to Susanna's way of thinking was taking a fondness for children to ridiculous extremes. Milla's nails were always manicured, and not once in the eleven years she'd known her had Susanna seen Milla when her toenails weren't polished. Even when she'd given birth, her toenails had been painted a delicate shell pink. Probably she'd had David paint them for her, because there was no way a nine-months-pregnant woman could bend down that far. And David would have done it without hesitation; he'd been absolutely crazy about Milla.

But the villagers who had witnessed the kidnapping said Milla had fought like a tigress for her baby. And even though she'd just come within a hairsbreadth of dying from a vicious stab wound, from the moment she'd regained consciousness, she'd been like a woman possessed, with only one thought in her mind, only one purpose in her life: finding her child.

She had sublimated her personality, forged herself into someone tougher. She had gone into places where armed men would have hesitated to go, talked to thugs and drug addicts, thieves and murderers—and for some reason, though none of them had given her any real information, neither had they harmed her. Maybe, on some cellular level that never reached conscious thought, they hoped their own mothers would have searched so relentlessly for them. Perhaps even those who knew better had wished that their mothers had been like Milla.

It hadn't hurt that she was so young, with a world of heartbreak in those big brown eyes. The silver streak in her hair drew the eye, reminded everyone of her suffering. She had been everywhere: on television, in magazines, in the Mexican president's office, talking to the Federales and the Border Patrol, talking to anyone and everyone who might be of help. She'd become the personification of bereaved, outraged mothers, the face of heartbreak—and of determination. She'd even broken with her own family over her dedication to searching for Justin.

David had fallen by the wayside. It must have been damn hard to be married to a crusader, Susanna thought. Milla had revealed a backbone of steel, and a stubborn streak that went all the way to her core. She had adored David, and yet she had walked away from him.

And True thought he could do better? Susanna didn't think so. But he'd insisted, and what True wanted, True got. She wasn't fool enough to turn him down. She knew better than most how ruthless he could be, and she'd always been careful not to run afoul of him.

The door leading from the house into the garage opened, and Rip appeared. "Are you going to sit there all night?" he asked.

Oh, God. Why was he still up? Normally she would have been gratified that he'd waited up for her, but not now, not tonight. He was probably pissed about True and Milla, and she was too exhausted to dance a verbal fandango with him.

"I'm so tired I could sleep right here," she said as she got out of the car. "I probably should have stayed at the hospital."

"Probably," he agreed, stepping aside so she could enter the house. "Then you would have been there when I checked."

She froze in mid-step, then continued through the house and up the stairs, all but hauling herself up them. Damn it! She should have covered herself somehow, but since he'd accused her of having an affair with True, and he knew True wasn't with her, she hadn't even considered he would check up on her.

"Nothing to say?" Rip asked behind her.

"No. If you're going to have a shit fit because I didn't hear a page, or the staff didn't know where I was, there's nothing I can do about it. I'm going to shower and go to bed."

"I didn't call. I went to both hospitals. You weren't there. Neither was Felicia D'Angelo. So I looked in your patient Rolodex and got Felicia's number, and called to check on her. She said she's feeling fine, in case you're wondering."

Damn. Double damn. Fuck. She always kept a record of her current patients' home phone numbers here at the house, for her convenience. When had Rip turned into fucking Sherlock Holmes?

"We'll talk tomorrow," she said, because she couldn't think of anything to say tonight. She needed to talk to True. She was losing control and she knew it, because she didn't swear, even to herself, unless she was pushed to the wall. She didn't dare get into an argument with Rip now, or she'd say more than she should.

She went into the bedroom and closed the door, leaning back against it while she waited to see if Rip would follow, if a push would send her stumbling across the room. But after a moment she heard his footsteps continue down the hall to the room where he was sleeping, and with a sigh of relief she locked the door and went into the bathroom.

She used her cell phone to call True. He answered on the second ring, his voice alert and full of authority, as always.

"Rip checked up on me," she said. "He knows I wasn't at either hospital. He even called the patient I said I was meeting."

"Find someone and let Rip catch you fucking him, and he won't check any further."

She closed her eyes at True's crude reply. The hell of it was, he was right: if she did that, Rip would think he'd solved the mystery and would stop prying. But she'd never cheated on Rip, and she wasn't going to start now, no matter what he thought or what True said.

"How did things go with Milla?"

"They didn't." She could hear the banked fury in his voice, and she knew Milla had reacted just the way she'd expected.

She was too smart to say "I told you so" to True. Instead she said, "She's obsessed with finding her kid. Nothing else touches her."

"Not even reason, apparently. I have to have some way of keeping tabs on her. She was never a threat before, but she is now. Who told her about Diaz? I've headed her off, but she might decide to do some investigating on her own, and the last thing we need is Diaz in the picture."

Susanna didn't know Diaz, but she knew *of* him. She also knew that True Gallagher wasn't afraid of the devil himself, but he was wary of this Diaz guy. There was history between them, there had to be. She got the feeling Diaz would be more than happy to do anything that caused trouble for True. Diaz's reputation was downright scary; if Milla somehow made contact with him and talked him into helping her, they'd have to take steps to protect themselves.

"Feed her some more false leads," she suggested. "Get her busy chasing ghosts."

True chuckled. "Good idea." He paused. "I just realized. It wasn't your home phone that showed up on Caller ID."

"I'm on my cell phone."

"Shit! You know they can be intercepted."

"If I call from the home phone, Rip can pick up and listen."

"Then find some other way, but don't use your cell." The receiver clanged in her ear.

Grimacing, Susanna ended the call. "Fuck you, too," she muttered. There she went again with the swearing. She stood for a moment, swaying with exhaustion; she was tempted to fall into bed and shower when she got up, but after what she'd been doing, she didn't want to go to bed without bathing. She'd washed up before coming home, of course, but that wasn't the same as an all-over bath. Perhaps this was how Lady Macbeth had felt, scrubbing out invisible spots of blood.

True got out of bed after hanging up on Susanna. He trusted her as much as he trusted most people, but sometimes she could do things that were incredibly stupid. He'd told her over and over, no cell phones or cordless phones. Use land-lines. They were safest. He had cordless phones for convenience, of course, but the phones by his bed and in his office were corded.

He'd have to update his security eventually, he thought. Scramblers on his phones. Electronic countermeasures to prevent anyone from eavesdropping with a parabolic mike. Right now, though, he wasn't a big enough fish for anyone to go to that much trouble to catch him. He was still medium-sized, but growing. He intended to keep on growing. Give him another year, two years at the most, and he'd be able to walk away clean with a sizable fortune that would require overseeing and investing, but would grow under its own momentum.

If he could just get through those couple of years without things blowing up under him.

Milla had never been very worrisome, despite her persistence. He'd made certain no one would tell her anything. He'd kept tabs on her through Susanna and other contacts, and he even—somewhat to his bemusement—admired the way she never gave up. Certainly his own mother had never been that devoted. Eventually, when Milla got into fund-raising for that group of hers, he'd made a point of showing up, contributing, and slowly getting to know her and getting her to trust him. What better way to stay on top of her efforts? He was a sponsor. She talked to him, and though she normally limited her conversation to what Finders was doing, if he asked about her personal situation, she would tell him. He'd made a point of always asking.

The unwelcome surprise was that he liked her.

Hell, he wanted to sleep with her. He wanted her naked. He wanted to tangle his hands in that soft curly hair and hold her while he fucked her. He didn't understand it, because she wasn't his usual type. She wasn't voluptuous, or flashy, or even really pretty. But she had style, and presence, and brown eyes that invited a man to get lost in them.

It would be a bitch if he had to have her killed.

He didn't want to. For one thing, she was too high-profile. People knew her name, her face, her story. It would be national news if anything happened to her, which meant the cops would go all out on the investigation.

She was enough of a threat that he'd had her watched, had kept watch on her himself, for ten years. He'd minimized her effectiveness, and taking her out now would be like using an elephant gun to shoot a bird. He didn't want to overreact and bring unnecessary attention his way. There were other ways to keep her in check.

Having an affair with her would have been the best way to keep tabs on her every movement and control the situation until he was ready to get out. He knew she was attracted to him, knew she'd had a couple of short-lived affairs that proved she hadn't completely given up living. But he'd underestimated the strength of her devotion to her cause, and after the way she'd stiffened in his arms when he kissed her, he had to accept that she wasn't going to change her mind. If he persisted, he would completely turn her off and she'd stop regarding him as a personal friend.

He'd have to cut his losses there, but he didn't like it. He'd felt almost like a teenager again, in a lather of anticipation. He saw now that he'd handled things clumsily with that "accidental" meeting at the restaurant, Susanna knowing she'd have to leave and arranging for a watcher in the restaurant to call her pager as soon as Rip sat down at their table. Very high-schoolish, and Milla had immediately seen through it.

So he'd back off. That didn't mean he'd give up. Eventually, he'd have her, because he was like her in one critical area: he never gave up.

* * *

Milla noticed when she changed her birth control patch the next morning that she had only a month's supply left, with no refill, so she made a note to call Susanna's office and get a prescription called in. She was always careful about birth control because she was aware of the risks she ran of being assaulted. She literally made a note, writing it down, because she didn't trust herself to remember otherwise. She felt both lethargic and nervous, wiped out from the stress of the night before and yet oddly on edge, waiting for something to happen.

She had slept like the dead. Handling True had been stressful, but Diaz—the short time she'd been with Diaz had left her feeling as if she'd been caught up in a tornado and hurled over half the country before being dumped into an ice-cold bath. Terror, fury, laughter, desire, despair—all had chased through her in rapid succession. The effects of so much adrenaline dumping into her system had left her shaky, and then she'd crashed.

And yet, the first thing she thought of when she awoke was how Diaz had looked crouched before her, smiling in the lamplight. And because she wasn't completely awake, her imagination had then drifted and placed them in different positions altogether, with him crouched *over* her, his eyes heavy-lidded and that same small smile on his lips as he slowly penetrated—

She blocked the fantasy, shuddering with delight even though she refused to let her imagination take her any further. That was far enough, anyway, to shock her. She had desired other men before, imagined making love with them. But none of them, not even David, had ever tempted her to veer from the course she had set herself.

Diaz did. Sleeping with him would be a mistake on a personal level, but what scared her was the chaos it could cause in their working relationship. For Justin's sake, she didn't dare change their status. And yet, knowing that, she still *wanted* to, yearned to taste him and touch him and feel him inside her.

Diaz had never kissed her, had scarcely touched her hand, but with one smile he had completely wiped out her memory of True's taste.

She had to get herself under control before she did something stupid. If she read him right, Diaz would disappear if she got clingy and started making any emotional demands on him, and she didn't trust herself not to do that. She hadn't felt this way since ... well, she'd never felt this way. With David, she had felt absolutely secure in his love. There hadn't been any reason for emotional insecurity. Diaz, however, was David's polar opposite, and he might offer her a few things, but emotional security wasn't in his repertoire.

She was doing what women always did, she realized: obsessing. She should put him out of her mind, concentrate on controlling herself and doing what had to be done every day. The day-to-day business at Finders was way more important than her libido.

While driving to work, she put in a call to Susanna's office, only to be told, after holding for five minutes while she threaded her way through heavy morning traffic, that Susanna wanted her to come in for a checkup, since it had been two years since the last one.

Damn. Sighing, Milla made an appointment, scribbled the date on her note reminding her to call Susanna in the first place, and hoped she'd be in town to keep the appointment.

The first thing she saw when she entered the office was Brian hanging over Olivia's desk. But his voice was only a murmur, and his eyes had that intent, sleepy look men got when they—

Her eyes widened, and she shot a disbelieving look at Olivia, who was leaning forward with her arms folded on top of her desk, which pushed her breasts together and upward. She was smiling up at Brian.

So it wasn't just her, Milla thought. Lust was busting out all over.

Joann stuck her head out of her office. "Amber Alert in Lubbock!"

Within a minute they all had descriptions of the child, a three-year-old girl snatched from her front yard; the vehicle, a dark green, late model Ford pickup; and the driver, white male, early thirties, long blond hair. The Lubbock police would handle the actual apprehension, but Finders called all their associates in the Lubbock area and got them on the streets and highways, armed with cell phones and a description of the truck and driver. People going about their daily business might be listening to tapes or CDs and not hear the alert over the radio, or just be remarkably inattentive to what was going on around them.

Forty-five tense minutes later, the truck was spotted and police notified. The driver, when a cruiser flashed his lights at him, pulled over without fuss. It turned out to be a dispute between a divorced couple, the little girl was his daughter, and not only was she happy to be with her daddy, she began crying when the officers took her away from him.

"People," Milla said in disgust, lightly banging her head against her desk. "Why do they do that to their kids?"

"Because," was Joann's informative answer. Then she caught her breath in an audible gasp. "Guess who just walked in," she said in a high, squeaky tone.

Milla raised her head, her heart already thumping as she watched Diaz walk toward her office with that catlike tread of his. Heads were turning, watching him, and conversation stuttered to a halt in his wake. Brian stood up, his attention on high alert as he automatically reacted to the presence of a predator in his group. He recognized Diaz, surely, from the search for little Max the week before, but that didn't seem to make any difference.

Diaz stopped in her office doorway, turning slightly to the side so he couldn't be approached unawares from the rear. "Let's take a trip over the border," he said. His face was set in its usual emotionless mask.

"Right now?"

He shrugged. "If you're interested."

She started to ask, "In what?" but he wouldn't have been here if it wasn't something that concerned Justin.

"I'll change clothes," she said, getting to her feet. She was wearing a sundress and sandals.

"You're fine as you are. We'll be in Juarez."

She got her purse, checked to make certain everything she needed was in it, just in case, and said, "Let's go."

As they reached the bottom of the outside stairs, he said, "We'll use my truck," pointing her toward the dusty blue pickup.

"Are we driving across, or walking?"

"Walking. It's faster."

"Should I call and arrange for another car?" she asked as she gathered her skirt and clambered up into the high cab.

"No need. I've got another one on the other side."

"What are we doing? Who are we seeing?"

"Maybe the sister of the man who stabbed you."

15

THEY WALKED ACROSS ONE OF THE BRIDGES AND PRESENTED their drivers' licenses, which was all that was required for tourists staying inside the border free-zone. He hooked his cell phone off his belt and made a brief call; within ten minutes, a grinning teenager drove up in a slightly rusted brown Chevrolet pickup. Diaz passed him a folded twenty-peso banknote, and the teenager tossed him the keys, then turned and took off into the crowd.

This truck sat higher than the other one did, and when she opened the door, she looked for a handle to help her pull herself up. Before she could manage the feat in a skirt, Diaz stepped behind her, put his hands on her waist, and lifted her onto the seat.

She settled herself in the seat and buckled up while he went around and vaulted behind the wheel. She was shaking inside, her nerves knotted. "*Maybe* the man's sister?" she asked.

"I don't know for certain. We'll find out." He leaned over

and opened the glove box, took out a big, holstered automatic and laid it on the seat beside him.

"How did you find her?"

"It doesn't matter how," he said briefly, and she understood. His informants were his own, as were his methods. She didn't want to look too closely at either.

He deftly navigated through Juarez's noisy, crowded streets, going deeper and deeper into a neighborhood so rough she didn't know whether to weep with pity or duck down in the seat and hide. She was glad Diaz was armed, and she wished she were, too. The streets were narrow and crowded, with ramshackle buildings and shanties pressing in on each side, and trash littering the ground. Sullen-faced men and teenage boys stared at her with unconcealed resentment and vicious intent, but when they noticed the man driving the truck, they quickly looked away.

She said, "I think your reputation precedes you."

"I've been here before."

And done considerable damage, judging from the way these people were reacting to the sight of him.

Battered and rusty vehicles lined the street Diaz drove on now, but he found a gap big enough to wedge the truck in. He got out, strapped the holster around his thigh, and checked how the automatic was seated. Satisfied, he came around the truck and opened her door. After he lifted Milla down from the seat and locked the doors, he made eye contact with a man sullenly watching them from ten yards away, and made a brief motion with his head.

Warily the man approached. "If my truck is unharmed when we return," Diaz said in rapid Spanish, "I'll pay you a hundred dollars, American. If it is harmed, I will find you."

The man nodded rapidly, and took up his sentry position guarding the truck.

Milla didn't ask if the precaution was necessary; she knew it was. The pistol, however–"Should you wear the pistol out in the open? What if the Preventivos see you?" They were the Mexican equivalent of regular beat cops.

He snorted. "Look around. Do you think they come here very often? Besides, I want it where everyone can see it, and where I can get to it in a hurry."

The thigh holster made him look like some modern-day outlaw; even the way he walked–loose-limbed, perfectly balanced–seemed like a throwback to some rougher, more violent time. She could easily imagine him with bandoliers crisscrossed on his chest and a bandanna pulled up to cover the lower half of his face.

He set an easy pace as he wound through a warren of increasingly small and nasty alleys. She clutched her bag tightly in front of her and stayed close to him, but he must not have thought she was staying close enough, because he reached out with his left hand and caught her right wrist, pulling her to him. He tucked her hand inside his belt. "Hold on, and don't stray."

As if, she thought.

She tried to watch where she stepped; since she was wearing sandals, she was doubly concerned. Evidently his definition of "You're fine as you are" differed from hers. She would much rather be wearing pants and boots–and a Kevlar vest, if she had the choice–while she waded through trash and other things she didn't stop to identify.

His right hand was on the butt of the pistol, not gripping it, just resting lightly in a way that said he was ready to use it. He turned down an alley even narrower than all the rest and came to a door that had once been painted blue, but only specks of paint remained, and some holes in it had been patched with pieces of cardboard that were duct-taped in place. He rapped on the rotted wood frame, and waited.

She heard scuffling noises from inside; then the door opened a tiny crack and one dark eye peered out. The owner of the eye made a muffled sound of alarm, as if she recognized him.

"Lola Guerrero," he said, the tone of his voice making it a command.

"*Si,*" the woman said cautiously.

Diaz reached out and pushed the door open. The woman squeaked a protest and retreated a few steps, but when he didn't come into her home, she hesitated, looking back at him. He didn't say anything, just waited. The light was dim inside the little room, but still Milla could see the anxious look the woman darted at her. Perhaps she was reassured by the presence of another woman, though, because she muttered, "*Pase,*" and motioned them inside.

The smell inside was sour. A single naked lightbulb burned in a small lamp in a corner, and an old electric fan with metal blades and no guard whirred noisily as it stirred the air. Lola herself looked to be in her mid- to late sixties, with plump, shiny skin that said her room might be a dump but she was getting enough to eat.

More money appeared in Diaz's hand, and he offered it to the woman. Warily she eyed his outstretched hand, then snatched the money as if afraid he would think better of offering it. "You have a brother," he said in Spanish. "Lorenzo."

He had an interesting interrogation technique, Milla thought. He didn't ask questions; he made statements, as if he already knew the facts.

A bitter expression crossed the woman's face. "He is dead."

Milla was still holding Diaz's belt, and her hand tightened convulsively on the leather. So this was another trail that led only to a blank wall. She bowed her head, fighting the urge to howl in pain and protest. As if sensing her distress, Diaz reached back and pulled her to his side, tucking her within the circle of his arm and absently patting her shoulder.

"Lorenzo worked with a man named Arturo Pavón."

Lola nodded, and spat on the floor, which made Milla think even less of her housekeeping than before. Hatred darkened Lola's face. A flood of Spanish poured out, too fast for Milla to completely follow, but she gathered that Pavón had either killed Lorenzo or been the cause of his death, and that Pavón was one of any number of unsavory animals who performed sexual acts with assorted other animals and also with his mother.

Lola Guerrero didn't like Pavón.

When Lola's invective finally ran down, Diaz said, "Ten years ago this woman's baby was stolen by Pavón."

Lola's gaze darted to Milla, and Lola said softly, "I am sorry, señora."

"*Gracias.*" Lola must have children of her own; her gaze had carried the instant, almost universal link between mothers that said, *I understand this pain.*

"She was injured in the attack, stabbed in the back by a man I believe was Lorenzo," Diaz continued. "Your brother was known for his knife work; his specialty was going for a kidney."

Oh, my God. Milla shuddered at the realization that the man who'd stabbed her had been *trying* to hit her kidney. She wanted to bury her face in Diaz's shoulder, shut out the ugliness that surrounded her.

Diaz paused, his cold eyes raking over Lola. "You used to care for the babies who were stolen," he said. Milla went rigid, her head snapping up. Lola had been *part* of the gang? The woman's expression hadn't been one of commiseration, but of guilt. Milla heard a low growl, and in shock realized it came from her own throat. Diaz's arm tightened around her, clamping her to his side and preventing her from moving.

"My friend clawed out Pavón's eye as she was fighting for her baby. Lorenzo would at least have told you about it, even if you did not see Pavón yourself. You would remember this, remember the baby."

Lola's gaze darted from Diaz to Milla and back, as if she was trying to decide who was the greatest threat. Like all rodents, she had a sound instinct for preservation, and decided on Diaz. She stared at him, frozen in alarm that he knew so much. She would have lied; Milla saw her consider it, saw the thoughts chasing across her expression as clearly as if she spoke aloud. But Diaz stood as still as a rock, waiting, and Lola had no way of knowing what he already knew and what he didn't. Either way, she must have figured he would see through any lie. She swallowed, and muttered, "I remember."

"What did you do with the baby?"

Milla's nails dug into his chest as she waited, unable to breathe, for the answer.

"There were five of them," Lola said. "They were flown across the border that day. The gringo baby was the last one brought in." She spared a cautious look at Milla. "There was much trouble about him; the police were looking for him; we could not wait."

Flown out. Milla squeezed her eyes shut. "Did the plane crash?" she asked in a hoarse tone.

Lola brightened at being able to impart some good news. "No, no, that was later. Different babies."

Not Justin. He was alive. Alive! After all these years, she finally knew for certain. A sob caught in her throat and now she did bury her head against Diaz, almost breaking down at the release of an unspoken, unceasing tension that had held her for ten years. He made a low, wordless sound of comfort, then returned his attention to Lola.

"Who was in charge of stealing the babies? Who owned the plane? Who paid you?"

She blinked at the barrage of questions. "Lorenzo paid me. I was paid from his portion."

"Who was the boss?"

She shook her head. "That I do not know. He was a rich

gringo; he owned the plane. But I never saw him, or heard his name. Lorenzo was very careful; he said his throat would be cut if he told. This gringo, he told Pavón how many babies he needed, and Pavón found them."

"*Stole* them," Milla corrected violently, her voice muffled against Diaz's shirt.

"What happened to Lorenzo?" Diaz asked.

"His throat was cut, *señor*. By Pavón. Just as he said it would be. He did not talk to me, but he must have said something to someone else. Lorenzo, he was always stupid. His throat was cut as a warning to others not to talk."

"Who else knew anything about the rich gringo?"

Lola shook her head. "I knew only Lorenzo, and Pavón. They said it was best. I do know there was another woman helping them, a *gringa*, but they never said her name. She did something with the paperwork that said where the babies were born."

"Do you know where she was? What state?"

Lola waved a vague hand. "Across the border. Not Texas."

"New Mexico?"

"Perhaps. I don't remember. Sometimes I tried not to listen, *señor*."

"Do you know where the rich gringo lived?"

Alarm flashed across her face. "No, no. I know nothing about him."

"You heard something."

"Truly, no. Lorenzo thought he lived in Texas, perhaps even El Paso, but he did not know for certain. Pavón knows, but Lorenzo never did."

"Have you heard where Pavón might be?"

Lola spat again. "I have no interest in that pig."

"Take an interest," Diaz advised her. "I will perhaps feel more friendly if you have information about Pavón when I return."

Lola looked horrified at the idea of Diaz returning. She looked wildly around her cluttered, nasty, dark little room, as if wondering how fast she could pack up her things and disappear.

Diaz gave a slight shrug. "You can run," he said. "But why bother? If I want to find you, Lola Guerrero, I will. Eventually. And I never forget who helps me, and who does not."

Lola nodded her head very fast. "I understand, *señor*. I will be here. And I will listen for news."

"Do that." Diaz loosened his arm that was around Milla, turning her toward the door.

Milla dug in her heels, glancing back at the woman who had helped steal her baby. "How could you do it?" she asked, pain lacing every word. "How could you help them steal children from their mothers?"

Lola shrugged. "I am a mother, too, *señora*. I am poor. I needed the money to feed my own babies."

She was lying. As old as Lola was now, even ten years ago her youngest child would have been, if not grown, at least an adolescent. Milla stared at her, frozen in place by fury that roared through her with the force of an avalanche. She could have at least understood if there *had* been babies to feed, but obviously Lola had done it purely for the money. This was no victim, no poor and desperate mother doing whatever she could to feed her children. This woman was as bad as her brother Lorenzo, as Pavón. She had been part and parcel of the scheme, a willing participant in robbing grieving mothers all over Mexico of their babies.

"You lying *bitch*," Milla said through clenched teeth, and hurled herself toward the woman.

She must have telegraphed her intentions, because Lola sidestepped and quick as a flash had Milla's arm twisted up behind her and a knife at her neck. "Stupid," she hissed in Milla's ear, and the knife pressed harder. Milla felt the cold sting on her neck.

Then there was a faint *snick*, the sound of a safety being thumbed off, and Lola froze in place.

"It seems your family has a propensity for the knife," Diaz said very softly, his voice scarcely more than a rustle. "Mine, however, has a propensity for bullets."

Off balance in more ways than one, Milla cut her eyes to the left and saw Diaz holding that big pistol flush against Lola's temple. There was no quiver in his hand, no uncertainty in his eyes; instead they were narrowed in cold rage. "You have to the count of one to drop the knife. On–"

He didn't wait even that long for her to drop it. His left hand snaked out, caught Lola's hand, and twisted it down and away from Milla. There was an odd sound like a brittle branch snapping and Lola went rigid, a long, strangled moan reverberating in her throat. The knife clattered to the filthy floor and that lightning-fast hand transferred to Milla, snatching her to his side, holding her there with an iron grip on her arm. All the while the pistol in his right hand remained pointed at Lola's head.

Lola reeled backward, keening and holding her hand. "You broke it," she moaned, sinking down on a rickety chair.

"You're lucky I didn't take the knife from you and carve out your eyes," he said, still in that soft, soft tone. "You cut my friend. That makes me unhappy. Are we even, do you think? Or do I owe you more, perhaps another bone–"

"I will find out whatever you need to know," Lola babbled, rocking back and forth and staring at him in horror. She was no longer watching the pistol, but him, and Milla could understand why. His face was terrifying in its stillness, with only his eyes alive, glittering with rage. She could feel the force of his anger in the coiled strength of his body, hear it in the almost inaudible softness of his tone. He wasn't a man who lost control in his anger; he gained it to an even greater degree.

"You will do that anyway, *señora*. So I think there must be something else."

"No, no," Lola moaned. "Please, *señor*. I will do anything you ask."

He tilted his head as if considering. "I don't know what I want, yet. I'll think about it and let you know."

"Anything," she said again, half weeping. "I swear."

"Remember this," he said, "and remember that I don't like it when anyone harms my friends."

"I will, *señor*! I will!"

Diaz all but dragged Milla out of the room, and hustled her down the alley. She grabbed his belt again, hooking her fingers in it in a death grip, and pressed her other hand to her stinging throat. Warm blood wet her fingers, dripped through them. He glanced over his shoulder at her, his gaze going to her neck. "We need to get that cut cleaned and bandaged. It isn't deep, but it's making a mess of your dress. Keep your hand over it."

The truck was right where they'd left it, with the sullen man standing guard. He straightened when he saw them coming, and his expression changed to alarm when he noticed the blood on Milla's neck and dress, as if he might somehow be found at fault for whatever had happened. Diaz handed over the folded hundred dollars, then fished out his keys and unlocked the door. He lifted her in, nodded to the man, and went around to the driver's side.

"We'll go to Wal-Mart," he said. "I can pick up something for you to wear as well as an antibiotic and bandages."

The Wal-Mart was on Avenue Ejército Nacional. She sat with her fingers pressed to the cut on her throat as he worked their way out of the slum. "What exactly did you do to her hand?" she asked. He'd moved so fast she wasn't certain, plus she'd been a tad distracted; had he crushed it with a quick, hard squeeze?

Diaz glanced at her. "I broke her right thumb. It'll be a while before she can hold a knife again."

Milla shivered, sharply aware all over again of the kind of man he was.

"I had to," he said briefly, and she understood. Fear was his greatest ally. Fear was what made people talk to him when they wouldn't talk to anyone else. Fear gave him an edge, an opening; it was a weapon in itself. And to earn that fear, he had to be willing to back it up with action.

"She'll run," she said.

"Maybe. But I'll find her if she does, and she knows it."

They reached the Wal-Mart, and she sat in the truck with the motor running and the air-conditioning on—and the doors locked—while he went in to buy what he needed. He returned in no more than ten minutes, proving that the shoppers inside had taken one look at him and realized he belonged at the front of the checkout line. At least he'd removed the thigh holster before he went in, she thought, or there would have been wholesale panic.

He had a bottle of water, a package of gauze pads, a tube of antibiotic salve, first-aid tape, some butterfly bandages, and a cheap skirt and blouse. She started to say she'd just put the blouse on over her dress to cover the bloodstains; then she looked down and realized the blood had dripped on her skirt, too.

He drove into the parking lot behind the store, away from the crowd of shoppers, and parked the truck facing away from the lot to give them as much privacy as possible. She started to tear open the package of gauze, but he took everything from her and said, "Just sit still."

He wet one of the gauze pads and put it over the cut, then

took her hand and pressed it there. "Hold that." She did, pressing firmly to staunch the bleeding that had slowed but not completely stopped. He wet several more of the pads and began wiping her neck and chest, washing away the dried blood. His fingers dipped impersonally down the front of her dress, down to the edge of her bra.

"Okay, now let me see," he said, taking her hand away from the cut. He peeled back the gauze pad and grunted with satisfaction. "It isn't bad. You don't need any stitches, but I bought some butterfly bandages just to be on the safe side."

He applied the antibiotic salve, then a couple of butterfly bandages to hold the edges of the cut together. Then he taped a gauze pad over the butterflies to further protect the cut. When he was finished, he said, "Use the rest of these pads to wash your hands and arms before you change clothes."

She complied, glad to get the blood off of her, but she said, "I don't need to change clothes; I can go home like this."

"You're going to cross the border in bloody clothes? I don't think so. And we're going to get something to eat before we cross back over."

She was so frazzled she'd forgotten about the border crossing. She finished cleaning her arms, then took the skirt and blouse out of the bag and tore off the price tags. "Turn your back."

He gave a low laugh and got out of the truck, standing with his back to the window. She sat for a moment, blinking in astonishment. Had he actually *laughed*? He'd said he did, but she hadn't really believed him, and now she'd heard it for herself.

Dear God. He'd had his arm around her, his hand down the front of her dress. She'd had her head on his shoulder, her nails digging into his chest.

Intimacy was a slippery slope, with one thing leading to another, and without thinking, today she had slid dangerously close to peril. His arm around her had felt too natural; his shoulder had been too comforting and right *there*, as if meant for her use.

Hurriedly, she pulled her dress up and skimmed it off over her head, then donned the blouse and wiggled into the skirt. Both were a little tight, but they would do until she could get home. When she was dressed, she leaned over and rapped her knuckles on the window, and he got back into the truck.

"What would you like to eat?"

Her insides were shaky, telling her that she needed to eat something, even if she wasn't certain she could hold a fork. "Anything. Fast food will do."

Instead of a fast-food restaurant, he stopped at a *fonda*, one of the many small, family-run restaurants. There were three tables outside on a small shaded patio, and he led her there. The waiter, a tallish young man, politely did not look at the bandage on Milla's neck. She ordered tuna empanaditas and bottled water; Diaz went for the enchiladas and a dark beer.

While they waited for their food, she played with her napkin, folding and refolding it. She fidgeted with her blouse, because it was tighter than she liked. Then, because she couldn't ignore him and she knew he was silently watching her, she said, "You're very at home here."

"I was born in Mexico."

"But you said you're an American citizen. When did you get your citizenship?"

"I was born with it. My mother was American. She just happened to be in Mexico when I was born."

So he had dual citizenship, just like Justin.

"And your father?"

"Is Mexican."

She'd noticed he said "was" when talking about his mother, and "is" when it concerned his father. "Your mother is dead?"

"She died a couple of years ago. I'm fairly certain they weren't married."

"Do you know your father very well?"

"I lived with him half the time when I was growing up. That was better than living with my mother. What about you?"

Evidently that was all the small talk he was prepared to make about himself. Tit for tat, though, so she told him about her family, and the rift between her and her brother and sister. "It's hard on Mom and Dad," she said. "I know it is. But I just can't be around Ross or Julia now without–" She shook her head, unable to find the right word. She didn't want to hurt either of them, yet at the same time she wanted to bang their heads against something.

"Do they have children?" he asked.

"Both of them. Ross has three, Julia has two."

"Then they should be able to understand how you feel."

"But they don't. Maybe they can't. Maybe you have to actually lose a child before you really understand. It's as if part of *me* is missing, as if there's nothing but a great big hole where he used to be." She bit her lip, refusing to cry in public. "I can no more stop looking for him than I can stop breathing."

Diaz regarded her with those somber eyes, eyes that saw straight through to the core. Then he leaned over the small table, cupped her chin in his hand, and kissed her.

16

IT WAS JUST A SMALL KISS, BUT IT WAS SO DAMNABLY UNFAIR of him that she just sat there, stunned. Too much had happened in too short a time; she felt dazed, off balance, totally unable to cope. She caught his wrist with both hands, then didn't know what to do or say when he released her chin and lifted his mouth, leaving her still hanging on to his arm.

That grim mouth was softer than she'd expected, and gentler than she'd ever imagined. The kiss hadn't been passionate; it had, in fact, been more comforting than anything else. She hated him for that. She shouldn't want any kiss from him, but if she had to have one, she certainly didn't want it to be for comfort.

She glared at him. "What was that for?"

One corner of his mouth quirked in his equivalent of a chuckle. "I don't guess," he said, "that you've ever seen what other people see in your eyes."

"No, of course not." When he didn't say anything else, she waited a minute, then, goaded, said, *"What?"*

He shrugged, and seemed to be considering the matter, picking his way through various words and discarding them. Finally he said, "Suffering."

The word punched her, hard. *Suffering.* God, yes, she had suffered. Only parents who had lost a child could possibly understand. Yet this man, whose contact with emotion seemed tenuous at best, had seen and responded. And she had slipped even further down that blasted slope.

The waiter brought their meals, and she was glad to devote herself to the empanaditas, which were one of her favorite Mexican dishes. The tuna-stuffed pastries suited her taste today, and she plowed through them, not stopping until her plate was clean. Getting her throat sliced seemed to have really revved up her appetite. There was nothing like a brush with death to make you appreciate food.

Diaz made equally short work of his enchiladas, though he drank only half his beer.

"Don't you like it?" she asked, indicating the bottle.

"Well enough. I just don't drink much."

"Do you smoke?"

"Never have."

"Vote?"

"In every election since I was of age."

And he wore his seat belt, too. She regarded him with exasperation. Had there ever before been such a sober, civic-minded assassin?

At some point during the day, she had lost her fear of him. She didn't know exactly when or why, but she couldn't have found comfort in his arms if she'd still been afraid of him. He hadn't changed. Had *she*? The past week and a half had been nothing but an emotional roller coaster, and the strain had to be taking a toll. She had to be losing her mind for her to be attracted to someone like Diaz.

She had at least kept him from realizing what she was feeling, she thought. She hadn't responded to his light kiss; in fact, her reaction had been perfect, though unplanned.

"Are you finished?" he asked.

She looked at her empty plate. "I am unless I lick it."

Again that little quirk of his mouth. "I mean, would you like something else?"

"No, nothing else, thank you."

He paid for their meal, and as they were walking to the truck, she realized how much money he had spent today. "I'll reimburse you for your expenses," she said. Let him think Finders was reimbursing him; she intended to pay with her own money.

He didn't say anything, and she wondered if she had offended him. He was half Mexican, after all, and had spent part of his formative years here. The machismo of the culture had to have affected him at least a little.

"Give me an itemized statement," she continued, unable to leave it alone.

His expression was blank again. "How should I list the bribe?"

"As a bribe. We pay them all the time. How else would we get information?"

"There are other methods. But sometimes a bribe will work." He took out his cell phone and called someone, presumably the same boy, to meet him and collect the truck. But it was a different boy who showed up, somewhat younger than the first one, and with an engagingly roguish grin. Diaz gave him the keys and some money, and the kid hopped behind the wheel and roared off.

"Brothers?" she asked.

"Not mine."

"I mean, are the two boys brothers?"

"Probably. They live in the same house, but they could be cousins."

Milla and Diaz walked across the bridge to El Paso and collected his other truck. "Where to?" he asked. "Back to the office, or home?"

"Home." She wanted to change clothes, because the skirt had become uncomfortably tight after she'd eaten. "Then, if you don't mind, take me back to the office." She had to pick up her car. "If you don't have time, I'll just call a cab."

"No problem."

"By the way, how did you get into my house the other night? I *know* the doors and windows were locked."

"They were. I unlocked one. You need a security system."

She hadn't before; her neighborhood was very low-crime. "Would that stop you?"

"Not if I wanted in."

He waited downstairs in the living room while she ran upstairs to change. She didn't bother looking for anything that would hide the bandage on her neck, because the weather was too hot. Instead she put on crisp yellow slacks and a white sleeveless blouse, and ran back downstairs.

He was examining the rocks scattered around the living room; she had used the prettiest ones as decorations. The rest were in various containers: a big blue bowl on the coffee table, two clear vases, a huge glass piggy bank. "What's with all the rocks?" he asked, his head tilted to the side like a quizzical dog's.

"I picked them up for Justin," she said, going very still. "I thought he'd probably like rocks. Don't little boys like to throw rocks, and carry them around in their pockets? I guess he's too old for that now, though. But sometimes I'll see an unusual rock and pick it up anyway. Habit."

"I liked bugs," he said. "And worms."

"Gross!" She wrinkled her nose and shuddered, imagining a pocket full of worms. Then she sighed. "I suppose I should get rid of the rocks, but I just haven't been able to make myself do it. Maybe one day."

"If nothing else, you could throw them at anyone who breaks in."

"*You're* the only one who has broken in."

"You probably throw like a girl, anyway."

Despite herself, Milla found herself smiling at him. "Well, of course. What else?"

What else, indeed? Diaz mused as he walked back across the bridge into Juarez. She was a girly girl. She tried to be tough, and was certainly competent and willing, but her instincts were completely female. Her bedroom was froufrou, with sheets that felt like satin, mounds of pillows, soft rugs underfoot, and crystal things hanging off her lamp shades. Her bathroom smelled sweet and perfumey.

She wouldn't like knowing that he'd touched her sheets and looked in her closet, but he'd been curious. He'd wanted to know about her, read her in the clothes and scents she preferred. She had jeans and pants and shirts, but for the most part her clothes were dresses and skirts, delicate blouses. Today, when she'd come back downstairs after changing, she'd looked neat and cool in yellow and white, with a couple of white freshwater pearl bracelets on her wrist. She'd somehow managed to make the bandage on her neck look more like an accessory than a necessity.

Because she tried to be tough but was inherently soft, he was going back to Juarez without her. Lola wouldn't be expecting him back so soon, so now was the perfect time to be there.

He would be surprised if Lola didn't have at least a couple of kids. Grown, now, of course, but it was possible one or more of them had still been living with her when she was taking care of the stolen babies for her brother and Pavón. Kids were nosy, and they heard things even when you thought they were nowhere around. Hers might well have overheard some conversation between Lorenzo and Pavón, something that would give him another thread to follow.

Very little scared him; he was stoic about pain and death, figuring very few people escaped the first and no one escaped the second. But when Lola had held the knife to Milla's throat and he'd seen the blood trickling down her neck, for the first time in a very long while he'd been scared. He could have killed Lola right there, had been within a hairsbreadth of pulling the trigger, but the thought of Milla's reaction if he blew Lola's brains all over her had stopped him. He'd reined in the impulse, though Lola had been able to see in his eyes how close he was to doing it.

He'd known going in that Lola Guerrero was a stone-cold bitch, with a reputation for meanness and a taste for drugs. But she had information Milla wanted, and he'd known he could get it. Taking Milla, though, had been a mistake, which was why he was going back alone.

He'd had to think very fast, before. If he didn't kill Lola at that point, he was in a quandary. He couldn't just walk away, not after she'd cut his woman. He'd called Milla his friend, but no one would believe that. Everyone who had seen them, everyone who would hear about the incident, would think she was his; he couldn't let anyone cut her and go unpunished. If he did, people would think he was going soft. They would think they could get away with crossing him, get away with the flood of killings and drugs that he was trying to help stem. And because they would think they could get away with it, innocents would die. Then he would have to kill even more people to convince them that they still didn't want to cross him.

All of that, and more, and had flashed through his mind in a split second. What should he do about Lola, if not kill her? Beat the hell out of her? That would have taken too long, Milla would have been in hysterics, and he had a distaste for such brutality against women, even scum like Lola. Shoot her? With a nine millimeter, there was no such thing as a minor wound. The big slug tore out flesh, ripped nerves and blood vessels. Cut her? Unless he sliced her to pieces, cuts were easily healed, and he hadn't wanted to remove any body parts, minor or otherwise.

The only option that had been left was breaking a bone, which would cause her trouble for a good length of time. He'd chosen the thumb because of the knife, because he was so enraged that she'd cut Milla. With a broken thumb, she wouldn't be holding that knife for quite a while. And there was something cold about the chosen punishment that fit the crime, and that let people know he hadn't gone soft. As soon as he'd thought it, the deed was done.

He realized the absurdity of trying to choose a punishment that was bad enough to make a statement on the street but wouldn't permanently cripple the woman. He didn't want to hit her, so he'd just break her thumb. Having been beaten himself on more than one occasion, he knew how long the pain lasted, how utterly debilitating it was. Lola's thumb would pain her, but she wouldn't be seriously handicapped—except for knife handling, of course. He wanted her mobile, able to get around; she couldn't find out anything for him if she was half dead from a beating.

He could have killed her without the faintest twinge of remorse; breaking her thumb had made his stomach knot with nausea, even though he hadn't shown a flicker of hesitation. If he had, Milla might now be dead, or at least seriously hurt.

Milla had been upset, but she had understood immediately why he'd had to do *something*.

He needed to get his hands on Pavón. Wasn't it interesting that the same person was connected to smuggling babies ten years ago and smuggling involuntary organ donors now? Maybe Pavón was just a man who got around, but maybe he was still working for the same boss.

Diaz got a nice warm feeling in the pit of his stomach at the thought of tying up both problems with the same bow.

Milla's son was gone. Only fools would keep a paper trail, and since adoption files were, for the most part, private, he didn't see how she would ever be able to track him down even if they did crack the ring and discover the fake birth certificate that had been issued for him. But it had meant a lot to her to find out that at least he hadn't been in that plane crash, or smothered in a car trunk. He'd seen the look in her eyes, the joy that had temporarily banished the sadness.

The plane crash was another avenue he could investigate. The FAA would have a record of things like that. He didn't remember anything in the news about a plane crash killing six babies, and he was certain a story like that would have stuck with him. So either the crash site had been sanitized and the little bodies removed before rescuers and investigators arrived, leaving only the pilot, or the site had never been discovered by authorities. New Mexico was a big, mostly empty state. There were thousands of square miles in which a small plane could go down without being seen.

The owner of the plane would have known it was missing, though, and mounted a search for it. If he'd found it, what then? Completely disposing of a plane, even a small one, would take quite a bit of effort. The best bet would have been to remove the bodies, strip the plane, remove all markings and serial numbers, and set fire to it. There were a number of accelerants that would produce a very hot fire.

That's how *he* would have done it, anyway.

He had a pretty good instinct for how the bad guys worked.

All he had to do was figure out how he would do something, and most of the time he was right on the money. That didn't say much for his personality, but it said a lot for his effectiveness.

He had to be more careful now, because Milla softened him. He didn't know why, but he knew it happened. He found himself doing things he shouldn't be wasting his time with, because of her. Conversation didn't come easily to him, but he could talk to her, tell her things about himself. It amazed him that she told him about herself in return. At first she had been afraid of him, but he was used to that. Now she wasn't, and he was pleased.

She wouldn't sleep with him if she was afraid of him.

Maybe she didn't know yet how he felt. He held himself back, not wanting to push too hard and make her run. When he'd kissed her, he had wanted to deepen the contact, taste her with his tongue, but he'd felt the way she'd gone still and she hadn't returned the kiss, so he'd kept it gentle and light.

She might not know yet how *she* felt, either, but he could read people and he knew she reacted to him. She too easily accepted his touch, had too easily leaned against him today, buried her head on his shoulder. As a woman she totally responded to him.

It had been a long time since he'd had a woman, but he intended to have Milla. He'd be patient, give her time to get used to him, but he had no doubt of the outcome. She was his.

He didn't call for his truck this time, but took a cab and had it let him out while he was still a fair distance from Lola's place. Then he walked, moving quietly, easily, approaching from a different direction, aware that his only weapon this time was the knife in his boot. She'd had time by now to have her thumb taken care of. She should be back at home, cradling her hand, popping pain pills, and cursing him. He was the last person she would want to see, which was why she would be so eager to get rid of him by telling him what he wanted to know. She would give up her own kids to him without even a protest.

He didn't knock on the sorry door this time. He tried to open it and found it was secured from the inside, so he simply kicked it in.

Lola was lying on her cot, her hand bandaged with her thumb stuck rigidly outward. She was dressed in only a dingy nightgown; evidently she had taken her pain medication and decided to turn in for the night, even though it wasn't dark yet. She gasped when she saw him, her face going slack with terror.

"I thought of another question," he said softly.

True wasn't in a good mood, so when his phone rang for about the thousandth time that day, he snatched it up with a snarl. "What?"

There was a hesitation; then a timid voice with a Spanish accent said, "*Señor* Gallagher?"

"Yeah, what is it?"

"You said you wished to know if anyone saw the man Diaz."

True straightened, all his irritation gone, his attention totally focused. "Yes, that's right."

"The reward, you are still offering it?"

"In cash. American." He never welshed on promises to pay. Money kept the information pipeline flowing.

"He was in Ciudad Juarez today."

Juarez. The son of a bitch was close, too close.

"He was not alone," the timid voice continued.

"Who was he with?"

"A woman. They came to our *fonda.* I served them myself. I am sure it was Diaz."

"Did you recognize the woman?"

"No, *señor*. But she was a *gringa*. She had a bandage on her neck."

True didn't see how a bandage on her neck meant the woman was American. "What else?"

"She had curly brown hair with a white streak on top."

True went cold. Automatically he got the information for where he should send the money and made arrangements for payment to be made that very night. With one sentence, Diaz's presence in Juarez had gone from annoying to catastrophic.

Milla was with him. Milla and Diaz, together.

Son of a *bitch*.

He had to start tying up loose ends immediately. He had to locate Pavón and make certain the stupid bastard didn't talk.

17

TRUE WAS VERY GOOD AT ANALYZING HIS OPTIONS. HE KNEW whom he was up against, and Diaz was nobody's fool; on the contrary, the bastard was one of the most cunning people True had ever met or heard about. Just his name was enough to send a certain element scurrying for cover, because Diaz always found his quarry, but he didn't always bring it back alive.

The word was that Diaz was government-sanctioned–both governments, United States and Mexico. Since Mexico didn't extradite criminals who might receive the death penalty, the country inadvertently became the safe haven of some very unsavory characters. The United States wanted these people either caught or dealt with by other methods. Mexico just wanted them to disappear and stop being a problem. So it was possible Diaz was being paid by both governments. Maybe. Maybe he was just a very good bounty hunter who was also very good at projecting an image. But he definitely had contacts and resources, and the nose of a bloodhound.

True had been able to keep Milla stonewalled all these

years, but Diaz was different. For one thing, people were afraid of him. If it came down to a question of who they feared most, him or Diaz, True wasn't certain what the answer would be.

The key, he thought, was misdirection. Keep Diaz occupied chasing down bogus rumors while he himself found and eliminated Pavón, which was something he probably should have done years ago. Pavón was the one person, other than himself, who knew everything–and True had certainly never intended that to happen. People underestimated Pavón; True had been guilty of the same misjudgment. Pavón was a vicious thug, but he had an instinct for survival and for handling things just right.

That had made him a valuable asset. Pavón could get things done. Tell him what you wanted, and it happened. But valuable asset or not, with Diaz on his trail Pavón's personal scale had tipped over to the liability side.

The good news was that Pavón had heard Diaz was after him and had gone to ground. The bad news was that Diaz never gave up and would eventually find Pavón. Which meant True himself had to find Pavón first. No one would care enough about Pavón to do more than a cursory investigation into his death.

True's other option–his *only* other option–was to have Diaz eliminated. Problem was, that was easier said than done. And if Diaz truly was government-sanctioned, that would bring down more heat than True was prepared to handle. You could hide only so much, and that was as long as no one was looking very closely. The Feds tended to look closely. He had to be very, very careful in how he arranged things.

So–buy some time by leaking bogus rumors and names, and keep Diaz occupied. Find Pavón and get rid of that problem, which would buy him even more time and allow him to finish covering his tracks. This was probably the end of a very lucrative business, which was a shame, because he had only about half as much as he'd wanted to accumulate before he got out.

But he would find some other moneymaking deal. He always did. And if the price was right, he could always do some special collections.

He smiled, thinking of all the people whose names he could drop into the rumor mill and get Diaz pointed in their direction. He could have some fun with this. Payback was always hell, wasn't it?

August slipped into September, bringing a slight lessening of the heat, noticeably shorter days, and a tantalizing hint of crispness in the air. School had started, and it seemed as if kids were swarming everywhere. Though it was painful, she had always compulsively watched the kids in Justin's age group, from kindergarten on up. He would be in fifth grade this year, she thought. Somewhere, he was starting school just like all these youngsters, yelling and running, full of energy and devilment. Were his eyes still blue, or had they darkened to the brown of her eyes? She thought they would be blue, because they had been the exact shade of David's eyes.

Diaz seemed to have disappeared–again. That day they'd gone to Juarez she'd felt such a connection with him, but she hadn't heard from him since. Of course, just because she'd felt a connection didn't mean *he* had, and no matter what she felt the truth remained that she knew very little about him. She wasn't even certain what his first name was, if he'd pulled "James" out of thin air that day or if it really was his name. She'd never thought to ask him, because in her mind he was "Diaz," not "James."

She didn't know where he lived, how old he was, if he'd ever been married–my God, what if he was married now? The thought of Diaz being married made her sick to her stomach. What if he had children? He'd been at ease with little Max that day, so it was possible he had a child somewhere. Perhaps that was where he was, at home with his family.

Milla knew she was being ridiculous. She'd never seen anyone less likely to be a family man than Diaz. He was so clamped down and solitary that she couldn't imagine him living with anyone, which in turn told her how foolish she was to be attracted to him in the first place. But chemistry was what it was, and it seemed she could no more stop thinking about him than she could flap her arms and fly.

Diaz wasn't the only one who seemed to have disappeared. To her relief, she hadn't seen True at all. Not that she'd seen him all that regularly before, but after the last time, she'd been afraid he would become even more persistent. He'd said he would back off, but she doubted he knew how. But relieved as she was, she'd still expected to run into him at some of the city's society functions she had to attend. He was either out of town, or he'd found a Miss September who was unusually engrossing. She hoped it was the latter, to deflect his attention elsewhere.

The second week of September, her mother called and asked her to come for a visit. Milla hadn't seen her parents since spring break, when both Ross and Julia had gone on vacation with their respective families and there hadn't been any chance of running into them at her parents' house. Right now, with school just starting and all the extracurricular activities, they would be busy and weren't likely to pop over to their parents' house. In addition, her mom would call and warn them that Milla was visiting.

Glad for the chance to get away and have something besides Diaz to think about, she took a few days off and flew to Louisville, Kentucky. There she rented a car and drove across the Ohio River to the small town in southern Indiana where they lived.

Her dad was sixty-five and newly retired from an accounting firm; her mother, at sixty-three, had retired from teaching grade school the year before. Already her dad was making grumbling noises about moving to Florida, where he wouldn't have to deal with shoveling snow ever again, but her mother was firmly planted in the house where she had lived for over forty years and where she had raised her three children.

The house was synonymous with "home" in Milla's mind. It wasn't fancy, just a fifty-year-old two-story frame house, with a deep porch, steep roof, and memories in every room. There were three bedrooms upstairs, and during a remodeling in the seventies, a large downstairs parlor had been turned into a master bedroom with connecting bath. The eat-in kitchen was large enough that they'd all been able to sit at the table, and they'd had many wonderful, exciting Christmases tearing into a mountain of wrapped gifts under the decorated tree in the living room. In the future they might hire someone to shovel the snow from their driveway, but Milla couldn't imagine her parents ever moving from this spot.

Milla had once thought her life would be a lot like her mother's: teaching and raising a family. Now she couldn't even imagine so peaceful a life. Hers had been torn apart so completely that the *After* bore no resemblance to the *Before*. She hated that there was a rift between her and her siblings, but they couldn't seem to grasp how deeply she had been changed. They wanted her to go with the flow, and it simply wasn't possible. She couldn't imagine giving up on Justin, and she couldn't forgive them for thinking she should.

Still, when she and her mother were gossiping in the kitchen and Mrs. Edge caught herself for the third time mentioning either Ross or Julia and then lapsed into an uncomfortable silence, Milla sighed. "Mom, I don't expect you to never mention them. Talk about them if you want; I'd like to hear what the kids are up to, keep up to date on what's happening."

Mrs. Edge sighed, too. "I just wish you three would settle things between you. I hate not having you here for the holidays."

"Maybe someday, after I find Justin. Though I doubt I'll ever completely forgive them for saying I should just forget about him."

Her mother's eyes filled with tears. "Oh, honey ... Do you still really think you'll ever find him? I don't see how it's possible."

"I'll find him," she said fiercely. It hurt that her mother had given up, too. Was Milla the only one who still hoped? "I have leads now that I didn't have before. I know he was flown out of Mexico, probably to New Mexico. I know a woman falsified a birth certificate for him. I know the name of the men who stole him from me. One of them is dead, but the other one–" She stopped. Without Diaz, her chances of finding Pavón had dwindled alarmingly. But maybe that's what Diaz was doing: tracking. It was what he did best.

Mrs. Edge looked stunned. "You–you've actually found out all that? Just recently? I know you haven't said anything when you called."

"Within the last month." She felt ashamed that she hadn't called her parents in over a month, at least. There was no excuse, no matter how busy she was. "Things have been"– she searched for a word that was accurate but unalarming– "hectic."

"I imagine so." Mrs. Edge glanced at the thin red scar on her daughter's throat. "How did you get that scar?"

Self-consciously Milla touched the scar. It wasn't a bad scar at all, and in time would probably fade completely. She doubted her mother would appreciate that little detail. "From a cut," she finally said.

"I see. You were shaving?"

Milla smiled appreciatively, then gave up. "No. A woman did it. She was part of the smuggling ring; she took care of the babies who'd been kidnapped, until they could be flown out of the country."

Mrs. Edge sat down hard in the nearest chair. Her cheeks were pale at the thought of her youngest being attacked, yet at the same time she was almost beside herself at the other news. "She—she saw Justin? She actually saw him? She remembered him?"

"She remembered. He was alive. He was okay."

"She—but why did she cut you?"

"Because I did something stupid." Trying to attack Lola had been very stupid, but she'd been blinded by emotion, the same way she had been in the cemetery when she'd first crossed paths with Diaz. Scolding herself hadn't worked; she'd done exactly the same thing again, and this last time she hadn't come out of it unscathed. She was good at several things, but evidently fighting wasn't one of them.

"Stupid, how?"

"I jumped her." Milla made a helpless gesture. "I was just so angry at her, I couldn't help it. She had a knife."

"You could have been killed!"

She could have been killed numerous times in the past ten years. Thank heavens, her mother had no idea of the type of places she had gone into, the people she had talked to, the things she'd done. She supposed she was lucky she hadn't been shot, beaten, or raped, but her personal safety had somehow never mattered. Her guardian angels must have been working overtime—that was the only reason she could come up with for none of those things having happened.

And if Diaz hadn't been there in Juarez, Milla had no doubt Lola would have sliced her throat from ear to ear, just because she could. Diaz was the most unlikely guardian angel she could imagine, but he'd served the purpose.

She'd come to Indiana so she could stop thinking about him for a while, but every subject seemed to bring her right back to him. It was almost like having a painful adolescent crush, she decided, though she'd escaped her teenager years largely unscathed. Maybe if she'd gone through the usual emotional upheaval then, she wouldn't be so hung up on Diaz now. He was the ultimate bad boy, she was in lust, and she needed to forget about him and concentrate on more important things.

"What are you thinking about?" her mother asked suspiciously. "You got the most peculiar expression on your face. Has something like that happened before, and you didn't tell me about it?"

"What? Oh, no—no. Nothing like that. I was actually thinking how lucky I'd been that nothing *had* happened before."

"Lucky? You mean you've done things that—"

"I mean I've been in some really rough places, trying to find someone who knew anything about the baby smugglers. I never go alone, though," she hastened to add. "Never."

"That's something, at least." Mrs. Edge blew out a shaky breath. "But how I'll sleep at night now knowing you make a habit of doing things like that, I don't know."

"I guess that's why I haven't told you before," Milla said, feeling guilty. There was nothing like a visit with your parents to make you feel twelve years old again.

A car pulled into the driveway, and Mrs. Edge got to her feet, peering out the kitchen window to see who it was. She gave a small gasp of dismay. "It's Julia. What on earth? I told her you were here."

"It's okay," Milla said to reassure her mom. She thought of going up to her room to avoid her older sister, but that seemed so cowardly she remained where she was. Their relationship was strained, not violent; she didn't care to be around either her brother or sister now, but that didn't mean she couldn't be polite.

Listening, they heard Mr. Edge open the front door, heard Julia say, "Hi, Dad. Where are Mom and Milla?"

"In the kitchen." His tone was that of a man who planned to absent himself from a likely unpleasant scene as soon as possible.

Then there were Julia's crisp footsteps on the hardwood floor in the hallway. Milla just stood and waited, leaning against the cabinets, declining to do anything that would make her look busy and casual.

Julia was three years older than Milla and two years younger than Ross. Instead of being the stereotypical middle child who got lost when the family's attention was doled out, Julia had always claimed attention as her due. She paused in the kitchen doorway, looking as stylish, collected, and determined as always. She had always been the pretty one of the family, with their mother's delicate features. Her hair was the same color as Milla's, but had great body and a hint of wave instead of Milla's crop of curls. Whenever she had time, Milla actually had a perm to tone *down* her curls and make them more manageable; Julia had never had to resort to a perm for anything.

They were both around the same height, five-seven, with the same general build. No one looking at them could ever mistake them for anything other than sisters, despite the stronger, more severe structure of Milla's face. Their styles were completely different: Milla moved with a floaty grace that was completely in tune with her love for rich fabrics and feminine clothes, while Julia strode through life, preferred tailored suits for work, and at home was often in sweatpants and a T-shirt.

Julia would have been much more suited for the life Milla had been living. *She* would never have lost control of her emotions and charged into danger.

"What's wrong?" Mrs. Edge asked, a trifle nervously.

"Wrong? Nothing. You said Milla would be here, so I came by." Julia was staring hard at Milla, as if daring her to say something to start a fight.

"You're looking good," Milla said with perfect civility, and truth. She wouldn't say she was glad to see her sister, because she wasn't.

As usual, Julia charged right to the point. "Don't you think this has gone on long enough? It's silly that we can't come over when you're here, and you're doing nothing but hurting Mom and Dad by staying away during the holidays."

There were a lot of things that Milla wanted to say, but she took a page from Diaz's book and remained silent, letting Julia have her say. This was distressing enough for their mother, without descending into a hurtful argument.

"It's been three years," Julia continued. "Don't you think that's long enough to pout?"

Had she been pouting? Milla wondered. Funny, she had considered her anger to be far more serious than that. The word "enraged" came to mind.

Evidently their mother took issue with Julia's word choice, too, because she said, "Julia!" in a sharp tone as she got to her feet.

Julia said, "You know it's true, Mom. We told her the truth, and she got in a snit about it. Milla, honey, I'm so sorry your baby was stolen, I would do anything in the world to undo it, but it's been *ten years*. He's gone. You're never going to find him. At some point, you have to start living again. It's better to do it now while you're still young. Get remarried, have a family. No one will ever replace your baby, but this isn't about replacing him, it's about *living.*"

"No, it's about making life more comfortable for you and Ross, because you feel guilty whenever I'm around," Milla said.

"Guilty!" Julia drew back, her pretty face astonished. "What do we have to feel guilty about?"

"Having your children safe and sound. Being happy. Being whole. It's a form of survivor's guilt."

"That isn't true."

"Then what does it matter to you how I live my life? If I were a drug dealer or a prostitute, I could see your point, but I look for lost people—children, mostly. And I still look for my son. How on earth is that harming you? What if it were Chloe?" Chloe was Julia's five-year-old daughter, an impish pixie of a child who lit up the world with her smile. "If some stranger snatched her away from you at, say, the mall, how long would it take before you said, 'Oh, well, I've looked long enough, time to get on with my life'? Would there ever be a night when you didn't go to bed wondering where she was, if she was hungry or cold, if some pervert was using her in unspeakable ways? And even then would you pray that she still be alive, so you at least had a chance of seeing her again? How long would you give yourself, Julia?"

The color washed out of Julia's cheeks. She wasn't the most imaginative of women, but she could picture how she would feel if anything happened to Chloe.

"So imagine how I felt when you and Ross said, 'Hey, it's been a while, you might as well give it up and stop bothering us with your sad face.' I personally don't give a damn how you feel about my sad face, and I don't know if I'll ever forgive you for saying Justin doesn't matter!" Despite her attempt to remain calm, Milla's voice was fierce as she finished.

"We never said that!" Julia was appalled. "Of course he matters! But he's gone, and you can't change that. We just want you to accept it."

"If I'd accepted it three years ago, I wouldn't have found the people who took him," she snapped. "Just last month, as a matter of fact. I finally have some solid leads, and even if all I can find out is that he was adopted, using a fake birth certificate, can't you see that's more than I've had before? Until two weeks ago, I didn't even know if he was alive when he was taken out of Mexico! So let's just say you and Ross made an error in judgment, and leave it at that."

"Leave it, period," said Mrs. Edge, a stern, angry look on her face. "That's enough. Julia, I love you dearly, but this isn't your home anymore; how dare you come here knowing you were going to start a ruckus? I can see the points both of you are making. As a mother, I know I would never stop looking if one of you went missing. Also as a mother, I hate to see my child tearing herself apart for a hopeless cause."

"But it isn't hopeless," Milla said.

"We know that now, but we didn't know it before! We have to go with what we can see, and what we saw was your life in ruins. You and David divorced, and you buried yourself in this Finders work until it seemed that there was nothing left of *you*, the person we all love. Milla, you have no idea how we've worried—"

"Uh." Mr. Edge hesitantly stuck his head through the doorway. "I hate to bother you, but Milla's purse is ringing." He held out his hand, and in it was Milla's purse, which, from the habit of a lifetime, she'd placed on top of the piano when she'd come in. The cell phone inside was both ringing and vibrating, making it sound as if the noise had disturbed a rattlesnake.

She hurried across the kitchen to take her purse and dig

out her phone. The office had her parents' number, and normally when she was on vacation she turned off her cell phone, but she'd turned it on while driving over from the airport to let her folks know she was on her way, and had forgotten to turn it off again. The call was probably related to Finders, but unless it was an emergency, she'd just refer the caller to the office number.

She punched the *talk* button and said, "Milla Edge."

"How soon can you meet me in Idaho?" The voice was low and rough, almost rusty sounding, as if the owner didn't use it very often. He didn't have to identify himself.

Milla sucked in her breath. She was already upset, already tense, and hearing Diaz's voice was like receiving a mild electrical shock. "What is it? What's wrong?"

"I found a name. I don't like taking you along, not after what happened with Lola, but I figure you have a right."

"That was my fault," she admitted. "I lost control. I promise it won't happen again." Her heart was racing and she was all but quivering with excitement. "I'll call the airline and see what's available, then get back to you. Where exactly am I going?"

"Boise. Plan on spending one night; then we'll fly home the next day."

"I'll get right back to you. Will you be at the number on Caller ID?"

"Yeah."

She pulled her return ticket out of her purse and looked at the phone number on it. Her fare was nonrefundable, but sometimes it could be transferred to a different flight.

"What's going on?" Mrs. Edge asked, coming to stand beside Milla as she dialed the number for her travel agency. She always used an agency instead of booking the flights herself, because last-minute changes had had to be made often enough that she'd found a travel agent could handle things much easier, having all the information for all the airlines right there.

"That was one of my contacts." Explaining exactly who and what Diaz was would take far too much time. "He's been tracking the men who took Justin, and he's located someone who might know something. I'm meeting him in Idaho."

"But you just got here!"

"This can't wait."

"I can't believe you're doing this again," Julia said.

Milla spared her a brief glance. "I can't believe you think I should pass up a chance to find out anything I can—Yes, hello." She turned her attention to the travel agent on the other end of the line. What she found was that, because it was late afternoon now, if she left today the only flights available would involve a couple of layovers, changing airlines, and still not get her into Boise until tomorrow morning. Or she could wait until tomorrow morning and take the first flight out; she would still have to change airlines, but she would arrive in Idaho only an hour later than she would if she left right now.

That was a no-brainer. Milla chose the second option, got all the details, then called Diaz back. "I can't make it today; tomorrow morning is the best I can do. If the flight's on time, I'll be getting in at eleven-oh-three." She gave him the airline and flight number.

"Are you checking your luggage?"

She thought of all she had brought, since she'd planned to spend several days here. "I'll have to, or have most of it shipped home."

He didn't gripe about having to wait for her luggage, just said, "I'll meet you in baggage claim. See you in the morning."

"Yes," she echoed. "I'll see you then." She hung up, her attention already far away from the people in the room. She brushed past Julia without really seeing her and made her way up the stairs, her mind on repacking her bags so her essentials were in one small bag that she could carry on with her, in case her checked luggage went missing.

"Milla!" Julia called after her, but Milla kept climbing the stairs.

18

Catching the first flight out meant getting up at three A.M. so she would have time to drive to the airport in Kentucky, turn in her rental car, and still have plenty of time to get through security. She bought some snacks out of vending machines in the Louisville airport, because it was a safe bet the airline wasn't going to serve anything and she was already hungry. From Louisville she flew to Chicago, then from Chicago to Salt Lake City, where she changed airlines and flew to Boise.

Diaz was waiting for her, and her heart gave a huge thump at the sight of him. He was dressed much as usual, in jeans and those rubber-soled boots, though in deference to the changing season he wore a long-sleeved denim shirt over his dark T-shirt, with the sleeves rolled up over his forearms. He stood apart from the small crowd, his expression as remote as ever. Several people darted vaguely uneasy glances at him, though he wasn't doing anything other than just standing there.

"What did you find out?" she asked anxiously as she reached

him. She'd been fretting during the entire trip, wondering who they were going to see and what he or she knew about the kidnapping.

"I'll tell you on the way. I have two rooms booked for us at a hotel," he said. "We'll drop off your luggage and you can change clothes before we leave."

"Why do I need to change clothes?" She looked down at herself. She was dressed for comfort, in slacks and a blouse, with a lightweight sweater thrown over her shoulders to keep off the chill. For someone used to El Paso's climate, both airplanes and Idaho were too cold for her.

"You need something sturdier, like jeans and boots, since we don't know what we'll find. I've done some advance scouting and the terrain looks rough." They collected her luggage; he took her heaviest bag and shifted it to his left hand, then used his right to guide her in the direction of the parking lot.

"How long have you been here?"

"I got here last night."

She hadn't seen him for three weeks, and until this moment she hadn't realized how starved she felt. Just his physical presence sent a wave of longing through her. He was like the pain of childbirth: away from him, she remembered that almost electric aura of danger, but she didn't *feel* it. Being near him made her heartbeat rev up, all her senses heighten; it was almost as if the fight-or-flight response kicked in—or maybe that was exactly what happened.

She recognized the giddy sense of euphoria, the butterflies in her stomach; she hadn't felt this way since David. She'd loved David and she most assuredly did *not* love Diaz, but she had also wanted David sexually. No other man she'd met since then had gotten that reaction from her, no matter how much she might like the man himself, until Diaz. She wanted him. She needed her head examined, but she wanted him.

She was expecting a rental car, or maybe an SUV, but the

vehicle he led her to was an enormous, black four-wheel-drive pickup, with the frame sitting so high she wondered how she could climb into the cab, even though she was wearing slacks.

Diaz put her bags in the bed of the truck, then unlocked the doors. "Where on earth did you get this thing?" she asked, looking up at the lights mounted on top of the cab. "I know you didn't rent it."

He put his hands on her waist and lifted her onto the seat. "It belongs to an acquaintance."

When he got behind the wheel, she said, "An 'acquaintance,' huh? Not a friend?"

"I don't have friends."

The blunt statement rattled her, hit her in the chest, and made her ache inside. How could he bear to live such a solitary life? "You have me," she said before she thought.

He froze in the act of putting the key in the ignition, and slowly turned his head to look at her. She couldn't read the expression in his dark eyes; she knew only that they burned. "Do I?" he asked softly.

For a moment she felt off balance, as if he'd asked one thing but meant another. Was he asking if she was his on an entirely different level, or was he expressing doubt? She had no idea; he was so unreadable she was left floundering, so she instinctively went to shallow water. "If you want a friend, you do. How can you live without friendship?"

He shrugged and turned the key, firing up the big motor. "Easy."

Yes, that was what he'd meant, that he doubted he had any real friends. She was both disappointed and relieved. However much she might want him, she wasn't certain she'd ever have the nerve to do anything about it. That would be like stepping into a cage with a tiger, no matter how tame the handler said it was. The doubt and fear would always remain.

She sought refuge in the original subject. "This 'acquaintance' knows and trusts you well enough to put this monster at your disposal?"

"He trusts me."

She noticed that he didn't say the man knew him. This was a dead-end subject, though, and she was anxious to find out what Diaz knew and why they were in Idaho.

"Okay, we're on the way. What did you find out?"

"Nothing, yet," he said, and she almost wilted in disappointment.

"But I thought—"

"After we talk to this guy, we might know something more. What I heard was that his brother was the pilot of the plane that crashed."

"You got the pilot's name?"

"Maybe." At her frustrated look, he said, "It's like a string. We'll pull on it and see if it goes anywhere. Most of the time it doesn't, but negative knowledge is almost as good as positive knowledge."

"Meaning then you know where *not* to look."

"It also tells you something about the person who put the string in your hand, too."

"But *maybe* you have the pilot's name?"

"I heard that a guy named Gilliland would fly any cargo out of Mexico, but that he crashed and was killed seven or eight years ago. The only thing anyone knew about him was that he had a brother named Norman Gilliland who lived in the Sawtooth Wilderness close to Lowman."

She stared at him, suddenly uneasy; after a moment, she realized why. "So no one knew anything about the pilot, but all of a sudden someone remembers his brother's first name and exactly where he lived? That's very specific knowledge for someone who didn't know anything else about the pilot."

He gave her an approving glance. "You might make a pretty good tracker yourself. You have good instincts."

She knotted her fists. "This is another wild-goose chase, isn't it? Why are we even bothering?"

He paused. " 'Another'?"

"That's what I've been doing for ten years, running in circles and getting nowhere." She stared out the window, her jaw set.

"Like someone's been feeding you false information?"

Slowly she turned her head to look at him. "You think that's it? I've been deliberately led away from the right track?"

"You're too smart and too good at what you do for it to be otherwise. When it's someone else's kid, you have damn good luck finding them, don't you?"

Mutely she nodded. She had an almost eerie knack for success, as if she could put herself in the mind of a lost child or runaway and figure out where they'd gone. That had made it doubly frustrating for her, that she could find other children but not her own child.

"That's another string I can follow," he said. "Maybe I've been asking the wrong questions. Maybe I should ask who's been telling people to give you the wrong answers."

She really had been chasing in circles all these years, and someone had made certain she stayed in the same rut by dangling a carrot in front of her nose. The only real lead she'd ever had was the one that had taken her to Guadalupe that night when Diaz was there, and she had no idea who her informant had been. Nor had Diaz ever found out, or he would have told her. On second thought—"Did you ever find out who tipped me that you'd be in Guadalupe?"

"No."

Another mystery, but evidently this one was in their favor. She was having a hard time dealing with this new slant on all the frustrations and dead ends, the constant rise of hope only to have it dashed on the rocks. She could understand if no one had told her anything, just stonewalled her, but to deliberately have her chasing wild story after wild story smacked of a deep malevolence.

She was so mired in thought she didn't realize they'd stopped in front of a small hotel until he opened the door and vaulted out. By the time she got her purse hooked on her shoulder and her own door open, he was there, reaching up to grasp her waist and lift her out of the seat. He set her on the ground in front of him, hemmed in by the truck, the open door, and his body. There were a good six inches between them, but abruptly she felt blasted by his body heat, carrying with it the warm, clean smell of his skin. He hadn't shaved; at least two or three days' growth of beard stubbled his jaw. She wanted to reach up and stroke his face, feel the bristles against her palm.

"Don't let it get you down," he said. She struggled to pull her mind back to reality. "Misdirection takes money and influence. Knowing that gives me another string. Hell, I've almost got a whole ball of yarn now."

She managed a smile, and he turned to lift her bag out of the truck bed. He led the way inside, past a small reception area, where the man on duty gave them a cursory glance, then went back to what he was doing. Everything was clean and well maintained, including the smallish elevator, which arrived with a smooth whooshing sound.

Diaz pushed the button for the third floor, and after the doors closed and the elevator began gliding upward, he said, "Your room number is 323; I'm in 325." He fished in his pocket and pulled out an electronic door card, which he handed to her. "Here's your card. Take a left out of the elevator."

He took both her Pullman case and carry-on bag, while she walked ahead of him and unlocked the door to room 323. The heavy curtains over the windows were closed so the room was dark, and she flipped the light switch. It was a standard hotel room, clean and unimaginative, with a king-sized bed, a twenty-five-inch television in an armoire, an easy chair with an ottoman, and another chair at a desk. The connecting door to the next room stood open, revealing a mirror image of her room.

Maybe he walked in his sleep.

"Where do you want this?" he asked, indicating her heavy suitcase.

"On the bed. I'll dig out my clothes and be with you in a minute."

"I'll wait outside." He left by her door, and Milla hurried to unzip her suitcase and search through it for her jeans, socks, and sneakers. Three minutes later she grabbed her purse, put her room card in it, and was out the door.

They retraced their steps to the parking lot. He boosted her into the truck, and as she buckled herself in, she said, with a touch of irritation, "Why did you get a truck so high I need a stepladder to get into it?"

"Where we're going, we'll need the extra clearance."

She gaped at him. "What are we doing, stump-jumping?"

"Part of the way."

The ride was going to be a rough one, then. Before they left Boise he said, "Hungry?" Thinking she needed to fortify herself, she nodded, and he pulled into a fast-food place. Less than five minutes later they were back on the highway, hamburgers in hand.

"We'll drive as far as we can, but we'll have to walk the last leg," he said. "This guy is a survivalist, and he made damn sure he isn't easy to get to."

"Will he shoot at us?" she asked, a little alarmed.

"He might, but from what I've been able to find out he isn't generally violent, just a little crazy."

Which was better than being a lot crazy, but anyone with a survivalist mind-set might get a little anxious at being approached by two strangers, especially if he'd gone to a lot of trouble to make sure people couldn't easily get to his house.

Three hours later, she realized "house" had been a generous term. After leaving the real road, Diaz had driven the truck over terrain so rough and mountainous Milla had simply closed her eyes and held on to the strap, certain they were going to overturn at any minute. When the trail finally ended—and "trail" was another generous term—at a mountain that seemed to go straight up, Diaz turned off the engine and said, "Here's where we start walking."

Milla stuffed her purse under the seat, then jumped out of the truck without waiting for his aid, and turned in a slow circle, staring up at the mountains surrounding her. From what she'd seen so far, Idaho was one of the most beautiful places in the world. The sky was the deep vivid blue of autumn, the trees were a glorious mix of evergreens and color, and the air was crisp and clean.

He took a backpack out from behind the seat and slipped his arms through the loops. "This way," he said, stepping into the silent forest.

"How do you know the exact way?"

"I told you, I scouted around some yesterday."

"But if you came this far, you could have already talked to him."

"It was night. I didn't want to spook him."

He'd come up here last night? The wilderness was so rugged and ... absolute that she couldn't imagine how he'd found the track, much less managed to stay on it. She knew he was totally at home in the southwestern desert regions, but had vaguely expected him to be more of a fish out of water up here in the mountains. Not so; he seemed to unerringly know the direction he wanted, and he moved through the massive trees like a silent ghost.

"Have you done mountain hiking before?" she asked, glad she'd made a point of keeping in shape. This wasn't terrain for a couch potato.

"The Sierra Madre. I've been in the Rockies before, too."

"What's in the backpack?"

"Water. Food. Ground sheet. The basics."

"Are we spending the night out here?" she asked in astonishment.

"No, we should be back to the truck before dark. I just don't take chances in terrain like this."

Following behind him as she was, she noticed the bulge under his loose shirt. Being armed was natural for him, but she hadn't seen him get the weapon out of the glove box, nor had he gone into his own room at the hotel. Surely he hadn't–

"Did you have that pistol with you in the *airport*?"

He glanced over his shoulder at her. "I didn't have to go through a metal detector."

"My God, isn't that a federal offense, though?"

He shrugged. "They might get upset if they caught me."

"How did you get it up here?"

"I didn't. I got it here."

"I guess I shouldn't ask if it's registered."

"It's registered. Just not to me."

"It's stolen?"

He sighed. "No, it isn't stolen. It belongs to the man who owns the truck. And even if I did get caught at the airport with it, I wouldn't be arrested. They'd *want* to arrest me, but it wouldn't happen."

"Why not?"

"I know some people with Homeland Security. I've–uh–done some work for them. Freelance."

She was amazed that he was answering her questions, because he was usually so reticent. She hurried a bit until she was more or less abreast with him. "You find terrorists?" she asked in amazement, her voice rising on the last word.

"Sometimes," he said, with that vague tone in his voice that said he wasn't going into any detail on that particular subject.

"You're a *Fed*?"

He stopped in his tracks and looked at her, his head cocked in mild exasperation. "No, I just said I've done some freelance stuff. That's all. I've done jobs for individuals, corporations, governments. I guess I'm kind of a bounty hunter, though I don't go after bail jumpers. Usually. Now, are we done with the questions?"

She made a derisive noise in her throat. "In your dreams."

His slow smile began transforming his face. "Then can they wait until we're heading back? I want to listen to what's around us."

"Okay, but only because you have a good reason." She fell back behind him and they continued the hike in silence, with only their muffled footsteps breaking the peace of the mountains. It was just as well; within minutes the trail went sharply upward, and she needed her breath for the climb.

After half an hour they heard the sound of rushing water. The almost invisible trail led them straight to the river. The water had cut a small gorge through the mountain; at this point, the sheer rock walls were about eight feet high and the river was narrow, no more than twenty feet wide, which forced the water along at a faster pace. The rapid current frothed and boiled over underwater rocks, whitecapping the surface and occasionally sending up a spray of diamond drops.

Diaz led them along the bank, with the sound of the rushing water growing louder and louder as the stream gradually narrowed until the width was about twelve feet. He stopped, raised his voice, and said, "Here we are."

Only then did she see the tiny shack on the other side of the river. "Shack" was a complimentary description. It appeared to be made out of rough plywood, with black tar paper nailed over it. The forest was making an effort to reclaim its territory, because moss was growing up the sides of the shack, and vines were growing down from the roof. The tar paper and vegetation did a good job of camouflage; the one tiny window and rough rock chimney were almost the only details that gave away the shack's location.

"Hello!" Diaz yelled.

After a minute the rough door opened and a grizzled head stuck out. The man regarded them with suspicion for a moment; then he stared hard at Milla. Her presence seemed to reassure him, because he eased out of the door with a shotgun cradled in his arms. He looked bearlike, standing about six-foot-six and weighing close to three hundred pounds. His long gray hair was in a ponytail that hung halfway down his back, but his beard was only a few inches long, proving that he did some personal upkeep. The beard was the only evidence of that, though. He wore camouflage pants in a forest pattern, and a green flannel shirt.

"Yeah? Who are you?"

"My name is Diaz. Are you Norman Gilliland?"

"That's right. What about it?"

"If you don't mind, we have some questions about your brother that we'd like to ask."

"Which brother?"

Diaz paused, because they had no first name. "The pilot."

Norman shifted a wad of chewing tobacco to his other jaw and pondered the matter. "That would be Virgil, I guess. He's dead."

"Yes, we know. Did you know anything about his–"

"Smuggling? Some." Norman heaved a sigh. "Guess you might as well come over. You carrying?"

"Pistol," Diaz replied.

"Just keep it holstered, son, and we'll do all right."

Norman carefully propped the shotgun against the shack, then lifted a long, rough plank that looked to be hand-hewn, about fifteen feet long, three or four inches thick, and a foot wide. It had to be heavy, but Norman handled it as if it were a two-by-four wall stud. He positioned one end of the plank into a notch that had been carved into the riverbank, then got down on his knees and let the other end tilt down until it fit into a corresponding notch on their side of the river. "There you are," he said. "Come on over."

Milla looked at the plank, at the rushing water foaming beneath it, and drew a deep breath. "Ready if you are," she said to Diaz.

He caught her hand and carried it to his belt. "Hold on to me for balance."

She pulled her hand back. "No way. If I fall, I don't want to take you with me."

"As if I wouldn't go in after you anyway." He took her hand once more and put it on his belt. "Hang on."

"Are you coming or not?" Norman called irritably.

"Yes." Diaz stepped calmly onto the plank, and Milla followed. Twelve inches was really pretty wide; as a kid she'd balanced on much narrower edges. But now that she was an adult, she knew how reckless kids were, and she'd never walked across a roaring river even as a child. She did remember that you had to just do it, that a sure step was much better than a hesitant one. She didn't crowd Diaz, just maintained a grip on his belt, and it did help with balance. In no time they were across the plank and stepping onto solid ground.

Neither Diaz nor Norman offered to shake hands, so Milla steeled herself and held out her hand. "I'm Milla Edge. Thank you for talking to us."

Norman eyed her hand as if he wasn't quite sure what to do, then gingerly folded his big paw around her fingers and gave it a barely noticeable shake. "Glad to meet you. I don't get many visitors."

No joke. He'd made damn sure of that by living where he did.

He didn't invite them inside, and she was just as glad he hadn't. Not only was the shack tiny, but she'd bet Norman hadn't won any housekeeping awards lately. There were a couple of nice-sized rocks nearby, though, and he indicated they should sit there. Norman himself took a seat on a stump. "Now, what can I do for you folks?"

"You said you knew about your brother's smuggling," Diaz said.

"Course I did. Marijuana. He made a bunch of money, but Virgil never did have any sense about money and I guess he blew it all. God knows, when he died there wasn't anything left."

"He died in a plane crash?"

"Virgil? Naw. He died of liver cancer, in November of ninety."

Before Justin was kidnapped. Milla sighed in sharp disappointment, even though after their conversation in the truck, she hadn't really been expecting any useful information.

"Did he ever smuggle anything except weed?"

"That was pretty much it, I reckon, though there could have been some cocaine runs."

"How about people? Babies?"

"Not that I ever heard."

"Did he work for just one man?"

"He never was that steady. He moved around a lot, until he got sick. The cancer took him fast. By the time he knew he had it, he only had a couple of months left."

"Where was he when he died?"

"Why, right here. I got him buried back in the woods. Nobody wanted to foot the bill for his funeral, so I took care of it myself."

There wasn't anything else to be said. They thanked Norman, Diaz slickly passed him some folded green for his time, and they went back to the plank bridge.

Milla felt confident enough not to hold on to Diaz's belt on the return crossing, though he insisted. As long as she didn't look down at the water, which gave her a mild sense of vertigo as it rushed past, she was fine.

They were almost halfway across when Diaz made a sharp sound of warning. The board tilted wildly beneath their feet; Milla released Diaz, both arms waving as she scrambled for balance. It happened so fast she didn't even scream as thcy both plunged down into the swift, icy river.

19

THE WATER WAS SO COLD IT WAS NUMBING, AND DEEPER THAN she'd expected. The current pushed her below the surface even as it tumbled her along, tossing her like a rag doll in a child's careless grip. Instinctively she began kicking, trying to go with the current rather than fighting it, and as if rewarding her, it promptly shot her upward.

Her head broke the surface and she gasped in air. Her hair hung in her face, blinding her. She thought she heard a distant shout; then the current tumbled her under again. Rolling, she took a glancing blow to her left shoulder, but it scarcely stung; what it did do was tilt her back to the right, toward the middle of the river, and she fought for the surface once more. Somehow she got turned so she was going with the current again, swimming as hard as she could, and she popped up like a cork.

"Milla!"

The voice calling her name was rough from strain, but she knew it. She turned her head and saw Diaz behind her and to the right, swimming toward her with desperate, powerful strokes. "I'm all right!" she yelled, then felt the current tug at her again. She kicked harder, concentrating on keeping her head above water.

Diaz was a stronger swimmer, but he was heavier, and he couldn't gain any ground on her. If she stopped swimming so hard, in order to let him catch up, the current would pull her under again. The banks rose steep and high on both sides of the river, and the water swept them along as if they were in a chute, with no way out even if they could fight their way to the side.

Ahead, the river curved to the left. A tree had fallen on the right bank, its limbs reaching almost to the water.

"Tree!" she heard Diaz roar behind her, and understood. She angled to the right, fighting to get within reaching distance of one of the limbs. Her head went under just as she gasped for air and she choked on a mouthful of water. She fought to the surface once more, but the effort and the cold were taking their toll. Her arm and leg muscles ached, and her lungs were burning. Maybe if she could catch one of the limbs, she could rest there for a minute; maybe they could even climb out that way.

It wasn't by her efforts that she succeeded; the current obligingly pushed her to the right, where the bank was hollowed out by the water's force. Desperately she reached up and caught a limb; the water jerked at her and the dead limb broke off in her hand, and she went under.

She was tiring rapidly, her kicks becoming less forceful, her arm motions jerky instead of smooth. Still she once more gained the surface and sucked in much-needed air, and just before the roil of water pulled her under again for what was probably the last time, a hard arm wrapped around her and held her up. The tree hadn't stopped her, but it had slowed her enough for Diaz to catch up.

"Angle to the right!" he yelled. "That's the side the truck is on!"

It was comforting to know that he thought they'd make it, at least, otherwise he wouldn't have cared which side they got out on, just that they got out.

She had no idea how far the water had carried them, but the current was so swift they could already be half a mile downstream from Norman's shack. Then, abruptly, the river widened and the current slowed.

It was still a fast current, so fast she couldn't fight it, but at least the water smoothed out and stopped battering at her. The riverbanks were less steep, but choked with huge boulders. She could stay on top with less effort and give her burning muscles some rest, but the cold was going bone deep, and she knew they didn't have much time left before they became too sluggish to swim.

"Catch the end of my belt and wrap it around your wrist," Diaz said hoarsely, and a length of leather slapped the water in front of her.

She caught the belt, but said, "I'll drag you under."

"No you won't. We can't be separated. Do it!"

What he meant was, if they got separated, she was a dead woman. On the other hand, if she dragged him down, they'd both be dead.

"We don't have much time!" he yelled. "We have to get out before we go over a waterfall!"

There was a waterfall on this river? Her blood chilled even colder. The force of the water would push them to the bottom and they'd drown, assuming they weren't battered to death on rocks. She didn't know what he had in mind, but she was game for anything. She clutched the belt and twisted her hand several times, wrapping the leather around her wrist.

"There's a right bend!" He coughed, and spat out water. "Just ahead. The current is slower on the inside of a curve, so that's our chance. Just hang on, and I'll get us out."

"I can kick," she said, surprised at how guttural her tone was.

"Then kick like hell."

She kicked like hell.

Her thigh muscles had gone beyond tired, beyond burning. Her legs were in agony, but she kicked. Diaz's arms scissored like an automaton's, dragging them on a diagonal through the water. Forward progress was swift, his diagonal progress was measured in inches, and the bend was coming up much too fast; they were going to get swept past it before they could make it to the slower current. She growled like an animal as a burst of adrenaline sent her surging forward, almost even with Diaz. Without the drag of her on his arm, he gained even more ground as the current swept them into the bend.

A big tree was clinging to the earth right at the water's edge. As they passed it, Diaz reached out with his right hand and caught one of the big roots.

He stopped, but the water didn't and neither did she. When the belt reached the end of its length, her entire body snapped backward like the end of a whip, but she didn't lose her grip on the leather. Diaz's face was twisted with effort, his teeth gritted, as he hung on to the root with his right hand and with the left tried to pull her against the current. She kicked, swinging her body, and suddenly the grasp of the water eased and seemed to push her against the bank on the far side of the tree. They were stretched out with the tree between them, tethered by the belt.

Milla caught one of the roots, too, and managed to wedge her feet against an underwater rock that was just past the tree. The current still pushed at her, but she locked her trembling knees and managed to hold her position.

"I'm letting go of the belt," she managed to say. "I'm braced. How about you?"

"I'm good," he said. She untwisted the belt and the leather floated free. For a split second she panicked as the water seemed to tug at her, as if it had just been waiting for her to release her lifeline. But she pushed back harder against the tree and held her position.

Her lungs were pumping like bellows, dragging in air for her oxygen-starved muscles. She couldn't hear anything now except the water and her own heartbeat thundering in her ears.

Diaz hooked his hands under her arms from behind, and dragged her up and back, onto a shelf of rock and out of the water.

The effort seemed to take all his remaining strength, because he collapsed on his hands and knees on the rock, wheezing and groaning. Milla lay facedown where he'd let her drop, too exhausted to move. Her body felt as if it weighed a thousand pounds, as if even twitching a finger would take gargantuan effort.

The rock was in full sunshine and felt warm under her chilled body. Water streamed from their clothes and hair. She closed her eyes and listened to their laboring breaths, listened to the pound of blood through her veins. They were alive.

Maybe she dozed, or fainted, or both. After a while she managed to turn over, onto her back, and let the sunshine wash over her face. Still breathing hard, almost giddy with relief, Milla tilted her face up to the warmth.

That had been so close. She still couldn't quite believe they'd managed to make it to the bank; she definitely knew she wouldn't have been able to make it on her own. The water rushed and swirled only a foot beyond where Diaz lay, sucking at the rock and the stubborn tree, knowing that eventually it would claim them. Time, after all, was on the water's side.

Only Diaz's strength had enabled them to break free of its clutch.

Still gasping a little, she said, "What happened? Why did we fall?"

He said, "The ground crumbled under the other end of the plank and tilted it."

Her next question was "How did you know there's a waterfall on this river?"

He was silent a minute; then he said, "There's always a waterfall. Don't you watch any movies?"

Overwhelmed by relief and an almost effervescent joy at being alive, she began to laugh.

Diaz had rolled onto his back beside her, his own chest heaving as he fought for breath, but now he turned his head toward her and the hard line of his mouth moved in a slight smile. He watched her for a minute, his dark eyes narrowed against the glare of the afternoon sun. Then he said, "I'd give my left nut to be inside you right now."

Her laughter vanished as if it had never been, sucked away by the shock of his words. She'd daydreamed and fantasized and obsessed, but she'd never thought she'd have to deal with reality, and here it was, staring her in the face. Diaz? And *her*? The hard fact of what he'd said was so jarring that reality tilted for a moment, leaving her adrift on that warm rock with her head buzzing and adrenaline still burning through her veins. Then everything slammed back into place, and with it came a rush of carnal hunger that stunned her with its force. Diaz— and her. Her insides clenched at the thought of him on top of her, between her legs. She wanted him. She had wanted him the moment she saw him, and she wanted him now.

He'd never even really kissed her. That light comfort kiss in Juarez didn't count.

She'd wanted this, and now reasons for backing away

swarmed through her mind like locusts. If all he wanted was a quick fuck, she wasn't the woman he was looking for, and she couldn't imagine him wanting anything other than that. This was *Diaz*, after all; he wasn't the hang-around type of man, and she wasn't stupid enough to think she could change him. She'd been so careful not to give him any sexual reaction, any hint that she found him attractive; she'd kept it all inside, in her daydreams. But he'd known anyway; it was in those shrewd dark eyes, that knowledge.

"You're thinking too much," he said lazily. "It was just an observation, not a declaration of war."

"Women always think too much." She sniffed. "We have to, to keep things balanced." Odd that he'd chosen "war" as a metaphor . . . or perhaps it was fitting. Squinting up at the sun, trying to find something solid to hold on to, since the ground had just shifted beneath her, she said, "Why do men always offer their left nut and never their right one? Is something wrong with it? Or is the right one somehow more important?"

"You wrong us." He closed his eyes with a tired sigh, and that slight smile touched his mouth again. "A man takes both his nuts seriously."

"In that case, I'm flattered."

"But not interested."

Here was where she could lightly say "Sorry" and that would be the end of it. Instead, unable to lie, she closed her own eyes and let the silence grow between them.

She felt him move as he heaved himself up; then he was propped on his elbow, leaning over her and blocking the sun. "You'd better say no," he murmured, flattening his hand on her stomach. The heat from his palm burned through her wet clothing to her chilled skin; then he slipped his fingertips under the waistband of her jeans and she felt the heat go all the way through *her*.

"Not that I intend to do anything right now, anyway," he

continued. "We need to get back to the truck. A rock's a damn uncomfortable place for what I want to do, our clothes are wet, my balls are so cold it may take me a week to find them, and we don't have any condoms. But in a few hours things will be different, and if you don't want to go anywhere with this, you'd better say no right now."

He was right. She should say no.

But she didn't. Despite all the good reasons she'd given herself just a moment before . . . she didn't.

Instead she opened her eyes and turned her head toward him as he bent down to her. His lips were cold; hers were colder. But his tongue was warm, and the kiss was almost shy as he gently explored her mouth. His left hand tangled in her wet hair and he slowly deepened the kiss as he caught her waist and rolled her toward him.

The touch of that whipcord body sent a pool of warmth spreading through her insides. It was almost enough to dispel the chill, but still she suddenly shivered as the aftermath began to catch up to her.

He lifted his mouth and smoothed her hair back from her face, his gaze intent as he watched her. "We have to get to the truck and get warm. The sun will be going down soon, and we don't want to get caught out here in wet clothes."

"All right." He moved back, and she struggled to a sitting position. "Do you think Norman will call the authorities, have them looking for our bodies or something?"

"I doubt it. I don't guess you heard what he yelled."

"I heard someone yell something, but I couldn't tell what it was."

"He yelled, 'Good luck.' "

Astounded, she blinked at him. Then she began snickering as she slowly climbed to her feet. She guessed Norman wasn't the type to worry about what happened to anyone except himself.

Swaying, she took stock. The backpack he'd been carrying was long gone, of course. She was aching from head to foot, but she couldn't tell if it was from the battering force of the water or if it was sheer muscle fatigue. She was lucky; she didn't think she'd hit anything hard enough to injure herself, and she thanked God for the depth of the river, which had probably saved their lives. If it had been shallower, they likely would have been killed on some rocks.

Both her sneakers were gone, as was one sock. How that other sock had stayed on she couldn't imagine. Her wristwatch was ruined, the face crushed. Likewise her sweater was gone, but she'd only had it around her shoulders, not buttoned.

Diaz was looking down at her feet. "You can't walk like that," he said, and began unbuttoning his denim shirt. He stripped it off, then took a knife from his pocket and sliced off the sleeves. Going down on one knee in front of her, he draped a sleeve over his thigh and patted it. "Put your foot here." Gingerly balancing on one foot, she placed her other foot on the sleeve, and he swiftly wrapped the ends of the sleeve around and around it, then tied a knot on top. After repeating the process with her other foot, he said, "How does that feel? It isn't like having a leather sole, but is it enough protection for you to walk? If it isn't, say so instead of tearing up your feet."

She walked across the rock, testing the thickness of the fabric. Like he'd said, it wasn't like leather. She could feel every pebble. "How far do you think it is to the truck?"

He glanced at the sun. "If I'm right, we're not all that far. The truck was downstream, and the river carried us in that direction."

"But there was that bend to the left."

"And then this bend to the right. I'd say . . . maybe a mile."

A mile through a mountainous forest, virtually barefoot. He evidently came to the same conclusion she'd reached, because he shook his head, then looked around. Abruptly he took out his knife again, and went to the tree. He stabbed the point into the bark, then began slicing downward.

"What are you doing?"

"Cutting off a sheet of bark to use as a sole."

She stood to the side and watched with interest as he carved off a square of bark roughly ten inches by ten inches. She sat down and began unwrapping her feet. He split the square of bark in half, then knelt on one knee in front of her again. He balanced one slab of bark on his other knee, with the smooth underside up, and laid the sleeve over it so she'd have a double layer of cloth between her foot and the wood. Then he rewrapped her foot, binding the bark to the bottom with two swaths of cloth, and tied the knot on top again. After repeating the process with her other foot, he stood and pulled her to her feet. "How does that feel?"

"Much sturdier, though I don't know how long the bark will hold together."

"Anything is better than nothing. If it falls apart, I'll cut some more."

They left the riverbank and set out at a right angle into the forest. She had to walk gingerly, because the makeshift shoes didn't give her feet any support, but the bark at least protected their tender bottoms from the worst abuse. She tried not to step on sticks or rocks, tried not to make the bark flex very much, which would cause it to break apart. That made their pace necessarily slow, when they couldn't afford any delay.

Under the canopy of the trees they didn't have the sun's warmth, and within minutes Milla was shivering violently. Her wet clothes felt like ice on her, and she realized they were in as much danger from hypothermia as they had been from the water. Diaz, with his greater muscle mass, would do better than she at producing body heat, but he, too, was shivering.

He stopped once and wrapped her in his arms, hugging her close so they could share what meager heat they could generate between them. They stood pressed against each other, and she tiredly rested her head on his shoulder. He felt so hard and vital, but he was as vulnerable as anyone else to the chill of these conditions. She could hear his heart thumping steadily, strongly in his chest, sending warming blood through his veins, and after a while she began to feel a little warmer.

"We'll make it," he murmured against her temple. "We have a lot to look forward to tonight. Besides, I have a couple of sweatshirts behind the seat of the truck."

"Why didn't you say so?" With effort, she straightened away from him. "The promise of a sweatshirt will work miracles."

The "mile" he'd estimated was a straight line, but unfortunately they couldn't walk in a straight line. They climbed up slopes, down slopes, always working their way around to the direction he wanted. They had to hold on to trees when the mountainous terrain grew so steep they couldn't stand upright. What would have taken them twenty minutes on the flat took them over two hours, and twice he had to replace the bark in her improvised sandals. His sense of direction was unerring, though, and eventually they cut the trail that led them back to the truck.

By the time they reached it, the sun had set and twilight was deep, and the day's warmth had long since fled. Milla could barely walk, she was so cold. She shuffled along like an old woman, every muscle screaming in pain. She kept thinking longingly of the missing backpack and the ground sheet in it; they could have wrapped it around themselves and huddled together, and replenished their body heat that way. Food wouldn't have been amiss, either; it had a way of revving up the system. She thought of coffee, a big steaming cup of it. Or maybe hot chocolate. Any form of chocolate.

She thought of Diaz, and what would happen between them tonight–if they made it back to the hotel.

Just when she thought she couldn't go any farther, she looked up and there it was, that monstrosity of a truck. Nothing had ever looked more welcome. "The keys," she suddenly croaked. "Are they still in your pocket?"

That was the good thing about jeans when they became wet: they clung. What was in the pockets tended to stay in the pockets, even in river rapids. With difficulty, Diaz dug his fingers into his cold wet pocket, and came out with the keys. "Thank God," she breathed.

The next hurdle was getting *into* the damn truck.

Diaz tried to pick her up, but couldn't. Finally he boosted her enough that she could crawl, giggling, onto the floorboard and from there up onto the seat. The situation wasn't funny, but the choice was either laugh or cry. He had to hold the steering wheel to haul himself up, and he was shaking so hard it took him three tries to get the key into the ignition. But it was warmer in the truck than it was outside, and after it had idled a few minutes, warm air began blowing from the vents. He pulled two sweatshirts from behind the seat; they were new, with the tags still on them, so he must have bought them today to have just in case. His caution amazed her, because there was no way he could have known they'd fall in the river.

He stripped off the sleeveless remnant of his denim shirt and his T-shirt. Milla wasn't so far gone that she wasn't interested in the rock-hard expanse of his lightly haired chest, or his ridged abdomen. She pulled off her own blouse and her wet bra, and suddenly he hauled her across the truck seat, wedging her between the steering wheel and his chest as he kissed her. Their bare torsos rubbed together, his chest hair rasping over her chill-tightened nipples and making them tingle. She wrapped one arm around his neck and snaked the other one around his back, pressing her palm to the smooth, thick muscles she found there. This kiss wasn't shy, or gentle. He kissed her as if he might not wait until they got back to the hotel, his tongue stroking, his teeth nibbling. He rubbed his hand over her breasts, stroking them, learning their shape and softness and how they fit in his palm.

She whimpered into his mouth. It had been a long time since she'd felt this, too long. She still couldn't quite believe it was actually happening, that Diaz wanted her as she wanted him.

He was shaking when he drew back, but no longer from the cold. "We'd better get dressed," he said gruffly, and pulled one of the sweatshirts over her head himself. It was a man's shirt and there was far too much fabric, but she didn't care. The garment was thick and dry, and she almost wept at the warmth. He pulled on his own shirt, then took off his wet boots and socks and stuck his bloodless feet up to the floor vent so the truck's heater could blow right on them. She followed suit on the passenger side. The cab quickly heated, but it was at least fifteen minutes before her shivering subsided and her numb feet began to tingle with warmth. Finally he felt warm enough to drive, and by then the darkness was thick around them.

They had a long drive ahead of them back to Boise, and even though she was warm now, she felt drained. He had to feel the same. She put her hand on his arm. "Can you make it, or do we need to stop somewhere?"

"I can make it. When we get back to the highway, we'll stop at the first restaurant we see, no matter what kind, and get something hot in our stomachs."

That sounded like heaven. She pushed at her wild crown of curls. Her hair had dried, but she knew she had to look like a wild woman. She'd be surprised if any restaurant other than a motorcycle gang hangout would let her in. "The pistol is long gone, huh?"

"Bottom of the river."

"Too bad. You might need one to make a restaurant serve us."

He glanced at her and smiled. "I'll manage."

They lucked out and found a hamburger joint with a drive-through window. After getting their food, he pulled over and parked so they could eat. By then she had recovered enough to be starving, and she chowed down on her second hamburger of the day. He'd ordered each of them a large cup of coffee, and they settled back in bliss.

"We have to find a place that sells condoms," he said abruptly. "I don't have any."

There was tension in his voice, and she glanced over at him. He ran a nervous hand over his face.

Suddenly uneasy, she said, "We can wait. This doesn't have to happen if you're having second thoughts–"

"No. It isn't that." He took his hand down and gave her a somber look. "It's just–I haven't had sex with anything other than my fist in two or three years and I–"

"Two or three years?" she echoed, then shook her head. "It's been longer than that for me. I'm not exactly a red-hot mama."

"I want to make it good for you, but I probably won't last long."

"I probably won't, either," she said truthfully. Since that last kiss, her body had been humming with anticipation.

Doggedly he plowed ahead. "But then I'm good for the rest of the night, and I'll make it up to you."

His nervousness was appealing; her nature was fastidious, and she didn't like promiscuity. His confession was reassuring, too. "Are you healthy?" she asked, because she'd be stupid not to.

"Yeah. I haven't been with many women, and never with a whore or a drug-user. And I give blood at the Red Cross, every three months, so I'm tested regularly." He said it with an earnestness that touched her. Diaz was so sure of himself in every other way; she liked this more human side of him. She sensed that he really had to trust a woman before he'd let down his guard enough to be intimate with her, and even then he probably kept a tight rein on his emotions.

Tonight, she would find out.

She leaned over and kissed him. "Forget the condoms. I'm on birth control."

He took control of the kiss, and he might not have had a great deal of sexual experience, but he knew what he was doing. He kissed her deeply, a little roughly, and with growing urgency. When he set her back from him, his eyes were narrowed and fierce. Without a word he put the truck in gear, and they roared down the highway toward Boise.

20

THE TENSION BETWEEN THEM GREW MORE THE CLOSER THEY got to the hotel, until it was thick and smothering. She tingled from head to foot, her thoughts feverish as she thought about what she was going to do. Against all common sense, she was going to bed with Diaz. This might just be a very human reaction to the danger they'd survived together, she might regret it in the morning, but she was going to do it.

She was so hungry for him that she ached with need, so desperate to feel him inside her that she thought she might climax as soon as he touched her. She wanted to tell him to pull over to the side of the road so she could straddle his lap and get it done, now, before she died from tension. But, like him, she wanted a bed for what was going to happen between them, so she kept silent and gritted her teeth against the sheer lust that gnawed at her.

Finally they were there. He stuffed his feet into his wet boots, left his socks on the floorboard, and got out. Milla wasn't about to hop out with only fabric and pieces of bark to protect her feet, so she sat there while he came around and opened the door to lift her out. She thought that this time he might let her slide along his body, but he held her at least six inches away and set her gently on her feet. She looked up into his face, expecting the hard, remote expression so natural to him, and finding exactly that. But he tucked her against his side and walked with her into the hotel.

The night desk clerk looked at them with curiosity as they approached, and she knew he didn't often see a woman with rags wrapped around her feet. At least with the new sweat-shirts they didn't look homeless. If it hadn't been for that, she suspected the desk clerk might have called security.

On the way up in the elevator, she and Diaz stood side by side, not talking. She could feel every heartbeat; even her fin-gertips were tingling.

He tried his key card and wonder of wonders it still worked.

He unlocked his door and ushered her inside, turning on the light in the tiny entrance. Suddenly feeling like Little Or-phan Annie, Milla sidled toward the open connecting door to her room. "Uh–let me get my feet unwrapped and take a shower, and I'll–"

"Sit down," he said.

She blinked at him.

He pulled out a chair and pushed her down into it. After turning on the bedside lamp, he knelt and began untying the knots that held the sleeves around her feet. When her feet were bare, he carefully examined them, looking for scrapes or cuts, but she'd come through the ordeal in good shape.

When he was finished, he stood up and she did likewise, shoving a hand through her unruly hair. "I'll take a shower," she said again, trying to step past him, but he curved a hand around her waist and pulled her back to him.

"The shower can wait."

"My hair—the river water—"

"The water was clean."

"But I'd rather be fresh." She didn't know why she was making excuses now to delay what was going to happen, but she was suddenly nervous. It had been a long time for her, and Diaz wasn't an ordinary man. Both facts were staring her in the face, and she wanted to slow this down.

He unsnapped her jeans and said, "I want you just like this." Then he kissed her.

There was nothing romantic about Diaz, no murmured sweet things, no gallant gestures, just this kiss that went on and on, deep and voracious. She'd never been kissed like this before, with an intensity that stripped everything down to the simplest components: male, female. He held her with his hand burrowed into her hair, her skull gripped in his palm, her head tilted back while he fed from her mouth. That was what it felt like, a taking. And yet he gave, too. He gave pleasure. She burned with it, the flames fueled by nothing more than his mouth and tongue.

His erection bulged in the crotch of his jeans. It was a rock-hard presence pushing against her stomach, and her loins tightened with need. Frenzied now, she pulled back a little, fought with button and zipper and won, wrenching the damp cloth aside so she could grasp the hard length that thrust outward. She wrapped her fingers around him, delighting in the thickness, the silky slide of his skin. She moved her hand up and down, circling the thick crown of his penis and dragging a deep, raw sound from his throat as he shuddered convulsively.

His arms tightened and he bore her down on the bed and, in twenty tumultuous seconds, had her stripped naked. Another ten had his own clothes on the floor. He put his hands on her knees and pushed them apart, not waiting for her compliance, and moved into place over her. Milla put her hands on his ribs, holding on as he braced his weight on one arm while with his other hand he guided his penis to her and in the same rough motion pushed deep inside.

He froze in place, his breath panting between his parted lips as they stared at each other. She couldn't move; the feel of him inside her was too sharp, almost painful in its intensity. Their gazes met in the mellow lamplight, and she was mesmerized by the tension in his face, the way his steely muscles were locked as if he didn't dare move. It built and built, that clawing need, and yet she remained poised on the razor's edge of something she knew she couldn't control. His chest suddenly heaved on a convulsive breath, and he moved in a long, deep stroke that took him all the way to the hilt.

She clenched: her vagina, her entire body. She clenched around him and her vision blurred and she began to come, wave after wave of almost blinding pleasure. She had never come like that before, so totally lost in the physical that she had no sense of self, of surroundings, of anything beyond the moment and the ecstasy that spasmed in her belly, down her legs, along her nerve endings. He rode her through it, thrusting hard, demanding his own release and in doing so prolonging hers. He made that raw sound again and arched back, shaking convulsively as his hips jerked and plunged before, long seconds later and trembling in every muscle, he slowly collapsed on top of her.

The aftermath was like a wasteland, desolate and empty. She lay beneath him, too exhausted to move, barely able to breathe, and fought the urge to cry. She had never before been weepy after sex and didn't know why she should be now, but she felt a haunting need for comfort. She wanted to bury her face against his shoulder and sob like a child.

Because this had been a monumental mistake? Or because it was over?

Even though he lay heavily on her, sucking deep breaths into his lungs, she could still feel a fine, subtle tension running through his every muscle, as if he never quite relaxed—as if he was already thinking of moving on.

What did one say after an experience like this? "Wow" seemed both inadequate and out of place. "Do it again" was what she wanted to say. Right at this moment, she never wanted to be separated from his body again. Sanity would return, she was certain. Maybe in another few minutes. Maybe tomorrow. Until then, she wanted him inside her. She wanted to feel again what she had felt moments before, though she didn't know if she could muster the energy to try, or survive it if she did.

"Do it again." She said it anyway, because she couldn't *not* say it. She slid her legs up his sides and coiled them around him, clung to him with her arms, tilted her pelvis in an effort to hold his softening penis.

He laughed, that low, rusty growl of sound, and his breath was warm in her hair. "I'm not sixteen. You've gotta give me a few more minutes than this." He still sounded a bit breathless. But he didn't withdraw from her; he settled down a bit more heavily, as if he finally relaxed that last little bit, and snuggled in so that as long as they didn't move, his penis would remain inside her. "I think that lasted about fifteen seconds."

"I didn't last that long," she murmured, closing her eyes and inhaling the warm male scent of his skin.

"Thank God." He nuzzled her temple, then whispered, "Take a nap," and he closed his eyes and proceeded to do just that.

This was nothing like the first time he'd told her to do that. This time, the feel of him on top of her was so wonderful she was still fighting tears. How could he expect her to sleep when he weighed a ton and she could barely breathe, when she wanted to cling to him and cry and laugh at the same time? How could she sleep when she was afraid to relax her muscles, lest she lose him? And yet she did, too exhausted to do otherwise.

She woke to long, slow strokes that went deep into her, to his hard hands gripping her bottom as he tilted her up and ground her clitoris against his pubic bone. He might not have had vast experience, but he knew what he was doing, knew all the hot spots and pleasure points of her body, and he used that knowledge to push her high and keep her there, without letting her go over the edge. This time was as prolonged as the first time had been brief. After a while she began struggling with him for supremacy, fighting him for her release, but he was too strong and controlled her until he was ready. Then he rode her hard and fast and hurled them both into orgasm.

She finally got her shower, though with him in there with her it was more orgy than shower. He paused once, with the water pouring over them, and touched the patch on her hip. "What's this?"

"My birth control patch."

He regarded it with interest. "I've never seen one before. What if it comes off?"

"I've never had one come off until I take it off. They stick pretty good. But I check it every time I shower, just to make sure."

He trailed his fingertips over the slope of her breasts, then lightly circled her nipples. His expression was serious. "I've never had sex without wearing a condom before."

"Never?"

He shook his head. He watched his fingers as they moved down her stomach, over the gentle curve of her belly, before curving into the notch between her legs. His two middle fingers slid between her folds and up into her. Milla's breath hissed between her teeth and she lifted onto her toes, clinging to his shoulders for balance.

"I liked it," he murmured.

"What?" She had totally lost the thread of their conversation.

"Coming inside you. So don't lose that patch."

She had never been into kinky sex; oral was as far as she would go. But Diaz knew no boundaries on her body and she was drunk with physical pleasure; she let him do whatever he wanted. He took her in the shower, on the floor, sitting on the vanity. He put her against the wall and took her standing up. It was sex as she had never known it before, raw and powerful, surprisingly sophisticated in execution but primitive in design and intent. And she kept coming back for more, arousing him with his penis in her mouth, her hands cupping his heavy balls and feeling them tighten, and doing some of the same things to him that he'd done to her, just to hear the thick groans he gave.

By morning, she was raw and sore, and knew walking would be an effort. By morning, she could barely remember what it had been like to *not* know his body, not to have felt him inside her and held him in her arms and absorbed the power of his thrusts as he came. By morning, she was his.

She woke to see light seeping around the edges of the pulled curtains. He lay behind her, one heavy arm draped over her waist, his breath warm on her shoulder. She felt stupid. She was more than a little shocked at herself, but there it was: she was his, in a way she had never been David's. The knowledge hurt her. Though until the day Justin was stolen, her marriage had been a happy one, she had remained her own person and David had remained his. He had been absorbed in his work, of course, as he still was, and she had been content to have that small, almost imperceptible distance between them. It had felt good, that sense of autonomy, of controlling her own life.

But David was a civilized man, and Diaz . . . wasn't. He hadn't let her maintain that tiny sense of distance.

She knew very well she had bedded down with a predator. He was dangerous, unpredictable, and she had never felt safer than when she was in his arms. He had used her for his pleasure, but he had also let her use him in return. Last night hadn't been just sex, though she had thought it would be. Instead it had been a . . . claiming, raw and raunchy and unexpected.

How could she have known he wanted that? She could have handled her emotions better if it *had* been only sex. But he had known what he was doing, and ruthlessly used the physical to cement the emotional. Claimed, and bonded. No matter what, now, they were linked, and not just by memories of what had passed between them. No, there was something else, something primitive and elemental that she couldn't quite grasp.

Love? She couldn't call it that. There was a powerful attraction between them that seemed to go all the way down to the cellular level, but it wasn't love. She was damn certain he didn't love her. It was almost a case of like calling to like, a sense of ease as if they were two halves fitting into one perfect whole, and that made her even more uneasy than thinking about love. Was she like Diaz? Was she that ruthless? Had she become like him, in her relentless search for Justin?

He stirred and pressed a kiss to her shoulder. "We need to get to the airport," he said sleepily.

She didn't want to move. "I have two more days of vacation left." She should go back to El Paso, she knew. Diaz should renew his search for Pavón, and now that they were fairly certain someone had been misdirecting her all these years, they had another angle to explore. But for ten years she had been battering herself against a blank wall, and she was tired. Yesterday she had nearly died in that river. Would it be so horrible of her if she stole two days just for herself, away from the constant struggle? Two days, that was all she was asking. She had never even considered doing such a thing before.

"What will happen if we go home?"

"I'll probably go back to work," she said honestly. Things would be different when she was home. El Paso was the center of it all; she couldn't be there and *not* work. Boise was a different world, away from everyone she knew.

He rolled over and picked up the phone. "I'll cancel our flight reservations."

21

Arturo Pavón liked to tell everyone that he never forgot an insult. He enjoyed seeing the caution in their faces, the way their gazes skittered away from him. And it was true; he forgot no slight, real or imagined. There was only one who had harmed him and gotten away with it, and the knowledge was a bitter little knot in the pit of his stomach, a knot he lived with every day. But he hadn't forgotten, hadn't given up on vengeance. His time was slow in coming, but come it would. One day their paths would cross, and he would make the American bitch regret the very day she was born.

For ten years he had waited to make her pay for the loss of his eye.

He could have had her any number of times, the way she constantly came into his country with her silly questions, her prying. But Gallagher had said no, she was too visible, if she disappeared that would raise too many questions and would, at the least, cost them a great deal of money to ensure certain officials looked the other way; at worst, they would end their days in either an American or Mexican jail, depending on where they were caught. If it came to that, Pavón very much wished for an American jail, where they had air-conditioning, cigarettes, and color television.

Gallagher. Pavón didn't trust him, but only because he trusted no one. Their association was a long and profitable one. Gallagher let nothing get between him and money. He'd been dirt poor when Pavón first met him, but full of fire and nerve and ideas, powered by an absolute lack of scruples. Gallagher knew how to make money; if he couldn't make it, he would steal it, and he didn't care how many people he trampled into the dust in the process. A man like that would go far.

Pavón had known it would be better to ally himself with such as Gallagher than to go his own way and perhaps become a rival that had to be eliminated, so he had made himself indispensable. If Gallagher needed someone to disappear, Pavón handled it. If he needed something stolen, Pavón stole it. If someone needed to be taught a lesson, Pavón took great pleasure in making certain this person never forgot it wasn't wise to cross *Señor* Gallagher.

Things had gone well for Arturo, until ten years ago. The assignment was so simple: take the blond baby from the young *gringa* who visited a small village marketplace at least three mornings of the week. So he and Lorenzo had gone to the village, and waited, and they were lucky: the very first morning, she had been there.

It would be easy, they thought. The only problem was that she carried the baby in a sling across her chest, rather than in her arms or in a basket. But Lorenzo always had his knife, and the plan was that they would flank the *gringa*; Lorenzo would slice the strap of the sling, Pavón would grab the baby, and they would run. Some rich Americans had agreed to pay a lot of money for a blond baby to adopt, and this one was an easy target. The young *gringa* was distracted by her shopping, and she was a typical American, soft and unprepared for danger.

They had underestimated her. Instead of becoming hysterical and helplessly screaming, as they had expected, the woman had fought with unexpected fierceness. He still woke from nightmares, feeling her fingers clawing at his eye, reeling from the bursting pain and horror, his entire face feeling as if it were on fire. Lorenzo had stabbed the bitch in the back and they had escaped, but unfortunately she had lived. He himself had spent many days recovering, cursing her and swearing vengeance. Where his eye had once been was now a scarred pit; his cheek was permanently furrowed from her claws. When he had recovered enough to begin moving around again, he'd found that his depth perception was altered, that he could no longer shoot so well. And he could no longer blend into a crowd without being noticed; people stared at his ruined face.

She had caused him a great deal of trouble, and he would never forget.

But he had bigger trouble now, trouble that alarmed him. The matter of the woman, he would settle in his own good time. The matter of Diaz . . . he must be doubly cautious now, with Diaz on his trail, or he was a dead man.

Everyone knew Diaz hunted for money; Pavón, while proud of his justly deserved reputation, had still taken care not to come too much to the attention of the authorities. Under the radar, as Gallagher liked to say. So whose ire had Pavón drawn who also had the money to hire someone like Diaz? He had thought and thought, and there was only one answer.

It had disturbed him afterward when he heard that Milla

Boone had been in Guadalupe the same night they had transferred the Sisk woman for her trip to heaven. She had been very close to him, in the same area at the same time, which for the past ten years, on Gallagher's orders, he had taken care would not happen. Was it coincidence that she had announced then, to an entire crowded cantina, that she would pay ten thousand American dollars to anyone who could give her information leading her to Diaz? If she had ten thousand just for information, how many more thousands did she have? And why would she want Diaz, if not to hire him? Diaz was not a man one called simply to say you admired his work, and one certainly did not pay ten thousand dollars for that.

Pavón had put two and two together. It was obvious Milla Boone had hired Diaz to find him, because shortly thereafter he had received word that Diaz was looking for him. Pavón hadn't lingered to find out why; Diaz didn't hunt people just to chat with them. The people he hunted simply . . . disappeared. Except for the dead ones. They were always easy to find. The others were simply never seen or heard from again. What Diaz did with them was a matter of great speculation.

Pavón had immediately left Chihuahua, and his future was now uncertain. Diaz did not give up; time made no difference to him.

For the first time in his life, Pavón was frightened.

He had gone to the Mexican Gulf Coast, where a distant cousin kept a small fishing boat for him. The area, with the jungles and wetlands, the mosquitoes and the offshore oil fields, was not crowded with tourists, as the rest of Mexico seemed to be. He had supplied his boat and put out into the gulf, where no one could approach him unseen—unless Diaz had taken up scuba diving, which Pavón wished he had not thought of, because since then he had been uneasily watching the depths around his boat as well as the surface.

The weather was miserably humid and he, a child of the desert, hated the heaviness of the air. This was also the prime time of the year for hurricanes, so he made a point of listening to his weather radio every day. If one of the huge storms got into the gulf, he wanted to be far inland at the time.

Once a week, he went to shore for supplies, and also to call Gallagher. Gallagher did not trust cell phones, though he had one; he simply never conducted any business over one. He was so careful he did not even use a cordless phone. Pavón had tried to tell him he could get a secure cell phone, one whose conversations could not be intercepted, but it was one of Gallagher's quirks that he was so distrustful.

Since learning Diaz was asking about him, Pavón appreciated such caution. Perhaps it would keep him alive.

The only long-term solution he could think of was if he killed both Diaz and Milla Boone: Diaz because he was the immediate, and strongest threat, and the woman because she would just keep hiring people until one of them succeeded. How she had finally linked Pavón with the kidnapping, he didn't know; someone had obviously talked, despite Gallagher's influence.

To kill them would require a game of delicate balance, at least where Diaz was concerned. The woman would be easier, so he would take her last. Perhaps he would even show her what a real man was, before she died. Ah, he knew the perfect ending for her! After he finished using her, he would *donate* her to the cause, an act of tremendous goodwill on his part. He chuckled at his own play on words, then quickly sobered.

The difficult part would be getting close to Diaz; the man was like smoke, appearing and disappearing with the wind and leaving no trace of his movements. To find Diaz, Pavón would have to offer himself up like a tethered goat, and it must be done carefully. He would have to lead Diaz into a place and situation in which he, Pavón, had the control—and he would have to prevent Diaz from realizing that the tethered goat was armed and ready until it was too late to save himself.

This required much consideration and planning; it wasn't something that could be done overnight. Everything must be perfect—or he himself would be dead.

No one was more cautious and meticulous about detail than Gallagher, so when Pavón went to shore that week and made his regular call, he broached his plan. "We must lure Diaz to me," he said, "but in such a way that he doesn't know he's being lured."

Gallagher paused, then said, "That's a good idea. Let me think about it. Where are you now?"

"In a safe place." Gallagher wasn't the only one who could be cautious.

"We need to meet."

Ah. That meant there was something he didn't wish to say over the phone. "I cannot get there today." He could, but he preferred to have Gallagher think he was much farther away, perhaps even in Chiapas, the southernmost Mexican state.

"When, then?" Gallagher sounded annoyed, and . . . something else. Worried, perhaps? But why should Gallagher sound worried? Diaz was not after *him*—in an instant, Pavón perceived that he was in danger not only from Diaz. He was a link, not only between Gallagher and what was going on now, but between Gallagher and Milla Boone's kidnapped child, ten years ago. The best way for Gallagher to protect himself was to break that link.

"Perhaps . . . two weeks from now?" Pavón said slyly.

"Two—goddamnit, you can get here faster than that."

"Perhaps I don't want to leave this wonderful place. I have everything I need here, and no one knows how to find me. If I come there, many people know my face. I have to ask myself, who will people be most afraid of: *Señor* Gallagher or *Señor* Diaz? If *Señor* Diaz has a knife to a man's throat and asks if he has seen me, will that man lie, or will he tell the truth? I think he will piss himself, but he will tell the truth."

Gallagher dragged in a long, exasperated breath. "All right. If you're afraid, then you're afraid. When you find your *cojones*, call me and we'll set up a meeting."

An insult to his machismo was supposed to suddenly make him stupid? Pavón smiled to himself as he hung up the phone. The smile quickly faded, though; what did he do, now that he couldn't count on Gallagher's help?

He would have to take care of Diaz by himself. There was no other option. How to do it, though, was a problem. Perhaps he could take the woman and use her as bait? If Diaz was working for her, he would come to her aid, so long as he didn't suspect a trap. How could he take her and make it look like something unrelated?

He kept coming back to using himself as bait. But for *her*, not Diaz. He would somehow have to make certain Diaz was occupied elsewhere, then get a message to the Boone woman that he knew she wouldn't ignore, nor would she wait until Diaz was available. She would come by herself, and then he would have her. When he had her, he would also have Diaz. Perhaps not right away, but he could enjoy himself while he was waiting.

Yes. It was a good plan.

The days slipped past and cooler weather settled in. Except for that one heat wave the summer hadn't been a hot one, but Milla was still glad to see it go and autumn arrive. She kept her appointment with Susanna and got a new prescription for the birth control patches just before she used up her supply, which was a good thing considering the drastic change in her love life.

"I want to apologize for what happened," Susanna said contritely. "I was out of line. I should have listened to you and not thought I knew best."

Milla blinked at her, totally at sea for a moment. She never felt chatty when her feet were in stirrups, and she'd been determinedly thinking of other things. These days, to an alarming degree, "other things" meant Diaz.

The world clicked back into place, and she remembered the scene with True. "It's okay," she said. "Everything's fine. He didn't like taking no for an answer, and I guess he needed to hear it one more time. He hasn't called since."

"That's good. That he isn't bothering you, I mean. But what about Finders? Is he still one of your sponsors? You can sit up now."

Clutching the paper sheet for the meager modesty it provided, Milla took her feet down and scooted back so she could sit up. The nurse began doing the paperwork for the Pap smear, and Susanna turned away to wash her hands.

"He said that turning him down wouldn't affect his support, so I have to take him at his word."

"That's good. I don't think he'd be petty. I don't know him that well, but he doesn't seem to be a man who pouts."

Milla laughed. No, True didn't strike her as a pouter. She hadn't thought about him at all recently, she realized. Two things had occupied her mind: work and Diaz.

"I called and apologized to him, too," Susanna continued. "We got to talking about other things, and he said you had a lead on the man you think took Justin. Diego? Diaz?"

"No, nothing that panned out," Milla said, instinctively not wanting to say anything about Diaz. Now that she knew what kind of work he did, the less said about him the better.

"Damn. I was hoping this time—well, never mind. Keep me up-to-date if you do get any information, though."

"I will." But she already knew a lot more that she was keeping to herself. Given Diaz's theory that she had been deliberately led down blind alleys all these years, she thought that the less said the better. She trusted Susanna, but did she trust everyone Susanna knew? Or everyone Susanna's other friends knew? Not likely. So she borrowed a page from Diaz and kept her mouth shut.

Susanna picked up her pad and scribbled the prescription. "Everything looks fine. We'll call when the results come in."

"Leave the message on my answering machine if I'm not at home."

Susanna made a note on Milla's chart, smiled, and said, "If I can wrangle any free time for lunch, I'll give you a call."

Milla smiled in return; then Susanna and the nurse left the examination room to let her get dressed. As soon as they were gone, her smile vanished. Worry nagged at her. Since they'd returned from Idaho, Diaz had been prowling Mexico. On two nights he'd shown up at her condo, scruffy and snarly, lean from the hunt. A wise woman would have stayed far away from him when he was so lethally edgy, but Milla had decided that where he was concerned, she wasn't wise at all. Both times she'd fed him, put him in the shower, and washed his clothes. Both times he'd let her, though he'd watched her with narrowed, feral eyes that made her knees go weak, because she knew he was biding his time. And both times, as soon as he was out of the shower, he was on her before the towel hit the floor.

After his sexual appetite was slaked, he was usually hungry again. Whatever he was doing, he wasn't getting enough to eat. She would make him a sandwich and they would sit at the table while he ate and told her anything new he'd learned, which was precious little. Still, she at least felt that those tidbits were solid information, not a smoke screen.

"The word I get is that Pavón has been working for the same man from the beginning," Diaz had said the last time she'd seen him, four days before. "They smuggled babies; now they smuggle body parts. But the information on the street is thin; they've done a good job of scaring the hell out of everyone."

"Did you find Lola's children?"

"The oldest, a son, was killed in a knife fight over fifteen years ago. Lola hasn't seen her youngest in eight years, but I've tracked him to Matamoros. He's a commercial fisherman, and was out in the gulf. He's supposed to be back three days from now. I'll be there waiting for him."

When she'd awakened the next morning, she had lain there for a moment, so ... *content,* feeling him there beside her, that it frightened her. Almost as soon as she woke, he seemed to sense it and stirred, pulling her close before his eyes were even open. He was relaxed with her, she thought—as much as he ever relaxed, anyway.

She slid her hand over his chest, feeling the hair rough under her palm, the warmth of his skin, the strong, steady beat of his heart. His morning erection rose, inviting her touch, and obligingly she slipped her hand beneath the cover to envelop him. "I can't believe this," she murmured as she kissed his shoulder. "I don't even know your first name."

"Yes you do," he said, frowning. "James."

"Really? I thought you made that up."

"James Alejandro Xavier Diaz, if you want the American version."

" 'Xavier'? I've never met anyone named Xavier before. What's the Mexican version?"

"Pretty much the same. Ouch!" he said, giving his rusty laugh and dodging when she darted her hand to pinch him in a very tender place. It always melted her when he laughed, because he did it so rarely.

While she had him weakened with hysteria, she slithered on top of him, positioned his penis, and slid down to take him tenderly inside. He took a deep breath and let his eyes close, both hands going to her bottom and kneading. Milla adored morning loving, when she was still sleepy and lethargic, when time didn't seem to matter and in a way climaxing didn't either. It was enough, almost, to just lie there and hold him with arms and body. Almost. Eventually she had to move, or he had to move, and it was as if that first stroke broke the bands of self-control. She rode him hard and fast, and when her climax shook her and left her collapsed on his chest, he rolled over with her and took his own satisfaction.

After breakfast he was gone, and she hadn't heard from him in four days. The first week of October was almost behind them. Was he all right? Had he found Lola's son?

After Milla left, Susanna went into her private office and called True. "I just saw Milla. We're still safe; she doesn't know anything about Diaz. She thinks it was bad information."

True was silent; then he cursed luridly. "She's *met* Diaz, you fool! They were seen together last month in Juarez."

Susanna's blood ran cold. "She lied to me?"

"If she denied knowing anything about him, she did."

"But why would she do that? We've been friends for years."

True snorted at that. Friends? God save him from friends like Susanna Kosper.

"Maybe she suspects *you*," he snapped. "Maybe Diaz is closer to us than I thought."

For once he didn't have the chance to hang up; Susanna dropped the receiver into its cradle and sat staring at the phone as if it were a snake. She'd always thought Milla, while admirable in so many ways, was a touch naive. Now she wondered if *she* wasn't the naive one. Was Milla playing her?

Panic rose in her throat, threatening to choke her. She'd worked too hard to let things fall apart now. She had to do something, and she had to do it fast.

22

DIAZ ENTERED THE SMOKY CANTINA AND FOUND HIMSELF A place against the wall, partly shadowed, where he could watch the patrons come and go. The music was loud, the metal tables were crowded with empty bottles, and the urinal consisted of a barrel in a back corner. Two prostitutes were doing a lively business; the Mexican farmers and fishermen were relaxed and having a good time, singing along with a folk song, giving one another numerous and enthusiastic toasts, which called for more bottles, which called for more toasts. The *cantinero*, the bartender, looked like a man who kept a loaded shotgun close to hand, but in the convivial little cantina Diaz doubted he needed it very often.

Running Enrique Guerrero to earth had taken a lot of time and patience. Diaz thought he'd probably chased him over half of Mexico. But he'd finally caught up with the little fucker, in the port city of Veracruz, in this crowded, aromatic cantina where he felt safe, surrounded by all his *compadres*.

Lola must have warned him, Diaz thought, or his friends in

Matamoros had. Enrique had run. Now why would he do such a thing, unless he had something to hide? Watching him, Diaz figured he had a lot to hide. Enrique was one of those furtive weasels who watched the people around him and, when they were too drunk to notice, relieved them of some of their cash. He was slick, but the cantina was dark and smoky, and there was some serious drinking going on; a five-year-old would have had some success doing the same thing. Enrique was drinking, but not much, which gave him a huge advantage. Still, not a few of the *campesinos* carried machetes; it was their weapon of choice, and hacking at one another was almost a national sport. Enrique was risking more than a black eye if he got caught.

Diaz wasn't drinking at all. He stood very still, and most people never even noticed him. He didn't make eye contact with anyone. He just watched Enrique, and waited for his chance.

Because he wasn't drinking very much, Enrique didn't have to make any visits to the barrel in the corner. If he had, Diaz could have moved up behind him and gently escorted him out the nearby door that led into the *callejón*, the alley. In this crowd, no one would have noticed or given a damn even if they had. So Diaz waited, moving deeper into the shadows, his attention never wavering.

Dawn was only minutes away when Enrique stood and slapped his pals' backs, trading loud and hilarious insults if the drunken laughter was anything to go by. Probably he'd lifted all he could reasonably expect to get; it was a good gig, because when everyone sobered up, they would simply think they'd had a very good time and spent all their money.

When Enrique opened the door, the fresh air outside didn't even make a dent in the almost palpable wall of smoke that filled the room. Diaz moved without haste from his post, timing his arrival so he stepped through the door right behind Enrique. No one seeing him would have thought there was any purpose at all to his leaving right then, because his gait had been leisurely.

As soon as the door closed behind him, he had his hand over Enrique's mouth and his knife point sticking just under his ear as he dragged the weasel into the darkness of a narrow alley.

"Talk, and you will live," he said in Spanish. "Fight, and you will die." He removed his hand from Enrique's mouth. Just to make certain Enrique got the point, Diaz gave him the point, about an eighth of an inch. It stung like hell and blood began pouring, but Diaz had taken care not to cut anything major.

Enrique was already slobbering with fear, promising anything, everything, whatever the *señor* wanted. Here, he had money—

"Don't move your hands, *cabrón*." Diaz dug the knife point in a little deeper. With his other hand he did a swift search and relieved Enrique of the blade he'd been trying to pull out of his pocket. "I don't want your friends' money, just answers to a few questions."

"Yes, anything."

"Your mother sent me. My name is Diaz."

Enrique's knees wobbled. He let loose with a number of colorful curses at Lola, who, even if she'd heard them, likely wouldn't have cared. Diaz figured there wasn't any love lost between mother and son, or she would never have told Diaz how to find Enrique. Essentially, Lola cared about no one but herself, a trait she had passed on to her son.

"Ten years ago you were living with Lola when she was caring for the stolen babies."

"I know nothing about the babies—"

"Shut up. I'm not asking about the babies. Who did Arturo Pavón and your uncle Lorenzo work for? Did you ever hear a name?"

"A *yanqui*," Enrique babbled.

"Not his nationality, *cabrón*; his name."

"No . . . no name. All I heard was that he lived in El Paso."

"Is that all?"

"I swear!"

"I'm disappointed. I already knew that much."

Enrique began to shake. "I never saw him. Pavón was very careful to never mention his name."

"But was Lorenzo as careful? Or did Lorenzo like to brag?"

"He bragged, *señor*, but it was empty noise. He knew nothing!"

"Tell me some of the things he said. I'll decide if it is nothing."

"That was a long time ago; I don't remember–"

Diaz made a *tsk*ing sound. He didn't move the knife at all; he didn't have to. Terrified beyond reason by that regretful *tsk*, Enrique shuddered and began to sob. The strong odor of urine wafted up.

"Do you remember when Pavón lost his eye, stealing a gringo baby? The mother clawed out his eye, tore it from his head. Surely you remember that."

"I remember," Enrique said, weeping.

"Ah, I knew you didn't have amnesia. What is it you have recalled?"

"Not about the man in El Paso, I know nothing about him! But that baby, the gringo baby . . . Lorenzo said the woman doctor helped them."

The woman doctor.

Milla's friend Dr. Kosper had delivered her baby, and had kept in touch all these years. She even lived in El Paso.

A big piece of the puzzle clicked into place.

The eviscerated victims hadn't been butchered; their organs had been neatly removed, indicating some surgical skill was used. A damaged organ had no value. An undertaker could be doing the organ removal, but a doctor was the more likely choice.

Who was the one doctor who had lived nearby at both the little village where Milla's baby was stolen and the border where the bodies were being found?

None other than Susanna Kosper.

He had to warn Milla.

By the middle of October, Diaz still hadn't returned and Milla was so worried she couldn't seem to concentrate on anything. Had anything happened to him? Mexico was, by and large, an extremely friendly and hospitable country, but like every other country in the world, it also had a very rough element. She would have bet on Diaz against almost anyone, but even the most efficient predator could be outnumbered and overwhelmed. He wasn't proof against a high-caliber rifle, either.

When she wasn't sick with worry, she was furious. Didn't he have any idea how it would make her feel to have someone else she cared about just disappear? There was no comparison between Diaz and Justin, of course, except for their ties to her heart. Her son and her lover: surely she couldn't lose them both in such a cruel way, with no closure, just pain and emptiness and uncertainty. When Diaz did show up again, she'd give him a piece of her mind he wouldn't soon forget, and if he didn't like it, that was just tough. He could sever their relationship if he wanted, but as long as there *was* a relationship she refused to be treated like nothing more than a sexual convenience whenever he got around to visiting.

She had tried his cell phone number several times without

luck. He was either unavailable, according to the canned message, or not in a service area. If he had a voice mail option with his service, he hadn't activated it.

She kept busy. Unfortunately, Finders kept busy. There was a rash of runaways and kids being snatched, as well as the inevitable hikers getting lost in the mountains. The reason didn't matter; if feet on the ground were what mattered, Finders provided them. In just one week, Milla flew from Seattle to Jacksonville, Florida, to Kansas City, then San Diego, and finally back to El Paso. She was exhausted when she got back, but the first thing she did when she got home was check her answering machine for messages. There were plenty of them, but none from Diaz. She didn't think he'd called on her cell phone, either, but the caller log feature had totally stopped working and she had no way of telling if she'd missed a call or not.

Come to think of it, she'd had no calls on it at all for a couple of days. She hadn't thought anything of it because she'd been on so many different flights, and she had always called the office as soon as she could. She'd had no trouble making calls, but what if she couldn't receive them?

She picked up her home phone and called her cell number. She listened to the ringing in the earpiece, but the cell phone in her hand did absolutely nothing.

In disgust she hung up and tossed the cell phone back into her purse. First thing in the morning she would drop it off for repairs and pick up a loaner, or even buy a new one if necessary. She couldn't bear thinking that Diaz might have tried to get in touch and that stupid phone wasn't working. Did he have her home phone number? She couldn't remember ever giving it to him. Surely, though, if he'd needed to get in touch with her and couldn't get her on the cell, he'd have called Finders and left a message, or called Information and got her home phone number and left a message here.

Where in hell *was* he?

Her home phone rang and she snatched up the receiver. Maybe–

"*Señora* Boone."

"Yes, this is she." Milla didn't recognize the voice. This reminded her of the call back in August, telling her where she could find Diaz. But the voice wasn't the same; she was certain of it. The first voice had been lighter, smoother; this voice was coarse, and the accent was different.

"You are interested in Arturo Pavón?"

My God. Milla swallowed hard to contain the sharp rise of excitement. Please, please let this be some real information and not another false lead, she prayed. "Yes, I am."

"He will be in Ciudad Juarez tonight. At the Blue Pig Cantina."

"What time?" she asked, but the caller had already hung up. She checked Caller ID; it said, "Unavailable."

Desperately she called Diaz's cell phone again. After three rings the canned voice said the customer was not in a service area.

She checked the time: four-thirty. Because this past week had been so busy, the office staff was scattered over the country. Brian was in Tennessee. Joann was in Arizona. Debra Schmale and Olivia were both sick with a vicious stomach virus.

She knew better than to go alone. She didn't know what kind of place the Blue Pig was, if it was a regular cantina, in which case she wouldn't be welcome in there, or if it was a club where women *were* allowed without it automatically being assumed they were prostitutes. She couldn't see Pavón going into any of the more exclusive clubs; no, if he was there, then this was a regular cantina. For her to step foot inside one of them was to invite big trouble.

She racked her brain, trying to think of someone who was both available and capable.

Only one name surfaced.

Diaz had told her to stay away from True Gallagher, and she assumed he had a good reason other than just being territorial. He'd said that before they became lovers, as more of a warning than anything else. She should have asked specifically why he mistrusted True. But other than Diaz and Brian, he was the only man she could think of who would be capable in a situation like this.

She realized that it didn't matter. Diaz wouldn't have said what he had without reason, so she had to trust him. Just as soon as she saw him she'd find out exactly what he had against True, but until then she had to rely on her own sense of trust, and that lay with Diaz.

There had to be someone else. The problem with concentrating on work and on her quest to find Justin was that her social life was limited; she knew a lot of people, but none intimately, and in circumstances like this she needed someone she knew she could rely on.

Then she drew a quick breath of relief. There was one other, if she could just get in touch with him: Rip Kosper. Quickly she looked up his office number; of course he didn't see patients in the office, since he was an anesthesiologist, but he and his partner had an office for handling the paperwork and billing, and taking messages.

He hadn't yet left the hospital, the woman who answered said. Milla said it was urgent, gave her name and number, and the woman promised to page him. While she waited for him to return her call, Milla ran upstairs and changed into jeans and sneakers.

More than an hour passed before Rip called. In that time Milla paced, tried Diaz's cell phone three more times, and forced herself to eat a sandwich. The caller hadn't given a time, so this could well be an all-nighter.

"Milla?" Rip sounded concerned when he finally called. "What's wrong?"

"I need someone to go with me into Juarez tonight," she said. "My regular crew is either gone or sick, and this isn't something I can do by myself. Can you go with me? I know this is way out in left field, but you're the only friend I can think of."

"Sure, no problem. Where and what time?"

She told him which bridge to meet her at, and when. "You'll need to change clothes, if you can. The cantina we're going to will probably be on the rough side."

"All *riiight*," he said with relish. "It's been a while since I've done any cantina crawling."

"Oh, one more thing: I have no idea how long this will take. It could be all night."

"I have a light schedule tomorrow anyway. Nothing until almost noon. I'm good."

"Thanks, Rip. You're a doll."

"I know," he said smugly.

An hour later they walked across into Juarez. Milla had previously used Chela's services only if they were leaving the border zone, but under no circumstances would she ever willingly be near Pavón without being armed, so she had placed a call to the arms dealer and arranged to meet her. "Do you know how to use a pistol?" she asked Rip when they were on the Juarez side.

"Never have. I've hunted, but with a rifle. Haven't hit anything yet." He gave her a concerned look. "You really think we'll need guns?"

"I know I'd rather have them and not need them, than vice versa. I didn't tell you, but the man who took Justin is supposed to be at this cantina tonight. If he is, you can bet he'll be armed."

Rip stopped in his tracks, an uneasy expression crossing his face. "Don't you think you should call the cops? The PJF or the PJE, whichever would handle things like this."

"And tell them what? I think he's the man I saw very briefly ten years ago?" She didn't want to deal with either the state or the federal judicial police. Both were highly unpopular in Mexico.

"You took out his eye. That makes him easy to identify."

"Unless I think all one-eyed men could be the same man. I don't even know that he'll be here. I had an anonymous call that said he would be. Do you know how many other calls I've had over the years? Take a guess how many of them have actually been worth anything."

"I'm guessing not any," he said, relaxing.

"One, actually."

"So this is more of a wait-and-see."

"Probably. I won't know unless I show up. But I definitely don't want to hang around a rough cantina without some means of protection."

Rip knew the score on cantinas, knew she couldn't go inside—which meant she would be on the street. Even sitting in a car, as she intended to do, had its risks.

Her old friend Benito met them with a grin and a Ford Taurus in fairly good shape. He also knew where the Blue Pig was and gave her careful directions, along with a warning. The Blue Pig had a very bad reputation. Most cantinas were friendly places where men relaxed and got shit-faced drunk, but the Blue Pig was where the very rough element gathered.

Milla began to think Pavón might actually be there, if the place was that bad.

They met Chela, who silently handed over a shopping bag,

took her money, and walked away. "Is it always that easy?" Rip asked in surprise.

"So far. If a policeman ever wants to look in the bag, though, I'm dropping it and running."

"I'll run with you," he said, grinning.

They got back into the Taurus, with Milla behind the wheel. Without hope, before they went to the Blue Pig, Milla tried Diaz's number one more time. To her absolute astonishment, he answered.

"Where have you been?" she all but shouted at him, then caught herself and felt her face getting hot. She'd said that as if she had a right to know. Then she thought briefly and decided she *did* have a right to know. They were lovers, and she'd been worried about him.

There were three beats of silence; then he said, "I was going to ask you the same thing."

"My cell phone won't receive calls. I can call out, but that's it."

"I've had my phone turned off most of the time."

"Why?"

"Because I didn't want it to ring."

This time she was the one who waited before she spoke, fighting the urge to beat her head against the car's dashboard. She had the feeling that if she could see him, he'd be wearing that tiny smile of his. "Why not?"

"I didn't want the noise to attract attention."

He'd been on stakeout, then. "Did you find out anything?"

"Something very interesting. Where are you?"

"Juarez. That's why I've been trying to reach you. I got a call this afternoon saying Pavón will be at the Blue Pig Cantina tonight."

"I know the place. Stay where you are until I can get there. Don't go there alone."

"I'm not alone. Rip Kosper is with me."

His voice was suddenly tense. "Kosper?"

"Remember my friends Susanna and Rip?"

"She's involved, Milla. She's part of it. Get away from him, go back to El Paso. Do it now."

She actually took the phone away and stared at it in astonishment for a second before putting it back to her ear. "What did you say?"

"Susanna. She set up Justin's kidnapping. She's probably neck-deep in the organ smuggling, too. Someone with skill has been removing the organs, and a doctor is the most likely bet."

She was so stunned she couldn't think. Susanna? The idea was preposterous. Susanna was her friend, she had delivered Justin, she had made a point of staying in touch all these years and offering support and friendship. *She had kept track of Milla's efforts to find the kidnappers.*

Milla was hyperventilating. She caught her breath and held it before she got dizzy, her eyes squeezed shut.

"Milla?" Rip asked, his voice worried. "Are you all right?"

"Get away from him," Diaz's voice said in her car, the tone deadly.

"How soon can you be here?" she asked with a calm that took every ounce of control she possessed.

"I'm seventy kilometers away. An hour, at least."

"I won't pass up a chance at Pavón. We know he probably won't show, but maybe he will."

Evidently realizing the futility of telling her to go home, Diaz took a deep breath. "Are you armed?"

"Yes."

"Is he?"

"Not at the moment."

"Keep it that way. What kind of car are you driving?"

She described the Taurus to him.

"Stay in the car. Keep the doors locked. Park on the street where I can find you. I'll be there as fast as possible. And if Kosper does anything the least bit suspicious, shoot his ass."

"Yes. Okay," she said to the staccato list of commands.

He disconnected the call, and she did the same. She felt shell-shocked, and she didn't dare look at Rip. He couldn't be involved. Not Rip. He had a gentle heart, that of a true gentleman. The only time she had ever seen him be less than friendly was the night Susanna had tried to set her up with True; he'd made it obvious that he didn't like the man.

Neither did Diaz. How odd that both of them would so intensely dislike the same man, and knowing that Rip disliked True, how odd that Susanna would try to throw Milla at him anyway. Why would she do such a thing?

True and Susanna talked. Nothing incriminating about that. He was wealthy now, but he'd dragged himself out of poverty. She had heard that he'd come from El Paso's meanest, toughest section. She knew that he still had contacts in that world, that he knew all sorts of unsavory characters such as smugglers.

Susanna . . . and *True*?

It made sense. She was going solely on instinct now, without a shred of corroborating evidence, but it made sense.

She took one of the pistols out of the shopping bag, then put the shopping bag in the floorboard on the other side of her legs.

"What's wrong?" Rip asked. "Who was that?"

"A man named Diaz."

He heaved a weary sigh. "I've heard about him."

"How?"

"I overheard Susanna and True talking." Rip stared out the window. "I'm guessing he knows about Susanna."

Startled, Milla stared at him, and kept her hand on the pistol. He rubbed his eyes. "She's careless sometimes. She says things she shouldn't, forgets how sound carries. Her home office, for example, seems to amplify sound. I've overheard conversations for years, but only in the past few months have things started to come together for me. She was talking to him on the phone one day, and–I don't remember exactly what she said, but the meaning was pretty clear. Something about how much money they'd earned with the babies, though the hullabaloo about Justin had nearly gotten them caught. *Earned.* She actually said they *earned* the money."

"Why didn't you say something?" Milla asked. "Go to the cops?"

"Lack of evidence. Hell, *no* evidence. Just some phone calls that I heard only her side of. She asked True if he was sure this Diaz guy was coming up empty and they didn't have to worry. I don't know what True said, but it was obvious he took Diaz seriously. So I did some investigating on my own, did more eavesdropping, and found out there was going to be a transfer of some kind of cargo behind the church in Guadalupe. I know a few hard-asses in Mexico myself. I contacted one of them, told him Diaz would appreciate knowing about this, hoped it worked. Then I called you, used a fake accent and told you Diaz would be there. I didn't know for sure, but there was a possibility. Guess I was right, huh?"

Rip was the anonymous caller. He had to be; otherwise he couldn't have known about that night. "He was there," she said, her throat tight.

Rip bowed his head. "When I found out what she'd done . . . I've loved that woman for twenty years, and I never knew her. It was the money, I guess. We were almost bankrupted paying back our student loans, credit card bills, you name it. She isn't good with a budget. I'm not either, truth be told. That's why we went to Mexico, to get away from the bill collectors for a year.

The money situation got much better that year, and now I know why. She was selling babies. Hell, she delivered them, she knew their sex, age, general health."

And the poor Mexican women had traveled considerable distances to reach the clinic so they could have a real doctor in attendance during birth. The kidnappings would have been spread out over a sizable area, and who would ever think to ask who had delivered the babies? Since Susanna had had no contact with them once they left the clinic, she had never even blipped on the radar of suspicion.

"She sold Justin," Rip continued. "They got a lot of money for him. I'm sorry, Milla, I don't know where they sent him. I've gone through all of her paperwork, but there's nothing about what happened to the babies. I don't think she cared." Tears gathered in his eyes. "She said they'd kept you busy chasing your own tail for ten years. They've been hindering you every way they could."

"What are *you* going to do?" Milla asked, her voice thin. This hurt. She was shocked and hurt and angry. Susanna was lucky she wasn't within reach at that moment, or Milla would have done physical damage to her.

"I don't know. Divorce, obviously. I haven't left her because I wanted to be in a position to snoop. Can I testify against her? I don't know if I can make myself do it."

"Diaz thinks she's involved with black market organ transplants, that they're killing people and selling their organs."

Rip stared at her, his mouth working soundlessly. Finally he managed to say, "She—she couldn't do that. That's beyond—"

"The 'cargo' that was transferred in Guadalupe that night was a person."

"Oh, my God. Oh, my God." All color washed out of Rip's face and he closed his eyes. He looked as if he was going to vomit.

Milla felt as if she might be sick, too. She checked the time and a spurt of adrenaline had her starting the car with quick, jerky movements. "We have to get to the cantina. Pavón might already be there."

"I thought you said he probably wouldn't—"

"There's always a chance."

23

PAVÓN REACHED THE BLUE PIG EARLY; HE WANTED TO BE here when the bitch arrived, he wanted to watch her wait for him. Talking to her on the telephone had made his heart beat faster, and the excitement had given him an ache in the crotch that he wanted to rub. He had waited and waited, hiding out in that foul boat, every day that he spent cowering like a little girl eating at his soul. He needed to find out where Diaz was before he made a move on the woman, and that was not easy.

But fortune had at last smiled on him. One of the fishermen mentioned to his cousin that the tracker Diaz had been to Matamoros looking for Enrique Guerrero. The news was both frightening and reassuring: it was good because this fisherman also said that Enrique had fled south, from which Pavón could assume that Diaz had followed; it was bad because he had no doubt Diaz would find Enrique, who could not be trusted to keep his mouth shut about anything. He would sell his mother to the devil to keep himself safe, though with Lola as a mother, one couldn't truly blame him. Still, Pavón had to assume that what Lorenzo had known, Enrique knew. And what Enrique knew, Diaz would shortly know.

There could not be a better time to sever the relationship with Gallagher, and disappear for good. There was a chance that Diaz would be content to go after the bigger fish, and leave the minnows alone. But he had a reputation for being both ruthless and relentless, letting no one escape, and Pavón couldn't take the chance of looking up one day and coming face-to-face with that devil. His original plan was better, to take the woman and use her as bait to catch and kill Diaz. Only then would he truly be safe.

So he sat in the cantina and waited–and waited, consoling himself with several bottles of Victoria beer. Where was she? Was he so unimportant to her that she wouldn't bother to walk across the border to see him? He'd made it as easy for her as possible, short of presenting himself at her front door.

He was on his fourth bottle of beer before he realized that perhaps she would not come into the cantina. Only whores did, or women looking for trouble. A good woman did not, and the bitch was a good woman.

Swearing to himself, he got to his feet and was halfway across the floor to the front door when he suddenly reversed himself and went to the back. Fool! What if she was parked directly outside? That would be foolish of her, but it was possible. He definitely wanted to see her before she saw him, so he would go out the back door.

He worked his way around, which was not easy, because here the buildings had been built flush against one another and he had to walk through the narrow, smelly back alley to the end of the street, then double back. He stayed in the shadows against the buildings and near other people as well; she would be looking for a lone man, not a group. Luckily this street teemed with people, especially at night, and most of them were men of the type a good woman would not like to meet.

He moved carefully. She might be parked on the other side of the street, or facing him. He had to examine each vehicle–there! And so conveniently parked, on this side of the street, with her back to him.

It had to be her. It was a woman with light-colored curly hair, so light a brown that it was almost blond. And the curls; he especially remembered the curls. Even at night and in silhouette they seemed to float around her head with a life of their own; they looked as soft and feathery as a baby chick. He wondered if her lower hair was as curly, and chuckled to himself because he would soon find out.

For ten years he had not fucked a woman who was not a whore–not a willing woman, anyway–because this curly-haired bitch had ruined his face. She would pay for that. He would use her until she screamed for mercy.

Perhaps he would keep her for a while, even after he killed Diaz. He could charge others to use her. He did, after all, need to make a living.

There was someone else in the car with her. A man.

He stopped, his blood turning to ice. Diaz–how could he have returned so fast? *Idiota!* He mentally slapped himself. Just because he himself would not go in an airplane–too much security and checking of papers–didn't mean others had the same need for secrecy. Diaz could return from anywhere in the country in a matter of hours.

But this could be to his advantage. Both of them together, and oblivious of his presence behind them. He could kill Diaz right now. A bullet through the window into his head; that would do the job. The woman ... he would probably have to kill her now, too, and he sighed with regret. Ah, well. Shooting Diaz first, as he had to do, would give her time to react. He didn't dare approach from the front, which would give him two quick shots at both of them; he would have to move in from behind and to the side, out of the view of the side mirror, until he had an angle on Diaz's head. After shooting Diaz, he would have to move forward even more to be able to see the woman and have a decent shot at her. She would be screaming, moving around, perhaps even trying to drive away. He would have to be fast, and accurate, which was not so easy now with only one eye. To make things worse, it was his left eye that was missing, and they were on his left.

The man got out of the car. Pavón froze in place. This was not Diaz! This man had light-colored hair. He was older, shorter, stockier. Shocked, he recognized him. It was Dr. Kosper's husband, the other Dr. Kosper.

Son of the great whore! What was he doing here?

Whatever the reason, it didn't matter. This Dr. Kosper was going into the Blue Pig, presumably to look for him, Pavón. This could not be better. The woman was watching Dr. Kosper; she wasn't paying attention to—she looked into the rearview mirror, checked her side mirror, and Pavón froze. She couldn't see him in the mirrors, but she was more alert, more cautious, than he'd believed. He needed to come at her from her left, his right, so he would be best able to see her. But if he did, she would be able to see him.

He had underestimated her once, to his cost. He would not do so again.

She would have the car doors locked; she wasn't stupid. The windows were up. But had she relocked the passenger door after Dr. Kosper got out?

The four beers he'd had to drink said there was only one way to find out.

He strode forward at an angle, staying away from the mirrors until he was right at the car. He pulled on the door handle, the door opened—miracle!—and he leaned in with his pistol pointing right at her head.

"*Hola!*" he said, grinning as he slid into the passenger seat and closed the door. "Remember me?"

He saw her eyes grow huge, a most satisfying response—then quick as a snake her hand snapped up and he found himself also staring down the barrel of a pistol that was pointed at his good eye.

"*Hijo de la chingada,* do you remember *me?*" she said in slow, careful Spanish. *Son of a bitch, do you remember me?*

Her hand wasn't shaking. Her eyes were cold with hate. Pavón looked at her and saw his death, unless he could pull the trigger faster—

The door beside him opened again and another pistol jammed under his right ear. "Pavón, you pig," said a soft voice so laden with menace that he nearly pissed himself with terror, because he knew whom the voice belonged to and he also knew beyond a doubt that he had fucked up beyond all chance of recovery. "You threaten my woman? That makes me very angry."

Rip stood off to the side, shaking uncontrollably. When he'd returned to the car, he'd almost passed out at the sight of Milla holding one of the pistols to a man's head, that man also holding a pistol pointed at *her*, and a second, dark, lethal-looking man standing in the open door also with a pistol to the man's head. By Rip's panicked count, that was three pistols and two threatened heads. Someone was going to die.

Things had then happened fast. The man in the front seat with Milla was disarmed, and Rip found himself in the backseat sitting beside that living, breathing weapon who simultaneously held one pistol to the back of Pavón's head and another trained on Rip himself. He'd figured out that this was the infamous Diaz, and after seeing the man, he understood completely the rather gory reputation that followed him. He was absolutely the scariest person Rip had ever seen, and it wasn't anything he said or did; it was just that aura of lethal competence. He himself had been speechless with fear at having that pistol pointed at him, but Milla had talked fast as she drove out of Juarez, following the stranger's directions, telling him everything that Rip and Milla had discussed. At hearing that Rip was the anonymous informant who had brought them together, and everything he had to say about True Gallagher, Diaz shoved the pistol he'd been holding on Rip into a holster strapped to his leg like an honest-to-God gunslinger.

Now they were in the desert, far from the lights of Juarez and El Paso, and he was shaking not from the cold or from any lethal aura. He was shaking because he had watched Diaz at work with Pavón, and now he knew Diaz's reputation was well-deserved, even understated.

Pavón was, quite literally, scared shitless. He was naked and staked out, spread-eagled, on the ground. At first he had cursed long and loud; then he had tried to bargain, and now he was simply begging. Diaz kept asking questions in that soft voice, and what Rip heard made him turn away and vomit. Pavón told it all, starting with the babies who were sold like so many cattle, how the smuggling ring had worked, Susanna's role in it, the name of the woman in New Mexico who worked at the rural county courthouse and who had stolen blank birth certificates and falsified them. With birth certificates bearing new names, the babies had immediately become different people.

Pavón had told everything he knew about True Gallagher, and Rip shook with rage. Diaz, if anything, became even colder and his work with the knife more diabolical. The people who had been murdered for their internal organs that were sold for millions on the black market—Susanna was doing the organ removal, and Gallagher was getting rich. That was when Rip turned aside and vomited, shaken to the core by the knowledge that his wife was as cold a murderer as this disgusting thug staked to the ground and spewing out his filth.

When Diaz had asked all his questions, he stopped and wiped off his knife and slipped it into a sheath inside his boot. He stood looking down at the sniveling, sobbing mess at his feet, then pulled the pistol from his thigh holster.

Pavón began begging again.

Diaz reversed the pistol in his hand and extended it to Milla butt first. "Do you want to do it?" he asked with grave courtesy. "It's your right."

Milla stared at the pistol for a long moment, then slowly stretched out her hand to take it.

"Milla!" Rip said in shock. "This is murder!"

"No," Diaz corrected, his tone going hard and giving Rip a searing look that told him to keep out of it. "What they do is murder. This is an execution."

Milla looked down at Pavón, the weight of the pistol heavy in her hand. This was a larger caliber weapon than the ones she'd bought from Chela, guaranteed to do the job, which was probably why Diaz had given it to her. She had wanted Pavón dead for the past ten years, dreamed about killing him. She had dreamed about choking him to death with her bare hands. But she had always seen herself killing him in a rage, not in cool deliberation.

Pavón was going to die here tonight. It was a given. If she didn't kill him, Diaz would. Because of what Pavón had done to her, Diaz was offering her retribution.

Slowly she lifted the pistol and aimed it. Pavón closed his eyes and flinched, waiting for a sound that he wouldn't be alive to hear.

She didn't pull the trigger, and her hand began to tremble from the weight.

Pavón opened his eyes and began to laugh. One way or another he would die here tonight, and he knew it. It made no difference to him who pulled the trigger, but if he had one last chance to torment her, he would take it. "You stupid whore," he jeered, then coughed on his own blood. "You are too soft, too useless. Your stupid little boy was soft and useless, too, but the buyer wanted a pretty baby boy. He loved little boys. Do you understand, slut? Your baby was sold to a boy lover who wanted to raise his own little love slave. Your baby boy probably likes it by now; he likes getting it in his–"

Those last disgusting words were never said.

Diaz handled everything. He left Pavón's body there to be found, his clothes and identification neatly folded and placed on the ground beside him, with a large rock on top to hold everything in place.

There were the pistols to be taken care of–he didn't destroy them, as Milla and Brian always did; instead they were put away for future use. His own vehicle was there; he had flown into Chihuahua and taken care of some detail he didn't explain, then driven to Juarcz. It wasn't one of the pickups Milla had seen before; he seemed to have an inexhaustible supply. He arranged for it to be picked up at the border crossing as before; he called Benito and told him where he could pick up the car Milla and Rip had used; then he got them back across the border.

Rip and Milla were totally silent, in shock at the events of the night. It was only when Rip was unlocking his car that he looked up with agony in his eyes. "I can't go home," he said. "I can't look at her again. What happens now? Will she be arrested?"

"We have no proof," Diaz said. "If we were in Mexico—" He broke off and shrugged. If they were in Mexico, True and Susanna would already be in jail, and charges didn't have to be filed for seventy-two hours . . . or as long as was necessary. But this was the States, and what a dead Mexican thug had supposedly told them wouldn't get them the time of day in a police station. "But we know where to look now, and there are people here who are much better at this than I am; I'll turn it over to them."

Rip looked startled. "Whaddaya mean? You're some kind of—I mean, you're *official?*"

Diaz ignored that. "Stay in a hotel. Don't speak to your wife; you're too emotional. Don't spook her into running. If she runs, I'll have to go after her."

Rip had seen what happened to someone Diaz went after, and he shuddered.

Diaz ignored him after that, putting Milla in the passenger seat of her SUV and then driving off without speaking again. Rip stared after them for a moment, then shuddered again. He got behind the wheel of his car and sat there for a minute, different scenarios running through his mind and none of them pleasant. He thought of Susanna. Then he bowed his head against the steering wheel and cried.

There was such a storm of emotions roiling through Milla that she couldn't pin one down long enough to examine it. There were both relief and regret, triumph and sorrow, shame and grim satisfaction. She leaned her head back and watched the streetlights loom and then recede in a dizzying parade. The dash clock said the time was only eleven P.M.; she had thought surely it was almost dawn.

Tonight she had seen in action what she'd always sensed about Diaz, from the very first moment he'd knocked her down and threatened to snap her neck. The destruction he was capable of was truly frightening—and yet she wasn't frightened. He had taken those aspects of his own character and molded them into a weapon to be used against the enemy, the dregs of society who ignored its laws and wreaked their own destruction. He won by being even more brutal, even more ruthless. What he didn't do was turn that force against those he perceived as innocent. Ever. She felt safer with him than she'd have felt sitting in the middle of a police station.

"Thank you," she said.

"For what?"

"Helping me." She didn't know if she could have finished it without him. When Pavón started spewing his poison, Diaz had simply put his hand over Milla's and together they'd pulled the trigger; his hand had steadied hers, his finger had added its strength to hers. She was ashamed that she hadn't been able to do it herself, and yet so relieved that she hadn't had to.

"You'd have done it," he said with cool confidence. "I just didn't want you to hear any more of what the bastard had to say."

"Do you think he was lying?" She squeezed her eyes together, because his filthy words had spread cold horror through her heart.

"He didn't know what happened to any of the babies; he just wanted to say something to hurt you."

And he'd succeeded, all too well.

They reached her home and a touch of a button raised the garage door; he slotted the Toyota inside before the door had finished lifting, and had it lowered again almost before Milla could get out of her seat belt and open the door. She dug out her keys and unlocked the door from the garage into the kitchen, stepping inside and turning on the lights.

He whirled her against the refrigerator, his hands hard on

her waist. Startled, she dropped her purse and keys to the floor and looked up at his set face and narrowed savage eyes. "Don't *ever* do that to me again," he said with clenched teeth.

She didn't have to ask what he meant. Those moments when Pavón's pistol had been trained directly at her head had been long and terrifying.

"I stayed in the–" she began, but he cut her off with a kiss that was wild and hungry and deep. He lifted her onto her toes and pressed in hard against her, grinding his erection into the softness of her mound. She yielded immediately to that outraged male aggression, wrapping her arms around him and transforming it into sheer lust. He moved one hand to the waistband of her jeans and unsnapped them, dragged down the zipper, then thrust his hand inside her panties and curled his fingers up into her while his palm rode her clitoris. She bucked under the lash of abrupt desire, growing wet around his fingers, hugging them with her body.

He took her there, shucking her out of her jeans and dropping his own, then bending her over the kitchen table. Milla clutched the edge of the table to brace herself against his hard thrusts, pushing back to take all of him. He reached around and under to fondle her, his talented fingers wringing a fast orgasm from her. Then he simply gripped her hips and pumped into her until he began coming, slumping over her as he jerked and thrust. He shuddered with completion, his mouth hot on the back of her neck. "God," he muttered indistinctly, "when I saw him with that pistol in your face–"

"I had one in his, too."

"Would that make you any less dead if he'd pulled the trigger?" He bit her shoulder, then gently pulled out of her and turned her around. He buried his fingers in her hair, holding her head as he sank into a kiss as hungry and devouring as if they hadn't just made love. She gripped his wrists and let that steely strength wrap around her, soaking it up and using it to bolster her own. There was so much still to be done . . . tomorrow. She would spend the rest of the night just being with her lover.

Tomorrow she would go to New Mexico. Only part of her mission had been accomplished. She still had to find her son.

24

In the night, while she drowsed with her head on his shoulder and one arm draped across his stomach, he said absently, "I think I should tell you something."

She woke enough to murmur, "What?"

"True's my half brother."

She sat straight up in bed. *"What?"*

"Get back down here," he said, tugging her down into place once more on his shoulder.

"Neither of you go out of your way to broadcast the relationship, do you?" she demanded sarcastically.

"He hates my guts and I hate his. That's the relationship."

"So he knew exactly who you were and where to find you when I first asked!"

"No. He's never known where to find me."

Wow. They were *really* close, weren't they? "You have the same mother, obviously."

"Had. She's dead. But, yeah. He was around five, I guess, when she left him and her husband and went to Mexico with my father. She had me, she left *my* father, she found another guy."

"But she took you with her when she left him."

"For a while, until I was about ten. Then she sent me to live with him. I doubt they were ever married, and now that I think of it, unless True's father divorced her before I was born, my last name might legally be Gallagher." He sounded only mildly interested, and she knew he'd never go to the trouble of looking up the legal documents to find out.

"Why does he hate you? Does he even know you?"

"We've met," he said briefly. "As for hating me, his mother left him for my father. Then when she left my father, she took me along. She didn't take True when she left his father. Old-fashioned resentment, I guess. And I'm half Mexican. He hates Mexicans, period."

She had never picked up on any prejudice from True, but that would be something he kept hidden, wouldn't it? Especially in El Paso. He was a man intent on climbing as high as he could go, and it wasn't smart to offend the people who would help him along the way.

"What happens now? Shouldn't you tell whoever you deal with"—she waved a hand to indicate the universe—"about Susanna and True?"

"I did that as soon as I talked to Enrique Guerrero. They're being watched to make certain they don't try to leave the country. As for gathering the hard evidence, I leave that to the other guys. They have the crime labs, the forensics experts. Normally I just find people for them; I don't get involved in the crime solving."

She felt flat. Perhaps she'd watched too many crime dramas on television, but she wanted a big showdown, with violence and a full confession and True being led away in handcuffs. Played out this way, she wouldn't even get to ask him the question that burned in her mind: *Why?* She couldn't go near him now, not without tipping him off, because there was no way she could act normally around him, and she probably wouldn't be allowed to see him later.

She didn't care about his confession, about the careful gathering of evidence. She wanted to see him staked out the way Pavón had been staked out. She wanted him to suffer the way she had suffered. She wondered what it said about her as a person that she wasn't suffering agonies of the conscience about Pavón, but she wasn't. She was glad he was dead. She was glad she'd been involved.

"Tomorrow I'll try to find this woman in New Mexico," she said, changing the subject because she couldn't let herself focus on True right now. Her job wasn't finished. "She's the next link in the chain. She knows which birth certificates are false."

"Adoption papers are usually sealed. In these cases, you can bet they are. It's a dead-end road."

She shook her head. "I can't accept that. I still haven't found my son, so I have to keep trying. Finding the people who took him—that was just part of it, the smallest part."

Diaz fell silent, his hand rubbing up and down her bare back. Milla breathed in his scent and warmth, and felt comforted, strengthened by this short lull before she once again had to throw herself into what seemed like a never-ending effort. She nestled closer against him, feeling herself lapse back into sleep, and this time he let her.

He was gone when she woke in the morning. She sat up in bed and stared in bewilderment at the empty space beside her. He was gone. He wasn't just downstairs making coffee, or in the bathroom; she could sense that the condo was empty except for herself.

She got out of bed and looked around for a note, but of course there wasn't one. His communication skills were rusty, to say the least. Or rather, he communicated just fine when he wanted to, but a lot of times he simply didn't feel the need. She tried his cell phone number. The irritating voice said the customer was not available, meaning he didn't have the damn thing turned on. She growled in frustration.

Thinking about his cell phone reminded her of her non-working one. She had to do something about it today before she went to New Mexico. She put on coffee and got out her atlas to locate the town where Pavón had said the woman falsified the birth certificates. It was located exactly where it needed to be to make getting to it from El Paso difficult. She glanced at the clock; the travel agency wasn't open yet. Depending on what the airline schedules were, she might well be able to get there faster by driving. "Fast" was a comparative term, of course. The earliest she could get there was probably late afternoon. Even if she did fly, she would have to either go to Roswell, rent a car, and drive north, or go to Albuquerque and drive east.

She had waited ten years. If she didn't find the woman today, she'd find her tomorrow.

As it turned out, that was exactly what happened. When the travel agency opened, she learned there were no direct flights to Albuquerque or Roswell at the time she needed, on any airline. Of course. The next direct flight with an available seat was late afternoon. She'd have to either spend the night in Albuquerque and get an early start the next morning, or drive across lonely, unknown territory at night, not knowing if this little town even had a motel where she could stay.

Or she could forget about flying and drive. It was a hefty distance but still easily done in one day, if she'd been able to get an early start. By the time she could get away today, though, she'd be able to get to Roswell before dark—barely—then spend the night there and finish the trip tomorrow morning. The decision was a no-brainer.

Rip called her as she was packing for the short trip. "Are you okay?" he asked in a subdued voice.

"I'm fine." She was; she hadn't had nightmares, hadn't dreamed at all that she could recall. "How about you?"

"Exhausted. I can't believe last night actually happened. Is there . . . will there be any repercussions?"

The way Rip saw it, he had participated in a murder. Milla's view was more like Diaz's: it had been an execution. Considering what Diaz's job was, doing pretty much what he'd done last night—though maybe without the questioning session first—she doubted there would even be an investigation. "No, I don't think so. You're safe." She would have gone into greater detail, but she was mindful of saying too much over a telephone. Rip was being careful, too; with Susanna's example of saying too much in a nonprivate situation, he knew what a mistake that could be.

"I spent the night in a hotel, then got my partner to cover for me today. Good thing my schedule was light, huh? I just couldn't—she would probably make an effort to track me down at the hospital, since I didn't go home last night. I can't talk to her right now. Maybe tomorrow."

Poor Rip. His life had been torn apart, his marriage of twenty years was shot, his view of the world turned upside down. But he was soldiering on, because that was what most people did.

Milla made a fast decision. If no one from Finders was available to go with her today—she had no idea if anyone had returned last night or this morning—then she'd ask Rip. That would get him far away from Susanna, give him time to get his composure back. Though after last night, he might refuse to go anywhere with Milla ever again, and if so she couldn't blame him.

She'd prefer to take someone from Finders, though, so she wanted to check out the situation there before she asked him. "How can I reach you today?"

He gave her his cell phone number, plus his hotel and room number. He didn't intend to check out of the hotel today, but he was going home after he was certain Susanna had left, to get some clothes and toiletries.

After hanging up with him, she called the office. Olivia answered the phone, sounding dragged out. "I'm functional," she said when Milla asked. "But I'm weak and I still don't feel great. I talked to Debra and she's still puking her guts out."

"How are we looking today?"

"Joann's search is still going on. It isn't looking good for the kid; this is the fourth day. Brian will be home about six tonight."

"What happened there?"

"Bad outcome."

Milla sighed; she didn't ask the details. "I'm driving to Roswell this afternoon, spending the night there. I have another lead on Justin, the woman who supposedly falsified the birth certificates so the babies could be adopted."

"That's great!" Olivia said, her tone perking up. "Who's going with you?"

"I'll ask a friend to go, since we're still so understaffed. Rip Kosper. I don't know if he'll be willing, but he and Susanna are having trouble and he may want to get away."

"Oh, no," Olivia said. Most of the staff knew Rip and Susanna, since they'd been Milla's friends for years and Susanna often called Finders to talk to Milla. Now that she knew why Susanna had stayed in such close touch, Milla wanted to scream with rage.

She told Olivia about her cell phone situation; then after hanging up she called Rip and explained her plans to him, asking if he wanted to go.

"Let me call my partner," he said. "I'll get back to you."

Of course he had to clear it, she thought. He had a medical

practice; he couldn't just leave whenever he wanted. But the day was not getting off to a fast start; it was grinding along, ignoring her impatience.

She turned in her cell phone, and found that since the phone was out of warranty, the repairs would cost almost as much as a new phone, so she bought a new one and extra battery packs, plus the home and car rechargers. Doing so, for one reason and another, took over an hour. The need to be on her way ate at her, demanding she hurry, and there was nothing she could do about the situation.

As soon as she was in her Toyota, she plugged in the phone to charge the battery and also to use the car's power to call Diaz again. He still wasn't available. She wanted to wring his neck. Why couldn't he have left her a damn *note*?

Rip called; he'd cleared things with his partner and taken off the rest of the week. He could leave anytime she was ready.

Deep twilight had fallen by the time they drove into Roswell, and Milla felt as if she'd been nibbled to death by ducks. The entire day had been filled with delays and irritations, and Diaz still wasn't answering his phone. She and Rip checked into a motel, went for supper at a steakhouse, then returned to their separate rooms and turned in for the night.

They left Roswell early the next morning, heading north. Rip was quieter than usual, lost in his thoughts. He'd left a message with Susanna's office that he was going out of town and wouldn't be back for a couple of days; then he'd turned off his phone.

The country they were heading into was dry, but not desert. The morning was cool and clear, and didn't get a lot warmer as the day progressed. She lost her cell phone service, which wasn't surprising considering the emptiness around them. New Mexico was a big, beautiful state with fewer than two million people living in it, but the vast majority of them were grouped around the cities. This section averaged something like two people per square mile, which didn't mean each square mile had two people in it. In fact, she saw many square miles that had zero population. She was glad she hadn't done this trip the night before.

The small town where the county seat was located had a population of around three thousand. The courthouse was a small adobe building, with the sheriff's department occupying an adjacent adobe building. Milla's first step was to find out if the woman, Ellin Daugette, still worked at the courthouse in the probate office.

The probate office was the first door on the right, and when they approached the counter a smiling, overweight woman with an improbable shade of red hair came over and said, "May I help you?" Her name tag said she was Ellin Daugette, and Milla had to grip the edge of the counter.

"My name is Milla Boone," she said, using the name she always used when on a search. "This is Rip Kosper. May we speak privately with you?"

Ellin looked around the office. They were the only people there. "This looks pretty private to me."

"It concerns kidnapped babies and falsified birth certificates."

Ellin's face changed, the friendly smile vanishing. She stared at them a second, then sighed and said, "Let's go into the judge's office. He won't be back from lunch for another hour, at least."

She led them to a small, crowded office and closed the door behind them. There were only three chairs in there, including the one behind the judge's desk, so she took it and heaved another sigh. "Now, what's this you're asking about falsified birth certificates? I don't know that it's possible, with everything computerized now."

"When was this office computerized?"

"I don't know exactly."

"Ten years ago?"

Ellin surveyed Milla, the look assessing. "No, not that long ago. Five or six years, maybe."

Ellin was keeping her composure, trying to find out how much they knew. Milla decided to oblige her. "My son was one of the babies kidnapped."

"I'm sorry to hear that."

"It's taken a long time, but we've finally broken the smuggling ring. Let me name some names for you: Arturo Pavón." She watched closely as she said each name. Ellin showed no sign of recognition. "Susanna Kosper." Still nothing. "True Gallagher was the boss." Ah, there was a telltale flicker. "Ellin Daugette."

"Damn it!" Ellin slammed her hand down on the desk. "Damn it all! I thought all that was over with. I thought it was over."

"You thought you'd gotten away with it."

"It's been a long time, of course I thought that!" She seemed to realize there was no use in prevaricating now. "Are you two cops?"

"No. I don't know that any cops are coming. I can't promise you that they won't, but I don't intend to tell them anything about you—in exchange for information."

"You're looking for your baby, aren't you?"

"That's more important to me than anything else."

"What makes you think I'd keep incriminating evidence around? Do I look stupid to you?"

On the contrary, Ellin looked like a cagey woman who knew how to look out for number one. "Yes, I think you'd keep it. It would give you an edge, wouldn't it? Something to bargain with, whether it's with someone private like me, or a district attorney, or even True Gallagher. If you ever felt that you couldn't trust him, you'd need some way of keeping him in line."

"You're right about one thing. I wouldn't trust Gallagher as far as I could throw him."

Milla leaned back in her chair and crossed her legs, pinning Ellin with a cool look. "I really, really hope you have what I need, because otherwise you're no use to me."

"You're threatening to turn me in."

"No, I'm promising it. Just as I promise not to if you help me. Like I said, I don't know if the cops will come calling or not. The people you dealt with are involved in a series of murders, and they're going down. The investigation will probably concentrate only on that." She felt Rip tense beside her, and wanted to pat his arm in comfort. Instead she concentrated on Ellin, pouring all her force of will into her face and voice. "If they hadn't been the same people running the smuggling ring all those years ago, I wouldn't have made the connection to you. But I *will* turn you in, in a heartbeat, if you don't help me."

Ellin said "All right" so easily Milla could scarcely believe what she was hearing. "I believe you. Let me get my list."

"You kept a list?" Milla couldn't believe it.

"Well, how else would I remember which birth certificates were legitimate and which weren't? It's not like I wrote 'FAKE' across the bad ones."

They went into the outer office, and Ellin sat down at a battered metal desk. "See, I've had this job for almost thirty years; it's not like I had to worry about anyone going through my desk, finding this list, and getting suspicious. It's just a list of names, doesn't say anything about them. And if I get killed in a car wreck or drop dead from a heart attack, then I guess I don't care if anybody finds it, right?"

"No worries," Milla said, shaking her head.

"You got it." She opened a desk drawer, pulled out a fat file, and placed it in front of her on the desk.

Milla was astonished. "That many?"

"Hmm? No, of course not. This is a bunch of other stuff."

She began thumbing through the papers. She reached the end, grunted, and started back at the beginning. "Must have overlooked it." She didn't find what she was looking for on the second thumb-through, either. An alarmed expression crossing her face, she went through the file a third time, one sheet of paper at a time. "It isn't here. Damn it, I know it was here!"

For some reason, Milla believed her. Ellin's upset was too genuine. A new worry crept into her mind. "Could someone– like perhaps True–have broken in and taken the list?"

"He didn't know it existed. Why would he do something like that? The sheriff's department is right next door; it isn't like breaking in would be an easy thing to do. Besides, we're on camera." She nodded toward a huge metal shelving unit that was stacked high with huge ledgers.

Milla looked, but didn't see any cameras. "Where?"

"Tiny little bastard; the upper-left-hand corner. See the holes in the braces for moving the shelves around? Third hole down."

Ah. Now she saw where the third hole looked as if it had been blocked. "That's the camera?"

"Sneaky, isn't it? See, one of the county commissioners suspected his wife was having an affair with the probate judge before the one we got now, coming down here at night for some private, extracurricular activity. So one weekend he sneaked in a security company and had the offices wired. Caught them, too."

"Can we look at the tape? Or is it possible you moved the list?"

"I never moved the list," Ellin said flatly. "Ever. And it was here just a month or so ago, I saw it when I was going through the file looking for something else. But all is not lost, as Shakespeare would say. Like I said, do I look stupid? There's a copy in my safe-deposit box."

Milla went weak with relief. Thank God, thank God, she

thought fervently. To come this close and hit a wall was more than she thought she could bear.

"Let's have a look at that tape, though; I'm curious if someone came snooping around." Plus Ellin needed to know exactly where she stood, so she could protect herself if maybe True had known about her list after all, and decided he needed some leverage in his present situation. The same thought occurred to Milla. If that was the case, Ellin would do better to come forward immediately and use the list for her own protection, before True could use it.

She led them down a set of narrow stairs to the dusty, musty basement level. An older Hispanic man sat at a metal desk reading a newspaper. "Ellin," he said in greeting.

"Morning, Jesus. We want to take a look at the security tapes."

"Sure, no problem. Or is there?"

"We don't know. Someone could have been in my office."

"Last night?"

"Have no idea. Could have been any time in the last month or so."

"The tape resets and records over itself every seven days. If it was that long ago, you won't find anything."

He fetched the tape from the security system's recorder, and slapped it into a VCR hooked up to a thirteen-inch television. He punched *Play*, then *Rewind*, and they all gathered around to watch everything in reverse. Milla and Rip were the most recent visitors, of course. There had been several more during the morning, plus one fairly busy stretch when there was actually a line three people deep waiting for Ellin's help.

Then there was a long stretch, before the office opened, when nothing happened. They watched daylight reverse into night, with only one light left burning in the office. Then, suddenly, there was a dark figure in Ellin's office.

"There!"

"Well, how about that," Jesus said, sitting up alertly. "How did that rascal get in? There's no sign of a break-in, everything was locked up tight as a drum when I got here this morning." He let the tape continue to rewind until it picked up the dark figure coming in the door, then he stopped it and played it forward.

Milla's heart skipped a beat, then another. Beside her, Rip said, "Son of a bitch!"

They watched the man, dressed head to foot in black, walk calmly around the office orienting himself. He came to Ellin's desk, saw her name plaque on it, and sat down in her chair. He began opening drawers, taking out files and going through them as casually as if he had all the time in the world, as if there wasn't a nerve in his body. Eventually he came to the correct file, and leafed through it one page at a time. When he reached a certain page, he paused and seemed to read it, then pulled it out of the file and laid it aside. He continued his systematic search of the desk, but pulled out no other papers. He even examined the undersides of the drawers.

"What in tarnation is he looking for?" Jesus said. No one answered.

Then the man extended his search to the rest of the office. Finally, evidently satisfied he'd found what he wanted, he went back to Ellin's desk and picked up the single page. He took the sheet over to a machine and fed it into it.

"That's the shredder!" Ellin said.

Then, thorough to the end, he lifted the shredder off the trash can and pulled out the shredded paper, stuffing it into a small plastic bag he'd pulled out of his pocket. He put the shredder back in place, restored Ellin's desk to order, then left as quietly as he'd entered.

Pain expanded in Milla's chest, smothering her. Rage followed, and she had to clench her fists to hold herself in.

The man was Diaz.

* * *

No wonder he'd had his phone turned off. No wonder he'd slipped out in the middle of the night. There wasn't any possibility he'd gotten the list to search for Justin himself, to do this for Milla, because he'd destroyed the paper. For whatever reason in his convoluted brain, he didn't want Milla to find her son.

Jesus wanted to call the sheriff, but Ellin said no, it was a personal paper she was missing and not anything she wanted to pursue. Milla pulled herself together and shoved everything she was feeling to the back burner. There were still things to do.

The small community bank closed for lunch from one until two, after everyone else's lunch hour, so people could do their banking then if needed. Promptly at two, Ellin was there with Milla and Rip to get into her safe-deposit box.

There it was, a single sheet of paper with three rows of single-spaced names. They returned to the car and looked over the list. Each name had a numerical code next to it. "Is that the birth certificate number?" Milla asked.

"No, that's the date, so I know exactly where to look. Only I wrote the date backward. See, December 13, 1992, is 29913121. Easy."

Milla told her the date Justin was stolen and that she'd found he was flown out of Mexico right away.

"Huh," said Ellin, running her finger down the list of dates. "That narrows it down, because there's only one Caucasian male name during the next week. The babies were moved fast, you know. The adoptions went through almost right away. Anyway, there are two Hispanic male names, and three females. That's gotta be your boy. The name I gave him was Michael Grady, 'Michael' because it's the most popular boy's name. That's the name he was adopted under, though of course the adoptive parents would rename him."

They returned to the courthouse basement, where Ellin looked through the microfiche files and came up with the birth certificate for Michael Grady. "There. The father is listed as unknown. I made up the mother's name, too."

"What about the mother's social security number?" Rip asked, staring at the microfiche screen.

"You think that's actually checked out? Especially in a private adoption, ten years ago? Things like that may be checked now, but as long as the mother's signed and notarized consent is provided, who's going to check if that's her correct social security number? Besides, the adoptive parents get the baby's social security number for him."

Hoping against hope, Milla asked, "Do you have any idea where the babies went? What attorney handled the private adoptions? Anything?" Without that information, she wasn't in a much better position than she'd been in before.

Ellin grinned. "Well, now. For that list to be much good, you gotta have some backup information, don't you? There's a lawyer here in town who handled the legal stuff on this end. He knew there were a lot of adoptions, but he didn't ask a lot of questions as long as he got paid, and he was told an adoption service was working with poor Hispanic families to ease their burden, plus you know Hispanics frown on their unmarried girls messing around. It's a real social no-no for them, so any Hispanic girl who got pregnant was likely to give up her baby. At least, that's what we told Harden. We'll go see him now; at the very least, he should have the name of the lawyers on the other end of the adoptions."

Two hours later, Rip drove them back to Roswell, because Milla was crying too hard to see. She was holding a copy of Justin's fake birth certificate, as well as a copy of everything Harden Sims had had in his file concerning that particular adoption. The attorney on the other end practiced in Charlotte, North Carolina.

As everyone had kept telling her, the adoption records were probably sealed, and she would have to get a court order to unseal them. But she'd get the information she needed from the attorney in North Carolina, even if she had to sue him to get it, and then she'd get that court order. Considering the circumstances and how well publicized her own case had been, she knew she'd win.

The future wasn't a fog of heartbreak now. She'd done it. A lot of legwork remained, but at the end of it she knew she'd find her son.

When they got to Roswell, they decided to drive straight through. It was a long drive, they wouldn't get home until late, but both of them wanted to get home.

"What are you going to do?" Rip asked soberly. He was talking about Diaz.

"I don't know." She couldn't let herself think about it too much, or she would break down. His betrayal sliced through her, so much more painful than the sense of betrayal she'd felt about Susanna. She had trusted Diaz more than she'd ever trusted anyone, trusted him with her life and her body and her heart. Why would he do such a thing, knowing how long and hard she'd searched for Justin? He might as well have stabbed her in the back himself. Looking back, she examined their times together, looking for some clue, but there was nothing. He'd either gone absolutely crazy during the last night they'd spent together, or he'd had a different agenda the entire time.

They were exhausted when they reached El Paso. It was after midnight, and they'd had an early start that morning and been on the go for over eighteen hours. She had taken over the driving at Carlsbad, so she dropped Rip off at his hotel and drove home, taking extra care because she was so tired.

When she opened her garage door and drove inside, she almost didn't notice the pickup truck parked in the other bay of the double garage. Slowly she slid out of her seat, staring at it. The bastard had his nerve, after what he'd done. She hadn't wanted to have this scene now, while she was almost punch-drunk with fatigue, but she wanted him out of her house and out of her life.

She let herself in through the garage and went into the kitchen, dropping her purse and the file on the table. A light was on in the living room, and then he was there, leaning against the door frame and watching her.

She didn't look at him. She couldn't. A tremor ran through her every muscle and she leaned against the table.

"Susanna rolled," he finally said. "She's been arrested. True, too. Just a few hours ago."

"Good," she said briefly, noting that there wasn't a word of explanation about where he'd been, why he'd left in the middle of the night, or any questions about what she'd been doing for the past two days. Finally she looked at him, her fury and hatred clear in her eyes. "Get out."

He straightened from the door frame. His expression had been faintly quizzical, but now it shut down, in an instant as blank and remote as she'd ever seen it.

"You didn't check closely enough," she said. "There was a security camera. Caught you in the act."

He was silent for a moment, watching her, letting the time tick by. Then he said softly, "It was the best thing to do. It's time to let him go. It's been ten years. He isn't your kid now, Milla, he's someone else's. It would have wrecked his life if you'd shown up."

"Don't *talk* to me!" she said fiercely. He didn't understand;

he had no idea about her or how she felt. *"You ... had ... no ... right!* He's my child, you bastard!" She screamed it at him, then caught herself and knotted her hands into fists.

"Not now, he isn't." He stood there like judge and jury combined, untouched by human emotion, and she wanted to kill him.

Tears began running down her face, tears of rage and hurt and from the superhuman effort it took to keep from attacking him. "It didn't work. She had copies." She swiped at the tears on her cheeks. "I've got all the information I need now to find him, and that's exactly what I'm going to do. Now get out of my house. I never want to see you again."

Because he was Diaz, he didn't stand there arguing his side. He didn't even shrug, as if to say, *If that's what you want.* He simply walked past her and left. She heard the garage door open; then his truck started, and he was gone. Just like that.

She sat down at the table, laid her head on her crossed arms, and sobbed like a child.

25

He looked like David.

Milla kept the field glasses trained on him as he darted around the fenced schoolyard with an excess of energy that seemed to be shared by most of the boys his age. He seemed to have three or four particular buddies, and they shoved one another, laughed uproariously at one another's jokes, and generally postured and strutted all the while they pretended they were cool. Maybe, to other ten-year-olds, they *were* cool.

Her heart was right in her throat, pounding so hard she could barely breathe. Her eyes kept stinging with tears and she kept blinking them back, because she couldn't bear to miss a single second of watching him. She picked up the expensive camera from the seat beside her, and focused the zoom lens on him, then snapped several shots in rapid succession.

She had parked far enough away from the private school that no one would notice her. She didn't want to alarm anyone, least of all Justin. But she'd had to see him, had to watch him just a little longer to feed these memories into her starving heart. This morning she had parked down the street from the Winborns' house and noted what he wore when he skipped and hopped down the steps to meet the bus that took him to school. Rhonda Winborn had stood at the front door and watched until he was safely on the bus, and he'd given her a cursory wave. He'd been wearing the khaki pants and blue shirt that was the school uniform, and a bright red windbreaker. The windbreaker, which he wore now as protection against the chill breeze, helped her pick him out from the other boys.

She had sobbed aloud this morning when she'd watched him get on the bus, watched him wave to another woman. Everything about him was so familiar, from the color of his hair to the shape of his head, even the way he walked. His face was still a child's face, but it was taking on the stronger lines of approaching adolescence even now. His hair was blond, his eyes were blue, and his grin was pure David.

Milla was so shaken and ecstatic that she wanted to get out of the rental car and throw her head back on the loudest, longest yell she could muster. She wanted to run up to the fence and scream his name, though of course everyone would think she was crazy and the school authorities would immediately call the cops. She wanted to dance, she wanted to laugh, she wanted to cry. There were so many emotions storming inside her that she didn't know what to do. She wanted to stop strangers and point to him and say, "That's my son!"

She'd never been able to do that, claim him in public, and she couldn't do it now. Protecting him was the most important thing in the world to her, and she wouldn't mess this up by scaring him, by breaking the news to him in the worst possible way.

The past week had been a nonstop roller coaster of emotions. Events had happened so fast that she could barely react to one before another was upon her. Once she'd found the information Diaz had tried to destroy, she'd been able to follow the trail that led straight to Justin.

Rhonda and Lee Winborn were both blond, and they had wanted a blond child, preferably a boy, to adopt. They were desperate for children, having lost three to miscarriages and a fourth had died only a few hours after birth. They weren't rich people who went out to buy a child much as they would buy a car; they had all but beggared themselves to come up with the amount of money True had charged, and both their families had chipped in to make up the difference. Since then Lee had done very well in business; four years ago they had moved to this upper-middle-class neighborhood in Charlotte, and they could afford to send Justin to private school, but from everything Milla had been able to find out they were nice, likable, solid people who adored their son and were doing their best to raise him to be a decent human being.

They couldn't have had any idea he'd been stolen from her arms. They'd been told that his mother wasn't able to support him, and she needed so much money because she had other children to support, one of whom needed corrective eye surgery. The violin strings had been singing when that tale was told, but they'd had no reason to disbelieve it. The lawyer who'd handled the private adoption hadn't known, so there was no way the Winborns could have known. All they knew was that they finally had their son.

Not their son. *Her* son. Her heart whispered it, insisted on it. *Hers.*

If there was anything of her in him, she thought as she watched him, it was perhaps his nose and jawline. Everything else about him resembled David.

Joy bubbled in her veins. He was alive, he was well, he was loved. Her baby was all right.

The Winborns had named him Zachary Tanner, for each grandfather. They called him Zack. He was Justin to her; that was the name that had been in her desperate prayers all these years, the name engraved on heart and mind and memory.

She had to tell David. Until she actually saw him and knew for certain it was Justin, she hadn't wanted to get his hopes up. She could have been wrong; it could have been another child. Even after seeing the paperwork and knowing with her brain that this child was Justin, she had still needed to see him with her eyes before she could let herself believe.

It was Justin. And he looked like David.

Milla dropped the field glasses and buried her head in her hands, her shoulders shaking with sobs. Laughter kept mixing with the sobs, until even she didn't know if she was laughing or crying. She sat there until play period was over and the teachers herded the boisterous youngsters back into the neat, yellow-brick building. She watched him go inside, the November sun glistening on his blond hair; he jumped the last step and was laughing as he went through the double doors and disappeared from her sight.

When she could, when she'd stopped shaking enough to hold the cell phone, when her throat wasn't so clogged with tears that she couldn't speak, she called David's office and made an appointment to see him the next day. If she'd been a patient, she never would have seen him that soon, but he'd always told her he would see her any time, any day, and evidently he had instructed his office staff to accommodate her, because as soon as she told the receptionist her name, the woman had given her a noon appointment. She would be intruding on David's lunch hour, but she didn't think he would mind.

This wasn't something she wanted to tell him over the phone. She wanted to see his face, wanted to share this with him as they had shared Justin's birth. She could have called his home, gone there rather than his office, but she was selfish enough to want this just between herself and David, rather than sharing it with Jenna and his two other children. For this one time only, this one last time, she wanted just the two of them.

She had the legal papers in her briefcase. She'd had them drawn up before she even came here, because she wanted to have everything ready.

Taking a deep breath, she drove to the Charlotte airport and turned in her rental car, then caught a flight to Chicago.

David's office was in a professional building adjacent to the hospital where he practiced. The decorations were tasteful and fairly shouted "money." The surgical group he was in featured all heavy hitters, and David was one of their stars. He was young, he was handsome, he was brilliant. At just thirty-eight, he had many years left in which to shine.

Evidently he'd had his secretary clear his appointment calendar when he was told she'd called, because the waiting room was empty. Milla closed the door to the hallway and started across the taupe carpet to the receptionist's desk, where a middle-aged blonde and a perky brunette wearing a nurse's uniform were avidly watching her. Before she reached them, however, the door to the left opened and David stood there, tall and better-looking now than he had been when he was in his twenties. Age sat well on most men, and David was no exception. His face was stronger, with a few lines at the corners of his eyes, and his shoulders seemed a little heavier.

"Milla," he said, extending his hand toward her and smiling the great smile that just yesterday she'd seen on their son's face, the one that lit him up like a Christmas tree. His blue eyes were warm. "You look great. Come on into my office."

He held the door for her and she stepped into the interior hallway, which was lined with examination and treatment rooms. Three different women, of diverse race and age, looked up from various tasks and watched as she walked by. The two in the reception area also poked their heads out.

"Don't look now," she said to David out of the side of her mouth, "but your harem is curious."

He laughed as he ushered her into his private office and closed the door. "That's what Jenna calls them, too. I call 'em my bodyguards. I feel very safe when they're around."

"They keep the wild women away from you, huh?"

He grinned. "They won't even let me do surgery on one. They send the wild ones to my partners. I get the old farts and battleaxes."

Her heart lightened to see him so basically unchanged. She could understand his office staff being protective of him; David was one of the good guys. She knew beyond a shadow of doubt that he was completely faithful to his wife, that no flirtatious nurse or patient had a chance with him, because she knew *him*. He threw himself heart and soul into his work and into his family. Whatever wonderful happened in his life, he deserved it.

There was a small grouping of photographs on his desk. Knowing what she'd see, she walked around to look at them. One was of a pretty redhead with an infectious grin, who had to be Jenna because there was another candid photo of the same woman and David with their arms around each other, hamming it up for the camera. There was a small heart-shaped frame that contained a photo of a plump toddler with smooth, shiny hair, holding a doll by its hair and looking like a little doll herself in a long lace dress. Another shot was of Jenna holding a baby and looking radiant, and Milla assumed that was their newest addition. "They're gorgeous," she said honestly, and she smiled because she was happy for him. "What are their names?"

"The little princess is Cameron Rose, called Cammy, and

the baby is William Gage. We plan to call him Liam, but he hasn't quite grown into the name yet. For some reason, Cammy calls him Dot."

Milla snorted with laughter; then, while she was still smiling, she couldn't hold it in any longer and said, "I found him. I found Justin."

David's legs visibly wobbled, and he sat down hard in one of his visitors chairs. He stared at her, pale with shock and unable to say anything. Slowly, tears welled in his eyes and trickled down his cheeks. His lips trembled and he finally choked out, "You're sure?"

Milla bit her lower lip, fighting her own tears, and nodded. "We broke the smuggling ring. The woman who falsified the birth certificates kept detailed records, I suppose for either protection or blackmail."

"Is he–" He gulped and fought back a sob, but his voice was thin and shaky as he asked the parent's universal question: "Is he okay?"

Milla nodded again; then David lunged toward her and somehow they were clinging to each other as they both wept, his body heaving with sobs. She tried to comfort him, patting his shoulder, his hair, saying, "It's okay. He's fine. He's safe," but she was crying, too, so she didn't know how much he understood of what she was trying to say. Then he did what she'd done, and burst into uncontrolled laughter. He alternated between laughter and sobs, swinging her around, releasing her to wipe his face, then grabbing her again.

"I can't believe it," he kept saying. "My God. All these years . . ."

Finally Milla pulled herself away from him. "I have pictures," she said, fumbling with her briefcase in her eagerness to show him. "I took them yesterday."

She pulled out the snapshots she'd taken, and handed them

to David. He looked at the first one and froze, his expression that of a starving man as he stared at his son. His hands were trembling as he looked at each photograph in turn, then went through them again. Delight began breaking through, like the sun on a stormy day. "He looks like me," he said triumphantly.

She burst out laughing at such blatant maleness. "Dummy, he's *always* looked like you, from the day he was born. Don't you remember what Susanna–" She broke off abruptly, remembering that he didn't know about Susanna.

He was still staring at the pictures. "She said I'd cloned myself."

"She was in on it," Milla blurted.

David looked up, shocked. "What?"

"She's the one who told the smugglers about Justin, and that I went to the market several days a week. They were waiting for me. They had an order for a blond baby boy."

"But . . . *why*?" His voice was full of bewilderment that a woman he had considered a friend would do such a thing.

"Money," Milla said bitterly. "It was all about money."

His right hand tightened into a fist. "The fucking bitch. There was a reward! I'd have given her everything I had to get him back!"

"The reward didn't come near matching what they'd charged the adoptive parents for him."

"He was *sold*? What kind of people would buy a baby they knew was–"

"They didn't know," Milla said quickly. "Don't blame them. They were totally in the dark."

"How do you know?"

"Because the lawyer who brokered the deal didn't know. It was a slick operation, with falsified birth certificates and legal documents from the fake mothers. The people who adopted the babies all thought it was legal."

"Where is he?" David asked. "Who adopted him?"

"Their names are Lee and Rhonda Winborn. They live in Charlotte, North Carolina. I've checked them out, and they're good people. Honest, upstanding. They named him Zachary."

"His name is Justin," David said fiercely. Still clutching the pictures, he sat down at his desk and looked at them again, examining every detail of Justin's face. "I didn't believe you'd ever find him," he said absently, as if to himself. "I thought you were breaking your heart in a worthless cause."

"I couldn't stop." The words were simple, the truth behind them fathoms deep.

"I know." He looked up at her, studying her face as intently as he'd studied the pictures. "I didn't know you, afterward," he murmured. "I was devastated, but the basic *me* didn't change. You . . . you turned into . . ." He paused as if searching for the right word. "An Amazon. I couldn't keep up with you, couldn't even touch you. You were so fierce, so determined, that you left me in the dust."

"I didn't mean to," she said, and sighed. "But I couldn't see anything else, couldn't listen to anything else. I knew he was out there, and I had to find him."

"I wish I'd had that conviction. I envied you your focus, your belief that he was still alive. I couldn't believe it. I've had him dead and buried for years, and I thought I'd handled it, b-but now I know he's alive and I feel like such a shit because I gave up on him." He buried his face in his hands.

"No, don't." Moving swiftly to him, Milla put her arm around his shoulder. "My biggest fear was that he was dead, and I couldn't stop looking for him because I had to know for certain. There was nothing you could have done that you didn't do—"

"I could have looked for him! I could have been beside you, helping you."

"Don't be silly, of course you couldn't. David, how many people would have died if you had stopped performing surgery?"

He considered that. "Maybe none. There are a lot of good surgeons in this town." Then his natural surgeon's ego kicked in. "Okay, maybe twenty or so. Or thirty."

She smiled. "There's your answer, Doogie. You did what you had to do. I did what I had to do. There's no right, no wrong, no woulda coulda shoulda. So get off the pity train, and let's talk about the future."

Five minutes later, after she'd explained what she wanted, what they had to do, his face was once again white with shock.

26

THE TIME WITH DAVID WAS WRENCHING BUT NECESSARY.
When she walked out of his office, Milla knew she would
probably never see him again, so she told him good-bye, kissed
his cheek, and wished him a wonderful life. "You can stop with
the alimony payments, too," she'd said, smiling at him through
her tears. "There's your reason for practicing medicine: you
funded the search. I couldn't have done it without you in the
background, supporting me and making sure I had the financial freedom to look for him."

"But what will you do now?" he asked, looking troubled.

"The same thing, I guess. Look for lost kids. I'll have to
draw some kind of salary, though." The truth was, she had no
idea what she was going to do. For so long her life had re-
volved around one thing, finding Justin, and now that she had,
she felt as if she had hit a wall that she couldn't see over. She
was exhausted in every way, mentally, physically, and emotionally. She thought of going back to El Paso and felt nothing
but blankness. So much had happened there, maybe too much.

After she went back to North Carolina and handled matters there, then she would sleep for maybe a couple of days, and when she woke up she would feel better. Then she'd be able to think about the future. She was good at finding the lost ones. How could she stop now, just because she'd found *her* lost one?

David caught her as she started out the door, and fiercely hugged her to him as if he, too, knew that the last tie binding them had been severed. "Now you can move on, too," he said.

Move on to where? she wanted to ask. Maybe one day she would know. For now, all she could focus on was what she had to do next.

She had booked a return flight to Charlotte late that afternoon, and by the time the flight landed she wanted nothing more than to check into her hotel, crawl into bed, and not move for at least twelve hours. Instead she ordered room service and unpacked while she was waiting for her sandwich to be delivered. She even had time to iron the outfit she planned to wear tomorrow.

After she ate, she put the room service tray outside the door and paced around the limited space, getting her thoughts in order. Finally, cell phone in hand, she looked up the Winborns' number in the local telephone book and dialed it.

A woman's pleasant voice answered on the fourth ring, with the particular *ooo* sound to her *o*'s that Milla already recognized as Carolinian. "Hello?"

"Mrs. Winborn?"

"Yes, it is."

"My name is Milla Edge. I'm the founder of an organization called Finders, which helps locate lost or kidnapped children."

"Yes, of course," Rhonda said kindly. "That's such a worthy cause; I'll be glad to donate—"

"No, this isn't a telemarketing call," Milla quickly interrupted. "It concerns your adopted son."

There was utter silence on the other end. She couldn't even hear Rhonda breathing.

"What do you mean?" Rhonda finally choked. "How can it concern–He's *adopted*," she said in a fierce whisper. "We went through a lawyer to make certain everything was legal. Don't you dare–"

"It's a complicated matter," Milla said, and hurried to reassure her. "There's some paperwork that needs to be done. Could I make an appointment to meet with both you and your husband tomorrow? I promise it won't take long."

"What kind of paperwork?"

"Legal," Milla said, unwilling to go into more detail on the phone. She didn't want to spook the Winborns into grabbing Justin and disappearing in the middle of the night. She knew that's what *she* would do, rather than risk her son. "It's just some signatures. No one is questioning the adoption."

"Then why–How is Finders involved?"

"That's complicated, too. I'll explain all of it tomorrow. What time would be convenient?"

"Just a minute." Rhonda's voice was faint; there was a clatter as she laid down the receiver, and Milla closed her eyes as she pictured Rhonda whispering to Lee where Justin–Zack–couldn't hear her. Lee would pick up on his wife's panic, alarmed that something seemed to be threatening his son, and he would hurry to the phone–

"This is Lee Winborn. What can I do for you?"

"I'm afraid I've frightened your wife," Milla said apologetically, "and I didn't mean to. It's important that I meet with the both of you to explain something about your son's adoption, and give you some legal papers."

"You can explain over the phone–"

"No, I'm sorry, I can't. It's complicated, as I told Mrs. Winborn. You'll understand much more when you read the papers. Is there a convenient time tomorrow? While your son is in school would be best." She softened her voice. "Please. It's nothing threatening."

"All right," he said abruptly. "One o'clock. Do you need our address?"

"No, I have it. Thank you for seeing me. I'll be there at one sharp." She clicked off the phone and closed her eyes, and realized she was shaking in every muscle. She'd done it. Now all she had to do was hold together through the next step. Since she had been able to get an appointment so early, she called the airlines and managed to get on a six o'clock flight out of Charlotte. Tomorrow night, she thought as she went to bed, she would be back in her own home for the first time since . . . she couldn't remember, exactly. Longer than a week, she thought.

The next day she slept as late as possible, ate a late breakfast, watched some morning talk shows, showered and washed her hair and took extra care styling it, as well as with her makeup, keeping the effect subtle. It was vain of her, but she wanted to make a good impression.

She dressed carefully, in a trim navy skirt and a fitted, long-sleeved blouse in seafoam green, with matching navy buttons. The outfit was both feminine and professional. It was an old trick; the more nervous she was, the more attention she paid to how she looked. By concentrating on her clothes, she could ignore the screaming of her nerves, the nausea that knotted her stomach, the tension that pounded in her temples. She had learned how to remain calm in the face of unspeakable pain, and she did so now, at least on the surface—and that was all that mattered, anyway. The mirror reflected back a face that was almost expressionless, like Diaz—No, don't think about him, she thought fiercely. He was out of her life.

The Weather Channel said Charlotte's high temperature today would be sixty-three, but with a brisk north breeze, so she laid her camel coat aside as she packed. She did the video checkout on the television, and then it was time. Twelve-fifteen. She took a deep breath, made certain her lipstick was even, left the room key on the bedside table with a tip for the maid, then checked once more that all the necessary papers were in her briefcase. Satisfied that she hadn't left anything undone, she squared her shoulders, balanced her coat and briefcase on top of the suitcase, slung her purse on her shoulder, and opened the door. And stopped dead, all her momentum lost.

Diaz leaned against the wall beside her door.

So many thoughts and emotions stormed through her that she could scarcely focus on any of them. Shock was uppermost; she'd thought, hoped, that she would never see him again. And, somehow, she'd forgotten all over again how powerful his physical impact was, what it was to have those cold, dark eyes leveled on you.

They hadn't been cold when she was lying naked beneath him, whispered the animal in her, and she wrenched her thoughts from that dark pathway.

My God, why hadn't someone called hotel security? Men didn't just lurk outside hotel rooms for God only knows how long without *someone* noticing. Even if another guest hadn't been suspicious, the hotel maids definitely should have been. She glanced wildly up and down the long corridor; a housekeeping cart was parked about a third of the way down the hall to the right. With just the one maid on the floor, perhaps he'd been able to avoid detection. Or perhaps he'd had a quiet word with her and scared the hell out of her, and she was hiding in that room waiting for him to leave.

"What are *you* doing here?" she asked, her tone cool and hostile, not at all like the tumult going on inside her.

He straightened and shrugged. "Curiosity. Like rubber-necking at a car wreck."

"How did you know where to find me?"

"That's what I do."

And that was explanation enough, she supposed. He'd known where Justin was, and that gave him a start. Even though Charlotte was a city of half a million people, he'd found her—probably with a few phone calls. The hotel wasn't supposed to give out room numbers, either, but he'd been waiting outside her door. How did he know where she was going? And how did he know she was going today? She burned to know the answers, but she would bite off her own tongue before she asked him. She didn't want to talk to him at all.

She pulled the hotel door shut and walked down the carpeted hallway to the elevator, pulling her suitcase behind her. Diaz fell into step beside her, as she had known he would. She didn't waste time trying to talk him out of going. She couldn't evade him, couldn't convince him to butt out; all she could do was ignore him, so she did—as much as one could ignore a wolf.

Details of his appearance registered with her. He had shaved, and he wore a decent suit in a dark blue-gray; his hair actually looked brushed, instead of looking as if he'd run his fingers through it and left it at that. Some people might think he looked respectable. She knew better, knew that the cold, enigmatic dark eyes in no way reflected the streak of violence that ran just beneath his surface. He probably had a knife strapped to his leg, a pistol holstered in the small of his back, and God only knows what other weapons hidden on his body.

But why *was* he here? This didn't concern him. They had parted on bitter terms, and he was the last person Milla wanted with her during the wrenching hour she faced. She was still so *furious* she could barely tolerate being this close to him. She felt the rage bubbling up all over again, tightening her throat. How *dare* he–?

She stopped the thought before it could completely form. Going over and over things wasn't going to change what he'd done, wasn't going to make her change her mind. Oh, she could try explaining things to him, but what would that accomplish? He had totally misjudged her, he was wrong, and even if he apologized she doubted she could ever forgive him. He knew–*knew*–how important Justin was to her, knew the hell she'd gone through searching for him, and still he'd kept her son's location secret from her. How could she ever forgive him?

It enraged her even more that Diaz was still convinced she was in the wrong. She wanted to slap him so hard his teeth rattled. Instead she ignored him.

"Do you need to check out?" he asked.

"No." If she had to talk to him at all, it would be as briefly as possible.

They left the hotel by the front door, and she started to give her car receipt to the parking attendant, but Diaz said, "Leave it here. I'll drive."

"I don't want to ride with you."

"You can do it the easy way, or the hard way. Up to you."

She didn't even glance at him, just continued walking beside him as he led the way to a dark blue Jeep Liberty. The easy way was hard enough; she didn't want to contemplate what the hard way would do to her. The north wind the weather forecaster had talked about bit through her clothes, and she wished she'd put her coat on before coming outside; she concentrated on how chilled she was, anything rather than think about him or what she was facing.

He put her suitcase in the back with his battered duffel, then opened the passenger door and put her inside. The sun had warmed the interior of the Jeep, and once she was out of the wind she was comfortable. She preferred being chilled, preferred being anywhere else, with anyone else. She prayed for strength, for control, for help in doing this right. She had to put Diaz out of her mind and concentrate on Justin, or she'd never be able to do this.

"Do you know where they live?" she asked distantly as he got behind the wheel and started the motor, then put the vehicle in gear and pulled out of his parking slot.

"Yes. I drove by there yesterday."

So he'd been a day behind her. She was surprised he hadn't been closer, that he hadn't shown up at her hotel in Chicago. But unless he was here to prevent her from talking to the Winborns, why bother? She went rigid as it occurred to her she was now locked in a vehicle with him, helpless to do anything but go where he took her. Stupid!

She whipped around as far as her seat belt would allow, her gaze lethal. "If you take me anywhere but to the Winborn house, I swear I'll—"

"That's where I'm taking you," he said grimly. "Though it's a little late for you to think of that, if I'd decided otherwise."

"So I'm not as good at being dirty and underhanded as you are," she snapped, and turned back to face the windshield. She paid close attention to the turns he took, making certain she didn't look up and find herself on a highway heading out of Charlotte. If he took one wrong turn, she would scream, she'd hit him, she'd pull on the steering wheel—anything to attract attention.

Though if he really intended to kidnap her, she realized,

none of that would stop him. He'd just knock her out and do as he'd intended. But what use would that be, unless he intended to keep her locked up somewhere for the rest of her life? She was never going to change her mind about seeing the Winborns. She had set her course, and she would keep to it.

The rest of the drive was made in silence. At twelve fifty-seven he pulled the Jeep into the Winborns' short concrete driveway. Rhonda's champagne Infiniti SUV was in the right bay, Lee's more serviceable extended-cab Ford pickup in the left. Milla's heartbeat suddenly doubled, leaving her feeling weak and light-headed. Don't let me faint, she silently begged. Please don't let me faint. She took slow, deep breaths, forcing her heart rate to calm.

Diaz got out and came around to open the door for her. His dark eyes narrowed as he surveyed her, but he didn't say anything, just took her arm and all but levered her out of the seat. If it hadn't been for him, she didn't know if she'd have had the strength. She grabbed the briefcase but left her purse on the floorboard. Diaz noticed, of course, and locked the doors behind them.

The small front yard was immaculately kept, with thick grass that had turned brown, and pots of bright red chrysanthemums. More potted plants were on the steps leading up to the sheltered front entry; someone, probably Rhonda, had a green thumb. Milla found she liked the picture of Rhonda humming as she carefully repotted plants, or trimming away the dead leaves and branches.

Before she could reach out to ring the doorbell, the door opened, and both of them stood there looking almost haggard with worry. Pity squeezed Milla's heart. She had tried to reassure them, but maybe she had handled this all wrong. If she had, it was too late now to change. Lee reached out and opened the glass storm door.

She managed, if not quite a smile, at least a friendly expression. "Hello, I'm Milla Edge. We spoke on the phone last night. This is James Diaz."

"I'm Lee Winborn, and this is my wife, Rhonda," Lee said, automatically reaching out to shake her hand, then Diaz's. Lee's hands were strong and slightly rough; he liked playing golf, fishing, occasionally hunting. He had coached Justin–*Zack's*–T-ball team, and helped coach his PeeWee football team. He was forty-four, eleven years older than Milla, a vital man with a few sun wrinkles at the corners of his blue eyes and no visible gray in his dark blond hair.

Rhonda was average height, her pale blond hair cut in a chic style, her makeup tasteful. She was slim, dressed in tailored trousers and a pretty French blue sweater that reflected color into her gray eyes. With their coloring, Milla thought, no one would suspect Justin wasn't their natural son unless they told. *Zack.* She had to remember his name was now Zack.

"Come in," Lee said, his voice nervous. He and his wife stepped back, and he gestured Milla and Diaz inside. Rhonda reached out and took his hand, lacing her fingers with his as if she needed his strength.

They went into the living room, which had the comfortable, lived-in feeling that meant they actually used it. There was a cozy fire going in the gas-log fireplace. There were shelves that held a number of books, children's mixed in with adult fiction, as well as the small mementos a family collected over the years: a starfish, a signed baseball in a Plexiglas box, photos and boxes and–

Photos. Milla looked around, and held a moan inside. Pictures of Justin as a fat baby, with one tiny white tooth gleaming as he laughed, his blond hair sticking straight up like a dandelion. She saw his chubby little feet, the fat dimpled hands, the rosy cheeks. There was one of him crawling, wearing nothing but a diaper. Another of him as an adorable toddler, holding a plastic baseball bat like a club; at the beach, with his little shovel and pail, wearing a small red baseball cap. A birthday party. What had to be his first day of school, beaming proudly as he clutched his little backpack. Missing his two front teeth, and wearing such a wide, mischievous grin that she almost whimpered. Her baby, and she had missed all of this. There he was in his T-ball uniform, looking fierce now as he held his bat the way he'd seen the big boys do. Another picture showed him in his football uniform, with his helmet threatening to completely obscure his face. He was so little, and so vital, so happy.

There were his school pictures, and other studio photographs that were more posed. Another was of him at perhaps one year, clutching a teddy bear that showed signs of severe wear. Sitting on a little John Deere tractor, gripping the steering wheel hard and pretending he was driving. She could just hear him making motor sounds.

"That's Zack," Rhonda said nervously, noticing how Milla was staring at all the photographs. "I know we went overboard taking pictures of him, but–" She broke off and bit her lip.

"Please, let's sit down," Lee said, indicating Milla and Diaz should take the two occasional chairs, while he and Rhonda sat side by side on the couch. "Tell us what this is all about. I don't mind telling you neither of us slept a wink last night, worrying that something has gone wrong. We can't think what, but–well, we're worried."

Milla set the briefcase down by her feet and took a deep breath, clasping her hands together. She had tried practicing what she would say, but the words never seemed right, so she fell back on the story she had told so many times, to so many audiences. But this time, she had an ending to the story.

"My ex-husband is a surgeon," she said, "a real Doogie Howser." She managed a tiny smile, thinking of David. "Eleven years ago, he and some other doctors took a sabbatical to work at a small rural clinic in Mexico. I had just learned I was pregnant when we went, but the team included an obstetrician I trusted, so we kept to our original plan and our son, Justin, was born in Mexico. I was at the village market one day when he was six weeks old, and two men grabbed him from me and ran. I had been stabbed in the back and nearly bled to death; by the time I recovered, there was no trace of our baby."

Rhonda reached out and grabbed Lee's hand again. "That's awful," she said, looking sick. Perhaps she was identifying with Milla as a mother, or perhaps she had a premonition.

"I looked for him anyway. I couldn't give up, when I didn't know what had happened to him. So many stolen babies are smuggled out of Mexico in car trunks, in the heat of the day, and a lot of them die. I couldn't stop looking until I knew for certain what happened to Justin, if he died, if . . ." She stopped and swallowed.

"My husband and I divorced a year after Justin was stolen. A lot of marriages break up after a child dies or is lost. The divorce was mostly my fault—no, *all* my fault, because I wasn't interested in being David's wife. I was too busy searching for Justin. Along the way I founded an organization of mostly volunteers, all over the country, who mobilize to help search whenever someone gets lost, or drive the highways during an Amber Alert. We look for runaways that the police don't have the money or the manpower to devote to the case. We—" She was going into her regular speech, she realized. She took another deep breath.

"Enough about that. The short of it is, all of this time I kept looking for Justin, for clues to who had taken him, what had happened to him. Just recently, with Mr. Diaz's help, the smuggling ring was broken and we found paperwork that allowed us to trace the stolen children."

This was it. Now. Her throat clogged and her hands clenched together so hard they were bloodless. "Zack is my son, Justin."

Rhonda fell back with a cry, her face paper white. Lee surged to his feet, his hands knotted into fists. "That's a lie," he said violently. "We didn't buy a black market baby; we adopted Zack through an attorney, and if you think you're going to take our son from us you're in for the fight of your life."

She'd already had the fight of her life, she thought. And it had lasted for ten long years. "Your attorney didn't know. The birth certificates were forged. The woman who forged them is the one who kept the records. I don't expect you to take my word for it; I brought copies of everything." She leaned down and picked up the briefcase, opened it, and handed a sheaf of papers across to them. Lee took the papers and rapidly thumbed through them. A rough sound of denial rumbled in his throat.

Her hands trembling, Milla drew out two more documents. "These are the papers where David and I both relinquish our parental rights to Justin—Zack—to you."

Rhonda and Lee both froze, staring at the papers in her hand as if they couldn't believe what she'd just said. Milla tamped down on the agony rising in her throat, fought for control. Just a little while longer. . . .

"There are no conditions. To take him from you would be devastating to him, and we l-love him too much to do that. What you tell him about us, if you tell him, is totally up to you. You've raised him, you love him, you know him better than anyone else on earth. Does . . . does he know he's adopted?"

Mutely Rhonda nodded. Lee said, "But he's never asked any questions."

He was happy, healthy, well adjusted, and secure in his parents' love for him. He felt no need for anything else, Milla thought. One day he might ask, but only out of curiosity.

She took a thick manila envelope from the briefcase and also handed it over. "This is personal information about David and me, our medical histories, blood types, anything you might need if there's some medical emergency with Zack. There are phone numbers, addresses, and if either of us moves or changes numbers we'll send the information to you. Our parents' addresses are also included. There are some pictures, if . . . if he's ever interested, and you decide to tell him. Newspaper clippings about what happened. I don't want him to ever think we didn't want him." She dragged in oxygen. "His father has a genius IQ, and is one of the best men I've ever met. He's blond and blue-eyed; Zack favors him. We're both healthy, no genetic problems that we know about."

Dear God, how much longer could she hold out? Rhonda had both fists pressed to her mouth, and tears ran down her cheeks as she stared at Milla. Lee was audibly gulping as he fought for composure. Diaz, beside her, was a still, dark presence. She hadn't looked at him, hadn't glanced once at him.

Raggedly she continued, "I hope, one day, he'll want to know about us, meet us. But if he doesn't, don't feel you have to look over your shoulder. We'll never contact you except for updates on necessary information, if needed. You're his parents. If you decide never to tell him about us, we'll accept that." That was it. She couldn't go on any longer. She surged to her feet and held out her hand. "Thank you for loving him."

Lee took it, his chin trembling, and wordlessly folded his

other hand over hers. Diaz stood, too, bending down to close the briefcase and lift it.

Rhonda jumped up. She was sobbing so hard she could barely speak. "Wait–you were looking . . . Would you like some of his pictures? To take with you?"

27

SOMEHOW MILLA SAID GOOD-BYE TO THEM, SHOOK HANDS, made it out to the Jeep clutching one of the photographs; others were in the briefcase that Diaz carried. She sat frozen as he drove her away from her son's life, her gaze fixed straight ahead, her face as still as a statue's. She'd done it. Somehow, she had managed to hold together. She had given her son away, and she felt as if there were a great gaping wound inside her from which her life's blood was pumping. Pain was already gnawing away at her control, as great a beast as it had been when Justin was first taken from her; the quality of the pain was different, more poignant—and more bitter, because she'd been forced to this point as the years had crept inexorably past—but the beast itself was the same.

There was no hope left. She couldn't turn back the years and have Justin back as a baby, couldn't fill her walls with pictures of him as he grew. He was someone else's child now, and she had to live the rest of her life without him.

In a remote, almost casual tone, Diaz said, "Nothing much impresses me, but that was the bravest thing I've ever seen."

She felt rage building inside her, like steam forming in a kettle as water heated. Helpless to stop it, she felt it build and build and build, rising up, choking her; her vision blurred with red haze and she heard an animal sound coming from her throat. Then the rage burst free, and despite the seat belt holding her in, she launched herself across the console at him, screaming and punching him, slapping any part of him she could reach. "Shut up! You bastard, you tried to keep me from finding him! I could *kill* you, I hate you—"

He jerked the steering wheel to the right, pulling them out of traffic and to the side of the street while he fended her off with his right arm. His features were blurred by her fury and tears, but she could see enough to tell that his expression hadn't changed, that he was still so damned *untouched*—

He put the gear in park, then just sat while she pounded on him. The sounds coming from her had deteriorated into wordless screaming, the raw, wounded sound of unbearable pain that started from deep inside and tore its way out of her throat. She wanted to destroy something, she wanted someone else, anyone else to feel just a portion of what she was feeling. She felt as if she would burst from the force of it, as if her heart would give out under the immense pressure.

Then she collapsed forward on herself, sobbing so hard she couldn't draw a breath. She hadn't known she could cry like this, not even in the early, desperate days. She'd had a goal then, a cause. Now she had nothing. Her voice broke and she choked, began coughing convulsively. Diaz seized her shoulders and hauled her upright, propped her against the door. Distantly she heard him say "Drink this," and he put a bottle of water to her lips. She managed to swallow a sip, though she was vaguely surprised at how difficult swallowing was with her throat so raw and swollen.

The storm passed as abruptly as it had come on, and she slumped in exhaustion, her eyes closing. She heard Diaz on the phone, talking quietly, but she was too numb to listen. She wanted to go to ground somewhere and die, because there was no way she could live with this pain.

She didn't die. Instead she sank into a stupor, so emotionally drained that she was unaware of anything except being on the move again, Diaz driving in silence. She thought they stopped once, maybe twice, but she wasn't certain. She slept, starting awake occasionally to stare out the windshield in total blankness, not knowing where they were now or where they were going, not caring, not even fully comprehending.

Darkness fell, and the headlights of oncoming traffic hypnotized her to sleep again. She roused when he stopped the Jeep and got out, watching dully as a man got out of the car parked beside them and handed something to Diaz, then gave a tiny salute and got back into his car and left.

Diaz came around to the passenger side and opened the door. "Come on."

Milla got out, moving slowly, like a very old woman. They were parked at what looked like the tiny back porch of a small clapboard house. A cold wind whipped at her legs, went through her clothes. The ground beneath her feet was fine and gritty, and there was a strange roaring sound in her ears.

She had no idea where they were. She said, "I have a six o'clock flight," and was surprised at how raspy her voice was.

"You didn't make it," Diaz said briefly, taking her arm and leading her up the three steps to the door. He opened the storm door and held it open with his body while he unlocked the wooden one, pushing it wide and reaching in to feel for a light switch. He found it, and bright light from an overhead fixture made her blink. He ushered her inside and she found herself standing in a smallish kitchen. Permeating everything was a peculiar smell that was somehow familiar, a not unclean smell, just . . . peculiar.

Diaz went back outside and she stood there, too tired and

beaten and apathetic to care where he was going. She heard doors slam; then he was back, carrying both his duffel and her suitcase.

He walked through the kitchen into another room and more lights came on. Milla closed her eyes and waited for him to come back. He always came back. . . .

He took her arm and led her forward. "I figure you need the bathroom," he said.

Vaguely surprised, she realized she did. The bathroom she found herself standing in had green and gray ceramic tile on the floor and in the rather large shower. Diaz closed the door and let her have the necessary privacy, but he must have been standing right outside, because as soon as she began washing her hands, he opened the door again.

"I'll put on some soup to heat," he said, and led her back to the kitchen.

She sat at the table and looked vaguely around while he poked through the cabinets and found what he needed. After a while she said in her croaky voice, "Where are we?"

"The Outer Banks."

For a moment she had no idea where that was. A tiny frown knit her brow as she tried to get her tired mind to sort through the available information. Finally she remembered that she was in North Carolina, and the Outer Banks was part of the coast. In another moment, she realized that the roaring sound was the ocean. They were right on the beach. The peculiar smell she'd noticed was the tang of salt water.

Diaz set a bowl of steaming vegetable soup and a glass of milk in front of her. Dipping a bowl full for himself, he sat down across from her and dug in.

Cautiously Milla dipped her spoon into the soup and sipped at the broth. It burned her raw throat, but at the same time the heat felt good. She had never before in her life lost her appetite, but the very act of lifting the spoon was almost too much effort and she had to make herself continue. She kept her head down, her gaze focused on the bowl of soup. She couldn't let herself look at anything else, think about anything else; right now she was numb, but the pain waited just on the edge of her consciousness, ready to consume her again.

When she was finished, Diaz cleaned the kitchen, then led her back to the bathroom, where he'd laid out a couple of towels and washcloths. "Strip," he ordered. "Get in the shower. I'll bring your nightgown."

If she'd had more energy, she might have argued with him, or even locked the door while he was gone. Instead she ran the water in the sink and obediently took off her clothes while it was getting hot, then turned off the faucet and stepped into the shower. The glass door was clear, which gave no privacy at all. She couldn't bring herself to care.

She had just finished drying off when he returned with his hands full, carrying everything she could possibly need. He set her toiletries and cosmetics on the vanity, put her blow dryer in one of the cabinet drawers, laid her nightgown on the vanity stool.

She put on the nightgown, then sat down on the stool and stared at the toiletries, trying to remember her normal skin care routine. "This one," Diaz said, nudging the toner forward. He had watched her get ready for bed on more than one occasion, leaning against the bathroom door frame and waiting patiently enough, but watching her with narrowed, hungry eyes.

Lethargically she poured toner on a cotton pad and wiped it on her face. Diaz pushed the moisturizer forward, and obediently she smoothed the cream on her face and neck. Then he leaned down and lifted her in his arms, carried her out of the bathroom and down the short hall to a bedroom. The bedside lamp was on, the covers turned down. He placed her between the sheets, pulled up the covers, and turned off the lamp. "Good night," he said as he walked out and closed the door behind him.

She slept immediately, as if her brain simply switched off, and several hours later woke crying. She touched the tears on her face and stared at them in bewilderment for a moment, then memory rushed back and brought with it that clawing pain.

The agony was so sharp she couldn't lie in bed. She got up and paced the small bedroom, her arms folded over her middle as if she could hold the pain in, but the same deep, tearing sounds she'd made earlier tore free from her chest and throat. She almost howled in her grief, and for the first time understood why in some cultures the bereaved tore out their hair and ripped their garments. She wanted to smash the furniture, throw something. She wanted to run screaming down the beach and throw herself into the ocean. Drowning had to be less painful than this.

Eventually exhaustion and that odd numbness claimed her again, and she fell back into bed.

Morning dawned clear and slightly warmer. She got out of bed, dressed, and looked out the window. Now that it was daylight, she could see the Atlantic looming just over a sand dune, all that water seeming to come right at her in an endless procession of waves. There was a row of houses much like this one marching up and down the beach; some were newer and bigger, others were older and smaller. During the summer the beach would be crowded with vacationers, but this morning it was devoid of people. After a while, she trudged to the kitchen.

Diaz had made coffee. He himself was nowhere in sight, nor was the Jeep parked outside. There was a note on the kitchen table that said, "Gone for food."

Milla poured herself a cup of coffee and walked about the small house, familiarizing herself with it. Besides the kitchen, bathroom, and her bedroom, there were two more bedrooms, equally small. The one Diaz had slept in was right next to hers, the pillow dented, the bed unmade. The kitchen was an eat-in, with a laundry alcove off it that was just large enough to fit in a washer and dryer. In front was the living room, filled with cozy, overstuffed furniture and a twenty-five-inch television. Across the front of the house was a screened porch with a set of white wicker furniture with colorful floral cushions. From the porch she looked straight out over the ocean, blue today from the reflected sky. The morning air was cold, and after a few minutes she went back inside to sit at the kitchen table and drink another cup of coffee.

Desolation filled her. For over ten years she'd kept herself focused; there had been pain, yes, but also purpose. Now there was nothing.

She would have to get rid of the rocks in her house. Justin wouldn't be needing them.

She had known for over three years now that even if she found him, she would still never have him. On his seventh birthday, she had awakened to the realization that he was irrevocably gone. Even if she found him that very day, his life and security were centered around other people, and to take him away from that would be devastating to him. Because she loved him, she knew she would have to let him go. She still had to search, she had to make certain he was okay . . . but he was gone. He would never be hers again.

She had hoped she would find comfort in the fact that he'd had a good life, good parents. And she did—she *did*—but the grief was still so immense she didn't know how she could survive it.

It was as if he had died, as if she had lost him all over again. What she had done was irrevocable. David had been aghast when she told him what they had to do. He'd wept, he'd raged—all the stages she had gone through in private. "We've just found him!" he'd shouted. "How can we do this? Without even seeing him, talking to him?"

"Look at his face," she'd said gently, once more directing him to the photographs she'd taken. "He's happy. How can we take that away from him?"

"We could still meet him," David had insisted, desperate. "He doesn't have to know who we are. I—damn it, Milla, I agree we can't totally disrupt his life by taking him away from these people, but we finally have a chance now to—"

"No. If we show up without giving his adoptive parents this security of knowing he's irrevocably theirs, what are they likely to do? I know what I'd do. I'd take him and run."

"But we could see him," he pleaded, worn down by the truth in her argument.

"That will have to be up to his parents. It *has* to be. This is what's best for Justin, not what's best for us. David, you have a family you love. You have to think about them, too. We can't tear up everyone else's life because of our own selfishness."

"Is it selfish to want to see our son? You, at least—you've sacrificed your own life to look for him, you've done so much more than I ever could. How can you not want to at least talk to him?"

"I do," she said fiercely. "I want to grab him and never let him go. But it's too late now, it's been too late for years. We aren't his family now. If we ever know him, it'll have to be his choice. Otherwise the damage to him will be terrible, and I haven't fought so hard and so long to find him just so *I* would be happy. I had to know if he was safe, if he was loved. He is." She swallowed and repeated, "He is."

In the end, his vision blurred with tears, David had signed the papers, then scribbled a handwritten letter to Justin telling him how much he loved him and hoped that one day they'd meet, and given the letter to Milla to put in with the other papers, which included her own letter.

She only hoped that one day Justin—Zack—would read the letters and be curious enough about David and her to get in touch. She hoped the Winborns wouldn't destroy the papers. She didn't think they would, especially the legal papers, but they might well put them in a safe-deposit box and never tell Zack about his natural parents. She hoped not, but she wouldn't blame them if they did. She knew how fiercely she herself had fought to protect him, so why should she expect them to do less?

She had accomplished what she'd set out to do, all those long years ago. She had done it knowing that she would be left with ashes. She just hadn't known the taste of them would be so bitter in her mouth.

The kitchen door opened and Diaz came in, carrying some paper bags. She'd been so preoccupied that she hadn't heard him drive up. He gave her a sharp look but didn't say anything, instead concentrating on putting up the groceries he'd bought.

She wasn't fully aware of him, certainly not with the hyperawareness she normally felt around him. He was just there, like part of the furniture. The grief and pain that filled her blotted out everything except a peripheral acknowledgment of his presence.

"Which do you want?" he asked. "Cereal or bagel?"

He wanted her to decide? What difference did it make what she ate? "Bagel," she finally said listlessly, because it wouldn't involve having to deal with a spoon.

He toasted the bagel and even spread the cream cheese on it, then put it on a saucer in front of her. She tore off a piece and chewed. And chewed. The bite kept growing bigger and bigger in her mouth until she thought she was going to choke.

She was sitting here eating just as if she hadn't given her son away yesterday.

She shoved back from the table, overturning her chair. Cat-like, Diaz whirled to face her, balanced to respond to any attack she might level at him. In a sudden burst of blind fury, she grabbed from the dish drainer the pot he'd used to heat the soup the night before, and threw it as hard as she could at the wall. It hit with a clang and crashed back to the floor. She grabbed the spoons and threw them, then the bowls. The bowls broke with a satisfying crash.

Sobbing, she wrenched open the cabinet doors and began grabbing out whatever she could reach: plates, saucers, bowls, cups, and glasses. She threw each one with as much force as she could muster, screaming in wordless agony as she hurled plate after plate, sending shards of glass flying around the room.

Diaz didn't move except when a thrown missile came flying too close; then he merely ducked a little to the side and stood his ground. Silently he watched her systematically destroy the kitchen, staying out of her way until the enraged burst of energy was abruptly spent and she collapsed to her knees, sobbing.

Then he picked her up and carried her back to her bedroom, placing her on the bed. Milla curled on her side and cried herself to sleep.

When she woke several hours later and stumbled out of the room, the kitchen had been cleaned and swept, and once again Diaz was gone.

He finally returned, carrying a cardboard box containing a mismatched set of dishes, including saucers and coffee cups. He went back outside and returned with another box, from which he unloaded about a dozen drinking glasses and several bowls. Nothing matched. He unpacked everything, then put it all in the dishwasher and turned it on.

Her head pounded with a dull headache, her eyes were sore and swollen, and her throat ached. "I'm sorry," she croaked.

"No problem."

She took a breath. "Where did you get the dishes?"

"I found a yard sale. It was either that or drive to Kitty Hawk to a Wal-Mart store."

Considering how deserted the Outer Banks were this time of year, finding a yard sale was nothing short of a miracle. In a moment of clarity, she had a sudden image of this dark-clothed predator prowling through a yard sale and buying up old dishes. He wouldn't even notice how out of place he seemed, but anyone else who happened to be there certainly would have.

He made sandwiches and she ate hers, then she put on her sneakers and coat and headed out to the beach. She walked for what felt like hours, with a cool breeze blowing in her face and her mind so numb she could barely think. Not thinking was good. At last she turned around to go back, and when she did she stopped short at the sight of Diaz following her. He had stayed back about thirty or forty yards, giving her privacy but still watching over her.

He stopped and waited. He had his hands stuffed in the pockets of a black jacket, and his dark eyes were narrowed against the breeze as he watched her approach. She knew it was irrational, but his following her made her angry. As she walked by she snapped, "Afraid I'll drown myself?"

She was being sarcastic, but his quiet "Yes" stung her to silence. She walked on, blinking back tears. She didn't want to cry. Her eyelids were so puffy and sore that she wanted never to cry again. She remembered thinking the night before about running into the ocean, and though the grief and pain were so agonizing almost any relief would be welcome, she knew she'd never do that. Surrendering wasn't in her nature. If it had been, she wouldn't have been able to hold on to her determination all those years.

She'd always been the idealistic dreamer in her family. Who would ever have thought that just beneath her skin was a layer of stubbornness that went all the way to the bone?

By the time they made it back to the house, her steps were dragging, and the sun was sinking low, taking the temperature with it. Exhausted, she lay down for a nap and woke only when Diaz shook her and told her it was time to eat.

The succeeding days passed like that, in a blur of grief and numbness, punctuated by bursts of rage. The sameness blended them all together in her tired mind, so it seemed as if time was merely creeping. She ate, she slept, she cried. The fits of rage would take her unawares, exploding when she least expected it, and afterward she was always ashamed of her lack of control. She screamed, she beat on the wall with her fists, she cursed the fate that had let her find her son, but too late.

She walked long miles on the deserted beaches, trying her best not to think of anything. At some point she realized she hadn't called in to the office, and mentioned it to Diaz. "I called them," he said. "When we were on our way here."

She remembered very little about the trip, except being mired in hellish misery.

Some days she hated Diaz with an intensity that prevented her from even looking at him. Rage seethed through her, and the fact that they had both wanted the same thing for Justin in no way mitigated his actions. Keeping her from Justin hadn't been his right, his decision. He seemed to know exactly what she was feeling on those days, because he would keep his distance from her, not speaking except for what was necessary when he called her for meals.

He made certain she ate and slept. He did the laundry, because the thought of it never even crossed her mind. She would hear the washing machine or the dryer running, and it meant absolutely nothing to her. It was just background noise. Clean clothes would reappear in her bedroom, and she would wear them. It was no more complicated than that.

One day she asked how long they'd been there, and he said, "Three weeks."

The answer stunned her, shook her up a little. She stared at him without the dullness in her eyes that had characterized her over these past weeks. "But . . . what about Thanksgiving?" Her comment was stupid, but it was the only thing she could think of.

"They had it without us."

Three weeks. That meant this was . . . the first week of December. "I don't have anyone to have Thanksgiving with," she blurted.

"You have your family."

"I don't spend holidays with them, you know that." Then she fell silent, because she'd found Justin and she hadn't called her mom, who might expect her to forget and forgive all concerning Ross and Julia, and she just couldn't. Not yet. Whether she ever could remained to be seen.

Diaz shrugged. "Then you just spent your first Thanksgiving with me."

Doing what? Screaming? Crying? Beating the wall? She hoped it wasn't the start of a new tradition.

The days were very short now, and the temperature had dropped even more. Diaz brought her some thicker socks to wear when she was out walking. Being outside helped, even though the sunshine was weak. Staring at the ocean helped. Sometimes it was gray, sometimes it was blue, but it was a constant, immense presence.

The periods of rage became less and less frequent, as did the bouts of horrible, devastating weeping. She was so tired mentally and emotionally that she functioned within a very narrow range. She didn't know what she would have done if Diaz hadn't brought her here. She hated being beholden to him, but maybe this was his way of making amends. The thing was, she didn't know if his efforts made any difference in the way she felt about him. She could only deal with one thing at a time, and right now was not his time.

Sometimes she tilted her face up to the winter sun in search of its meager warmth, and knew that she had survived.

28

MILLA WAS ALWAYS AWARE, ON THE DIMMEST EDGE OF HER consciousness, that Diaz constantly watched her. She also knew that he was a man who never gave up, who never lost sight of his goal. Exactly what his goal was wasn't always clear to her, but she had no doubt he was perfectly clear in his own mind what he wanted.

He wanted *her*. She knew it, and yet she couldn't imagine how they could ever be together again. The rift between them, to her, was final and absolute. He'd betrayed her in the most wounding way possible, and forgiveness evidently wasn't her strong suit. She had found that grudges weren't heavy at all; she could carry them for a very long time.

Diaz wasn't taking care of her out of the goodness of his heart. He was taking care of her the way a wolf cared for its wounded mate.

She had sensed that claim the first time he made love to her, that bonding of like to like. He wouldn't willingly relinquish it.

She knew she was in danger from him; she *knew* it. Not physically. Physically, Diaz wouldn't harm her. But emotionally he could devastate her, and she didn't think she could bear any more devastation right now. She knew she should start making a push to leave this little house that had seen the total breakdown of her soul and then the first tentative steps toward healing. Finders needed her. She needed to be doing something, anything, rather than vegetating. She needed to get away from Diaz. But insisting on anything took more mental energy than she could spare; she was so horribly tired of thinking, of feeling. She had her hands full just existing.

One day while Diaz was outside she actually tried to call Finders, just to check in with Joann, but she had evidently left her cell phone on when they came here and the battery was dead. Next she tried the house phone, and discovered that long distance calls were blocked on it. She sat staring at the phone, trying to remember her code for charging a call to her home phone, but the only number that came to mind was her social security number and she knew it wasn't that.

Diaz came in and noticed her sitting beside the phone. "What are you doing?"

"I'm trying to call the office."

"Why?" he asked simply.

She stared at him, because the answer seemed obvious to her. "Because it's been over three weeks and I need to check in."

"They're doing okay without you."

"How do you know?" she asked with a flash of irritation.

"I called."

"When? Why didn't you let me talk to Joann?"

"I've called a couple of times, once to let them know where we are and another time to say we'd be here a while yet."

She noticed he had totally ignored her question about talking to Joann. "It's time to go home."

He rubbed his neck. "Not yet."

"Yes, it is!" To her surprise, she began crying. She said, "Damn it," and went to her bedroom. She hadn't cried in a couple of days, not even about Justin, so why was she crying now over something so inconsequential? This just proved Diaz right, and she didn't want him to be right. She wanted to have something to do, to get back into a routine where she would *have* to think about something besides her own misery.

Did she really want to fly home if a flight attendant asking her if she wanted peanuts might easily reduce her to a sobbing heap?

After an hour of wiping her eyes and blowing her nose, she decided to take a walk before dark. She put on two pairs of socks and her coat; when she emerged from the short hallway, Diaz looked up and said, "Where're you going?"

"For a walk," she replied. Wasn't it obvious? Then she opened the back door and realized why he'd asked. A slow, steady, gray rain was falling. She checked the clock on the wall and discovered the time wasn't as late as she'd thought; it was the low cloud cover that made the day so dark. "Or not," she said with a sigh.

He turned on the gas-log fireplace in the living room, and the coziness of it drew her. She didn't want to sit in there with him, but the alternative was to return to her bedroom and stare at the four walls. The television was on satellite, which meant there was a multitude of channels available. To her surprise, Diaz was watching a decorating show on the Home and Garden Television channel with all the puzzlement of someone from another planet, as if he couldn't figure out why anyone would want to glue tasseled fringe to a lamp shade.

"Are you thinking of taking up interior decorating as an alternate career?" she asked, surprising both of them by initiating the conversation.

"Only if someone holds a gun to my head."

Milla surprised herself again by smiling. It was just a tiny smile, and it vanished immediately when she realized with astonishment what she'd done.

A smile, when she'd thought she would never smile or laugh again. He hadn't noticed, but she had. She curled in a chair and watched the rest of the program with him, but the rain made her sleepy and she dozed on and off for the rest of the afternoon.

They ate an early supper; then Milla showered while Diaz took a last turn around the property. There was no threat for him to guard against, but watchfulness was ingrained in his nature, and every night he walked around checking to make certain the Jeep was locked up and no strangers were lurking around. *They* were the only strangers on the Outer Banks at this time of year, but that made no difference to him.

Milla had just pulled on her nightgown when the bathroom door opened without warning and Diaz said, "Put your coat and shoes on and come outside."

Without question, spurred by the urgency in his tone, Milla hurried to put on her coat over her nightgown and slip her bare feet into her shoes. She stepped out onto the back porch with him and said, "Oh!" in hushed delight.

The rain had changed over to snow flurries. There was no chance of having an accumulation; the temperature, cold as it was, was still above freezing and the ground was still too warm and too wet. But the snow looked magical, swirling down out of a black sky.

Diaz looked down at her sockless feet, shook his head, then simply swung her up in his arms and went down the steps with her. Milla automatically clutched his shoulders for support. "Where are we going?"

"To the beach."

He carried her over the low dunes to the beach, right to the ocean's edge, and stood there in the darkness, the silence broken only by the rhythmic rush of the waves. Tiny snowflakes swirled around them and disappeared as soon as they touched down. She had grown up accustomed to seeing snow every winter, but since moving to El Paso snow was generally something she saw only if she was traveling. She certainly hadn't expected to see it here, on a southern beach. She started shivering almost immediately, but she didn't want to go inside and miss a minute of this.

The snow shower was of short duration, and after it ended she spent several minutes staring up at the black sky waiting for more, without success. "I guess that's it," she said, and sighed.

Diaz's arms tightened around her, and he carried her back into the house.

Milla went to bed soon afterward and went right to sleep. Since coming here she had slept twice as much as she normally did, as if her body was trying to make up for years and years of erratic hours and unending stress, and also to give her battered mind a rest. Her dreams were slowly becoming more normal, so she didn't wake up crying every night. She wasn't dreaming at all that night when she started abruptly awake to find a dark shadow looming over her, and a naked, heavy weight pressing down on her.

"Shh," Diaz said as he pulled her nightgown up to her waist and spread her legs. "Don't think."

"What—" she began, then inhaled sharply as he rubbed the head of his penis around her opening to moisten it, and pushed inside. Her nails dug into his biceps. She was moist, yes, but not ready; she felt every inch of him as he stretched her soft tissues and settled deep.

Don't think? How could she not think? But her mind was so tired, so bruised from the long weeks of grieving, and with intense relief she felt herself sinking into purely physical sensation. She should tell him no, but she didn't. When he kissed her, she tilted her head and kissed him in return. She needed this escape from herself, and he had known it.

She moved her hands to his shoulders and clutched them as he settled into a slow rhythm. Because she wasn't already aroused, her body only gradually responded to his hands on her breasts, his kisses, the back and forth motion inside her. She felt tension grow in him as he fought the rise of his own climax; sweat gleamed on his hard shoulders and along his back, making her palms slippery, but he didn't falter in the rhythm. There was just enough hallway light coming through her open bedroom door for her to see the glitter in his eyes as he watched her, waiting for and reading each tiny response in the quickening of her breath and heartbeat, the way her legs climbed to hug his hips. Her body began lifting to his to meet each slow thrust, and her arms slid around his neck.

She didn't want this to end. She knew it had to, knew he couldn't last forever, but as long as he was inside her the world was held at bay. What he was giving her, besides pleasure, was surcease. He had watched her for weeks, waiting, and tonight he had acted. She'd known he would, eventually. The only wonder was that he'd waited so long.

She felt both relaxed and protected with him, at least from outside forces. Nothing, it seemed, could protect her from him, and tonight she wasn't even certain she wanted to be. Claimed, and mated. She was his, but was he hers? And if he was, what in hell did they do about it?

"I don't even know what you want," she said fretfully, beginning to lose herself in rising sensation.

"This," he muttered in a dark, rough tone. "You. Everything."

Her head tilted back, her spine arched, and she began climaxing. He cradled her close and kept up his slow rhythm until her unconscious cries had faded, her fingers had stopped digging into his back, and her legs loosened around his hips. Milla relaxed against the pillows, her eyes closing, her muscles limp and her body replete.

Diaz gently kissed her forehead, then withdrew and tucked the covers around her again, and left as quietly as he'd entered.

Milla lay there, drowsing and trying to decide what was different, for about a minute. She needed to get up and clean herself as she usually did after they made love, but she was so sleepy now and, really, she didn't feel wet–

She came fully awake, aware of what had happened. Or rather, what hadn't happened. He hadn't come. He'd seen to her pleasure, then left without taking his own.

She was out of bed and moving before the thought finished. As soon as she entered the short hallway, she heard the shower running in the bathroom. She pushed open the door and saw him through the clear shower door. He stood with his head bowed and one arm braced against the shower wall in front of him, water beating down on him as he slowly worked his other fist up and down.

No. As she pulled her nightgown over her head and dropped it to the floor, everything in her rebelled at leaving him to this lonely release after he'd so unselfishly seen to hers. She jerked the shower door open and stepped in. "I believe that's mine," she said, reaching out to still his fist, then replacing it with her own.

Slowly he raised his head, and she was taken aback by the

fierceness in his dark gaze. "Don't do this unless you mean it," he rasped.

She didn't hesitate at the ultimatum. She shook her hair back out of her face as the warm water rained down on her head. His shaft was iron hard in her hand, and in her hand wasn't where she wanted it. She didn't let herself think; she just reached up and gripped the shower pipe and used it to lever herself up so she could wrap her legs around his hips. She wasn't high enough, so she braced one arm on his shoulders and pushed herself higher, trying to maneuver so she could ease down on his thrusting erection.

With a growl he wrapped one arm around her hips and pulled her against him, dipping his head down to close his mouth over her left nipple. His penis pushed up between her legs; gasping, she adjusted her position just a little, then let herself begin to slide down, stretching, enveloping him in her wet heat. He released her nipple as she slowly dropped down, a rough sound catching in his throat.

Just as he'd done to her, she slowly moved up and down, caressing him with her body, drawing out his response. He ground his teeth together, fighting not to come when she was just as determined he would. Frustrated, she wondered why he was holding back—until she heard herself moan, and realized the friction was working on her, too.

The battle there in the shower was in close-combat conditions. With the clinging grip of her body she tried to wring a climax from him, locking her legs around him and pumping hard. He slowed her down with that one arm around her hips, grinding her against him and sending her response rocketing.

The warm water began to go, but the heat generated by their bodies was so intense she scarcely noticed. Diaz turned her so they were out of the spray, breaking her grip on the shower pipe and bracing her against the tile wall. Milla gripped his head with both hands, kissing him with all the fierceness she could muster; then she lost the battle and her head arched back as she began to climax. With an inhuman sound, as if he'd been pushed beyond his limits, he jerked convulsively and began pumping into her with short, hard thrusts that took him to the hilt and made her cry out.

Afterward he slumped against the wall, pinning her to the tile. She was beyond limp, beyond drowsy. He kissed her shoulder, then let his legs bend so that they slid down the wall to sprawl on the shower floor.

Again, silence fell. She didn't know how to explain what she'd just done, and in any case, she was acutely aware of his stated condition: *Don't do this unless you mean it.* Don't do it unless she accepted him as her lover, though arguably what had just passed between them made that a moot point. Don't do it unless she tore down the wall she'd erected between them. Don't do it unless she was his and he was hers, with all the ramifications of what that meant. She'd done it, and God help her, she meant it.

Somewhere along the way she'd been stupid enough to fall in love with him. If she hadn't loved him, his betrayal wouldn't have hurt so much. Enraged her, yes, but not *hurt.* She couldn't imagine how, in her lifetime, she'd managed to love two such different men as David and Diaz. One was sunshine, the other was darkness. Perhaps, though, it made sense: the woman she'd been before couldn't have loved Diaz, but she was no longer that woman. She'd wanted to be, but she wasn't. The terrible things that had happened had changed her, and there was no going back. She would always love dressing up and fussing with her hair, love decorating her surroundings, the way people did in that program that had so bewildered him, but she was a stronger, harder, fiercer woman than she'd been when Justin was snatched from her arms.

The big question now was: Where did they go from here? She was just as lost now as she'd been that morning. The difference was, now she wasn't alone.

29

MILLA WOKE THE NEXT MORNING CUDDLED IN DIAZ'S ARMS, her head on his shoulder, the warmth of his body a source of comfort in the cold, gray December morning. Rain was pouring down, much heavier than the day before. As usual, he woke almost simultaneously, either too attuned to her to sleep after she was awake, or too inherently cautious to leave himself so vulnerable. Knowing him as she did, she assumed it was the latter.

She sat up and stretched, easing muscles that were stiff from lying in the same position too long. Still lying beside her, he reached up and rubbed one hand over her bare back. Her hair hung in her eyes and she pushed it back, aware of what a mess it must be, since it had still been wet when they'd tumbled back into bed last night. His bed this time, not hers. Though she doubted there would be any *his* and *hers* after last night, just *theirs*. The prospect made her uneasy, knowing that while one essential question had been answered last night, a multitude remained undecided.

"I'll turn on the heat," he said. She sat with her arms propped on her drawn-up knees and looked out the window, while he got up and left the bedroom. The house next door was empty, as was the one on the other side. In fact, theirs was the only inhabited house in this entire stretch of rental property. It made her feel as alone as if they were the only people on the planet, though she knew the locals were still here. A few times when she'd been walking on the beach, she'd passed one or two people who were also out getting their exercise, but for the most part she'd had the beach to herself. The windswept desolation had appealed to her aching heart, and in a way the pouring rain did now, too. Her mood was somber; had she made a colossal mistake last night? And even if she had, was there any going back?

Diaz returned with her robe and slippers, then left to put on the coffee. He wasn't very talkative in the morning–or any other time–and that suited her. She crawled out of bed and hurriedly pulled the robe around her, then dashed to the bathroom.

The bathroom had its own radiant heater, and he'd also turned that one on. Because the bathroom was so much smaller, it heated more rapidly, and it was already almost comfortable. Milla stared at her reflection in the mirror and made a face; her hair was definitely a mess. For the first time in a long while, though, her eyes weren't dull with misery. They weren't exactly sparkling, but there was life in them.

She turned on the shower and let the water heat, then got in and briskly washed her hair. The hot water felt good on her sore muscles, reminding her how demanding Diaz had been during the night. He'd been a patient lover but, after the first time, not a gentle one. He'd been hungry in a way he hadn't been even the first time they'd made love, in a way that wasn't completely physical. She tried to analyze the difference, but it eluded her, and she wondered if it wasn't because Diaz himself was so elusive and remote. What was startling was that he'd been neither the night before.

As she was drying off, she automatically touched her hip to make certain her birth control patch was there, and froze. Her fingers found only smooth skin. Horrified, she stared at herself in the mirror as she realized that not only was the patch not there, it hadn't been there for quite some time. For about three weeks, in fact.

She'd had a period. She remembered that, vaguely, because Diaz had gone out to buy tampons for her. Normally she wore the patches for three weeks, putting on a new one every week, then went without for one week, and that was when she'd have her period. That meant she had either removed the patch or it had fallen off after having been on for way longer than it was meant to be; it would have lost its effectiveness after a week anyway and she'd have had a period then. She had absolutely no memory of dealing with the patch, and putting on a new one hadn't crossed her mind.

None of which would have mattered, if it hadn't been for last night.

Realistically she knew her chance of getting pregnant was very small; her body wouldn't return to normal for a couple of months after going off the patches. But accidents happened, and women got pregnant all the time when it wasn't supposed to be likely.

Troubled, she dried her hair and actually took some pains styling it before the smell of coffee lured her out. She went to the bedroom and dressed in the warmest clothes she had, sweatpants and a flannel shirt, and frowned as she realized for the first time that she hadn't brought them with her. Diaz must have gotten them. She hadn't paid much attention to his comings and goings–or anything else–over the past few weeks. She just hoped that inattention didn't come back to haunt her.

He was cooking breakfast when she left the bedroom. She poured herself a cup of coffee and said, "I'm not wearing a birth control patch."

He turned the bacon with a fork. "I know."

Of all the things he could have said, that flabbergasted her the most. She gaped at him. "Why didn't you say anything?"

"I figured you knew."

"No, I hadn't realized." She sipped her coffee. "This could be a problem."

"Not for me, it isn't."

For a moment the callousness of the remark made her mute with surprise; then the truth struck her: the idea of her getting pregnant didn't upset him at all.

She didn't want to go there.

"It's probably all right," she said. "It takes a while for the system to get back to normal."

"When will you know?"

She groaned and rubbed her face. "I don't know exactly. Do you remember when I had my period?"

"It started two days after we got here."

She should have put on a new patch before going to see David, she realized, but she'd totally forgotten about it. Mentally she worked out the timing; if she was going to ovulate this month—which she hoped she wouldn't—the time for it, midcycle, would be right about ... now. Perhaps. She'd worn the patches for so long that she had no idea of the exact timing of her natural cycle now. But she wasn't going to take any additional chances; if—when—they had sex again, they'd have to take precautions.

"I'll get some condoms," he said as he broke eggs into a mixing bowl, added a little milk, then stirred the mixture with a fork. He was either reading her mind or had been following the same path of logic.

He finished cooking breakfast with the same competency he did everything, and as she tucked into the scrambled eggs, bacon, and toast, she realized she had done absolutely nothing while they'd been here, other than bathe and feed herself. Diaz had done everything else, from the shopping to the cleaning. Uneasily she shied from examining his motives, because she was just now becoming capable of dealing with herself again, on a very limited basis. She wasn't ready to start thinking about what he wanted.

She helped him clean up afterward, though, and other than a faintly surprised look he showed no reaction. Right after breakfast he showered and left on his condom-hunting expedition; he wasn't likely to leave something that important to the last minute.

After he left, she wandered around straightening the house, rearranging the decorative pillows on the living room furniture so they were color-coordinated, making his bed, stripping hers and putting the sheets in the wash, since she doubted she'd be sleeping there again. She didn't know how she felt about that, if she was worried or relieved. Just yesterday she had thought she'd never forgive him for what he'd done, that the breach between them was total and final. Then with one blow he'd smashed down the wall dividing them and she was right back where she'd been: flat on her back beneath him.

Last night, she hadn't wanted to be anywhere else.

At last, with nothing else to do in the house, she made some fresh coffee and got a blanket from the closet, then carried that and a cup of coffee out onto the screened front porch. She wrapped herself in the blanket and sat down on the wicker love seat, pulling up her feet for warmth. The darkly overcast sky, the gray and turbulent Atlantic, and the cold gray rain all blended together, robbing the day of both sunlight and color. She wrapped her hands around the warm coffee cup and inhaled the fragrant steam, staring into the curtain of rain as she tried to bring order to the multitude of thoughts swirling around her brain.

Today, for the first time, she realized how much the sharp edge of agony had dulled in the last few days. She could function, she could think of other things, she could carry on a conversation. She could smile. The hurt would never go away, but it had become manageable, and would become more so in the weeks, years ahead.

She wondered what she would have done if Diaz hadn't been there. Even though she had cursed his existence, she'd been totally dependent on him. Mostly he'd left her alone, staying in the background and going hours without even speaking to her, while taking care of the basics of life. At first he had followed her during her walks, but lately he hadn't even done that. He had, uncomplainingly and silently, done everything he could to help her through this.

He loved her.

The realization was almost blinding, and she bowed her head to rest her forehead against her updrawn knees. How on earth was she supposed to reconcile what he'd done concerning Justin with the care he'd given her these past few weeks?

She heard the sound of a motor; then it stopped and was followed by the slam of a door. He was back. She listened to the sound of his progress as he opened the back door and came inside, but then she lost track of his movements because his walk was so damned catlike and she couldn't hear a sound.

The door to the front porch opened and he stepped outside, his sharp gaze sweeping over her in a lightning assessment, as if checking that she was all right. He put his hands in his pockets and moved to lean against the frame of the screen door, his profile somber as he stared out at the gray ocean.

"I'm sorry," he said in a low voice.

The words lay there between them. He wasn't apologizing for last night–she couldn't imagine that–but for Justin. She doubted he'd ever apologized to anyone before in his life, but there was a simple grace to the offering that told her it was sincere.

"I know you meant to protect him," she said, and wondered why she was making his argument for him.

"I didn't know what you planned to do. It never occurred to me."

"You could have asked."

Except he wasn't a man who easily trusted, who opened himself up and let people get close to him. How could he have predicted how she would react? His own mother had virtually abandoned him, dragging him back into her life whenever it was convenient to her. What he knew of mothers came from his own experience, and though intellectually he knew, had seen, that most mothers truly loved their children, he'd had no personal connection with that kind of love.

Until she'd handed those legal papers over to the Winborns, she hadn't been certain herself that she could actually go through with it, and her soul had wept. If she hadn't been certain, how could she expect him to have intuitively known that she would never harm Justin in any way?

But she was still unable to let it go. She said, "One night while we were in bed you could have asked me. 'Milla, what will you do if you find Justin? How can you take him away from the only family he's ever known?' Then you'd have known what I felt, what I'd already realized."

He glanced at her over his shoulder. "It never occurred to me," he repeated. "I–when you turned over those papers, I felt like I'd been shot. I wanted to get down on my knees and kiss your feet, but I figured you'd probably kick me."

"No 'probably' to it. I would have."

He nodded and turned back to once more watch the ocean. "I didn't love you." His tone was low and almost absent, as if he were musing over the words. "Or I don't think I did. Not at first. But when you kicked me out, I felt"—he paused, and frowned as he considered his own feelings—"cut in half."

"I know," she said, remembering her own sense of loss.

"Looking back, I know when it happened. When I tilted over." He rocked his hand, demonstrating the slight degree between loving and not loving. "In Idaho. I dragged you out of the river and you rolled over on your back and started laughing. Right then."

And he'd done something about it right then, too. Until then the attraction had been building between them—she'd been half-crazy with wanting him—but neither of them had acted on it. Until that moment, with the sun beating down on them and the relief of being alive sweeping through them, when he'd looked at her and said—

She chuckled. "Some declaration of love that was. Offering your left nut."

"That wasn't a declaration of love; that was a declaration of intent. *This* is a declaration of love." He had his head tilted in that quizzical way she loved, and for a man who found communication difficult, he wasn't doing badly at all.

Silence fell between them as they both digested what had been said. She felt him waiting to hear her say that she forgave him, that she loved him, too, but though she was certain of the one she didn't know if she'd ever be able to do the other. The hurt and anger were still there, but no longer on boil. The most she'd be able to do, she thought, was put it behind her and say, okay, we go on from this point. If one wanted to argue the quality of forgiveness, perhaps that *was* forgiveness, just the willingness to go on. But this was Diaz, not your average blue-collar Joe, or even your white-collar Joe. With Diaz, where did they go on *to*?

She couldn't see a future with him, but neither could she see one without him.

"You might as well say it," he murmured, still looking out at the ocean. He hadn't looked at her once since telling her he loved her. "I know you do."

"Love you? Yes." She sighed and sipped her coffee. It had gone cold and she grimaced, setting the cup aside. "I do love you."

"Enough to marry me and have my kids?"

Her breath left her and she felt herself tilt sideways before she caught her balance. "What?" she asked, her voice reedy with shock.

"Marriage. Will you marry me?"

"How could that possibly work out between us?"

"I love you. You love me. It's a natural progression."

She raked her hand through her hair, more upset than she'd thought possible at a marriage proposal from him. It was unexpected, and tantalizingly sweet, but the enormity of the problems facing them if they got married was almost too much to comprehend. And part of her was terrified. He'd mentioned not just marriage, but children, too. How could she?

"Getting married wouldn't be smart," she said.

He turned and watched her with those dark, grave eyes, studying her, waiting for her to continue.

"Between us, we have enough emotional baggage to fill an airliner. I probably need to be in therapy." She gave a cracked laugh. "And you're an assassin. What kind of job security is that? I don't even know what I want to do, if I should keep on with Finders or go into teaching the way I'd always planned. Part of me wants to quit, but how can I? I'm good at what I do. I'm just so tired and–"

"Afraid," he said.

"Of the future? You bet."

"No. You're afraid to be happy."

She stared at him, frozen by the accuracy with which he'd seen behind the smoke screen of solid reasoning.

"Have you really convinced yourself that you don't deserve anything because you let Justin be taken from you?" he asked, relentlessly pinning her down. "You think you can't have a husband, another baby, because—what?—you were a bad mother and didn't hold on to him tight enough?"

Her throat worked as she tried to swallow. She felt as if her lungs had seized, her heart stopped. No one had ever said it was her fault; she'd fought for her baby, had fought nearly to the death. Only a knife in her back had stopped her. And yet, for over ten years, she'd struggled with the bone-deep knowledge that she'd failed to protect her child. "I . . . I shouldn't have had him at the market," she said, her voice stifled. "He was just six weeks old. He was too young—"

"You couldn't have left him by himself. What else were you going to do?"

Her lips trembled. God, how that question had gone around and around in her mind! What else could she have done? There had to be something else, something she hadn't thought of, hadn't seen, because she'd let those men take Justin from her.

"Haven't you bought enough redemption for yourself, with all the other lost kids you've found? What will it take for you to forgive yourself?"

Her baby home, safe and sound, and that was never going to be.

Diaz left his post by the door and squatted down in front of her, folding her hands in his. A cold, wet wind tangled her hair, lifted the curls. "Is that why you gave him up? To make yourself pay?"

"No. I gave him up because it was the right thing to do." She saw him shiver, and realized he'd been outside all this time without even a jacket. Impulsively she opened up the blanket and invited him inside its warmth. He was fast to accept, but when they settled back down, she was somehow sprawled half across his lap, with the blanket tucked over and around them and her head resting in the hollow of his shoulder. Their combined body heat quickly chased away the chill.

"It's okay to live," he said softly, stroking her face, tracing the lines of it with one finger. "It's okay to be happy again."

Just the idea made her feel as if she were balancing on the edge of a cliff, with a stiff wind trying to push her over. "It's too soon."

Even admitting that she might one day allow herself to be happy, to get on with life, was like lifting one foot and letting it dangle over the cliff.

"It's been ten years. You've found your son, and you've done what was right by him. How is it 'too soon'?"

"It just is." Once again, she sought refuge in logic. "By being happy, you mean getting married to you."

"I can make you happy."

And she could make him happy, she thought, feeling dizzy at the prospect. He was a complicated, difficult man; if she turned him down, given his solitary nature, he would in all likelihood never marry. She was his one shot at a family, at a halfway normal life.

As if any life with James Diaz could ever be normal.

"How can we get married? What do we know about each other? I don't even know how old you are."

"Thirty-three."

She paused, taken aback and immediately sidetracked from the other salient points she'd been about to make. He seemed older, even though there was no gray in his hair and his face was unlined. "That's my age. When's your birthday?"

"August seventh."

"Oh, my God, I'm older than you! My birthday is April twenty-seventh."

She was so dismayed that the corners of his mouth kicked up. "I've always wanted to sleep with an older woman."

She thumped him on the chest, which earned her a kiss that was deeper than she'd expected, and longer. When he released her she buried her cold nose against his throat, inhaling the warm scent of him. She wanted to say yes. She loved him, more than she'd thought she would ever love a man again. As difficult as he was, in so many ways they perfectly complemented each other. With her he talked, he joked, he even laughed. Something about her opened him up; something about him pulled her away from the rigid path she'd set for herself.

But she was right about the problems they'd face, and she knew it. Getting married would only compound those problems. "What would you do for a job? If we got married, you couldn't keep chasing all over Mexico looking for the bad guys, maybe getting killed–" She stopped, because she couldn't continue with that thread.

"I don't know what else I could do, but I'll find something."

There weren't many job openings for retired bounty hunters/assassins. She couldn't see him in any kind of office setting, or doing anything that required him to work with the public. Just what kind of job could he do?

She was thinking about the future, she realized. Things were moving too fast, and she still didn't have her feet under her, emotionally speaking. "I can't say yes," she said. "Not yet. There are too many problems we have to work through."

He kissed her again, closing his eyes as he hugged her to

him. "I'm not going anywhere. I'll ask again next year," he said, standing up with her in his arms and maneuvering to open the door.

Ten minutes later, as he moved between her opened legs and settled into place, she realized that this was December. Next year was in three weeks.

30

"Mama! Thane's tearing up my homework! Make him *stop*!"

Milla stirred the spaghetti sauce and cast a harried eye toward the living room, where the shrieks were growing louder. "James! Get Thane away from Linnea."

He was already on his way. The screams grew louder, evidently while he was in the process of peeling Thane away from his eight-year-old sister's homework, but in just a few minutes blessed peace settled over the household, except for an occasional grumble from Linnea as she set about redoing her pages. Diaz appeared in the doorway with a giggling Thane draped around his neck. "What do I do with him now?"

"Play with him. Or tie him to a chair. Something."

Six-year-old Zara was sitting at the kitchen table industriously practicing her letters, working to get them exactly right. Her dark eyes were serious as she said, "He won't like being tied to a chair."

"I was joking, honey." Of their three children, Zara was the most like Diaz, with his somberness and intensity. Linnea was bustling and confident, meeting life head-on, while Zara stood back and watched. Milla took the time to give her youngest daughter a reassuring hug, while Diaz carried Thane outside to distract him with something energetic and, Milla hoped, nondestructive.

Thane was a surprise baby, born two days after her forty-first birthday. They hadn't intended to have any more children, content with their two daughters, but a broken condom had resulted in a little boy that they should more accurately have named Hurricane. Even before he could crawl, Thane had been squirming to be put down so he could explore. When he learned to crawl, the entire household was off and running, trying to catch him before he could get into whatever mischief he'd found. Now that he was two, Milla was beginning to consider a straitjacket—for herself.

It was funny how things had worked out. She and Diaz—she still had to remind herself to refer to him as James—had been married for nine years now. She'd held out on marriage until some of their problems had been worked out, namely her own work and his. She was still executive director of Finders, but the day-to-day operation had been turned over to Joann Westfall, while Milla herself concentrated mostly on fund-raising, which never ended. She drew a salary now, her hours were more regulated, and she was never away from her children overnight.

Diaz field-tested weapons for a firearms manufacturer and did some consulting work with the El Paso police department, the sheriff's department, and private security firms. She'd been relieved almost to the point of tears when he told her what he was doing, because she'd been worried to death there was no legitimate job where he could use his particular skills. They would never be rich, but they had enough money to support their children and afford a few luxuries, so that was fine.

Living in her condo, with so many close neighbors, had made him antsy. He hadn't complained, but Milla had seen how restless he was, and increasingly jumpy. By the time she was five months pregnant with Linnea, he was getting on *her* nerves so much she knew they had to do something, so Diaz had scouted around and found a house far enough away from other people that he could relax, but not so far away that Milla felt isolated. It was an older house, pleasant, with shade trees in the yard and four roomy bedrooms. At the time, they hadn't known they would need all four of them. They had bought the house, fenced in the yard for the baby's safety, and settled in.

She'd been happy. Though she'd still had her doubts when they finally did get married, almost a year after he first asked her, she'd been almost deliriously happy with him.

Watching him with their children was a delight that still made her heart squeeze. He'd approached Linnea cautiously, as if she were a time bomb, but he'd doggedly learned how to change diapers and all the other things one needed to know with a baby. Discipline was a theory he hadn't quite managed to understand; he'd explained to Milla, with complete and rather baffled seriousness, that the kids cried if he scolded them, so he'd had to stop. The situation had to be dire for him to get stern, with the result that all three children were shocked into instant obedience if he so much as raised his voice. It wasn't fair; Milla sometimes felt she could scream her head off and the children wouldn't pay the least bit of attention to her. That was an exaggeration, because they were normal, bright, inquisitive, generally obedient kids, which meant that some days they were a real pain.

She loved that she could be exasperated with them. One of her greatest fears, while she'd been pregnant, was that the tragedy of the past had turned her into an obsessive, overprotective, stifling sort of mother. She hadn't been certain she was fit to be a mother. Thank God Linnea had been such a capable child; by the time Zara had arrived, Milla had relaxed. Then they'd had four peaceful, mostly idyllic years—until Thane. The two years since his birth had been joyous, but definitely not peaceful.

"Want to wash your hands and help me set the table?" she asked Zara, who obediently moved her homework off the table and ran off to wash her hands.

Linnea said, "I want to help," and rushed out of the living room, following Zara to the downstairs bathroom to wash her hands, too.

Milla set the big bowl of salad on the table, then checked on the rolls in the oven. They were a nice golden brown, so she took them out and put them in the bread basket. Diaz came back in with Thane, and took him to wash the worst of the dirt from his face and hands while Milla poured the spaghetti in a colander to drain.

The girls were busy putting out the plates and flatware when the doorbell rang. Milla sighed. It never failed; if there was going to be an interruption, it invariably happened as they were sitting down to eat. "I'll get it," she said, passing Diaz as he came out of the bathroom with Thane tucked under his arm.

She opened the door and looked up at a tall young man, with blond hair and blue eyes. Her knees went weak and she sagged against the door, tears burning her eyes.

She knew. From the instant she saw his face, she knew.

He was nervous. He cleared his throat. "I'm sorry to bother you, but I—are you Milla Edge?"

"Milla Diaz, now," she managed to say.

He cleared his throat again, and darted a wary look over her shoulder. She knew Diaz had come up even before his strong hand slid around her waist and drew her against him in support.

"I–uh–I'm Zack Winborn. Justin. Your son," he added, unnecessarily.

Her face was wet, her eyes overflowing; the tears blurred his features. A sob burst out of her before she could stop it, and an alarmed expression crossed his face. Just as suddenly the sob turned into laughter, and she reached out and took his hand. "I've waited so long," she said, and drew him into the house.

About the Author

LINDA HOWARD is the award-winning author of many *New York Times* bestsellers, including *Dying to Please, Open Season, Mr. Perfect, All the Queen's Men, Now You See Her, Kill and Tell,* and *Son of the Morning.* She lives in Alabama with her husband and two golden retrievers.